MY WIFE IS MISSING

My Wife Is Missing

D.J. Palmer

WHEELER PUBLISHING
A part of Gale, a Cengage Company

Wheeler Publishing, a part of Gale, a Cengage Company.

ALL RIGHTS RESERVED

Wheeler Publishing Large Print Hardcover.
The text of this Large Print edition is unabridged.
Other aspects of the book may vary from the original edition.
Set in 16 pt. Plantin.

LIBRARY OF CONGRESS CIP DATA ON FILE.
CATALOGUING IN PUBLICATION FOR THIS BOO
K IS AVAILABLE FROM THE LIBRARY OF CONGRESS.

ISBN-13: 978-1-4328-9930-1 (hardcover alk. paper)

Published in 2022 by arrangement with St. Martin's Publishing Group.

Printed in Mexico
Print Number: 01   Print Year: 2022

To Dr. Romy Valdez.
Thank you for setting me
on the path to mindfulness.

CHAPTER 1

Michael

As Michael Hart rounded the corner to his hotel room, he saw a small, lifeless shape lying on the floor of the hallway.

It was Teddy.

Teddy's arms were splayed open wide like the T-shape of a cross, legs straight as boards, feet pointed up at the ceiling. Still as stone, his two dark glassy eyes, black like onyx, gazed unblinking upward, seeing nothing. Wrapped around Teddy's neck was his familiar blue kerchief, frayed at the edges from time and touch.

"What on earth are you doing here?" Michael muttered to himself, bending at the knees to retrieve the beloved stuffed bear. He uncoiled his fingers from the pizza boxes he'd been carrying so he could latch onto Teddy's plush arm. Careful not to tip tonight's dinner, Michael rose to standing. In the back of his mind tumbled a thought:

7

Where is Bryce? Wherever Bryce went, Teddy went with him.

Michael endured a spurt of frustration — the kids dropping things everywhere, Natalie not thinking straight enough to keep track. Who was there to pick up the slack? He was, that's who. Chances were the old Natalie would have noticed Teddy had become separated from his owner. This new Natalie — his wife who managed only a couple hours of sleep on a good night, who suffered tremors, visions, and memory problems as a result, who these days had a fuse shorter than a matchstick — could have quite conceivably left one of the children behind (let alone a teddy bear) without realizing her oversight.

Michael exhaled his annoyance and concern in a single breath. No harm done. Teddy was safe. The cleaning crew hadn't swept him away. He figured Natalie and the kids had gone off exploring. Addison and Bryce had both been wide-eyed with wonder on their first trip up in the hotel's famed glass elevators so chances were they'd gone riding them again, and Teddy got left behind in all the excitement.

With the bear still dangling in his grasp, Michael gave the hotel room door a gentle kick, hoping the kids had returned from their adventures so he wouldn't have to fumble for a key. He waited. Down went the food (and Teddy) as Michael fished out a plastic rectangle from his wallet.

The room was dark when he entered. A heavy smell of vanilla and cedar clung to the air. It was a trick of the hotel trade, he knew; a little scent to help set the mood, like a new car smell. Normally the pleasing aroma didn't last long once the occupants arrived, but the vanilla odor was still quite strong. Something about it made Michael feel strangely alone.

Curtains thick as X-ray blankets blocked out the view of Times Square. He pulled them open to let in the last bits of daylight. They'd arrived close to sunset, and Michael couldn't wait to show Addie and Bryce the explosion of neon when darkness came. There was so much he wanted his kids to see and do here.

The city held a special place in Michael's heart. When he and Natalie were newly married, they'd make frequent trips from Boston to New York to take in shows and dine at fancy restaurants, but this was their first time coming to New York as a family. Today was all about getting settled and acclimated to the neighborhood. The plan was to check out Times Square from above and then on the ground. Of course Addison had already scoped out her primary stops, and no doubt the M&M and Disney stores would soon be getting some of Michael's hard-earned cash.

After setting the pizzas on a dresser, Michael tossed Teddy onto the bed Addison had claimed. The cot Bryce would occupy for the five nights remained folded up in a corner of the room. The cot wasn't exactly necessary, considering his son could sleep perfectly well in a sleeping bag on the floor. Michael knew the kids would be comfortable here, but he worried how Natalie would fare. She couldn't sleep at home, and it had been a shock to him when she suggested they take a family trip to New York during the kids' April vacation.

"Are you sure?" he said in response. "What are you going to do if you can't fall asleep? Wander the hotel halls like Marley's ghost?"

"I'll be fine. It'll be good for us," Natalie assured him.

He saw the outline of sadness in her tight smile and in her eyes, which were the color of the dark ocean. She was already anticipating the difficulty, but clearly she wanted to do it, so he made the reservation.

Good for us, Natalie had said. Goodness

10

knows they could have used some quality time together. It was something the marriage counselor had suggested. The truth was that he'd been planning to approach Nat about a getaway, just the two of them, leaving the kids with her parents for a stretch. More than family time, they needed time to reconnect, or at least hit the reset button on their marriage. The past few months had been, in a word, eventful. But Natalie had insisted on getting away with the kids as well, so family time it would be.

It took some fiddling, but Michael finally managed to get the room lights on — no small feat, given how modern hotels eschewed the old-fashioned switch for touch technology. Honestly, he was surprised everyone wasn't in the room eagerly awaiting his return, ready to pounce on the food. He checked his phone for a text from Natalie letting him know where they'd gone.

Nothing.

He checked the watch he wore obsessively — a throwback, Natalie called it. The Citizen timepiece with its thick leather band, darkened at the edges, couldn't send and receive messages, but it did tell him the hour was getting late.

They'd arrived in New York utterly famished after a four-and-a-half-hour car ride from their home in Lexington, Massachusetts. Michael had suggested going out to eat, but Natalie was too tired (no surprise there) and wanted takeout from a nearby pizza place she'd found on Yelp that had fantastic reviews. But given the dinner rush hour, delivery would take too long, so Michael was dispatched for pickup.

"Where is everyone?" he said to the empty room, plopping himself down onto the bed he'd soon be sharing with his wife. He sent her a text.

Food is here. Come and get it.

Wherever they were, he imagined the kids had to really be enjoying themselves to delay dinner for even a minute. A savory whiff of sauce and cheese tickled Michael's nose. He contemplated downing a slice, but managed restraint. He was a big believer in eating together as a family, and always made it a point to get home from his job at Fidelity in time for dinner. They'd only recently begun a new dinnertime tradition called Three Things, a conversation starter game that Natalie got off the internet. They'd take turns going around the table, each sharing one thing that had gone well that day, one thing they were grateful for, and one thing they'd have done differently.

Three things.

It wasn't easy getting the conversation going. Typically the kids launched half-hearted protests, but in the end Michael always felt the game brought him closer to the people who were closest to him.

He recalled Natalie's three things from the night before. They'd struck him as somewhat odd, just as this whole experience of returning to an empty hotel room felt odd.

Natalie had said:

"Today I got us all packed and ready to go."

"I'm grateful for the truth."

"I wish I'd done this sooner."

He had meant to ask his wife for clarification — what was it she wished she'd done sooner? Pack? And what truth was she grateful for? But then Bryce spilled his glass of milk and those questions got lost in the aftermath.

Now, thoughts of that game — specifically Natalie's reference to her packing prowess — brought Michael's attention to just how clean the room was. He took in that vanilla and cedar smell again. It was as if they'd not yet arrived. Normally there'd be clothes strewn about, the TV blaring, and suitcases left open on the floor, but not this time.

This time there was not an item in sight, as if Natalie had prepared them for a military-type room inspection.

In the bathroom, Michael splashed water on his weathered face and rubbed the dark stubble of a nascent beard. He looked aged well beyond his forty-three years, but stress can do that to a person. His marriage was on the rocks, but was there more to their troubles at home than he knew?

I'm grateful for the truth . . .

Noticing his reddish eyes, Michael went for his toiletry bag on the countertop, digging inside for the Visine. As he undid the zipper, a concern tugged at him, bringing with it an unsettled feeling not unlike the one he had experienced when he found Teddy all by his lonesome in the hallway.

All his senses were telling him something was wrong. He couldn't immediately identify the source of his unease, but as he scanned the bathroom, he realized what was amiss. He distinctly remembered Natalie getting her toiletries out of her suitcase because she had wanted to brush her teeth. Now there was only one toiletry bag on the counter, and it belonged to him. *Had she really put hers back in her suitcase?*

Michael's heartbeat picked up. Just a little.

He went to the closet directly across from

the bathroom. There he paused, not quite ready to open the door. His thoughts gummed up as he took another look around the perfectly ordered room.

Two rambunctious children aren't this neat.

The smell of vanilla taunted him.

He gripped the knob of the closet door, his stomach in knots, and gave it a yank. It was dark inside, but he had no trouble seeing the outline of his black suitcase pushed up against the back wall.

One suitcase.

Just one.

His.

CHAPTER 2

Michael

After dragging his suitcase from the closet, Michael fumbled with the zipper. Inside, he found all his clothes as he'd packed them. Shirts, socks, pants, underwear — they were all neatly folded and in their proper places.

His mind went blank. He called Natalie but was sent directly to her voicemail. He texted her but never saw the three dots signaling a return reply. There had to be a logical explanation for this: Why was his suitcase the only one in the room?

And then it came to him. It was obvious. There was a problem with the room — wrong view, too stuffy, a plumbing issue, something else he hadn't noticed — and Natalie had taken her suitcases to the new room, but his was too much for her to carry. She didn't bother with a valet because she can be quite the frugal Yankee. In the process of moving, poor Bryce dropped his teddy bear and didn't realize it. They were in the new room wondering what was taking Dad so long. Natalie had sent him a text, but sometimes those didn't come through right away, and hotels had notoriously spotty service.

Grabbing the hotel phone, he pressed zero for the front desk. He'd call her before she called him.

"Hello, Mr. Hart, how can I help you?"

Mr. Hart because it was his credit card on file, not Natalie's. They managed the finances by keeping their money pooled in joint accounts. To them it was a symbol of trust and respect — a what's-yours-is-mine kind of thing.

"Yes, I believe my wife changed rooms. I'm sure she sent a text message to let me know, but for some reason I didn't receive it. Could I have the new room number, please?"

He tried to put a smile in his voice while ignoring the light-headed feeling that overcame him. There was a moment of silence, which Michael used to check his phone, thinking her text must have reached him by now.

Seeing nothing, he waited, pushing down a gnawing concern.

"I'm sorry . . . um, no. There's no change

17

to your room number, Mr. Hart."

Michael's vision blurred.

"Well, that can't be," he said. "Their luggage isn't here. Did she maybe leave it with an attendant? It *must* be with a luggage attendant. Can you please check? It's Natalie Hart . . . Michael Hart . . . room 3541. Please . . . go check for me."

The room seemed to be spinning now. Michael dragged the phone all the way to the dresser, where the pizzas awaited hungry mouths. He pulled open the top drawer and found it empty. The second drawer was the same. A leather-bound Bible greeted him in the third drawer.

The blood in his head pounded like surf against his skull as he looked again for a note, scanning every surface multiple times, feeling his chest grow heavier with worry. There was hotel stationery and a pen on a desk near the window, but nothing scrawled on the pad. He rechecked his phone; his hands began to shake.

Eventually, the desk attendant spoke in his ear.

"I'm sorry, Mr. Hart. There's no luggage belonging to your family down here."

Michael dropped the hotel phone without bothering to hang it up. He raced out into the hallway, checking the long corridor in

18

both directions, hoping that he'd see his family coming toward him, hear the sweet voices of Bryce and Addie. But the only noise to hit his eardrums was the steady hum of the hotel air-conditioning.

Back in the room now, his mind empty, stomach tight, Michael stood at the edge of the bed, his arms hanging limply by his sides.

No note. No call. No text. No explanation.

Everyone and everything, just gone.

For a time, he paced the room like a caged animal. Nobody's here. Nobody's been here except to drop off luggage. That's what that vanilla smell was telling him. He looked over at Teddy. Poor Teddy. His eyes fixed and dilated, forever that way. Seeing nothing. Or maybe not.

Michael wanted desperately to breathe life into that bear so Teddy could tell him what had happened to his family. It was a ridiculous thought of course. It was all quite ridiculous.

Nat's three things flittered in and out of his mind again.

Today I got us all packed and ready to go.
I'm grateful for the truth.
I wish I'd done this sooner.

He was thinking . . . thinking . . . there

19

had to be a logical explanation. And then it came to him, a story that worked. He called the main desk, got transferred to the valet.

"Michael Hart here, room 3541. Has my wife been down there with some luggage? Did she have it put in the car?"

Poor Natalie must have gotten cold feet about their stay, and she'd brought all of the suitcases back to the car, or at least the ones she could take without calling for a bellhop.

He waited, biting the nail of his thumb.

I'm grateful for the truth.

"No, Mr. Hart," the valet attendant informed him after getting confirmation. "We haven't pulled out your car, and nobody has gone to it since you arrived."

"Thank you," Michael said weakly before cradling the phone.

He called Natalie a second time and again got voicemail straightaway, no ring. Either her phone was off (dead battery?) or she'd declined his call. But why would she do that?

Another thought now; they were coming to him quickly: she's downstairs at the restaurant with the luggage. She thinks she sent him a text, but it didn't go through. And her phone died and she doesn't realize it. That's it. That makes sense. Michael

20

could see his family in his mind's eye, the three of them sitting at a table with plates of French fries and glasses of chocolate milk, a little payoff to make up for the shortened (extremely shortened) trip.

Michael grabbed Teddy and headed for the elevator. The vanilla smell seemed to follow him into the hallway. Down he went, the glass windows of the elevator no longer holding any small thrill for him. The ride felt interminable. Michael ignored the other passengers, keeping his gaze locked on the digital readout counting down the floors, cursing softly to himself with each stop. He clutched Teddy the way Bryce did after a nightmare.

When at last the elevator reached the eighth floor, Michael shot out of the door, pushing past a younger man attempting to exit. No time to waste. He ran. He was a jogger, quite fit, but he had significant ground to cover. The hotel was a cavernous space with modern décor and enough square footage to house the reception desk, a box office, conference rooms, shops, and the restaurant, all on a single floor.

Crossroads served American cuisine, and the place could have been moved to any airport, USA, and would have blended in just fine. Michael breezed past the hostess, who didn't even blink as he went by. This was New York. Everyone here was in a hurry. He walked between tables, clutching Teddy at his side.

He checked every table twice, but Natalie and the kids weren't there.

There's an explanation . . . there's always a logical explanation, he told himself as he approached the hostess with the wide-eyed look of someone in shock. His skin felt clammy and cold even though he'd begun to sweat profusely.

"Excuse me," he said breathlessly. "I'm looking for my wife."

The raven-haired hostess, who stood a good deal shorter than Michael, peered up at him through coffee-colored eyes, a grave look of concern on her face. It was as if his anxiety had automatically transferred to her.

"I'm sorry," she stammered. "Um . . . how can I help?"

"My wife," Michael repeated in a low voice. He didn't want to make a scene. "Natalie Hart. Room 3541. Did she eat here recently?"

The hostess took a cautious step in retreat, and Michael wondered if she thought he might be unhinged.

"Please . . . just help me look for her," he said. "Talk to a manager. Room 3541. Did she eat here? Is there a room charge?"

The hostess left her station to find a manager, while Michael got out his phone. Natalie's number was the first in his recent list, but once again his call went straight to voicemail. He texted:

Where are you????? Why aren't you answering me????

No answer.

The hostess came back to her station.

Her face said *I'm sorry* before her words echoed that exact sentiment.

"Please call the other restaurant," Michael said briskly. "The View, I think that's the name, right? Ask them if Natalie is there. A woman, with two kids — boy six, and a girl, ten."

"What do they look like?" asked the hostess.

Michael unlocked his phone, but sweat from his thumb made it difficult to navigate to his photos app. Eventually, he got it open. Luckily he didn't have to scan for a picture of Natalie and the kids, as he had taken a group shot of his family in front of the hotel entrance moments after they'd arrived.

In that photo was Addie, beaming, wearing a gray Athleta sweatshirt and black leggings. Her hair was light blond like Natalie's had been when she was that age, but their daughter was clearly a blend of them both. She had inherited Michael's deep-set eyes, while getting (as luck would have it) Natalie's cute snub nose and full cheeks.

Bryce, who had hair several shades lighter than his older sister, looked sleepy, and true to form, wasn't looking at the camera when the picture was taken. No surprise, he had Teddy tucked under his arm, and there was a trace of a smile on his rosy lips.

Natalie, her hair once a cascade of chestnut, gorgeous in any lighting, appeared thinner now, perhaps from nerves and lack of sleep. Even so, she looked strong and assured, a natural beauty in every sense. She emanated a special sort of grace. To Michael's eyes, she appeared earthy and grounded, very much a Capricorn. Not that he was a believer in astrology, but he was a Taurus, so supposedly they were quite compatible.

A fan of the Grateful Dead, a devotee of yoga and meditation, Natalie was spiritual though not religious, and anyone who saw this picture, including the hostess, would think that his wife looked radiant. But Michael saw beyond the façade to the fatigue and sheer exhaustion lurking beneath the skin's surface. He knew that makeup could do wonders.

After studying the picture for no more than five seconds, the hostess returned Michael's phone.

"I'm sorry, I haven't seen them. Maybe try the concierge? They'll be able to call The View. And if they charged a meal from here to your room, it will be on your room bill."

Michael managed a curt thank-you before departing. He was back in the lobby, walking fast, Teddy swinging from his hand like a fuzzy pendulum.

Natalie's words again: *I wish I'd done this sooner. I'm grateful for the truth.*

Michael prayed with all his heart that it was a different truth from the one that haunted his dreams.

CHAPTER 3

Michael

By the time Michael reached the concierge desk, he was nearly out of breath. He was also third in line. From the snippets of conversation he could overhear ahead of him, a kindly looking elderly couple was having what would surely be a long chat about theater tickets. He barged to the front of the line.

The man he had interrupted grunted his protest.

"Hey, we were here first," he said in a raspy voice.

Michael ignored him.

"Excuse me."

Michael pressed his hands against the smooth surface of the concierge's podium. A nameplate, camouflaged on the lapel of the man's blue suit, read Raul.

"My wife is missing," Michael said, trying to keep the emotion out of his voice. "My

26

children are, too. I'm sure they're together."

In that moment, he suffered the strangest sensation ever. It was as if he were rising and falling at the same time; weightless. He didn't want to occupy his body. He wanted only to be with his family.

The elderly man he'd rudely interrupted sent Michael another scathing stare. His wife, however, put her hand to her chest, letting out a slight gasp before pulling her husband aside.

"Oh dear," Michael heard the woman say.

Calm. Stay calm, he urged himself. *There's always an explanation. This is just a misunderstanding. Everything is fine.*

"Could you call up to The View?" he asked Raul. "See if they're there."

Raul's brow furrowed and his expressive brown eyes became two slits.

"I'm sorry — I don't follow?"

In his head, Michael screamed: *What don't you follow?* But work, specifically the high-pressure world of managing other people's money, had taught him how to appear controlled in a crisis. He tapped into that power, sensing his fuel was running down to fumes.

Forget the call. I'll go up there myself, he decided.

Raul said something, but Michael was

already on the move and out of earshot. Back to the elevators. He'd go up, up to The View, because where else was there to go? *The pool? Maybe she took the kids for a swim. But with their luggage?*

It was as if he had an angel on one shoulder offering up one possibility and a devil on the other quickly refuting it. A feeling of cold dread sank into his bones, the devil on his shoulder whispering in his ear:

You're struggling here, Michael, because there is no explanation. You can't get your mind around this one, can you, old boy? That sick feeling in your gut . . . that uncomfortable worming sensation, the twisting knot of concern you can't shake? That's the knowing, Michael. That's your intuition talking to you, telling you things you don't want to hear.

As he rode the elevator up, Michael found it utterly impossible to stop the images in his mind, quick flashes that played out like mini-movies. He had no doubt that the devil was the director of this film, and the story line was quite grim: a family on vacation gets kidnapped from their hotel room at gunpoint.

His mind-movie showed a man, his face obscured by shadows, or maybe a hat — he settled on a baseball cap — marching his family away, a gun hidden inside his army jacket. Bryce led the exodus out of the hotel with tears in his eyes, shaking with fright. Addie was right behind him, her coloring a fever kind of pale, blue eyes brimming. Natalie did everything she could to stay calm and keep her family safe from this predator.

This mystery man had knocked gently on their hotel room door while Michael was out getting pizza, announcing himself as someone from maintenance. Natalie opened the door just a crack. Just enough. The gun was in her face in a blink.

"Get your stuff," the man growled. "Come with me."

And with him they went, but in the chaos and confusion, Teddy was dropped along the way.

Maybe . . . or maybe not. Maybe it's the other movie. The angel's film. Natalie at the pool. Natalie and the kids dining at The View, taking one last look at the city skyline before they headed for home, thinking she'd sent Michael a text, but insomnia had changed her. She was frequently confused. Forgetful. Panicky. Suffered from anxiety. Paranoia. Hallucinations.

But . . . I wish I'd done this sooner.

The View was the fancy restaurant. Michael charged forward into the dining area, bypassing the hostess without an explanation. The floor made a slow, three-hundred-sixty-degree revolution, turning in a clockwise direction to give diners a different city view every few seconds. Outside the tall windows, lights from the nearby skyscrapers twinkled with the brilliance of stars.

Michael ran the circle like it was a track. In his peripheral vision everyone was a blur, meaningless shapes. The food might have been savory, but the only smell he registered was that faint whiff of vanilla. He could tell some people were gawking. And why wouldn't they? He was a man with fear burned into his eyes, panic etched on his face. To them, he must have appeared utterly crazed, as if he'd just crawled out of a jungle following a plane crash, inexplicably clutching a stuffed bear in his grasp.

He didn't bother calling out the names of his family. No need. He could see with his own eyes they weren't here. And they weren't in the fitness studio, or the pool.

Some things were simply too hard to comprehend, some problems too big to wrap his head around. Michael went small, sinking into himself, going to that place where he could feel his fear, a molten thing, like a fire burning inside him.

He thought: *If she hadn't been kidnapped,*

then she cracked. What kidnapper takes time to pack luggage anyway? It's her insomnia. She broke.

He returned to the eighth floor. His eyes were downcast, but through his peripheral vision he caught glimpses of the people around him, worker bees and tourists flittering together, going about their lives. They had no idea his had just unraveled. He put Teddy to his face and breathed in deeply, inhaling the smell of Bryce and the sweet scent of home the bear held in his fur. He used his breath to center himself, and that gave him space to think.

In a crisis what would Natalie do? Michael asked himself. He decided she'd call a friend, that's what. A name came to him. Did he have Tina's phone number in his contacts? Tina Langley was Nat's closest confidante and coworker at Dynamic Media, a marketing company based in Waltham. Luckily, Michael found Tina's number in a group text message, one rife with memes and laugh emojis.

Tina answered after one ring.

"Hello?"

Her voice held an edge of concern. Michael's name must have come up on her display. He shouldn't be calling, but he was going to play it cool. He didn't want to hit

31

the panic button. Not yet anyway.

"Hey, Tina, Mike here. How are you?"

He worried his cheery tone sounded phony.

"Good, Michael. How are you? How's New York?"

"Yeah, fine, it's great," Michael said mustering some conviction into the lie. "Everything here is awesome." *Except I feel like I'm going to get sick and pass out.* "Say, has Natalie called you? We got separated in Times Square, and she's got the kids. I came back to the hotel to look for them, but they're not here yet. Wondering if she might have called you to chat, or whatever, and told you where she was?"

Less is better. Keep it simple. Listen to Tina's voice. Her voice will tell you what you need to know.

"No. I haven't heard from her," said Tina, sounding somewhat bewildered.

Michael picked up on her worry, but there was no hesitation, no pause before her answer.

She wasn't lying, he concluded.

"Okay, great, um . . . oh, hey . . . I think I see them. Yeah, here they are." Michael gave a little laugh to emphasize his relief. Acting was never his thing. "Okay, sorry to bug you, Tina. You know how it goes, city jitters.

We'll see you when we get back."

He found his parting words overly saccharine, but he ended the call before she could offer a goodbye.

Michael headed for the front desk, relieved there was no line.

"I need to speak to a manager right away," he said, barely able to muster the words. The young woman behind the counter took one look at Michael and lost her smile.

"It's my family," he managed. "They're missing and I need help."

Five minutes later, a man with thinning hair and puffy eyes, whose complexion told of too much work and too little sunlight, approached with hurried steps. Instead of the glad-to-see-you grin typical of anyone in the hospitality industry, this man conveyed the weighty look of a worried friend. He'd been briefed, and Michael couldn't help but wonder if his sole concern was for his family or if he was thinking also of the crisis he'd soon be facing over a kidnapping on hotel property.

"Mr. Hart, I'm Dan White, general manager here. Let's go somewhere where we can speak in private."

Dan led Michael to a small room down a short hall behind the reception desk. It wasn't nicely furnished, so chances were this was a shared space and not Dan's primary office.

"Can I get you something to drink? Water, coffee, anything?" asked Dan. He kept glancing at his phone, maybe because he couldn't face looking Michael in the eye. Sweat dotted Dan's forehead, glistening under the harsh fluorescent lighting. Michael had the passing thought that neither of them was equipped for this situation. Dan had come to work wanting nothing more than to have a good day, no troubles, no fires to put out. Instead, he had to listen to Michael recount everything that had happened, starting with finding Teddy in the hallway. Dan's expression said it all: this wasn't a fire; more like an inferno.

"So did you see a suspicious man following your family?" asked Dan, who couldn't hide the shake in his voice.

"No . . . I'm just . . ."

Just what? Michael asked himself. *Just making it up? Imagining things that aren't there, things that haven't happened, the way Natalie has been imagining things of late?*

"It's just that kidnapping is the only thing that makes sense," Michael said.

"I think we better call the police," said Dan, who might have been wondering

34

himself why a kidnapper would pack luggage.

Michael went cold inside. He imagined news cameras and reporters descending on the hotel (and him) with the buzz of locusts. Then what? He'd be putting up posters of his wife and children like they were beloved pets gone missing. But the answer to Dan's question was, of course, yes, call the damn police, call them right now. Better he find out this was all a huge misunderstanding, something he and Nat could laugh about years later.

But the movie still running in his mind wasn't a comedy. He kept seeing the man in the baseball hat with a gun in his hand. At least he knew what his family was wearing before they vanished. That was a plus. He had that picture.

"Cameras?" Michael suddenly thought to ask. "Do you have security cameras we could look at? Can we access them?"

"Yes, of course we do. I have my people working on that right now," said Dan. "I know you're nervous, Mr. Hart, and rightfully so, but we have an excellent security record at our hotel. If there was something suspicious as you've described, I'm sure someone working for me would have seen it."

"With all due respect, Dan, your security record means nothing to me right now. Nothing. Please. Just call the police."

CHAPTER 4

Michael

Detective Sandra Ouyang arrived at the Marriott Hotel thirty minutes after Dan White made his phone call. Michael's first thought was that dispatch had sent only one detective because the NYPD wasn't taking his case all that seriously. His family hadn't been gone for long and nobody else had seen anything suspicious, making his troubles either a big misunderstanding or a domestic squabble. Either way, in a city as large as New York, where police resources were scarce, someone had decided a lone detective could handle his situation just fine.

Detective Ouyang, an Asian woman with dark hair pulled into a tight ponytail and a full cherubic face, greeted Michael with a friendly enough hello, one tinged with empathy. Dressed in a purple blouse and black pants suit combo, she could have done any number of jobs, but the shiny badge and gun hooked to her belt elevated the detective to a position of authority.

The conference took place in the same small office where Dan had initially brought Michael. Hotel staff ferried in an extra chair, and it didn't take long for body heat to warm the room up to an uncomfortable degree. Even so, Michael knew that wasn't the reason he was sweating so profusely.

"Does that bear belong to one of your kids?" Ouyang indicated to Teddy.

Michael had forgotten he was holding the stuffed bear, clutching him really, in a white-knuckled grip on his lap.

"Yes, Teddy belongs to Bryce. He's my six-year-old. Addie, his sister, she's ten."

Michael sniffled and Dan White handed him a tissue, as if he'd been waiting for his cue.

"I found Teddy in the hall outside our room. That's why I think something horrible happened. Bryce would never leave his bear behind, not unless he was being rushed."

"Tell us what you know, Michael," Detective Ouyang said, her voice calm, her eyes kind. Michael sensed her genuine concern, but didn't trust it fully yet. He knew it could be an act, and that she might be suspicious of him. It's always the husband, after all.

Michael shelved that worry to go through it all over again. They'd arrived hungry, he told Ouyang. Delivery would take too long. He'd gone to get food. He came back and found Teddy in the hallway; the hotel room empty, suitcases gone. Searched high and low, no sign of his family anywhere. He showed the detective the numerous text messages and phone calls made to Natalie, all of which had gone unanswered.

"Who is *Maybe Tina*?" Detective Ouyang asked.

Maybe Tina? Then it dawned on him. When Ouyang looked at his phone she must have seen his call log. Tina wasn't a contact of Michael's, so that was how his phone registered her name. *Maybe Tina.* He was pleased to get a demonstration of the detective's powers of perception, and hoped that skill of hers would soon come in handy.

"Tina is Natalie's friend from work," Michael said. "I didn't know what to do when I couldn't find them, so I thought maybe Nat had called Tina or something. I had this notion that my wife got cold feet about the vacation and contacted her friend for support or guidance."

"And did she?" asked Ouyang. "Call her?"

"No," said Michael. "There was no call."

A slight hitch sounded in Michael's voice,

and then, without warning, a pit opened up in him, a trapdoor of sorts, and down went his spirits, free-falling into some abyss.

"What the fuck," Michael muttered to himself. "What the absolute fuck fuck fuck. Where *are* they?"

He gave the back of his hair a hard yank until it hurt, holding it so that a sharp pain radiated from his skull all the way down his leg. The brief flash of agony felt like a welcomed distraction from the other, far worse kind of suffering he was experiencing.

"Let's try to stay calm," said Ouyang. "Best for everyone. I know this is difficult. But we don't know anything yet, not really. We don't know what's happened here. It's possible it's all a big miscommunication, right?"

Michael wasn't sure what she was thinking, but something about the way Ouyang was eyeing him now made Michael more than a little uneasy.

"What else can I tell you?"

"Did you see someone following you?" asked Ouyang.

"No," said Michael, offering a slight shake of his head. "I thought everything was fine. Normal."

"So what makes you think they've been

kidnapped?"

Ouyang had her notepad out, pen in hand ready to scribble.

"Because what other explanation is there?" Michael said, exasperated. "We're here on vacation and suddenly they're all gone. All their things, gone."

"Sorry to say, but another explanation would be that she left you, willingly and willfully," the detective replied with stinging authority.

"Why would she do that?" Michael asked. "Leave me when we made these plans. She was looking forward to this trip. She *asked* to come here."

Michael locked eyes with Dan like he'd have the answer, which he of course didn't.

"You tell me," said Detective Ouyang, who pivoted to a slightly more menacing tone. "Did you two have a fight? Was she upset about something?"

"No . . . no, it's nothing like that. We've been good. I mean, yeah, it's been a struggle lately, but we've been okay."

"Why a struggle?" Ouyang wanted to know.

Michael took some audible breaths, hoping to purge any lingering frustration or animosity he felt toward his wife. It had been a hard few months. Perhaps the hard-

41

est. "Natalie, my wife, suffers from insomnia, and it's caused us some . . . difficulties."

"What kind of difficulties?"

The glimmer in Ouyang's eyes implied that she felt they were finally getting somewhere.

"She hasn't exactly been herself of late," Michael said. "Do you know the symptoms of insomnia? What it can do to a person?"

Ouyang's mouth formed the hint of a smile.

"I'm a New York City police detective," she said. "But why don't you tell me anyway."

"There's depression, irritability, anxiety."

But there's more, Michael, whispered the devil. *There's so, so much more.*

Ouyang's eyes widened slightly as if she'd heard that voice in his head. "So your wife had been acting strangely, and now she's vanished, with the kids. Is that about right?" The detective cocked her head slightly. "You see why I might not jump straight to kidnapping, don't you?"

Michael swallowed hard. He saw all right.

"Do you have a family picture, Michael?" she asked. "I want to get it over to the station right away so we can issue a BOLO. That's: be on the lookout in our parlance."

"Right," said Michael who then presented Ouyang with the same photo he had shown the hostess at Crossroads.

"Beautiful family," Ouyang said, in a way that conveyed the subtext, *and I hope you didn't do anything to them.* "Got another with your picture on it?"

So you can run me through some database, thought Michael. *Use facial recognition software to see what you might dredge up on me.*

He couldn't deny the request, however, so he ended up AirDropping two pictures to Ouyang's cell phone, one of which was a photo of the four Hart family members a kind stranger took at a rest stop on the drive to New York. Ouyang forwarded the pictures on to somewhere.

"What now?" Michael asked.

Now, the phone rang. Dan's phone, to be precise.

"It's security calling," Dan said briskly. "There's some footage we need to see. They're emailing me a link."

A short while later, Dan did some mouse clicking on a desktop computer, while Michael kept his eyes locked on Teddy. It was far easier to focus his attention on the stuffed bear than try to make small talk with the detective. Michael nervously drummed

43

his fingers against the desk, tapping loudly enough to get Ouyang's attention.

"Sorry, nervous habit," Michael said, pulling his hand back onto his lap. "My wife hates it when I do that."

My wife. It hurt even to say the words.

Dan spun his computer monitor around so everyone could have a good view.

"I had our security team use the photograph Mr. Hart provided, and they've been looking at our camera footage from around the time the Hart family checked in. Obviously we don't have cameras in the rooms, but we do have a state-of-the-art system with coverage in the halls and front desk and such. But my team said this is the footage we'll want to see first."

The video playback showed the outside of the hotel, looking toward the main entrance from the other side of the carport. Thanks to the camera's high vantage point, maybe the height of a basketball hoop, Michael could see the entirety of two single glass doors bracketing a revolving door. His gaze flickered to the date and time stamp in the lower left corner where a digital readout counted the hours, minutes, and seconds. Michael did some calculations of his own. He had been out getting pizza when this footage was taken.

In the foreground, cars and vans came and went with no discernible pattern. People who weren't his family did the same. Then, in an utterly surreal moment, they appeared in the frame — Natalie, Bryce, and Addison. He couldn't see them clearly, not their faces or their expressions, no way to infer a story in their eyes, but he knew their shapes so well that he recognized them even from a distance. They were leaving the hotel, carrying their luggage.

Michael searched the area behind his family for the man in the army jacket and the baseball hat — the one from his mind-movie, the kidnapper with a gun — but no one accompanied them. Natalie had two suitcases in her possession, one in each hand. Addie wheeled one bag, her own, a pink hard-shell case decorated with white polka dots. She pulled Bryce along with her free hand.

Michael had a flashback to their arrival, how the kids had struggled with the revolving door (who doesn't, with luggage?) He figured his children would want to go out the "moving door," as Bryce called it, probably after taking a couple extra spins around. But he could see this departure wasn't any fun. Natalie propped open a side door with her back, motioning urgently for

Addie and Bryce to pass that way.

Why that door? Michael asked himself. Because she's in a hurry, that's why. She has someplace she has to be. But where? He couldn't say, but as her head swiveled toward the camera, he could see there was tension on her face. What about?

Then it came to him: she was concerned he'd come back with pizza in time to see them all leaving.

Every second seemed to matter. There were a lot of bodies and luggage to maneuver, but Natalie did so in a calm and purposeful way. She did everything with intention. To Michael she looked clearheaded, not the least bit frazzled. It appeared to be, in a word, rehearsed.

Outside, in the carport, Michael could see his family more clearly. He didn't see fear in his children's eyes, though they did seem somewhat bewildered. They were looking about cautiously, taking in their surroundings. Or maybe they were searching for someone . . . perhaps even their father.

Whatever was going through Bryce's mind, he didn't seem to be aware that Teddy wasn't with him.

There was a black sedan parked curbside. The burly driver jumped out when he saw Natalie approach, and immediately set to work putting the suitcases into the open trunk. Their brief exchange wasn't without significance, Michael realized. The driver would have had no idea Natalie was his passenger unless it was prearranged.

Addison opened the rear door and climbed into the backseat, dragging Bryce inside with her. Natalie said something to the driver that the video didn't capture, and then calmly, purposefully, got into the rear with the kids. She closed her own door. The driver clambered back into the front seat.

A second later, they were gone.

Dan hit pause on the playback. Michael sat with it, processing what he'd just seen. It was Detective Ouyang who eventually broke the silence.

"Well, that sure was enlightening," she said. "I'd say, based on clear video evidence, that your wife is of sound mind and body. Looks to me, Michael, like she left this hotel willingly, of her own accord. Left you the same way."

Michael, too stunned to speak, searched his mind for any justification.

Someone had contacted her. She was being manipulated remotely by this person, blackmailed or coerced somehow. There's a threat nobody knows about. He thought about trying out his theory on the detective, but already it rang false in his head.

"Any reason your wife might have wanted to leave you, Michael, and take the kids with her?" Detective Ouyang asked.

Yes, Michael thought. *There's a reason. . . . a damn good one.*

But not one he could ever share.

CHAPTER 5

Natalie
Before She Disappeared

She could ignore most noises at work.

Over the course of seven years with the company, the muted chatter of Natalie's Dynamic Media colleagues had morphed into something akin to white noise. The sound of fingers tapping keyboards with the rhythm of woodpeckers also went unnoticed. Same for the noisy footsteps that carried far and wide because the firm had opted to go young with their design aesthetic — open plan, upscale flooring, an industrial feel. The youthful interior paired well with the employees, the majority of whom looked young enough to get carded. Their mobile devices chirped incessantly, but Natalie had learned to tune out the intrusive sounds — unless, of course, that chirping occurred during one of her meetings. Then, look out.

What caught Natalie's ear that afternoon was a sound unlike any she'd heard at work before. It was soft and plaintive, bereft. The sound of a woman weeping.

Natalie was on her way to the seventh-floor kitchenette to get coffee for her afternoon fix. Or was it hourly? There was a time, it felt like ages ago, when she had been a morning coffee drinker only. Now she was probably downing eight cups a day and afraid to go to the doctor. If she found out that caffeine was killing her, she might die on the spot. It was the only thing keeping her from becoming a full-blown zombie.

The seventh floor wasn't her usual domain, but she had ventured up for a two thirty meeting. Floor seven was where the finance department dwelled, while Natalie worked on four with the "creatives" and other account managers. She knew the layout of seven though — and specifically, where to find the kitchenette — because Tina Langley, her best friend at Dynamic Media, worked on this level. Tina actually ran the finance department, and considering how much money was going to be at stake at the two thirty meeting, it was no surprise they were spearheading the call.

Natalie poked her head into the kitchenette, where her eyes confirmed what her ears told her she would find: a woman in tears. The woman had her back to the entrance, her hands pressed against the red laminate countertop as if needing the support to remain upright. She had on a gray turtleneck tucked into a black skirt that called attention to her narrow waist and thin frame. Her auburn-tinged hair, cut stylishly short, was like a nod to Audrey Hepburn. A flash of jealousy passed through Natalie, more reflex than conscious thought, but just as quickly, empathy returned.

I should help.

But Natalie did not help. Instead, she stood awkwardly in the entranceway watching this private moment with a mixture of curiosity and uncertainty. Should she turn and go, leave the poor woman alone with her misery? No. Caring was in Natalie's DNA. If she hadn't gone into marketing, Natalie would have been equally content working as a therapist. In some ways, especially when dealing with her more difficult-to-manage clients, Natalie was that and more.

While she felt an urge to rush in and offer assistance, something held her back. A number of thoughts flew in and out of her mind: *does this woman even want help? Maybe she needs time to cry it out?*

Considering how much crying Natalie had been doing lately, she ought to have known how to help, but still she hesitated. She eventually decided that if the roles were reversed, she'd want someone to check on her, so that settled it.

Natalie cleared her throat, and the woman turned to face her. She was stunned. This wasn't a pretty woman. She was downright gorgeous. Her facial features were as delicate as porcelain, especially those high cheekbones, which would easily catch the attention of any casting director. The whites of her eyes might have been red from crying, but the blue of her irises shimmered like sequins. Judging by her smooth, unblemished face, Natalie thought she must be around ten years her junior. She also had to be new on the job. This place had a way of aging a person.

Embarrassed, the woman gave a slight gasp before offering an awkward smile.

"I'm so sorry," she said, sniffling and looking guilty, as if she'd been caught doing something wrong. She used a balled-up napkin to dab at her eyes. "I'm . . ." Her voice caught in her throat. She gave a laugh and dabbed those blue eyes some more.

"Are you all right?" Natalie asked.

Oh, good start, Natalie. Of course she isn't all right.

Natalie had never been this person, self-critical and uncertain. Before her world began to unravel, her biggest issue had been guilt. There was never enough time to do everything that had to be done and do it well. Like everyone else, she had twenty-four hours a day, not a second more, to be a wife, mother, and devoted employee.

It had seemed easy enough when she signed on for all those jobs — until she had to do them every day, all day long. Sure, Michael did the dishes without prompting, helped with the chores, the kid stuff, the cooking, all of that, but really the go-to person would always be Mom. She did the heavy lifting when it came to the worrying, the planning, and the endless stream of anxieties associated with parenting. Usually, she — not Michael — was the one the kids sought out for comfort when they were tearful or upset. That issue had come up in marriage counseling a couple of times, and never got resolved.

Was this woman married? Natalie wondered. She didn't wear a ring, but that didn't make it a sure bet in this day and age. No doubt though, she would transfix Michael with her youth and beauty. To

Natalie, she was the very picture of her imagination; a face that haunted her sleepless hours, one that no doubt belonged in Natalie's cadre of conjured concubines, an amalgam of the real woman destroying her marriage.

Natalie took a cautious step into the kitchenette.

"I'm fine, really," the woman said. The color of her cheeks betrayed the lie by flashing an even deeper red.

Natalie grabbed a few tissues from a box on the countertop.

"I'm Natalie Hart," she said. "I work on four with account services."

"Audrey . . . Audrey Adler."

Audrey.

Natalie's earlier thought, that the woman's hairstyle reminded her of Audrey Hepburn's, now seemed even more fitting.

Audrey took the proffered tissues, which sufficed as a handshake.

"At least it wasn't my ugly cry," Audrey said, dabbing away the last remnants of her tears. Black lines didn't drip from her eyes, which meant those long lashes were natural.

Damn.

"What's your ugly cry like?" asked Natalie, feeling more emboldened.

"I've been told it sounds like geese mating," Audrey said with a laugh.

Natalie's eyes went wide. "And this person is still alive?" she asked.

Audrey chuckled.

"I think I have to plead the fifth there."

At last there was a full smile. It was beaming and utterly brilliant.

"I work with the creatives," Natalie said. "We watch and listen to everything in pursuit of the perfect campaign, and that includes the sounds of mating fowl, and I can assure you that you don't sound a thing like that, no matter how ugly your cry can get."

At that, Audrey laughed, smiled, and may have swallowed a sob all at the same time.

"I think you saved me from drowning in self-pity," Audrey said, after collecting herself.

"You're over it that quickly?" Natalie's eyebrows arched. "Now I think I'm the one who needs your help."

"Why my help? I'm a bubbling, hot mess."

Natalie sent Audrey a crooked smile.

"Maybe so, but you're at least good at showing your feelings. I'm more likely to quietly stew while dwelling on mine."

Natalie didn't know what had possessed her to share, but she felt enough concern for Audrey to reach out and place a hand on her arm.

"Are you sure you're okay?"

She made certain they locked eyes.

Audrey smiled warmly.

"I'm fine. Really. It was . . . just a moment. It was nothing."

Now it was Natalie whose emotions welled up inside.

She'd imagined confronting Michael with her suspicions, imagined what he might say.

It was nothing.

Nothing. Just sex.

Just you inside another woman.

It was nothing . . . nothing but the destruction of our family.

Liar. Cheater. Bastard.

No wonder I can't sleep.

Natalie took a closer look at Audrey. Beautiful Audrey. Would Michael have gone for a younger woman like her? Of course he would have. Such a cliché. Old cow, new cow. Wasn't that some theory on male sexuality? Or maybe she'd read that in one of her chick-lit books. Natalie used to love to read — light stuff, heady stuff, paranormal, didn't matter. She'd read to fall asleep. When sleep left her, the reading left, too. Oh, how she missed it. But there were a lot of things she missed that she once took for granted.

"I'm sorry you had to see me like that," Audrey said.

"No you don't," said Natalie, wagging a finger.

A look of confusion crossed Audrey's face.

"What . . . I'm sorry . . ."

"There you go again," said Natalie. "Saying sorry when there's nothing to be sorry for. Since I saved you from drowning in self-pity, what I want in return is for you to refuse to say 'I'm sorry' to anybody, at least for the remainder of the day. You shouldn't be sorry for anything unless you do something to hurt somebody else. Don't apologize for being you. Do we have a deal?"

"Deal," Audrey said, as she stood straighter and taller. "You've been very kind to me. Thank you."

"I can be even kinder. Tina Langley is my dear friend. Since you're on this floor, I assume you know her."

Audrey blanched.

"Tina . . . you know Tina?"

"Let's just say they've named a margarita after us at La Hacienda."

Audrey looked too stunned to laugh.

"Tina is my boss," she said. "I've been here a year, but I don't think she's noticed me."

Natalie shrugged.

57

"Don't take it personally. Tina can be a difficult read, but deep down she's a softie."

"How deep are we talking?"

"Miles," said Natalie with a wink. "Say, why don't we go for lunch sometime soon. I've been with the firm almost a decade. I'd be happy to give you some pointers. I'll even put in a good word for you, help you get a leg up in the department. It would be my pleasure."

"I'd love that," Audrey said, and it was clear she meant it, too.

"Great," said Natalie, who was thinking about something else — or more specifically, some*one* else. Michael.

What Natalie had with Michael were her suspicions, and that wasn't enough to blow up her family, her life. She needed more, concrete proof of his infidelity, before she'd take such drastic action. Thanks to this chance encounter, she might be able to get what she needed. Natalie knew she'd just done Audrey a big favor. Hopefully, Audrey would be willing to repay her kindness, and in doing so become what Natalie needed her to be.

Bait.

Chapter 6

Michael

Michael got his wish, sort of. After viewing the video, Ouyang's phone rang. She stepped out of the room to take a call, telling him it was from the station. She returned with news that her boss was coming to the hotel to speak with Michael directly, which to him meant they were taking his case more seriously.

"I have some more questions," Ouyang said to Michael, "but I'm going to wait for Detective Kennett to get down here before asking them."

To her credit, Ouyang seemed to welcome the help, didn't seem at all annoyed by her supervisor's imminent arrival, which came twenty minutes after ending her phone call with him.

Detective Sergeant Amos Kennett (that was how he introduced himself) had that grizzled look of a seasoned vet, weathered face, dark hair, and hooded eyes that seemed to carry the weight of his caseload, all of which pleased Michael who believed experience was needed here. He soon realized, however, that this perceived advantage worked against him too, for it appeared, judging solely by the look Kennett sent Michael's way upon entering the back office, that he'd arrived already wary of the husband.

The detective greeted Michael with a tepid hello, which came out sounding more like "H'lo." And while he did express his sympathies, Kennett never really warmed up, as if his dark goatee was there to prevent his mouth from forming a smile.

To Michael's relief, Kennett eschewed small talk in favor for getting right down to it. He asked to watch the video of the security camera footage, and did so with his blue blazer off, revealing a shoulder holster and gun combo that served as reminders of Michael's grave situation.

Kennett sat transfixed during the viewing, offering no commentary. After it was over, Michael let out a long, audible exhale, emotionally spent from seeing his family on video for a second time. His thoughts were muddled, but he gave himself some credit: he hadn't broken down crying, even though that's exactly what he wanted to do. When he glanced over at Kennett, he thought maybe he'd get a genuine show of support. Instead he read judgment in the detective sergeant's piercing stare. By contrast, Ouyang, who had seemed quite harsh after she first saw the video, now appeared far softer and sympathetic. With the arrival of her boss, the roles were clearly defined. Ouyang would be the empathetic of the pair. Michael's mind flashed on the old trope of good cop/bad cop, with Kennett being the latter.

"So, Mike," Kennett said, with an expression that was equal parts curiosity and accusation. "Any reason why your wife appears to be running away from you? That's what it looks like to you, too, right? Like she's heading back out of town and didn't bother to tell you where she was going, or why. So . . ." Kennett clapped his hands together like an audible exclamation mark. "Why do you think that is?"

Michael swallowed a gulp. He tried to keep his face muscles relaxed to hide his fear.

"Did you two have a fight?" Ouyang asked. "Are you under any extra stress at home? Financial problems, maybe an affair, anything like that?"

For a moment, Michael was left speechless. His guilty conscience took over as he thought back to the many times in recent months when he lost his temper. He never touched Natalie and the kids, but one incident from long ago in particular haunted him still. He knew he had frightened Natalie, revealing to her a darker side of himself that he normally could keep suppressed.

"No," he said, with some bite in his voice. He didn't enjoy being put on the defensive. "I told you already, she's been dealing with insomnia. I don't think she's in her right mind. She shouldn't be alone with the kids. This could be a dangerous situation for them."

A fierce sense of foreboding sank into Michael's bones. Nothing made sense.

Except it did, didn't it? And if he was right, if his suspicions were confirmed, it involved the worst thing possible.

The truth.

"Look, Mike, there's not much we can do here," Kennett said matter-of-factly. "Last I checked, America is a free country and your wife can do as she pleases."

"But she has my kids," lamented Michael.

"*Our* kids, you mean," Ouyang chimed in. "As in her kids, too. And in the eyes of the law, that's kind of how it's supposed to be."

"You two don't have a custody arrangement, do you?" Kennett asked.

Michael swiveled in his chair. Facing Kennett, he did his best to ignore the steady thump in his chest.

"We're not divorced or separated," he said. He didn't mean to come off sounding irritated and snippy, but he wasn't feeling particularly in control at that moment. "What I mean to say is we're married. I told you that."

Kennett offered a shrug in return.

"I'm not a lawyer, Michael," he said. "Can't really advise you on what to do here. But I do know the laws around kidnapping pretty well, and I don't believe your wife has broken any of them."

"Until there is a court order changing the circumstance, both you and your wife enjoy equal rights to the care, custody, and control of your kids," Ouyang added.

Michael was sure he misheard.

"I don't think I follow," he said. His voice shook. "She can just . . . what? Up and leave me . . . with my children? Just take off like that?"

Ouyang did up a button on her blazer. Time to go.

"All I can tell you, Michael, is that right now you need a lawyer, not a detective."

She handed him her card.

"But if you need me for anything, feel free to call my cell. The number is on here."

Kennett slipped on his blazer, did up a button as well.

"Same goes for me, Mike," he said, handing over one of his cards. He plastered on a phony smile.

"I don't get it," Michael said to Kennett. "Detective Ouyang must have told you what was going on. Why did you bother coming here if you knew you couldn't help? Why get my hopes up like that?"

"Because this whole thing is kind of strange, Mike," Kennett said somewhat brusquely. "Even if your wife didn't break the law, at least not yet, it's unusual what's happened here, and it's good for detectives to team up when things take a surprising turn. Less chance of us missing something important. But right now, we don't have much to go on. Unless you've got something else you'd like to share with us. Do you, Mike? Have something else to share?"

Michael became acutely aware of his closed-off body language, and uncrossed his arms. Did he look shifty and uncertain? Was that the vibe he was giving off? These detectives had enough skills and resources to make things extremely complicated for him.

"I don't have anything else to tell you that you don't already know," said Michael.

Kennett's slim smile said: I don't believe you.

"Very well, Mike. We have pictures, better than descriptions. We'll keep a lookout and be in touch if we get any leads. We're happy to help you file a missing persons report, too. Though you should do that with your hometown police. Most police departments want you to wait twenty-four hours before filing, but I can make a call, push that along if need be."

"Why the waiting period?"

"Usually missing persons turn up, often it's a miscommunication or a fight, and so police try to cut down on needless paperwork."

Kennett didn't project much confidence that Michael's case would be of the sort-itself-out variety.

"Can I ask a favor of you before you go?" Michael said to Kennett.

"Sure, Mike. We're here to serve."

Subtext: *I still think you're hiding something.*

"Can you tell me the name of the car company my wife used to leave the hotel? You saw the license plate in the video. You could run it for me."

Ouyang didn't look ready to jump in and

offer her assistance. Michael pressed his case.

"Look, I can pay an internet service to get the info. Or hire a PI. Whatever. One way or another I'm going to get the company name. If you wanted to be helpful you could speed up the process for me."

Silence.

Ouyang and Kennett seemed to communicate anyway, talking with their eyes.

"We'll call you, Mike," Kennett said. "Save your money. We'll get you that name."

"Just curious though," Ouyang said. "What are you going to do with the information?"

"What do you think I'm going to do with it?" Michael answered coolly. "I'm going to use it to find my wife."

CHAPTER 7

Natalie
Before She Disappeared
Natalie and Michael were walking along a gravelly path, hiking a popular trail at Purgatory Falls in New Hampshire. It was a sunny day, but the temps were frigid. There was ice on this trail, and Natalie didn't have spikes on her hiking boots. *Why hadn't Michael advised her to bring spikes?*

High above, Natalie heard the stark caw-caw of a crow flying overhead, giving her something new to worry about. *Isn't that an omen?* Natalie wasn't sure, but she thought crows were once considered messengers of the gods. *Or was it harbingers of death?* She watched the black bird make ponderous circles, at times skimming the treetops.

Go away, thought Natalie. *Go away, you bad luck bird. I've enough trouble without you around.*

Why am I here? she asked herself, feeling

an ache of loneliness. They were the only hikers on this trail; the only people on the whole damn mountain, it seemed.

The cry of the crow bled off into the distance, but when Natalie looked up again, she saw not one bird but two circling now. Michael glanced back, at last taking notice of his wife.

"It's beautiful here, isn't it, Nat?" he said, shouting to be heard over a trumpet of wind that bellowed at them from the east.

One of the black crows cawed as if in response. Michael seemed at home in this stark terrain, far more so than Natalie. His rugged good looks appeared carved out of the very rocks on which he stood. He had a nose fit for a Roman emperor, and his penetrating dark eyes suggested a man who always seemed to have something on his mind. Buffeting winds revealed hidden grays that snaked through his mane of curly brown hair.

The warm feelings she still carried for her husband couldn't fend off the chill from the biting wind. She had on a light jacket and fleece underneath, but it wasn't nearly enough clothing for these temperatures. They should turn around, get back down, and find a cute little place for some hot chocolate.

Her gaze flickered between Michael's handsome face and the mountains far off in the distance. She took a step forward with her eyes on Michael, not the ground. In that moment, her boot found a patch of ice covered with pine needles, almost like someone had set a trap. One second Natalie was sure-footed, and the next her leg shot out in front of her as if the limb wasn't attached. She slid forward, fighting for balance, arms flapping like the crows' wings.

Her body lurched awkwardly in different directions, hips going to the right, torso to the left. When Natalie realized she was stumbling toward the ravine, that her feet no longer had stable purchase, she tried to force a scream, but nothing came out.

For a moment, she tottered between the trail and the abyss until gravity decided which way she'd go. She fell, arms and legs flailing as if to take flight. Her jacket flapped with the whipping sound of a sail catching a fresh breeze. Down, down she went, the sudden acceleration taking her breath away.

She heard Michael's terrified voice call out to her from high above.

"Natalie! Natalie!"

The scream stayed stuck in her throat, choking her.

"Natalie." The voice came again, but this

time it was softer and unquestionably female. "Natalie."

Light flooded Natalie's eyes as they came open. She took in the multitude of faces staring back at her. For a moment, she felt utterly disoriented, not recognizing any of the people who were gawking at her. Her confusion lasted only seconds, and then everything became clear. The woman staring at her from across the table was her friend, Tina Langley.

Next to Tina sat Dave Edmonds — that Dave, her employee who had made his crush on her painfully obvious — and next to Dave was a copywriter from the creative team, who was working with her on a campaign for —

A sudden realization hit her like a punch. This was the two thirty meeting. She was in a conference room on a conference call with the client.

Holy shit. I just had a nightmare in the middle of a meeting.

Panic and embarrassment enveloped her like a glove. Her face grew hot. *Oh my God, did I make a noise?* Everyone was looking at her as if she had. The shame was all-consuming. Her eyes burned as she tried to refocus them.

70

"Natalie, can we commit to a May delivery?"

It was Tina, seated across from her, dressed to the nines as usual in a pin-striped navy wool blazer and matching pants from Ralph Lauren, asking her the question. She sent Nat a look of concern along with a very subtle head nod.

Follow her lead, that's what she was trying to say.

"Yes," Natalie answered shakily. "April is fine. We can commit to that. No problem."

"You mean May," said Tina, calling her out gently.

"Right. May," Natalie clarified, shooting Tina an appreciative look.

Five minutes later, after next steps were agreed upon and the meeting adjourned, Natalie joined Tina in her office. Her heart was still thumping from the experience.

Tina got herself settled at her desk and didn't waste a moment's time digging in. "Sweetheart, what the hell was that?"

Natalie, who'd seated herself at the small conference table in Tina's spacious office, couldn't shake the jolt she'd gotten from the adrenaline rush of all those eyes on her.

"I was out," she said, in a disbelieving voice. "I had a goddamn nightmare during a meeting. Did I scream?"

Tina returned a weak smile. Sympathy sat prominent in her soft brown eyes.

"No, there wasn't any screaming. But don't feel too badly. That was a dreadful meeting. I'm surprised we didn't all fall asleep. And honestly, I don't think anyone noticed you had drifted off."

Natalie returned an incredulous look.

"You've got to be kidding me."

Tina shrugged her slender shoulders.

"Well, if they did, I'm sure they don't blame you."

Her smile was gentle but telling. Tina had a way of making bad news seem less dire. Many a company CFO had misjudged her friendly, agreeable demeanor during negotiations over contracts or acquisitions — to their detriment. Her shoulder-length mouse-brown hair might as well have been a lion's mane anytime she dealt with numbers.

"I appreciate you trying to sugarcoat it, but I'm utterly mortified."

"Don't stress, love," Tina said. "It's not nearly the worst thing that's happened in a meeting. Remember Roger Crosby?"

Natalie rolled her eyes.

"That poor man had Tourette's."

"Still, the client didn't know that."

"Be serious, Tina," Natalie said. "I think

I'm going to puke. Check your email, will you? Is anyone talking about it?"

Tina checked her inbox.

"No. But I do have an email from Steve, and now I have a bad taste in my mouth."

Steven Zacharius was the company CEO, and someone Natalie did her best to avoid. He was a nice enough boss, but he had a terrible habit of pitting his employees against one another.

"He wants to know why our P&L is all screwed up," Tina said. "Should I mention to him that he was the one who suggested we eat the Q2 revenue on the Broadcom deal?"

"Maybe not your strongest play," said Natalie, finally finding something to brighten her mood.

"Forget about Steven. Let's talk about you. What's going on?"

"I'm just not sleeping."

"You know they have pills for that, don't you?"

"Yeah, and they make me so drowsy during the day I can't function."

"Forgive me for stating the obvious, but I wouldn't say that meeting was a high-functioning moment for you."

"Very funny," Natalie said with a slight frown. "But I have to take the pills in the iiddle of the night because they've lost their effectiveness. That's why I get daytime drowsiness. My shrink is kind of at a loss, he's shooting in the dark with his damn prescription pad. We're trying everything, but I'm just not sleeping."

"Well, no shit. Look at your eyes. Careful a raccoon doesn't try to follow you home. What were you dreaming about, anyway? I know you said it was a nightmare, but were there any good parts? Anything sexy?"

Tina's aspect brightened ever so briefly. She liked talking about sex, especially because she complained about getting so little of it at home. She called Viagra a girl's other best friend. Despite the dwindling spark of her marriage, Tina loved her husband, Theo. She kept a framed picture of him — bald, with a round, ruddy face — and their two children (one in junior high, the other entering high school) on her desk in a glittery silver frame.

"Sexy? God, no," Natalie said. "It was a falling dream. It was awful." She recounted what she remembered.

"I think falling dreams and dreams where you can't scream are an indication of insecurity. Any chance you're feeling overwhelmed? Out of control? Maybe a sense of failure regarding some circumstance . . . eh?"

Natalie returned a come-off-it look.

"You know damn well what it's about."

"Have you tried confronting him? Tried being direct?"

"Yeah, point-blank."

"And?"

"And he said if I was sleeping better, I wouldn't be having those paranoid thoughts about him. He said I'm the only woman for him."

"And do you believe that?"

"I don't know what to believe anymore. Honestly, you're the one who got me thinking."

"Me?"

"Yeah, remember? I think we were on margarita number two and I confessed that Michael and I weren't having sex anymore and you said —"

"That it's a sign," Tina answered glumly. "Different with my marriage." Tina used her finger as a puppet to demonstrate a flaccid phallus. "Pills work, but it kinda kills the mood."

"No issues in that department for Michael. But he's more interested it seems in his phone than me, and he only recently became passionate about the gym and his appearance. You said it was like he was following the cheater's playbook. And remember the note?"

Natalie never saw who came into her cubicle, opened the drawer where she kept her purse, and slipped that note inside. It wasn't until she got home and went to put her car keys back in her purse that she saw the flash of white. She removed the paper, unfolded it, smoothed out the creases, and read the typewritten words. A pit opened in her stomach.

We work together. I see your husband at the gym . . . it's not my business, but he's quite flirtatious with the women. One woman in particular. They seem close. I felt compelled to tell you. I'm sorry.

Well before the arrival of the note, Natalie and Michael's relationship had cooled, and unsurprisingly sex was at the center of the trouble. The kids were hardly an aphrodisiac, one of life's great ironies Michael would sometimes joke, but he and Natalie still managed to carve out time once a week, or so, for a bout in the bedroom. Then one week became two, then became three, until sometimes a month would go by without intimacy of any kind. Add to that Addie's asthma inexplicably worsened, badly enough to land her in the hospital overnight, and Bryce was having some behavior difficulties at school.

Natalie was all set to make a grand return to the bedroom, recommit to their sex life, when a big project at Dynamic Media layered on the work and with it the stress. As those work pressures mounted, Natalie's libido downshifted even more until it stalled like a seized motor. She chalked it up to an extended dry spell, but her prolonged disinterest in sex stirred feelings of frustration and doubt in Michael as the weeks became months.

Around that time, Michael got really into the gym and his phone. All of which fueled Natalie's suspicions of infidelity that coincided with the start of her sleep difficulties. She found a direct correlation between her escalating sleep issues and her increasing questioning of Michael's fidelity. More often, she struggled to fall asleep only to wake up an hour later and be wide-awake staring at the ceiling in the wee hours of the night, her mind spinning theories about Michael's extra-curricular activities.

It was an unbreakable circle: he'd make a move in the bedroom, she'd think of him as tainted and pull away, which made Michael more embittered. Marriage counseling wasn't helping. How many times could she listen to her husband's denials?

The arrival of that note moved Natalie from the poor sleeper category into full-blown insomnia. For the last four weeks, it felt as if she hadn't slept at all. Natalie paraphrased the troubling note for Tina.

"Any idea who left it?"

"No," said Natalie. "But I'm sure Michael's not just flirting."

She looked teary-eyed.

"Oh, Nat." Tina got up from her chair, crossed the room, and motioned for Natalie to get out of her chair and give her a hug. "What an ass," she said, after the two women broke the embrace. Natalie still had moisture in her eyes, which would at least save her an application of the Visine she'd been using constantly.

"Why are men so stupid?" Tina asked, giving Natalie one more hug. "Just leave him."

Natalie slumped back into her chair.

"I can't do that. Not without proof. I need to be certain."

"Well, how are you going to do that?"

"Do you know a girl named Audrey Adler? Works in your department."

Tina mulled over the name.

"New girl. Short hair. A whiz with numbers. Not yet jaded. Love her. Why?"

"I found her crying in the kitchenette before the meeting and we got to talking."

Tina returned a curious stare.

"About what?"

"Nothing really." Tina looked skeptical. Guilt won out. "Okay, we were talking about you. I told her we were friends and that we could go to lunch and that I'd give her pointers how to get on your good side."

Tina looked aghast.

"Why on earth would you do that?"

Natalie shrugged.

"She's young and pretty and I got to thinking maybe she'd help me."

Tina eyed Natalie warily.

"Help you do what?"

"Set a trap for Michael. She could come on to him at the gym, because clearly that's his stomping ground, and tell me how he reacts."

"How do you know they go to the same gym?"

"Steve Z might be an ass, but he knows how to treat us. Everyone, spouses included, uses the gym membership. It's such a bargain. And I've seen Audrey's figure. That can't be a hundred percent effortless. Anyway, even if she's into some high-end boutique fitness studio, she still has access to the corporate gym, and Michael goes there all the time now, as you and I well know."

Tina took her seat again, appearing unsettled.

"Why not just hire a private eye like a normal person?"

"This is way less money," said Natalie, offering a devious smile. Certainly she hadn't expected Tina to jump on board with her plan, but she thought she'd be a little more enthusiastic.

"What are you worried about? It'll be fine. Worst she can do is say no."

"You're talking about bringing other people into your problems," Tina said. "I'm thinking the worst she can do is say yes."

CHAPTER 8

Michael

With a heavy thud in his step, Michael made his way back to his hotel room on the thirty-fifth floor. Drained and depleted, he moved as if in a daze, but still took notice of the place where he'd first spotted Teddy on the floor. Michael retrieved the room key from his back pocket, fumbling to switch a bottle of whiskey he'd just purchased from his right hand to his left. In the same pocket was a bottle of aspirin he bought for his future headache. The whiskey was also for his pain.

He stumbled into his room, where the emptiness quickly enveloped him. He'd never heard such silence before. An aroma of forgotten pizza vanquished the vanilla smell, but Michael wasn't sure which scent was worse.

He set the whiskey on the dresser beside the pizza before dashing into the bathroom,

81

thinking he'd puke, but no such luck. Instead, he splashed cold water on his face, not that it refreshed him. He spent a few moments silently staring at the specter in the mirror. It was a surreal sight for sure, twisted and warped, as though he were looking at a Dalí painting of himself. He was different now, a man without a wife and children. He felt unrecognizable.

He imagined what they'd be doing right now if she hadn't run away. At this hour, the kids would probably have been off the wall with sugar-induced giddiness, jumping on the bed as though it were a trampoline, while he and Nat tried their best to quiet them down, worried about neighbors and the noise.

Tomorrow they'd had plans to visit the Museum of Natural History. Michael had concocted a whole story in his mind about how that trip would go: Bryce, excited as could be at seeing a giant mammoth for the first time; Addie, who loved all things about space, would have sat awestruck next to him in the planetarium.

Despite wanting a distraction from the oppressive silence, Michael kept the TV off. He had to think, figure out what to do. He considered eating a slice of cold pizza, but his stomach felt like it was the size of a walnut. Instead, he poured two fingers of whiskey into a plastic cup from the bathroom.

He changed out of his clothes and put on sweatpants and a loose-fitting T-shirt. He wasn't in a rush. He knew Natalie wouldn't answer the phone, but he tried her anyway. Sure enough, his call went straight to voicemail, not even a ring. He pushed aside the raw emotions, the gutting fear and hurt, so he could speak clearly and from the heart. For sure the Jameson helped his cause.

"Hey babe," Michael said. His voice came out in a scratchy whisper. He downed a gulp of the brown liquid and let the burn linger before swallowing. "I'm not sure you're getting these messages. Maybe you're having them forwarded somehow, I don't know."

Here he paused, his breathing hitched and shaky. "I don't know what's going on with you, Nat, where you've gone, why you've run, but I need you to call me. I *need* to hear your voice, okay? I have to hear the kids' voices, too, so I know that they're all right. I know you're not sleeping — that you haven't been yourself — but it's okay. Everything is okay, or it can be. We can work this out, but only if you call me."

Michael felt his throat close up as though he were suffering an allergic reaction. His eyes itched, too, but there was no rubbing away the redness or the sting.

"I'm lost right now," he said into the phone to no one. "I don't know what's going on. I don't know anything."

Now, really Michael, I think you know something.

The devil again, perched upon his shoulder. He knew. The past was something Michael carried with him, even when he forgot it was there. His mind flashed on an image sourced from memory, one of blood and gruesome cuts to a body, of eyes open wide but seeing nothing. It wasn't over. It would never be over.

With a flick of his foot, Michael kicked off his shoes, flopped onto the bed, keeping the phone pressed to his ear. Somehow he landed without spilling his drink.

"Babe, just come back," he said. "Come back with the kids and we'll work this out. We'll work it all out, but please . . . please don't leave me like this."

He ended the call, letting the phone fall from his grasp. It landed on the carpeted floor with barely a thud. He stayed on the bed, eyes glued to the ceiling. Through the thick windows high above Times Square he could hear the sounds of the night, the honks and revving engines, the murmur of a thousand voices rising. People and life all around him, and yet he had never felt so utterly alone and adrift.

Where would she go? he asked himself. *Who would she stay with?*

One possibility came to him. She'd go home, back to her parents' place. Natalie could have had the town car that picked her up at the hotel drive her all the way to Massachusetts — Andover, specifically — or maybe to Amtrak, or the bus station. Her father could have collected her there. She's with them now, he imagined. Talking to them. Telling them everything.

Michael reviewed the day's events, thinking of Kennett, who had touted the benefits of using two detectives to lessen the chance of missing something important. And there was something important that he hadn't considered until now. It was Natalie who learned how long the pizza delivery would take, and she's the one who had suggested Michael go get the food.

A thought came to him, chilling, hard to process, but equally difficult to discount. Was it possible Natalie had done a dry run? Michael envisioned his wife calling that pizza place not from their hotel room but from home, days before they left for vacation. Could it be she wanted to find when delivery would take the longest, and then arranged it so that they would arrive in New York around that time?

The more Michael thought about it, the more it seemed possible. No, make that probable. He had watched the security video. The sedan was *waiting* for her in the carport. She knew exactly when she was going to be leaving. The timing was impeccable.

Three things, but only two stuck out to him.

I wish I'd done this sooner.

I'm grateful for the truth.

Why leave from New York City to backtrack home? Michael asked himself. The answer seemed obvious enough — she wouldn't. She wasn't headed east, back to her parents, Harvey and Lucinda, or even to stay with Tina. If she were going to run, she'd go west, he thought, or maybe south.

He decided then and there not to call her parents. All he'd accomplish by doing that would be to put them in a state of panic. And of course, they'd want to get involved in the search. He knew them well enough to know how they'd react, his father-in-law especially. Harvey was a retired attorney turned middling golfer. He had the time and resources to devote to a search effort, and maybe Michael would enlist his help, but not just yet.

Instead, Michael passed several minutes thinking of friends Natalie had scattered throughout the country, convinced she'd stay with one of them rather than at a motel. He retrieved his phone and accessed the app for their credit card company. The last purchase was the whiskey. If this was well planned, as Michael increasingly believed, it was likely Natalie had obtained a new card.

Hell, maybe she got a new name.

Friends, however, can't be changed as easily. Unfortunately, Michael's recall for names and faces was fragmented at best, and Natalie, not Michael, was the Facebook user. Despite this obstacle, Michael managed to jot down several names. Possibilities really. Calls he could make.

Then, since taking action, any action, was helping more than the whiskey, Michael decided to look up the plate information. Dan White had let him jot down the six characters that comprise a New York State license plate. No need to wait for the detectives. A Google search revealed a variety of internet sites offering free license plate lookup, but all were kind of dodgy. It seemed his best bet was to let the police do the work, or hire a PI, which would take time and wouldn't happen at this late hour anyway.

Michael finished his drink in a gulp before retrieving Teddy. The thought of Bryce separated from his beloved bear shot a pain into his heart. His vision turned watery. Michael wasn't a crier, but now it felt as though a bottomless reservoir floated right behind his eyes. He tamped down the sadness to focus on his web query.

Google would help. It always had some answer.

In the search field Michael typed: *Runaway Adult.*

The first link to appear was something of a "how to" guide, essentially an online instruction manual for ways and means to disappear. He wondered if Natalie had done the same search and come up with the same website. The lead paragraph opened with a reference to a Hindu practice that promoted running away as an act of spiritual illumination. According to the dogma, after twenty or thirty years of managing societal obligations, the time would be right to withdraw and seek the true meaning of life. The rest of the site was ludicrous, with tips on living as a vagabond, or backpacking around the country, even how to get a job aboard a yacht.

Is that what had happened here? Had Natalie embarked on some sort of pilgrimage? Had her sleep deprivation made her delusional?

Michael reasoned he should do as Kennett had suggested and call the police back home in Lexington to file a missing persons report. Too bad he didn't have access to Natalie's social media accounts. He did have Instagram, but never posted. Even so, the account gave him a view into Natalie's feed. Her last post was the same family picture Michael intended to send to the Lexington police. She captioned it:

Arrived safe and sound! Can't wait to explore the city. #familylife #familyluv #blessed #grateful #NewYorkCity

It sickened Michael to think she'd made that post knowing what she was going to do. There were about twenty likes and some comments, including one from Tina urging her to have a blast and get some sleep in a city that never does. At the end of her comment, Tina added a wink emoji.

He scanned the names of people who had liked and commented on that post as well as others she'd made over the years — pictures of their life together, trips to the beach, the mountains, the pond, the park. It wasn't long before he forgot all about his mission to identify someone with whom Natalie might have sought shelter and instead found himself lost in a sea of memories, snapshots of family life that left him feeling gutted and despondent.

He jotted down the names of a few people he thought lived out of state. Michael was about to go for his second two-finger pour when his phone rang. His heart leapt to his throat. The caller, from the 212 area code, wasn't someone in his contacts. He pressed to answer, feeling a dip in his stomach.

"Natalie?" he said, his quiet voice full of hope.

"Michael," a male voice answered with authority. "It's Detective Sergeant Amos Kennett. I have a question for you. Got a second?"

"Of course," Michael said. What other answer could he give? He had all the time in the world now.

"So we ran that plate. Wondering if you know a person named William Gillespie?"

Michael didn't have to think long to answer.

"No. Never heard that name."

"Natalie hasn't mentioned a William to you?"

"No. Not a William. Not a Gillespie. Why?"

"That's the name of the guy who picked her up. Drives for Uber."

Michael tried to tamp down his excitement. It wasn't much, a thin thread at best connecting him to his family, but even so, it was still a lead. It was something.

"Did you call him? Go there? Talk to him?"

"We called," Kennett said.

"And what did he say?"

"He drove them to Penn Station. Short ride. Cheap fare. Good tipper."

Michael puzzled that one out.

Amtrak. The vastness of the rail system meant that she could have gone anywhere. Still, there was cause for hope. There'd be security camera footage to look at. Plus Amtrak would have ticket information, and, assuming Natalie used her real name, the police could probably pinpoint a destination. It wasn't a home run, but it was a start.

"Did he say anything about Natalie? If she seemed okay, or in distress?"

"He said she was another fare and business hasn't been great, his words. He wished she was going to LaGuardia."

"Can you do something? Contact Amtrak? See if you can get a destination from her ticket?"

"If she used her real name, I think so,

Mike. That's assuming she didn't somehow acquire a fake ID. Then we'll really be at a loss. Any idea where she might want to go by train?" Kennett asked.

"No," he said. "I'm thinking about friends she might have gone to stay with."

"Okay. Well, listen. I doubled-checked the laws. You may have a case of parental interference here. Did you file a missing persons report with your local police?"

"No. I'm going to do that soon," Michael said in a quiet voice just shy of despair.

"Okay, Mike. Let me know if you need help there. I'll be in touch if we learn anything. What are your plans?"

Michael looked around the room, the emptiness caving in on him. He rushed to his suitcase. Grabbed the clothes he'd taken off earlier and tossed them inside. He did up the zipper.

"I'm going home," he said. "Right now. I'm leaving here."

"Whatcha gonna do there, Mike?" Kennett asked. There was noticeably more warmth, a little more compassion in his voice this time.

"I'm going to pull apart my wife's life bit by bit," he answered, "and hope to hell the pieces tell me where she's gone."

CHAPTER 9

Natalie

Before She Disappeared

Buckley's was the perfect spot to have lunch with Audrey. The restaurant had a nice selection of soups, always a good choice on a cold, blustery day. March was a sneaky month in New England. There were signs of spring here and there — birds that returned early from their southern journeys, muddy grass freed from layers of ice and snow — but really March was winter, and Natalie was never a big fan of the gray gloomy season. Sure, she'd make an effort to get outside as much as possible, encourage the kids to go skiing and snowshoeing, but really what she wanted the most during those long, cold months was hot cocoa and Netflix.

And sleep. God, how she wanted sleep.

Last night, she'd awoken at two thirty in the morning, her eyes snapping open like she'd been startled from a dream. At first she blamed Michael's snoring, but then realized he was quiet as could be, still as a stone, lying with his back to her. That was how they slept these days. Same bed, backs to each other, as if they occupied different rooms in the house.

What had woken her? Over the last few months she'd become something of a sleep detective. She ran through a series of questions she'd grown accustomed to asking herself. What was she feeling that day? *Emotional tuning* was what her therapist called it. Give the emotion a simple label — I feel sad, I feel happy, I feel lonely — and it helps to lessen the impact. That day she had no label, just the usual: I feel utterly exhausted and depleted.

Had she been extra upset about her husband and perhaps not realized it? No, she was living in a steady state of unease as far as that situation was concerned. All she had on Michael were her suspicions along with the anonymous note that proved nothing. She knew showing Michael the note would get his vigorous denials and cause a big fight, perhaps even a put up (ask for a divorce) or shut up ultimatum from him. To blow up her life, Natalie needed more than intuition to go on.

Tina's negative views of Michael might have tipped the scales toward ending things, but Natalie felt her friend's opinions needed to be tempered somewhat. Those two had never gotten along, probably because they were so damn alike. Headstrong. Opinionated. Driven. Ambitious.

Audrey sipped from her squash soup. No longer a stickler about cutting caffeine, which didn't seem to affect her sleep one way or another, Natalie got an espresso to go with her lunch selection — a bowl of minestrone soup. Audrey ordered hot water with lemon. Probably a consistent choice of hers, Natalie mused. No way would those pearly whites sparkle like they did if coffee or tea graced her lips.

While the two women sat sipping and chatting, butterflies flittered about Natalie's stomach as she contemplated how to broach the subject of Michael. More specifically, she wondered if she *should* reveal her plan. Tina's words came back to her, hard. This wasn't Audrey's problem to solve, but Natalie had reached a new level of desperation.

Maybe once she uncovered the truth, when she knew for certain that Michael was the player she suspected him to be, she'd be able to sleep again. That's all she really wanted. More than a stable relationship at home and a fantasy sex life, she wanted one damn night's sleep when she didn't wake up to darkness outside. It amazed her how slowly time could move, especially between the early morning hours of three and six thirty when the kids normally woke up. She felt every excruciating minute pass like the loud tick of a clock rumbling inside her head.

Natalie gave an involuntary yawn. She caught a slight grimace creep up on Audrey's face, as if she were the cause of her companion's boredom. They'd been doing the small talk — office stuff, project work, nothing of consequence, but it wasn't exactly riveting conversation.

"Sorry, it's not you," Natalie said by way of an apology. "I don't sleep well."

"Insomnia?" Audrey asked.

Natalie gave a nod.

"My mother had it. It's awful. She's had trouble sleeping since I was a young girl. She went through a lot back then."

Audrey trailed off.

Here it comes, thought Natalie as she forced her eyes to keep from rolling, *the litany of advice . . . all of it well-meaning, of course.* Natalie did her damnedest never to mention her troubles because she'd come to loathe the standard list of responses she'd get.

She knew the medicine aisle at CVS like a beloved childhood storybook, and drank enough NyQuil to turn herself green. None of it was a long-term solution, and to compound the problem, she'd quickly developed a tolerance to the natural, homeopathic cures.

She took every path, all the advice, always without success. Meditation. Check. No electronics at night. Check. Hot showers. Muscle relaxers. Reading before bed. Check, check, and check. There was her cannabis phase, which Michael couldn't partake in because his company drug tested. The weed helped her to sleep better, but it made her perpetually sluggish. She even tried counting sheep. One night she got to a thousand little ewes vaulting an imaginary fence in a verdant field before she envisioned impaling the annoying creatures with arrows.

After all the effort and energy expended, she'd resigned herself to a life of perpetual fatigue. Sandpaper-behind-her-eyes kind of exhaustion. It was as if nature had decided to make her the butt of a cruel joke. She was tired all the time, but not able to get a single restful night's sleep.

"You know what she did, my super religious, super straight, super strict mom, to cure it?"

Natalie took a sip of her espresso while giving Audrey an eager stare. In her head she was thinking: *essential oils.*

"Masturbation," Audrey said, delivering her reveal with a straight face.

Natalie got the napkin to her lips a split second before she spit out her drink.

Audrey gave a nervous but endearing laugh as her face went bright red.

"That's right. My sixty-eight-year-old, Catholic-to-the-bone mother asked me for tips on vibrators."

She was still laughing, and now Natalie could safely join in.

"What did you say?"

"What do you think I said? I told her Dame Zee, of course."

Natalie made an uncertain frown. She'd never heard of it, and Audrey picked up on her expression.

"It's relatively new . . . made from the same plastic as Legos, believe it or not, which means thinner material and more room for a high-powered motor."

Natalie held Audrey's gaze a couple beats before both women broke into a fit of laughter.

"Oh my God, if you knew my mother . . . she's like the Church Lady from *Saturday Night Live*. I mean, if she had any idea I told you this!" Audrey's expression suggested some sort of fire-and-brimstone type of event. "She calls it self-care, can't even bring herself to say the word."

Natalie kept a hand over her mouth, simultaneously feeling delighted and mortified.

"I have to say that's not at all what I was expecting to hear."

"Tell me about it," said Audrey with a smirk, still breathing heavily from the fit of laughter. "Anyway, my mother swears by it now. It must release some sleepy-time chemical, I don't know. I probably should research that myself, if you catch my drift."

"Caught," said Natalie with a smile. "Are you with someone?" Audrey just gave her an opening to make her request. Natalie figured if she were unattached, she'd be more willing to lend a hand.

It was as if the air had been suddenly sucked from the room. Natalie could see Audrey retreat into herself, felt the invisible wall come up around her. Sadness seeped into her eyes.

"Well," she said, clearing her throat. It was evident this was uncomfortable territory for her. "That's what I was crying about when you came into the kitchen area that day."

"Oh," said Natalie. She hadn't meant to go there, but now that a door of sorts was open, she felt safe to explore.

"I'm having some — troubles on the relationship front," Audrey confessed. "It's been a difficult, um, let's call it month."

"I'm sorry to hear," said Natalie. "Relationships are seldom easy." She wasn't sure what else to say, but felt confident that her words of comfort did little to ease Audrey's pain.

"Adler's actually my married name," Audrey revealed. "I'm divorced. Four years now. Haven't gone back to my maiden name because, well, it's a long story. Anyway, according to my then-husband, I wasn't cut out for marriage. I honestly agreed with him. There wasn't anything wrong with us exactly, but there wasn't anything really right about us either. We were just flat, or, according to him, I was. Then, I met the person I thought I'd be with forever and everything changed. I felt alive again, in every way." Audrey paused to make sure "every way" was perfectly understood. "Unfortunately, it didn't turn out that way."

A small part of Natalie felt shamefully disappointed. Now it would be quite awkward and utterly inappropriate to proposition Audrey for help with her own relationship troubles.

"Were you together long?"

"No," Audrey said with a pitiful shake of her head. "Eight months, about. But it was quite intense."

Eight months was about how long Natalie's marriage had been on the rocks, and that felt like an eternity. Einstein was right. Time really was relative.

"It was super passionate, the most — uh, most intense love affair of my life. God, I can't believe I'm telling you all this. I'm sorry. I shouldn't unload."

"No, no, don't be sorry at all. Didn't we talk about that? You apologizing for everything?"

Audrey offered up a half smile.

"It's fine, really," Natalie continued. "You need to vent and I'm an impartial ear, so if I can be helpful, I'm happy to do so."

"Thanks," Audrey said. Her sincerity carried a certain innocence to it that made Natalie want to embrace this young woman in a hug. "I've never been so in love before, so loved, but it was, um . . . kind of complicated."

"Why's that?" Natalie asked.

Audrey sighed, looking ashamed.

"Well, this person I was with for those incredible eight months . . . was married."

The harsh reminder of Michael's suspected infidelity made Audrey's admission feel like a slap to the face. One moment Natalie was all compassion and attentiveness, and the next she gazed at her lunch companion with a look of stunned disbelief, eyes wide as though she'd been stung by a wasp.

"Did you know he was married when you got involved?" Natalie asked, worried that Audrey might pick up the quaver in her voice.

"No . . . no . . . not at first, but eventually, yeah, I found out. But by then I was in too deep. I'm not proud of myself. Not at all. I never thought of myself as the home-wrecker type."

"His wife found out?"

Audrey paused, uncertain, it seemed, how to answer.

"No. Not yet. But there was talk of ending things. Divorce, all that."

Natalie had an entire catalog of fantasies about what she'd do if she could confront Michael's paramour. They ranged from the benign — a yelling fit, "He's my man, back off!" — to the truly sinister, such as driving the other woman off a cliff, like something

102

out of a movie. Of course there were no California-style cliffs in the Boston area for that fantasy to play out, but still, it was strangely satisfying to imagine the harlot's car careening out of control, hear the crunch of metal as the vehicle broke through the guardrail, listen to the terrified screams as Michael's lover plunged to her death on the rocky shore below. Never in all her imagining though did Natalie consider a scenario in which she'd confront a woman destroying another's marriage in such close proximity.

"I know it's awful, but it's not like there weren't problems at home before we got involved."

"Right, but it's hard to fix those problems when the focus is elsewhere."

Audrey looked deeply embarrassed.

"I know . . . you're right, and I feel sick about it. But you have to understand, the chemistry between us was instantaneous. It was like a magnetic pull. Honestly, it was overwhelming."

"Where did you meet?"

Audrey paused. How to share, her eyes were saying.

"At the gym," she finally confessed.

"Which gym?"

"Oakmont Athletic Club."

"Our corporate gym?"

I was right, Natalie realized. *Audrey does go to the gym just like everyone at Dynamic Media because Steve Z. provides it.*

"It's open to the public," Audrey said, making it clear it wasn't a work colleague with whom she'd started her liaison.

It's also open to spouses of employees, Natalie thought as a tickle of apprehension slipped under her skin.

It was impossible not to picture cute little Audrey on the elliptical, her tight body like a superhero's tucked into her Lycra workout outfit, catching Michael's eye as he sweated alongside her.

What would be his opening line? she mused. Something innocuous maybe, on the cusp of being cheesy. "You have really good form," he might say. Or, if they'd met on the weight floor, she could hear Michael counting his reps, *one, two, three,* until pert little Audrey walked by, then he'd up the numbers ridiculously: *one thousand one, one thousand two . . .* and then a little laugh, a playful look from her as she checked him over. *Hot,* she'd be thinking, because he was. Michael was an extremely good-looking man.

Natalie shook her head ever so slightly as

if to purge the vision from her mind like a reset.

"So you met at the gym," Natalie said, "and what? He just asked you out?"

"Something like that," Audrey said, keeping it vague. "Skimpy clothes and sweat can be quite the aphrodisiac."

Natalie forced out a smile.

"So what did you like about him?"

Audrey's eyes lit with excitement.

"You mean besides the obvious?"

Natalie gave a slight shrug, hoping her discomfort wasn't showing.

"There's a lot to love. Brown hair, fit, trim . . . super attractive."

Natalie resisted the urge to say that sounded like her husband, but the thought came out another way.

"What's his name?"

A flash of discomfort settled on Natalie's chest. She had no business asking. No business knowing, but the curiosity was like smog in her brain, clouding her better judgment. Audrey returned an uneasy laugh.

"Well, given the circumstances, I probably shouldn't say."

"Of course," said Natalie. "I don't know what came over me."

Yes, you do.

"Well, let's just call him . . . Chris, okay?"

Natalie smiled awkwardly.

Chris.

It took every bit of restraint Natalie could muster not to ask the question most prominent in her mind.

Is his first name Michael? As in Michael Christopher Hart. Natalie did not mention that Chris was her husband's middle name — a name given to him in honor of his grandfather Christopher Anders Hart.

A cold tickle danced across the nape of Natalie's neck.

"Okay, so Chris it is," Natalie said, hoping she managed to maintain a neutral expression. "I've been to that gym, but no guy has ever tried to pick me up."

Natalie tried for a light tone of voice, but thought she sounded bitter.

"Well, with Chris it was the other way around," Audrey answered.

"You came onto him?"

"Sort of. I needed a spotter, and next thing you know we were working out together. We'd arrange it so our schedules aligned, and we became workout partners. One thing led to another, and, well . . . we went out on a date."

"He didn't tell you he was married."

"Didn't come up. By the time I found out, it was too late. I don't know anything about

Chris's family. I didn't ask . . . didn't want to know. Somehow, it made it easier. I know it's selfish, horrible of me. But we couldn't get enough of each other. I just . . . couldn't let go. You must think I'm awful."

Audrey looked profoundly guilt-ridden.

"Well, I'm not here to judge. You really owe it to yourself to live your most authentic life, so perhaps you'll eventually be together again."

Audrey took in that bit of advice, which had pained Natalie to share, while absently drumming her fingers on the table in a rhythmic pattern — index finger to pinky then back again.

She noticed Natalie staring at her hand.

"Oh, sorry," Audrey said, pulling her hand to her lap. "Nervous habit I picked up from — Chris."

A lump sprang to Natalie's throat, making it hard for her to swallow.

Michael drummed his fingers nonstop whenever he was nervous, and it always made her crazy.

107

CHAPTER 10

Natalie

There were three things Natalie counted on happening after she ran. Three things, a slight variation on the family game they played at dinnertime, in another lifetime, it seemed.

One: Michael would call the police. Once he learned they weren't in the hotel, after he searched high and low, after he texted and called with no response, he'd contact the police. He'd probably think his family had been kidnapped.

Good. He needed to suffer.

Two: security cameras would capture them leaving the hotel, most likely show them getting into the waiting sedan. Upon their arrival, Natalie had surveyed the area, immediately spotting two security cameras in the carport. While Michael was taking a family photo, she noted a third aimed directly at the exit. There was nothing to be

108

done there. She wasn't a genius computer hacker who could bring down a surveillance system, so she accounted for it in her planning.

Three: the police would run the plate, confirm it was an Uber ride, and they'd probably get the destination. Amtrak.

They (the police/Michael/everyone) would soon be looking for Natalie Hart, who had boarded an Amtrak train to an unknown destination. Only Natalie didn't get on any train, or a bus for that matter. What she did, as soon as the Uber had dropped her and the children off curbside at Penn Station, was stick out her hand to hail a taxi.

She stood on the corner with Addie and Bryce on either side of her, cars whizzing past, horns honking as if barking at the other drivers. Life here moved with a frenetic energy that reminded Natalie of the jumbled thoughts constantly rumbling through her head as she tossed and turned in bed during those endless sleepless nights.

She found a strange cohesion in the chaos, like a frenetic orchestra playing something wild and untamed yet somehow synchronistic. The city felt dangerous but enticing. For a moment she imagined herself standing on the edge of one of the skyscrapers, readying to make an untethered plunge into the

109

depth of the darkness below. In a way, that's exactly what she was doing.

The children were unusually quiet — no, make that subdued — perhaps in shock. Natalie guessed their fight-or-flight responses were operating in overdrive, poor darlings, and since there was no place for them to run, and nobody to fight, they'd become somewhat frozen with confusion.

In time, she'd explain. What she was doing was mainly for them, their safety. Her only goal now was to get away from Michael, as far away from him as possible, someplace where she could think and plan. Up until now she'd done so much right. The pizza ruse had worked perfectly, as she knew it would at that hour based on the phone calls she'd made from home. It gave her just enough time to gather their belongings and go. The hasty departure, tense as anything she'd ever done, lingered in her mind.

"Where are we going?" Addie asked as she stuffed her flower-patterned pajamas back into her suitcase.

Natalie moved about the hotel room as though she were floating on air, going from one spot to another, grabbing all the things the kids had unpacked in a wild frenzy and

110

putting them into various pieces of luggage.

"I'll tell you later. We have to leave right now."

She used her stern voice, the one she reserved for times when the kids were really acting up.

"What about Daddy?" Bryce wanted to know.

"Your father is going to meet us," Natalie said. "There's been a change in plans and we're going on a surprise trip. It's going to be fun, you'll see."

Natalie's stomach tightened like a precursor to a bad cramp. She hated lying to her children, but the truth? Well, that was out of the question. For now.

"I don't want to go on a surprise trip," Addie said woefully, her expressive brown eyes brimming. "I want to stay in NewYork. This hotel is awesome."

"We're coming back," Natalie said, feeling that cramp again, only this time even tighter. "It'll be at the end of our trip, not the beginning. Okay, loves? But we have to go right now. We have to hurry."

"But Daddy," Bryce cried. "He's bringing the pizza. I'm hungry."

Natalie gave Bryce a Z Bar, one she knew he'd eat that she had at the ready. She needed everything to work in her favor.

"I'll get you something else to eat on our

way out of town. Okay, cutie?" Natalie said, kneeling before Bryce, rubbing the top of his head, her palm brushing the silken fair hair with great tenderness.

Bryce's bottom lip jutted out like a duck's bill as his whole mouth began to quaver.

Tears were coming.

"Grab your Teddy. I'll put on the TV," Natalie said, coaxing him onto the bed.

It took a few seconds, a minute at most, before she found a channel that would appeal to her son, one playing *SpongeBob SquarePants.* She never let him watch SpongeBob at home, it was a bit too fast-paced and a little mouthy for her standards, so this felt like an extra treat. Bryce quickly settled.

Still, even that little delay struck her as too much. If Michael returned from the restaurant sooner than expected, it would be trouble. Her whole plan could come undone. But worse . . . he'd have questions for her. She checked her phone. The timer was running. Then she checked her Uber app. The driver would be arriving in minutes. She had created a new Uber account using a new credit card she'd covertly acquired, one she hoped Michael didn't know anything about. She wasn't too worried about him tracking the Uber ride — she'd planned for that. But she couldn't allow him to be on her trail for long. From her research on how to disappear, she'd concluded money was the bread crumb easiest to follow.

Perhaps Michael, the police, or a private investigator would find her new credit card and track her that way. She had to use her real name and Social Security number to apply. Eventually though, that trail would go cold because she had every intention to live under the radar, so to speak, as soon as it was feasible. It wasn't a forever plan, but she'd be underground long enough to deal with the threat, to deal with Michael.

The movies made it seem easy. Get a fake ID from some nefarious type, new Social Security number, and then step right into your new life. Voilà! The reality, Natalie had found out, was something quite different. Despite all her searching, a few attempted forays into the dark web, she'd arrived at the jarring conclusion that disappearing was hardly a snap. She felt certain her new credit card wasn't the only wide-open hole in her plan that Michael could use to track her down.

Hunt her down was more like it.

Natalie put her toiletry case away last, leaving Michael's on the counter. Waves of sadness washed over her, along with feelings of guilt that she managed to tamp down with nothing more than willpower.

When all was packed and ready, she held open the room door using her suitcase.

"Let's go, children," she said, taking a clipped tone. "Time to leave."

Addie looked bewildered, but she came nonetheless. This was Mom after all, the person Addie trusted most in the world. Not that she'd ever confess to it, but there was an unspoken understanding with both children that Mom, more than Dad, had the answers.

Father knows best, my ass. Michael's show would be: *Father Knew More Than He Was Telling.*

As she expected, Bryce didn't budge when called, so Natalie took the drastic measure of shutting off the TV without warning. That was a mistake. Bryce howled at the black screen.

"I was watching," he whined.

"Not now," Natalie replied tersely, pulling him off the bed by his delicate wrist.

"I'm hungry," he said, sniffling.

"I have bars in my bag. You can have another when we're in the car."

"I don't want a bar," said Bryce, tears filling his eyes, poor thing. "I want pizza. I want Daddy."

He sank back down onto the bed, arms

folded across his chest in a brave act of defiance.

"Daddy will meet us soon. I told you. This is an adventure."

Bryce hurled Teddy angrily at Natalie's head. If it weren't for her quick reflexes, a remnant of her school years as a three-sport varsity athlete, the projectile would have struck her square in the face. Instead, poor Teddy hit the wall behind her. Natalie retrieved the bear from the floor and set him on top of the luggage. In normal times she'd have issued a stern rebuke for her son's outburst, but these were hardly normal times.

"Let's go," she said, adopting an even more commanding voice.

"When will Daddy meet us?" Addie asked as she marched out into the hall, her feet stomping in a huff.

"Soon," said Natalie.

Maybe that was all Bryce needed to hear. One word. "Soon." He was up off the bed, sprinting out the door.

"First one to the elevator gets to push the button," he shouted as he raced past his sister down the hall.

Addie took off after him.

What if they got into the elevator without her? Natalie thought with sudden alarm.

She rushed to the door, grabbed her suit-case, and took off after the children, who were no longer in her sight.

It wasn't until they were driving away from the hotel that Bryce asked for his bear. A sick, sinking feeling wormed into Natalie's gut. She remembered placing Teddy on the luggage she'd used to prop the door open, but had no memory of seeing him at any point thereafter. Was he in the trunk? He had to be. She strained to recall, trying to picture Teddy riding her luggage down the elevator and out into the carport, but it wasn't a clear memory; it wasn't a memory at all.

Her eyes burned with fatigue as her thoughts churned through a series of reassuring scenarios, each of which failed to placate her deepening worry.

It's your faulty sleep-deprived memory is all, Natalie assured herself. Teddy is in the trunk. The driver put him there. It'll be all right. He's in there.

They arrived at Penn Station after a brief car ride. Bryce wasn't panicking. He was curious now.

"Where are we meeting Daddy? When?"

"I can't tell you," Natalie answered. "It's a surprise."

Never in her life had she hated herself

116

more than she did at that moment. The guilt felt like a toxic gas swirling inside her. But what choice did she have? She'd read her fair share of true crime stories about women who had tried to flee a dangerous situation. She knew how they ended up. She'd learned about fathers who had annihilated their whole family, an unfathomable, unholy act, carried out with grim precision and evil desire. She had studied these men to better understand what made them tick, trying to get a clearer sense of her husband and what he might do in retaliation. These men all seemed to have one trait in common: they had to have it their way, had to have the last word — always.

The man thinks: *I want my mistress and not my family.*

Answer: *get rid of my family.*

The man again: *I don't have enough money to care for my family the way I think we should appear to our neighbors and friends — nice home, nice cars, nice clothes, my life is a lie, we're better off dead, so . . .*

Usually the murder-suicides are done with a gun, but there have been cases of smothering, strangulation, and knives that Natalie had read about.

How would Michael kill them? That gruesome question would rattle about her head in the horrible hours between three and six, when all she wanted was sleep, while the man she feared most slumbered peacefully beside her. He'd do it with a gun, right? Quick and painless. He doesn't want us to suffer. He wouldn't want that for his family. He's not cruel in that way, though he is cruel in a different way. And no question about it — her husband is quite capable of murder. He was capable of other things, too, cunning and deceitful in ways Natalie was only beginning to comprehend.

What Natalie did know was that Michael wasn't coming with them, and when Bryce and Addie finally learned the truth, the whole truth about their dad, she assumed (or prayed) that they'd be quick to forgive her for the deception.

The driver off-loaded them at the curbside. Nothing to sign. Uber. Natalie peered into the dark trunk, hoping with all her might.

Bryce soon confirmed her worst fears.

"Teddy's not here," he bellowed.

Natalie felt about in the interior, her hands brushing the carpet, searching every corner.

Please . . . please . . . please . . . be in here. Please. Oh God.

She felt again before resorting to her last

hope. The flashlight on her phone. She shined the blue-tinged light into the darkness.

Nothing inside but a few straps for securing baggage and part of a car jack.

Natalie turned to Bryce, getting low to face him. Gazing into the vast purity of his eyes, such tenderness and guilelessness, so much innocence there.

"Sweetheart, darling," Natalie said, brushing her hand against his warm cheek. "I'm so sorry, love, but I think Teddy must have fallen off the luggage when we were leaving."

He inhaled sharply, eyes gone wide. His shock and hurt felt like a knife in Natalie's heart.

"We have to go back and get him," he demanded.

"We can't go back," Natalie said, the ache in her heart deepening. "I'll call the hotel. We'll make sure Dad brings him to us when we all meet up again. Okay?"

Not okay, Bryce's tear-filled eyes told her.

Damn you, Natalie scolded herself, but then another thought overcame her self-recrimination. She imagined the crime scene tape around the house. Blue and red strobe lights pulsing in the dark night sky. Neighbors standing behind the cordoned off area, clutching each other for comfort. She could hear the whispered talk in her head:

"I knew something was wrong with that guy . . . had a feeling about him. I should have said something."

"I promise we'll take care of it," Natalie assured Bryce, vanquishing that horrible vision. She kissed her son gently on the top of his head, inhaling his scent, fresh and life affirming, her person that she helped to make, that she carried inside her body, a part of her soul forever, entangled in the fabric of her being. The love she had for her children felt as infinite as the stars hidden in the dark sky overhead.

She brought Addie over and hugged both her kids as the Uber driver merged his car into the flow of traffic.

"I love you two with all my heart," she said. "And I will never, ever let anything bad happen to you."

More lies, that voice inside her head scolded. *You can't make that promise. That's not how life works.*

Then she amended her words.

"I'll do everything I can to keep you safe."

Now they were here, and Natalie was determined to keep her promise. Cab after cab passed her. Not one had a light indicating its availability. She prayed, head tilted up to the heavens, eyes closed. *Please,* she silently pleaded. *Please help us. Please keep us in your heart, dear Lord. Please, watch over us.*

She opened her eyes and spied a cab with a single white illuminated light coming down the avenue. Out shot her arm, her hand waving frantically. The driver maneuvered over two lanes. He put the window down a crack. He wanted to know her destination.

"Avis Rental Car on Twenty-eighth and Broadway," Natalie said.

She heard the trunk latch come undone. The cabbie opened his car door, got out, and loaded the luggage into the back.

Natalie ushered her children into the backseat, got in herself, and closed the rear door behind her.

A few seconds later, Penn Station was no longer in sight.

Soon New York would be far behind them, but Natalie knew she couldn't relax. Michael would come looking for them, and he wouldn't stop until they were found.

CHAPTER 11

Michael

Michael kept the radio on for company while he wound his way through heavy traffic out of the city. Sports talk. Mindless stuff. He had his phone on the dash in a holder, Waze there to guide him. When traffic came to a stop, he'd drum his fingers restlessly against his leg. Sweat collected under his thick leather watchband.

It made him nauseated to think he was headed *away* from his family. They were on a train, heading south or west, to a destination unknown. Soon as the traffic thinned out he made a phone call to Amtrak, one that he should have made from the hotel but he'd been too eager to leave. Navigating a hellish phone tree while driving wasn't optimal, but he managed.

Eventually, after enduring a lengthy bit of Muzak, someone came on the line.

He knew from the gruff greeting that his

"ask" was going to go nowhere. Still, he had to try. He explained the situation to the woman on the other end of the phone.

"My wife is missing . . ."

"Kids with her . . ."

"Took an Uber to Penn Station . . ."

And, finally, "Can you look up her name and give me a destination on the ticket?"

"I'm sorry, sir, but that's against our privacy policy," the Amtrak employee replied.

"But this is an emergency," Michael answered, putting in a little extra effort to make sure his desperation came through. "She has my children." His voice cracked slightly. That was authentic.

"Yeah, I got that. But I'm sorry. We don't give out rider information. I suggest you —"

Michael ended the call before she could finish. He didn't need to hear her say the word "police." It would push him to the edge of insanity.

The rest of the drive passed in a blur, something akin to blackout time. One minute he was somewhere in New York and the next he was pulling into his driveway in Lexington, with only the thrumming of his caffeine-addled brain and his exhausted muscles to show for the trip. The tidy blue colonial gave him none of the warm feelings he usually associated with coming home. The porch lights were on, along with a single light in the kitchen, but really it was the alarm system — advertised with an ADT lawn sign — that kept the burglars out.

Michael parked the car, leaving his luggage in the trunk but taking the whiskey. He entered through the front door, silencing the beep of the alarm with the push of a few buttons. He headed to the kitchen, hating the quiet. On the built-in desk stood a mini-mountain of toys and kids' knick-knacks. Sadness tore through him at seeing the faces of his children peering out at him from the artsy black-and-white family photographs that Natalie had framed and hung on a nearby wall. The pain inspired him to try again, one more call, and once more he got pushed to voicemail.

In a daze, Michael made his way to Natalie's first-floor office, located off the kitchen. She'd taken her computer with her. "Emails," she'd said when he asked why she felt the need to bring her laptop on vacation. "I can't do emails on my phone, and I'm in the middle of a big project."

She was always in the middle of a big project, so Michael thought nothing of it —

until now.

What did she have on that computer? Something she might not want him to see? Something that could potentially explain what she'd done? Natalie's desk was spartan. The drawers contained a hodgepodge of office supplies, but nothing of consequence. Still, he sifted through every scrap of paper in that desk, and even dumped out the brown grocery bags destined for the recycle bin. Nothing. It was all just trash.

Her office, like the kitchen, featured framed pictures of the family hanging on the walls. Smiles and loveable expressions gazed back at him, echoing the past. In a moment of raw clarity, Michael saw something else: the fragility of it all. This house, sturdy as could be; a marriage lasting well over a decade; children; the bond, the glue that strengthened the foundation of their lives — all of it was an illusion. It was like a building on a movie set — realistic from the outside, but pass through a doorway and you'd see the struts holding a two-dimensional shell upright. Over the course of a day, Michael made thousands of decisions, but now he understood to his core how it took only one decision, one choice, one action, to dismantle an existence, one mistake to undo it all. That wasn't security;

it was living life on a tightrope.

Michael had had enough. There was nothing here. No clue. No insight to be gleaned. Two minutes later, he was pacing between the kitchen and his wife's office, on hold with the Lexington police department.

Lexington was a bedroom community of Boston, but police business didn't adhere to a nine-to-five schedule. Getting a detective to pick up his call dragged on for a few minutes, affording Michael a chance to think some more about his kids. Was Natalie with it enough to give Addie her inhaler? Could she pay proper attention to the children while on the run? Running from him, of all people, their father. Stress can easily exacerbate asthma symptoms. If Natalie wasn't careful, if she didn't watch for the triggers, Addie could be in serious danger.

The detective finally got on the phone. He introduced himself as Detective Alan McCarthy. Michael launched right into his saga, same story he'd told the Amtrak attendant, but this time with a different ask.

"I need you to issue an Amber Alert."

"Is she . . . it's Natalie, right? Is she your wife?"

McCarthy spoke in a low, nasally voice, and Michael pictured him as a heavyset man, further weighted with fatigue, but he knew that was conjuring a stereotype.

"Yes, Natalie is my wife. She's taken our kids, and I don't know where she went."

"Amber Alerts require certain criteria to be met, Mr. Hart, for us to issue one. She's got custody, right? You aren't divorced, or divorcing, so there's no court order here?"

"That's right."

"Well, then, that's a no. Your kids haven't been abducted. They're with their legal guardian."

Michael shouldn't have been surprised by this duplicate of his conversation with the New York City detectives. Even so, he staggered back as if McCarthy had just delivered him a body blow.

"But they may be in danger. Natalie isn't well. She's got a serious sleep disorder and my daughter has asthma. If my wife isn't careful, Addie could have an attack, and it could be fatal."

It was Michael who had shortness of breath.

"Is she suicidal? Any diagnosed psychosis?"

Michael couldn't lie.

"No. Not to my knowledge."

"So no self-harm, no mental health crisis, no custody violation."

"She has insomnia," Michael said in an imploring tone as if that would sway him.

"Who doesn't," replied McCarthy. "Listen, Michael, I feel for you, I really do. If I was in your situation I'd be doing the same damn thing, calling around, asking for help, but the law here is clear-cut. I can't order an Amber Alert for your kids when they're with their mother and legal guardian. I'm sorry. Have you filed a missing persons report?"

Michael revealed that doing so was Plan B. McCarthy then helped him fill out the correct paperwork, which took the better part of twenty minutes to complete. He provided all the pertinent information — names, dates of birth, and physical descriptions, which included a photograph of his family that he texted to a number the detective supplied.

He thanked McCarthy for his time and effort, though he wasn't feeling particularly thankful. After ending the call, Michael grabbed the whiskey bottle, which he'd left on the kitchen island, and poured some of the liquid into a glass. He went upstairs to lie down and think. His footsteps rattled like cannon shots in the quiet of the home. Was he imagining it, or was that scent of vanilla still haunting him?

In the bedroom, nothing looked as it once did. The bed he shared with his wife was neatly made and would stay that way. He'd sleep on the couch. It was almost midnight, too late to call Nat's parents. He'd do that in the morning. Maybe by then Natalie would come to her senses, but that felt like a dim prospect. In his gut, he knew: this wasn't his life anymore, and all these things they'd acquired over the years were illusions, too. It wasn't the possessions but the people residing within that made a house feel like a home.

Michael settled his gaze on the dresser. His clothes took up the bottom two drawers. Natalie had the other three. Something made him go there, a whisper of intuition perhaps. If she wanted to keep a secret from him, those drawers might be a good hiding place, somewhere he wouldn't accidentally stumble upon it. He riffled through piles of underwear he'd seen on Natalie's body, and thought that he might never see them grace her curves again.

Inside the other drawers, he found her socks and belts and a jewelry box filled with costume jewelry that had belonged to Natalie's grandmother, but no clues, nothing to point him in any direction.

He went to the closet, not to search, but

to get out of the clothes he'd had on in New York, purge himself of the reminders. He noticed a stack of shoeboxes, the ones Natalie left behind. A thought occurred to him that if she'd left the house knowing she was going to run, she knew what shoes she'd want to bring with her on her journey, and none of these made the cut.

The box with the red-soled shoes stood out to him. They were her most expensive pair — he should know, he had bought them for her as a gift. Well, she told him exactly which ones and what size to buy. She wore those shoes, often paired with a black spaghetti strap dress, whenever she got dressed up for a night on the town. The dress went with her to New York because Michael had insisted on it. It was so damn sexy on her, but the shoes had stayed behind, and he hadn't made the connection. That should have been a clue that Natalie had no intention of ever putting that dress on.

Michael opened the box and removed one of the insanely expensive shoes, which looked to him like a form of medieval torture. With one shoe out, he could see a flash of white at the bottom of the shoebox, contrasting with the beige interior — because fancy shoes evidently came in colored boxes. He soon realized the white was a folded-up piece of paper. A receipt, perhaps? Maybe he'd return the shoes. Vindictive? Sure. But maybe he'd do it anyway.

After unfolding the paper, Michael knew this was no receipt. It was a handwritten note. It was unsigned, but he knew who wrote it. He read the words with his heart in his throat.

There's something you need to know. I feel deeply ashamed and I don't think I'm capable of having this conversation in person. I've been having an affair with your husband. I didn't realize he was married when we first started talking. We were just friends and it progressed. As we got closer, I learned the truth, but I let my emotions take over, so I'm at fault as well. It's over now, but I think you should know that the man you're married to has been unfaithful. I'm sorry for the pain that I have caused you.

Oh shit, he thought. *This is bad. But does she know the rest?*

CHAPTER 12

Natalie

Before She Disappeared

The morning after her lunch with Audrey, Natalie awoke utterly exhausted. She made her way to the bathroom on achy legs, thinking she should make yoga a priority again. A splash of cold water felt rejuvenating, but the circles under her eyes suggested that to stay awake at work, she would have to forgo the Xanax she so desperately wanted to take for her anxiety.

After getting dressed, Natalie headed to the kitchen, where she prepped what would be the first of many cups of coffee that day. She looked around, seeing all the familiar sights of home. She had sought meaning and purpose within the kernels of the stories each of those items told: the couch where they lounged during family movie nights; an original oil painting that was supposed to be the start of an art collection but was still the only one they'd ever purchased. Every item, from the expensive to the mundane, told part of the same story: my husband loves me, we have a beautiful home together, a perfect life. It all rang hollow. Her possessions appeared as they did yesterday, as they always had, but now Natalie saw them as tainted, as if a coating of ash had settled over her life's accumulations.

Not only was Natalie convinced her husband was being unfaithful, but had she accidently stumbled upon the woman with whom he was having his affair? She didn't think to tell Audrey her last name. Perhaps Audrey didn't realize that she's Michael's wife, or could it be she was well aware and harbored some twisted curiosity about her lover's spouse? Tina's prescient words of warning came back to her with a sting. The bait had turned out to be the catch.

Natalie made waffles for the kids. More aptly, she put four quasi-edible frozen ovals in the toaster oven and heated them up. She had no qualms this morning about letting the children overindulge in the fake syrup Addie and Bryce liked so much. Natalie far preferred the Vermont variety, but little mattered to her at that moment.

Michael strode into the kitchen, knotting up his tie like he was stepping into a TV commercial: *Morning dear! Coffee dear? No time, hon, got to run. There's always time for [insert favorite brand of coffee here].*

But no, this wasn't a commercial. This was Michael's usual morning routine. He had his gym bag with him. That was different. Normally he kept his workout gear in a rented locker at the club, but Michael had lost his key and didn't want to pay the fifteen-dollar replacement fee.

"It'll turn up somewhere," he told Nat with his usual air of Michael confidence that everything was going to work out just fine.

Natalie eschewed the job of doting wife from that fictitious commercial to let Michael pour his own damn cup of coffee. He fixed it the way he wanted — milk with extra sugar, overly sweet, just like the kids and their syrup. Natalie drank her coffee black, the more bitter the better. Was that a sign of their incompatibility, one that she'd overlooked? Perhaps it was one of many. She wondered how many signs she may have missed along the way.

"Want me to pick up fish for dinner?" Michael asked all honey-voiced, face glued to his phone. Everything was on that blasted device, including, as Natalie now speculated, pictures of precious little Audrey Adler. Maybe there were some naughty shots, or sexts all hot and steamy. There certainly wouldn't be any pictures of that sort from their own bedroom, which had frozen over like an ice storm had passed through.

Michael wanted to blame her insomnia for what he called a "woefully lacking" (aka nonexistent) sex life, which Natalie now saw as a clever bit of misdirection. Sure, Natalie was the first to lose interest in sex, but it was a temporary hiatus she believed, work pressures and nothing more. The note about Michael's flirting habit was bad enough to send her into full-blown insomnia, but Audrey risked pushing her over the edge.

Natalie seethed. This was her life, too. Why should he get to indulge in his dark desires at her expense? No wonder her sleep troubles had only gotten worse.

In her groggy state, Natalie had a flash, something akin to a waking dream, of sticking the knife she was using to cut Bryce's waffle straight into Michael's arm, the blade sinking to the hilt, a splatter of blood going in all directions.

"Fish, babe?" Michael repeated.

The bloody vision left her, but the feeling of grotesque satisfaction lingered a few beats. Michael's handsome face beamed back at her.

"Sure," said Natalie, wanting to rip the phone from his hands and scour it for pictures. "If you're going to Wegmans, can you swing by CVS and pick up Addie's inhaler? She needs a refill."

"Happy to," he said with the charismatic smile that she'd fallen for so many years ago.

She often thought about the night she and Michael met. If she had said no to going to that party, she'd have had a different life, a different husband, one who didn't cheat.

That night, Natalie had set her intentions on bingeing bad TV and self-pity, but a friend of hers from work, Kate Hildonen, pressured her into going out.

"Morgan always invites cute guys to her parties," Kate had said. "We should go check it out."

Natalie was twenty-six at the time, living in Allston. She was happy(ish) with her career but frustrated with her love life, as were most of her single friends who endured the indignity of online dating.

"I want a connection that feels authentic," Natalie told Kate on their way to that party. "I want it to be organic."

"Then it's good we're going out tonight. Trust the universe," said Kate, who, despite having grown up on a dairy farm, could be prone to the mystical.

When they arrived at the cramped little apartment, the first person Natalie set her eyes upon after greeting their host was Michael. She was immediately struck by his handsome features and drawn into his soulful dark eyes.

"I'd say there's some high-quality grade-A organic material right there," Kate noted.

Almost immediately, like an inescapable gravitational pull, Natalie and Michael were drawn to each other. They struck up a conversation, and before long took a fateful walk around the block to get out of the smoke and the noise. That walk all but sealed the deal. Before the evening ended they'd made plans to take a hike at the Blue Hills nature reserve the following Saturday.

One hike led to one dinner, and after that meal Natalie knew she was in deep. From their first moments together, Michael's easygoing nature enveloped her with the pleasant joy of a warm summer breeze. She knew in her heart and soul that there was a rare kind of energy between them. By their fifth date they were already talking marriage, maybe in jest at first, but Natalie picked up the sincerity in Michael's voice and eyes. The eyes seldom lied.

The rest happened like a runaway train.

Natalie and Michael started integrating their friend groups, and then it was time to meet her parents, not his; his were gone, his father having abandoned him and his mother long before she died of cancer. It all felt right and normal, and the next thing Natalie knew, she was married. A year after that she was pregnant with Addie. Then came Bryce.

The anonymous note about Michael's flirting came many years later, and was the start of her full-blown insomnia. What wasn't as clear was when the gulf between them had started to emerge. The specific details were fuzzy, buried under an avalanche of experiences, so many moments that all blurred together. Natalie tried instead to pinpoint a feeling rather than a date or an event when her marriage hit the rocks, but there was nothing, no clear warnings, and no demarcation between the time when things were good and when they were not. Natalie likened her marriage to a frog trapped in slowly heating water, unable to sense the danger until it was too late to act.

The frog always died. The marriage seemed to be taking its final breaths.

She watched Michael fiddle with the thick leather strap of his watchband until it fully covered a nasty scar he picked up from a dirt bike accident when he was a teen. Bryce would never ride one, he swore. He ruffled Bryce's hair as he stuffed one half of a buttery English muffin into his mouth. He chewed slowly with a satisfied look on his face.

"What's going on at school today, champ?" he asked.

Champ — his nickname for his son since he was a toddler.

Bryce shrugged. It was too big a question for an answer. Michael winked. He wasn't expecting any grand revelations anyway, a moment of a connection, nothing more. He kissed Addie on the top of her head. Addie didn't even look his way, but Natalie had no doubt she was glad to receive her father's attention.

"Love you guys," Michael said, grabbing his workout bag on his way out the door. "See you, babe," he called out to Natalie, holding her gaze longer than normal. He came over to her. Gave her a kiss. "You look so tired, hon."

Because of you, she wanted to say.

"I'm fine."

"Okay. Fish and the inhaler. I'm on it."

After seeing the kids off to school, Natalie made her way to the office. She went from meeting to meeting hoping she'd start to feel better. It was as if she'd gone into shock and the gears driving her engine had seized up like a motor running without oil.

Toward the end of the day, a dose of anger kicked in and pushed the empty feeling away. Michael's selfishness, his horrible lack of judgment, had deeply hurt her. This wasn't like forgetting to put a stamp on the electric bill. They had a marriage worth fighting for, especially with the children. It became clearer to Natalie that what she wanted more than anything was to fight for her man — win him back, so to speak, possess him again as she had once before. Even though he had strayed, for reasons she couldn't quite process, she still wanted him. She longed to kiss him deeply, caress his back delicately with her fingers, to pull him in as closely as she could until their bodies came together as one.

She was having these surprising and sexy thoughts when Audrey emerged from around a corner, nearly bumping into Natalie.

"Hey there," Audrey said, her blue eyes brightening. "I came down here looking for you. Glad we caught up. I just wanted to thank you again for lunch yesterday and for being an ear. I so appreciate it."

"Of course," said Natalie, whose thoughts

went racing ahead.

It's a misunderstanding, she was telling herself. Michael isn't Audrey's Chris. All those connections she made could be just coincidences. Maybe the whole thing was in her head and he hasn't been anything other than a giant flirt. That's got to be it. Michael's a good man. She replayed how sweet he had been to her and the children that morning.

A man like that knows his boundary line and wouldn't cross it at the risk of everything he holds dear. But now the question was, how could she convince herself of that fact? While she may have been sleep deprived, Natalie was quite resourceful when the need arose, and soon an idea came to her.

"I love your top," she said to Audrey, who had on a cream-colored cable knit sweater. "You've got such great taste."

She tried not to put on too much of a show. Audrey returned an indifferent shrug.

"I'm far from an expert," she said.

"Well, I'm wondering if you ever shop for men? For . . . Chris?"

Audrey went red in the face.

"Um, sure. I guess."

Chatter on the fourth floor was at the usual high decibel level, but to Natalie's ears

141

the space had gone library quiet. She was letting nothing distract her.

"I want to go shopping for my husband's birthday," Natalie said. "Surprise him with a new wardrobe. Could you maybe suggest a store? Here, let me show you a picture of him. You can get a sense of his style."

Out came Natalie's phone like a quick-draw gun, and in no time, she had a picture of Michael up on the screen. She handed the phone to Audrey, all the while keeping her eyes locked on her target the way a raptor would a mouse. She assumed there'd be no subtlety if Audrey's Chris happened to be her Michael.

Audrey took the phone that was basically thrust into her hand and examined the picture of Michael intently.

"This is your husband?" asked Audrey. Her fingers moved in a way suggesting that she'd zoomed in on his picture. A quick hit of adrenaline sent Natalie back on her heels. Audrey was seeing something all right. Her face blanched as she brought the photo closer, and it seemed for a moment she'd forgotten about Natalie standing there. Then she handed back the phone, suddenly flushed. "He's handsome," she said, looking like she might vomit.

Oh my God, I was right, thought Natalie,

who blinked in disbelief.

But during that brief span when her eyes closed for just an instant, it was as if a complete transformation had taken place. Audrey no longer appeared disturbed or troubled in the slightest. The switch had come so quickly that Natalie had no choice but to question what she thought she'd seen. Did she imagine Audrey's reaction, the shock and surprise? Natalie assessed Audrey anew, this time seeing nothing in her demeanor to trigger any alarm. If anything, Audrey appeared utterly composed.

"I'm sorry," Audrey said. "But shopping for guys really isn't my forte. Though, I'm sure whatever you choose will look good on him."

Natalie focused in on a slight reddish color that had seeped into Audrey's complexion. Was that embarrassment for being put on the spot, or was it a carryover from the initial reaction that Natalie thought she'd witnessed?

Natalie's eyes burned with fatigue. She'd had two hours' sleep last night, and two the night before. She didn't want to use the word, but it came to her anyway.

Hallucination.

Was she seeing things now?

Visual hallucinations, paranoia, and disori-

143

entation are all common symptoms of insomnia. She felt fatigued for sure, had trouble keeping awake in meetings, but had she crossed some threshold into another level of sleep deprivation psychosis? The last thing she wanted was something new to talk about with her psychiatrist.

As if on cue, it happened again — another look from Audrey that Natalie found quite unsettling. There was something in it, something subtle and layered, but underneath it all, Natalie was sure she saw fear.

Then, just as before, the look was gone.

Audrey returned a weak smile.

"Thanks again for lunch," she said. "Let's do it again sometime. I'm late for a meeting. Gotta run."

And with that, Audrey bounded off down the hall at a hurried clip, her fast footsteps soon becoming a run, until at last she was out of sight.

CHAPTER 13

Natalie

An hour and a half after leaving the hotel, Natalie had made it all of two miles in the dense traffic of lower Manhattan. She calculated only a thousand-plus more miles to go. City lights swirled about them like they were driving through an electric meteor shower. The city was alive, and so were they, though Natalie's worries and fears about the upcoming journey only deepened with each West Village Italian bistro they passed.

At least the kids weren't begging to stop for something to eat anymore. They were both quiet and content now that they had bellies full of pizza and sodas, which helped soften the blow of their jarring transition. Bryce's inquiries as to the whereabouts of his father, when exactly he'd be joining them, and where the heck they were going came less frequently until they stopped altogether. He had a blanket to comfort him, soft with a satin edge, but it was a poor substitute for Teddy. Pile on the mother guilt.

Soon as she could, she'd find a toy store and get a new, bigger stuffed animal for him, though she was well aware it wouldn't really help. Teddy could never be replaced. Natalie made sure to check in with Addie as much as she did with Bryce. She was mindful of how stress could trigger her asthma, but so far, so good. Perhaps it was Teddy getting left behind that inspired Addie to act more compassionately toward her brother and less focused on her own distress. It wouldn't have been a conscious choice — she's too young for that kind of insight — but at least for now something was holding her worry at bay, along with her asthma. All that could change in an instant though, and Natalie only had two inhalers. She hoped it would be enough, as picking up another would risk exposure.

After twenty minutes of stop-and-go driving, Natalie was more than ready to say goodbye to the congestion and noise of the city. The kids perked up when they passed through the Holland Tunnel, and Bryce, as expected, won the breath-holding contest. Their delighted laughter from the backseat filled Natalie with some hope, but that didn't erase her fatigue. Her dry eyes felt like they were sprinkled with sand and dust. She knew her doctor would have sternly advised her against driving in this condition. Nobody needed a medical degree to reach that conclusion. Fatigue probably made her as impaired as a drunk driver. It was hard to pay attention to the road and her reaction time was undoubtedly diminished, but still she motored on.

At least she had a plan, a place to go where she was expected — a friend of hers whom (she hoped) Michael wouldn't think to contact. But with so many miles to go, there was no way Natalie could make the drive in one long leg, with or without insomnia. At some point, they'd have to find a motel, hopefully one that would take cash.

Natalie had known that money would be a constant source of stress. She had a thousand dollars in her suitcase, mostly in twenties, all fresh bills, neatly banded. That was all she could siphon out of the home cash supply and checking account without tipping off Michael, who was very attentive when it came to the finances. Each dollar mattered to her now more than ever, but such was life on the run.

The route through New Jersey was a slog, and if the kids hadn't had their devices, they would have been asking how much longer every few seconds. The late evening traffic clogging the long, flat highway puttered along at the speed limit, which Natalie found irritatingly slow. She wanted to blink herself into the next state, get herself and the kids as far away from Michael as possible. Eventually, she'd have to confront him. But she'd do so from a position of strength and only when she was certain he couldn't retaliate in all the horrible ways she imagined.

For the next several miles, Natalie stared out the window at the New Jersey scenery rolling past. It was a barren vista, dotted with oil refineries and desolate, radioactive-looking marshlands. The stark landscape echoed Natalie's emotions. Troubling memories of all she'd endured, all she'd witnessed, came back to her. She held on to these thoughts for a few miles, using them as reminders as to why she had to run.

New Jersey eventually faded into memory as the miles spun on. The kids, worn out from a long day of traveling, finally drifted off, even though the rented booster seats didn't provide much comfort. Addie slept with her head cocked in a neck-pinching way, while Bryce curled up cat-like into a tight little ball beside her.

She drove with the radio off, her phone off too, worried about GPS tracking. She assumed there'd be an accumulation of increasingly frantic messages from Michael. At first, Natalie reasoned, he'd probably think this was all about his infidelity. Thanks to a second anonymous note she'd received, one straight from Michael's paramour, now hidden inside a shoebox in her closet, she had proof of his affair. Of course it had to be Audrey, though she never did get official confirmation or that promised in-person confession. But now, in light of all that she knew, Michael's affair (or affairs) seemed insignificant. Knowing what her husband did, Natalie figured he would soon put it together and realize exactly why his wife and children had vanished.

And that's when his real worries would begin, and then he'd become truly dangerous to them. There were several instances of Michael's anger over the years that she could brush aside at the time, explain away, but in light of what she now knew, they took on a whole new significance. Natalie reflected on one particular event from her distant past, which at the time she had minimized. She would never forget the stranger her husband had become after a harmless fender bender in the grocery store parking lot. Addie, just an infant, had wailed in her car seat while Natalie tried to calm her as Michael pounded his fists on the other driver's window, looking ready to kill. Only Natalie's shriek, "Michael, stop!" had brought her calm, kind husband back to his senses.

The upsetting incident faded from her thoughts as they slipped into Pennsylvania without any fanfare. I-78 was a merciless highway dotted with a surprising number of fast-food restaurants and truck washes. By half past ten, they were closing in on Harrisburg. Natalie pulled off the highway and into the parking lot of a twenty-four-hour Walmart.

She needed supplies, very specific supplies.

The kids were awake now. Poor Bryce. He still carried the weight of his missing teddy bear in his bleary eyes.

Just inside the entrance, Natalie noticed a man with a thick beard, his heavy frame stuffed into a camo jacket — a hunter, perhaps. He seemed to be leering at her and the kids. Almost immediately, Natalie's radar went off.

Something about him seemed amiss.

They'd been gone many hours now, and it took only minutes to do a social media post.

Just one image on Facebook could go anywhere and everywhere. Michael could have easily offered up a hefty reward to anyone who helped him find his missing family. Perhaps the man in the camo coat had seen such a post.

Natalie kept her head down, averting her gaze, hoping not to attract the man's attention while her heart pounded in her chest like heavy-soled footsteps. *Don't look . . . don't make eye contact,* she told herself.

She passed him on the right, but couldn't resist a quick peek in his general direction. Her radar continued pinging too loudly to be ignored. She rotated her head ever so slightly, giving him nothing but a passing glance just to make sure he wasn't a threat. What she saw turned her blood to ice. He was staring right at her with a penetrating look, hard as granite. Even with his thick, knotted beard, Natalie could see a crooked smile upon his lips. He took a menacing step toward them, a glint coming to his dark eyes, and that smile morphed into something more sinister. Natalie's heart did a dance as he advanced stealthily.

Maternal instinct took over. She grabbed Bryce by the arm, hard enough to make him yowl. Michael had done something like that once, grabbed Bryce by his wrist when he wouldn't pick up his Legos. He'd given the arm a hard tug, then came a pop followed by a cry of pure agony. At the time, Natalie had thought it was an accident — Michael not realizing that the ligaments of a young child could easily slip out of place and get caught between the two bones of the elbow joint. While at the hospital, she heard the name for the injury: Nursemaid's Elbow, which gave quite the free pass to dads everywhere. Back then she'd thought of that incident as nothing but overzealousness on Michael's part, but now, in light of recent events, she saw it much differently.

He did it because he couldn't control himself.

There was darkness inside him.

The memory of that trip to the ER came and went as Natalie dragged Bryce down the detergent aisle. Without being told, Addie stayed in lockstep with her mother, thank goodness for that.

She advanced several feet before daring a glance behind her. *Please . . . please don't be there,* was her singular thought. She swiveled at the waist nonchalantly, feigning interest in the products on the other side of the aisle. But there he was — the man in the camo coat had followed them, and was approaching with a look of determination.

Terror flooded Natalie as she clutched Bryce's hand harder. Addie took no notice of the man approaching them. She had smartly stayed close to her mother and Bryce because that's what she'd been trained to do. But what training did the camo coat man have?

Maybe Michael *hadn't* put the word out on social media to find his family. What if instead he'd hired someone with the skills to track her down? And what if the camo man, now only fifteen feet away, hunted more than animals? How the tracker had found her so quickly was irrelevant. The bigger question was if this store had a rear exit, or better yet, armed security.

Natalie hurried down an aisle that felt like the length of a New York City avenue. In her mind, the shelves on either side of her grew tall as those skyscrapers, boxing her in. *God, how big is this Walmart?* The answer was big enough for Natalie to dare a second glance behind her, because she wasn't going to evade him.

Sure enough, Camo Man was still there and closing in fast, now taking quicker strides. Only twenty feet separated them. As he continued his approach, a flash of movement drew Natalie's gaze to the man's right hand, which had slipped innocently enough inside his jacket pocket. What was in there, she wondered? A knife? A gun? His piercing stare bore into her.

Natalie saw no chance for escape. He was gaining too much ground, coming too fast. Best she could do was scream for help. Coming to an abrupt stop, Natalie pulled her children in tight like a mother bird wrapping her wings around her chicks. She turned them a hundred eighty degrees so that they were now all facing the threat head-on. Her legs felt heavy, immobile. Watching with growing horror, Natalie observed the man slowly remove his hand from his jacket pocket. She caught a flash of silver, believing it to be the steel from some weapon. She felt a scream begin to materialize like a hurricane taking shape. She pushed the kids behind her — she would protect them at all cost.

Then she saw it. Not a knife, but the silver wrapper of a stick of gum. Camo Man removed the wrapper with one hand and slipped the gum into his mouth. The crumpled wrapper went back into his pocket. Natalie was stunned to see him walk past her, his face utterly placid, devoid of any hint of danger.

What the hell?

She was sure she'd seen it in his face, felt

a threatening intent, but the beard now gave him a genial quality, almost like a gentle giant type. He looked right past her and the children, settling his gaze on the selection of detergents. Eventually, he grabbed an orange plastic jug of Tide from off the shelf, tucked it under his arm like a football, and headed contentedly on his way.

It wasn't possible, Natalie told herself. She had watched him come at her with unmistakable hostility. What other motive could he have had but violence?

Still, she had to admit, perhaps she'd imagined it, just as she may have imagined Audrey's odd expression at seeing Michael's picture.

Sleep. God, she needed sleep.

"Anyone hungry?" Natalie asked, fake cheer in her voice.

Her breathing came in sputters as she tried to cool her engines. The kids had no idea she'd been alarmed. As far as they were concerned, their mother had brought them to the detergent aisle for no reason whatsoever, because they departed empty-handed. Now, they headed to her original destination — the beauty aisle.

"I want a cherry slushie," said Bryce in answer to Natalie's question about food. He'd spied the vending machine on their way into the store, already asked once, and got his answer.

"Slushies aren't real food," said Addie, parroting something she'd heard Natalie say in the past. Bryce was about to protest. If he raised a ruckus that might mean attracting unwanted attention. That couldn't happen.

Camo Man might not have been the threat she perceived, but that didn't mean there wasn't constant danger.

"It's fine," she said to Bryce, feeling herself snap back into her body. "I'll get you that drink on the way out."

Addie sent her mother a look of indignation.

"Well, I want one too," she said, exhaling a huff of air.

"Yes, of course," said Natalie, remembering the pizza and Cokes she'd already fed them.

Mother of the year, chided a voice in her head. But then she remembered: *I'm keeping them alive. I'm doing this for a purpose.* She knew the truth about Michael. Some secrets changed everything. It was like she'd taken a bite of the forbidden apple: one taste and there was no going back to the garden, ever again.

What she'd done was right. She had no

choice. They had to run.

With bouncing steps, Addie and Bryce headed for the slushie machine, but Natalie called them back.

"We'll get the drinks on our way out," she said firmly. "First, we've got shopping to do."

CHAPTER 14

Michael

Morning sun splashed into the bedroom, rousing Michael from a fitful night's sleep. He had drifted off, hoping for a different outcome before daybreak — a phone call or text message, something from Natalie that would bring an end to his nightmare. No such luck. He got up. Showered. Shaved. He didn't want to look scraggly when he broke the news to Nat's parents. The thought of that visit was already filling him with dread.

The day was going to be an eventful one, so Michael fortified himself by forcing down some scrambled eggs and toast. The coffee tasted bitter and failed to vanquish his lingering fatigue.

He asked himself: *Is this how Natalie felt all the time?*

Regrets hit him like punches.

I should have been more attentive. Done

more to help. I should have known she was
teetering. We should have doubled the mar-
riage counseling.

Three things.

Today I got us all packed and ready to go.

I wish I'd done this sooner.

I'm grateful for the truth.

On the kitchen island, Michael placed the
note he'd found in Nat's shoebox. Grateful
for the truth. She'd found out. Dammit.
Damn him. He'd been unfaithful to his
wife, deceitful, and Natalie knew, Lord help
him, she knew the truth. Sort of. He prayed
with all his heart that she hadn't learned all
the facts. A flash of blood hit Michael, his
mind seeing what he'd never forget, and
what he now feared Natalie had discovered.

Michael finished the breakfast dishes
while ruminating on the excuses he'd used
to justify his affair: they'd gone months
without sex (really without physical intimacy
of any kind); Natalie blamed work pressures, but he thought the children had
become more important than the marriage;
then he fell prey to temptation which roused
Natalie's suspicions and started the sleep
difficulties that only grew worse.

By then Michael had felt trapped in his
lies. He was desperately lonely in his marriage, in his life. He lived a grand façade, an

illusion. How many nights had he touched Natalie's shoulder, only to feel her shrug away, reject him? It happened with such frequency that approaching her felt like navigating a minefield.

Life became a grind. Work. Kids. Dinner. Rinse and repeat. The less Natalie slept, the more she pushed Michael away. Marriage took work, a lot more than he'd bargained for when he said "I do." Unhappiness and dissatisfaction with a spouse was as common as a cold. But still, it wasn't like he'd struck up a conversation with another woman thinking he'd end up in her bed.

It was innocuous, he told himself, in the beginning, back at the start of it all. Eye contact leading to a smile, leading to an offhand comment about the dearth of free weights on the bar; a little self-deprecating humor that allowed him to seem endearing instead of creepy.

When next he saw her at the gym, Michael didn't feel any great connection between them. The clouds didn't part, no golden ray of sunshine lit her like a spotlight — it was not a *This is your path, Michael* kind of thing. No, it was a slow burn, with the eye contact lingering a beat longer, his smile growing deeper, hers a little more welcoming.

They talked about fitness. Obviously it

was a shared interest, given where they met. The third time he saw her, Michael felt comfortable correcting her form on the tricep pushdown. She thanked him. The next day, she corrected his squat, letting him know to put more of his weight back into his heels. Soon after, they were working out together, and he felt an unexpected chemistry. Conveniently, he kept his wedding ring in his gym bag, and the gym bag in his locker, so the subject of his marriage didn't come up.

Not immediately anyway.

After a month or so of pumping iron, stirring the endorphins, it was a natural progression that the conversation turned more personal. Michael found it easy to open up to her about his marital struggles — the lack of intimacy, of touch of any kind — that sat at the center of his frustration and sadness.

Laura. That's what he called her, his wife.

It felt strange not to use Natalie's real name, but Michael had good reason for the ruse. The object of his desire (and yes, he now desired her) worked for the same company as Natalie. The more they spoke, the clearer it became to him that he was crossing lines that shouldn't be crossed. He understood he was playing with fire that would eventually burn him, but his brain

161

seemed to have shut down. Reason abandoned him and compulsion took over.

I'm lonely and alone. I'm getting older. Why should I live this way? Yes, they were justifications, but not without merit. The word "divorce" had rumbled in his head countless times, and eventually it came out to Natalie.

"This isn't working," he told her.

A sexless marriage, a loveless union — it was joyless for him, but it wasn't like they hadn't been trying to rekindle the romance. Michael made a point to be generous with his touches and gratitude, buy flowers and thoughtful gifts, and do his fair share of the chores and childcare duties. He talked openly about his desires and needs, and it was he who had suggested marriage counseling.

The counselor revealed that their real problem wasn't sex, but a lack of communication and support. He and Natalie simply didn't talk. She was too tired to hear about his day, to talk about hers, or to make plans for the future. He correlated Natalie's mounting work pressures with their subsequent relationship stress and lack of intimacy. It seemed to Michael that Natalie's insomnia came later, as she became suspicious that he was hiding something. Michael had no doubt his hurtful behavior was at the root of her sleep difficulties. She tried to get him to admit to his affair a month after it started, but he wasn't brave enough to tell her the truth.

"Are you seeing someone? I have this feeling you are."

"No," Michael assured her. "Of course I'm not. I would never."

Oh, how easily that lie came out. So convincing was his denial that he almost believed it himself.

He'd taken his new workout partner for coffee one afternoon following an extra strenuous, sweaty session. They chatted with ease. Without the weight and worry of running a home — bills, kids, job — he was free to be himself. He could vent a bit, and she could do the same. She recounted for his benefit her series of failed romances, and in those stories, they found a common thread of frustration.

"It's not about sex," Michael said as the two sipped on lattes and nibbled decadent desserts. "You want to feel wanted, feel loved. My wife and I stopped being friends. We're basically business partners now."

Despite the counseling, Natalie simply didn't want to talk about the state of their marriage. She avoided it at all costs, preferring instead to focus on things she could control: the kids' activities, treatment for Addie's asthma, her work. When relationship issues did come up it was more a list of grievances than a productive dialogue. Instead of coming together, they pulled further apart.

Did she notice the changes in him before the affair progressed? If so, she never commented on how he started losing fat and adding muscle, or bought grooming products he'd never tried before. He stopped asking for sex, too, because in his mind he was already having it with another woman.

Michael knew from discussions with the marriage counselor that he had grounds for divorce. He felt deprived in the marriage and couldn't imagine a fulfilling life without intimacy and a loving partner.

At least, that's what he told himself the day he crossed the line. It was a long, slow, tender kiss, the kind he remembered from his much younger years. There was freedom in it, and danger too, but it was more than that — he felt alive for the first time in ages.

He made all the trite excuses.

I deserve this. I need this. Nat's not committed to fixing our problems.

That's how a kiss became more, like the famous line about how one goes bankrupt, first slowly, then all at once.

There was no going back. He couldn't undo what he'd done. He could have stopped it at that though, a one-time-only thing. A fling. An indiscretion. Nobody needed to know. Nobody would have been hurt. But he couldn't stop. It was as if he'd mainlined a narcotic more addictive than heroin.

They had their ways of communicating in secret, using apps that allowed for discretion as they planned their next rendezvous. Sweaty sex. Tender sex. Glorious sex.

Eventually though, reality seeped into his bubble. His lover began to feel used, a second fiddle in Michael's life. She felt dirty, wrong, and sad all bundled into one. So instead of enjoying their liaisons, Michael spent those encounters coddling and reassuring her the best he could. But it was never enough. She wanted him all to herself.

That's when it hit him, like he'd awoken from a dream. This wasn't a game he was playing. There were real lives at stake, not just Natalie's and the kids', but his lover's as well.

It was as if an invisible switch flipped inside his chest. One second he was all in; the next he was all out. But getting out? Well, that was going to be a problem. He might have been ready to walk away, but she was not. She made all the threats.

I'll tell your wife.

I'll call you at all hours.

You can't just dump me like I'm trash. What if your kids find out? Have you seen that movie, Michael?

Up came his hand. He stopped himself though. Instead he pushed her hard onto the bed. She cried out, but more from fright than pain. He straddled her on the sheets where they'd made love only a half hour ago, pinning her down. He set his hands upon her throat, but resisted a powerful urge to apply exquisite pressure. He felt the desire though, palpable and pulling as a siren's call, one fueled by that rage that could go from a few flames to a conflagration in a snap, a snap of his temper, or a neck. He thought how easily it could happen, how quickly he could let his anger consume him, and his grip around her throat tightened ever so slightly.

Somehow, and thank God for that, he found himself dialing up the restraint.

Instead, his words of warning delivered a different kind of blow: "If you ever threaten my children again, I'll kill you."

He couldn't believe what had come out of his mouth, but it wasn't the first time he and murder had shared a close connection.

He climbed off her but stayed on the bed. Her eyes were as large as two saucers. He could see her trembling beside him.

"Stay away from my family," he warned in a low voice.

His kids.

That was the one place she couldn't be allowed to go. He might not have been the greatest husband, but his children meant the world to him. He'd die for his kids. He'd do more than that.

Michael got up off the bed. Got dressed. Left her place.

But that wasn't the last time he saw her.

CHAPTER 15

Natalie

Before She Disappeared

The elevator chimed, doors opened, and moments later Natalie emerged onto the seventh floor. There was no meeting today with the finance team, so technically she had no business being up on seven. She had no business sending Audrey Adler a Facebook friend request, either (which Audrey had ignored), or five emails asking for a private meeting and about an equal number of unanswered phone calls, but she'd done all that, too.

Probably not the wisest move, but her husband was probably screwing this woman, so what the hell? They should talk.

Rows of cubicles conjoining along a vast concrete floor gave the office layout the look and feel of a maze. If Natalie hadn't already sourced Audrey's cube number from the corporate intranet, she might have been wandering the aisles on the hunt. Instead, she was a woman on a mission and on the move.

A palpable rage simmered inside her, something molten and dark, but Natalie knew it had to be kept in check, especially at work. Twice now she'd tried confronting Audrey in person, wanting only confirmation of what she suspected to be true. Each time, Audrey intentionally avoided Natalie's gaze, as if doing so somehow rendered her invisible. Then, as casually as an afterthought, she changed course, slipping away before any words could be exchanged.

A three-walled cubicle would offer Audrey no easy way out this time.

Thanks to the company's shared Outlook calendars, Natalie had picked an hour when Audrey's schedule was clear. It wasn't a guarantee that she'd find Audrey at her desk, but the odds were in her favor. All she wanted to do was talk — well, that and elicit a confession.

Two days ago, Natalie had tried and failed with Michael. She'd said the name, Audrey Adler, before showing him a picture sourced from LinkedIn. It was a nice headshot that called attention to the blue of her pretty eyes and her delicate red lips. She caught a look in Michael's eyes, a flash of recognition that came and went as fast as a bolt of lightning. It was such clear and convincing evidence of his betrayal that Natalie had the urge to punch him in the face right then and there.

"I don't know who that is," Michael said rather flatly.

Natalie scoffed.

"Maybe that's because she's got her clothes on in this picture."

Michael groaned, rolled his eyes.

"Are we back to that again? My affair? I told you, I'm not seeing anybody, but I think *you* should see someone — your shrink, to be precise. You're getting paranoid now, making up stories. You need to stop with the accusations."

"I'm not just making up accusations," Natalie said, loud enough to be heard in the other room. "She works out at the same gym you do. She's seeing a married man named 'Chris' — your middle name. Chris drums his fingers, a nervous habit. Sound familiar? Brown hair. Good looking. Not to mention Audrey freaked out when I showed her your picture, so I know you're fucking her, Michael. Just admit it."

"Good God, Nat, keep your voice down, will you?" Michael seethed, gripping the upper part of her arm tightly in his hand. She felt the pinch on her bone as his fingers dug in, a sharp pain radiating down to her wrist.

Natalie knew the kids were within earshot, but she didn't much care. For once she didn't feel utterly enervated and fatigued. She had a pulse of fresh rage to fire her up.

"I saw the look in your eyes just now," Natalie said. "It was the same as Audrey's. You can't hide that. And I got a note from someone at work, too, claiming to have seen you flirting with pretty girls at the gym — with one woman in particular." Natalie held up the picture of Audrey again. "This woman."

Natalie long suspected that Dave Edmonds, her employee who had a crush on her, had left that note, but she didn't have corroborating evidence, or reason to doubt him given her husband's other telling behaviors.

Michael gave the image of Audrey a second glace, but this time she saw nothing in his eyes. Natalie couldn't help but wonder if she'd imagined his initial reaction, just as she may have imagined Audrey's.

For this coming confrontation, Natalie vowed to be ready. She would lock in on Audrey's face, not lose focus, not even for a second, and hopefully come away from the encounter without any lingering doubts.

Natalie found the right cube, and felt a spurt of gratitude when she spied Audrey seated inside. She had her back to the entrance, working away on a spreadsheet. Her two monitors glowed brightly, which gave Audrey's gorgeous auburn locks a halo-like effect. Natalie cleared her throat. No headphones meant Audrey couldn't pretend not to have heard her. Swiveling in her chair, Audrey's affable smile faded quickly when she saw who was calling for her attention.

"We need to talk," Natalie said.

Without reply, Audrey rose from her seat, aggravation dimming her usual radiance.

Natalie pressed her hands against the cubicle walls, forming a makeshift barrier with her arms.

"I know you're with him," Natalie said. "Michael is your 'Chris.' I saw the look on your face when I showed you his picture. Michael all but admitted it, too."

"I'm sorry, Natalie, but I'm afraid you're mistaken. I have a meeting. I have to go. Maybe we can talk later."

Her voice trembled, her tension palpable as a touch.

Natalie didn't lower her arms, but that didn't deter Audrey, who ducked low enough to get under the barricade as though

172

she were doing the limbo. After righting herself on springy legs, Audrey made a hasty departure for the elevators.

Natalie went to follow, but stopped when a strong tug on her arm pulled her in the opposite direction. She turned to see Tina Langley standing there. Tina kept a tight hold on Natalie's arm. Glasses magnified brown eyes that conveyed Tina's surprise and concern.

"What the hell are you doing, Nat?" Tina said, taking a sharp-edged tone with her friend.

"She's sleeping with Michael," Natalie answered back in a whisper. Evidently, she wasn't whispering quietly enough, because from down the row a young employee did what prairie dogs do and popped up from his cube to have a look around. He caught Tina's fiery gaze and down he went again.

"You need to come to my office. Now."

No debate there. Moments later, Tina and Natalie were seated together in her windowed office with the door closed.

"Look, I was going to call you," said Tina. "HR came to me with a complaint about you. Apparently, Audrey thinks you've been harassing her, and they've opened an internal investigation."

Natalie looked aghast.

"What? What the hell?? No! *She's* sleeping with *my* husband."

For Tina's benefit, Natalie rattled off the evidence, starting with where Audrey and Michael met — at the gym. She reminded Tina about the note.

" 'Flirting with one woman in particular,' " said Natalie, paraphrasing the confessional.

Natalie listed more connections, the same batch she'd given Michael. Then came the big reveal: Michael's reaction to seeing Audrey's picture, and Audrey's reaction to seeing Michael's. (She left out the part where she may have imagined both reactions because she'd been seeing things lately.)

"Hey, Encyclopedia Brown, I'm glad you've done your homework. And maybe you're right, maybe Michael is doing what you think he is, but if you keep going down this road with Audrey, you're going to lose your damn job. I'm saying this harshly only because I love you and I don't want to see that happen."

Natalie rolled her eyes the way a teenager might.

"Please . . . some random employee is more important than me?"

A sharp pain radiated around Natalie's temples. Her headaches were starting to come back. She'd gotten what, three hours of sleep last night, according to her tracker? This week was shaping up to be one of her worst yet.

"I'm sorry I said that," offered Natalie, adopting a grimace of embarrassment. "I'm not myself."

"Obviously," said Tina, her smile slight. "Just promise me you'll cool your jet engines, okay? We'll put our heads together and figure out a way to get the name of Michael's love interest without you getting tossed out on your ass."

"Right," said Natalie.

Tina tapped her fingers impatiently against her desk, her eyes demanding more of Natalie.

"Okay," Natalie said, with emphasis this time. "I promise."

To seal the deal, Natalie used her finger to make the shape of an "x" over her heart. Tina didn't look entirely convinced.

"Let's meet up after work for a drink. We can talk and plan."

She took that as her cue to leave.

"Let me see how I feel," replied Natalie, knowing full well she already had plans.

Hours after she'd bailed on drinks with Tina, following too many emails and meetings, the day's work was finally done. Natalie sat in her car in the employee parking lot, keeping an eye on things — one thing in particular. She moved to a new parking spot, one that offered the perfect sight line to a little red Kia Rio, the same car Audrey had driven to Buckley's on the day the two had shared that fateful lunch.

It was going to be a late day at the office — that's what Natalie had told the nanny. The kids were fine. The nanny was taking care of things at home, as she did Monday through Thursday. She agreed to stay as long as needed, freeing Natalie to go on a little expedition, though the right word, she knew, was tailing.

Natalie was texting with the nanny, making sure dinner was set (Bryce and his finicky eating these days), when Audrey finally appeared. She exited the building looking, to Natalie's eyes, hardened, determined. The sky was gray and overcast, the threat of rain hanging in the air, which seemed to suit Audrey's mood. This was a new look for her, and if Natalie were to infer anything from it, she'd say that Audrey didn't appear eager to go to wherever she was headed.

She watched Audrey get into her car. Moments later, the Kia abandoned its parking space after completing a tight turn. Thank goodness Audrey didn't seem to take notice of the midnight-blue Toyota Highlander that followed her out of the parking lot.

Natalie had never played PI before, didn't know the first thing about following somebody. She didn't think her SUV would attract much attention, but even so, she kept a few car lengths back. Twice she got a yellow light and had to switch lanes, gunning it to make sure she wasn't left behind. If Audrey became suspicious and checked her rearview, she likely wouldn't even recognize Natalie, who had donned a black baseball cap and wore sunglasses despite the gloomy day.

Until Tina had pointed it out, Natalie didn't think of her behavior as harassment. Clearly though, what she was doing now crossed a line. She could feel it like an insect bite on her neck, a tiny bump growing in size. That's what obsession felt like — a bite she couldn't scratch away.

Natalie followed the Kia onto I-95, and drove five miles south until Audrey flicked her blinker, bringing them both into a rest area with a McDonald's right off the highway.

The parking lot was half full, but Audrey settled on a vacant spot some distance from the entrance to the McDonald's. Was Audrey here for a bite to eat, or to meet somebody? Natalie drove her car into a spot a few rows behind the Kia. A light rain began to fall, a steady pattering on the windshield that left what looked like teardrops on the glass. Natalie kept the wipers off, allowing the rain to accumulate, making it harder for her to see and be seen.

Audrey stayed inside her car. Why? She had to be meeting someone. What other reason could there be?

She'd picked a good night to tail her coworker because Michael had texted to inform her that he, too, was working late. He smartly — or so he thought — offered assurances that it was *work* he'd be doing.

I know how you think these days. Don't get any wrong ideas. Ok? I love you.

He added two heart emojis after his message for emphasis.

Natalie's BS meter ticked up a few notches higher. *Guilty hearts,* she thought. Perhaps she'd be seeing her husband soon if she was right in thinking it was Michael that Audrey had come to meet. As the minutes passed and nobody showed up to rendezvous, doubt started creeping in.

You imagined it all, Natalie told herself. *The look on Audrey's face, then the one on Michael's, it's all in your head.*

Go home, Nat, that same voice urged. *Go back to the kids.*

Let the nanny go home.

Let this craziness go.

You're doing it to yourself.

Natalie's eyes burned with fatigue. She was tired. So damn tired all the time.

Again, she felt her eyelids growing heavy.

Don't.

Not now.

Audrey's here to meet someone. I can feel it in my bones. I know it in my heart. Something is going to happen.

But after so much time open, her eyes had other ideas. The patter of rain bouncing off the car roof made a gentle, rhythmic sound as the droplets hit the windshield, and its hypnotic quality eased her serenely into the place she wanted to go . . . but not now. Anytime but now.

Natalie fought as best she could, but it was no use. She heard Tina's voice ringing in her head: *you're going to lose your damn job!*

Next came Michael's.

Stop doubting me.

Then nothing, there was nothing at all,

but a blissful darkness. But from somewhere in that emptiness, Natalie felt a tug, not unlike the one Tina had given her arm some hours ago. This one, however, came from within, like a pull toward consciousness. As the sensation grew more imperative, Natalie forced open her eyes, allowing sips of light to hit her corneas. It took a moment for her vision to focus and when it did, she saw the taillights of Audrey's Kia on the move.

She had no idea how long she'd been sleeping. It could have been a minute or an hour. When she checked the clock on the car dashboard, she calculated that she'd been asleep for twenty minutes. *What had happened while she was out?*

Natalie snapped wide-awake. She got her finger on the button to start up her car engine. But before she could give it a push, something else caught her eye. A black Audi A8 had pulled directly behind the Kia as if the two vehicles were departing at the same time. Something about the rear of the car drew Natalie's gaze. Her vision was still slightly out of focus and the rain made it difficult to see, but Natalie could make out a dent on the right side of the Audi's back bumper.

She put her car in drive, then stopped short as a car she hadn't seen sped in front of her blaring its horn. She suddenly felt woozy, and wasn't sure she could maneuver her vehicle safely. Both cars faded from view, but not before she had made two observations:

Michael drives an Audi A8.

And his car has a large dent in the right rear bumper.

CHAPTER 16

Natalie

The motel was the kind Natalie would never have stopped at, the sort she'd expect to see on a *Dateline* episode, a place where the body had been found. The white clapboard siding had plenty of chipped paint, some of the shutters hung askew, and the grass, if it could be called such, looked like their lawn after they'd left it for two weeks in the heat of summer without setting the sprinkler. Still, the place had plenty of vacancies, it was cheap, and it happened to be directly off the highway, making Natalie's getaway much easier should the need arise.

She couldn't imagine how Michael would track her and the kids to this shabby place in the middle of Nowhere, Pennsylvania, but he was nothing if not resourceful. She found it easy to envision how the "reunion" might go should his efforts prove successful.

There'd be news coverage, of course. A father reunited with his missing kids was good for ratings. She had no doubt Michael would be all smiles and gratitude under the glare of the camera lights. He'd ooze his praise for the first responder types who had aided him in his desperate search. In the next breath, he'd tearfully express empathy for his poor, poor wife, who had such terrible insomnia that she'd suffered delusions, causing her to lose control and act impulsively. Once the cameras were off, however, Natalie was certain the real Michael would emerge.

And soon after, another news story would take place.

A family annihilated by their father.

Natalie often wondered how it might end. Would it be a murder-suicide, or was Michael too weak to take his own life? Probably he'd try to blame it on an intruder before the police put the cuffs on him. Either way Natalie, Addie, and Bryce would all end up in the afterlife, if such a thing existed.

That's why she had to get the kids to Missouri, to her friend Kate's farm. In a roundabout way, Kate owed her. It was Kate Hildonen who, many years ago, had suggested they go to the party where Natalie met

183

Michael. No party would have meant no Michael; no threat to her life. Kate owed her all right.

Natalie and Kate had lost touch over the years, but Facebook is a fabulous connector. In her messages Natalie kept it vague, revealing only that she and the kids were driving to St. Louis to meet family and could easily detour to Elsberry for a visit. Kate wouldn't dig into that story, though if she did, it was possible she'd find out that Natalie had no family in St. Louis.

She'd send Kate her new phone number in the morning, in case she saw a social media post about a missing family. Kate would call her and she'd explain the situation, at least in part. Once they were together, perhaps over a bottle of wine, Natalie would reveal the whole truth behind her unexpected visit. The real story would be far easier to digest in person, she reasoned.

From the safety of Kate's farm, Natalie would be able to plan her next move, map out her escape. She'd file for divorce. What she had on Michael might not put him behind bars, but it would be enough to grant her sole custody of Bryce and Addie. She was counting on it. Then, she could start the process of rebuilding her life anew.

That's how the story went in her head anyway.

It was almost midnight, but thankfully a night manager was on duty. Natalie took the kids with her into a wood-paneled office that had the feel of a 1970s basement. The portly man reading a newspaper behind the desk reeked of cheap cigars. He didn't ask any questions. His eyes didn't linger on Addie and Bryce. If he were at all suspicious, he kept it well disguised.

Natalie gave the room key to Addie. It was a real key attached to a big plastic keychain, and the novelty wasn't lost on the children, who went racing ahead to room 237 with gleeful innocence. Her poor kids were in the middle of all this, like it or not. And even if Natalie could explain the danger they were in, it was unlikely they'd believe it or be able to comprehend it.

Natalie brought the suitcases from the car into the room, along with the three bags of new purchases she had picked up at Walmart, including a new stuffed bear that Bryce lugged around like an obligation.

The kids had used up all their excess energy on the novelty key, so by the time they got the door unlocked, there was no magic left in them. After putting on their pajamas and doing a haphazard job of

185

brushing their teeth, each child fell into bed with the thud of a fallen tree. There were two twins; Natalie would sleep with Bryce.

Little Bryce said, "Will we get to see Daddy tomorrow?"

Natalie's heart did a stop/start. She brushed his cheek tenderly, gazing into those beautiful coffee-colored eyes he inherited from his father — a reminder that there'd always be a part of Michael with him, no matter what happened.

"Maybe not tomorrow, love," she said, stroking his cheek as he clutched his new bear. "It's been a long day. Let's get some sleep."

No sooner did their little heads hit the pillow than it was lights out for them both.

Natalie was not so fortunate. She did her evening ritual of soaps and creams, and brushed her teeth in a bathroom that was the size of a broom closet and dirty as a roach trap. She was worried about dust mites and other allergens that might trigger Addie's asthma, which was often worse at night. She turned up the heat, not sweltering, but warm enough to keep her daughter's airways from cooling too quickly. She regretted not bringing bedsheets from home, or at least a sleeping bag. It was an oversight she blamed (as usual) on exhaustion. If need be, she could use pillows to help elevate Addie's head. For now, all seemed fine, and Natalie kept the inhaler on the bedside table within easy reach.

When her prep was done, Natalie got into her pajamas, realizing they were the ones she should have been wearing to bed in the far nicer hotel in New York City. Had it really been seven hours since they'd left Michael?

She crawled into bed next to Bryce, who slumbered peacefully beside her. She stroked his fine hair and hoped the sound of his gentle breathing would soothe her to sleep. By this point, she should have been beyond exhausted, but the adrenaline hadn't quite worn off, and thoughts of Camo Man continued to trouble her. How had she been so wrong about him? The threat had felt so visceral to her, so real. Worry nagged at her. She was the one person her children depended on to keep them safe. What if her instincts couldn't be trusted?

That notion bounced around her brain, making sleep all but impossible. Natalie gazed at the dark screen of the small TV resting on a bureau across from the bed, thinking she might turn it on. Then she thought again. There could be news reports. One of the children might wake up and see their faces on the TV.

Tomorrow, in the light of day, Natalie would make sure the kids wouldn't be so easily recognizable. For now, she'd do what she always did this time of night: dream of sleep, pray for it, because she knew that going without for too much longer would put them all in a different sort of danger.

CHAPTER 17

Michael

He rang the doorbell at 16 Percival Way, unable to rid himself of his persistent foreboding. The lovely colonial, home to Natalie's parents, had weathered to a light gray over the years, giving the exterior the look and feel of a beachfront cottage. Michael was fond of his in-laws — they were good, decent people — but despite their years of spending holidays together and visiting the grandchildren, he didn't feel particularly close to them.

He couldn't say why he'd never quite hit it off with Harvey and Lucinda. There were no great disagreements, no issues with values or child-rearing practices to get in the way. However, there was a tension that had taken its toll over the years, like the wear and tear of waves eroding a beach over time.

Without another set of parents to compete

189

for time and attention, holidays were the exclusive province of Natalie's parents. Michael got the sense Lucinda was glad his parents were out of the picture, as the idea of mixing clans would never have meshed with her vision of family holidays. Knowing her, she'd resent a shared approach.

Lucky for Lucinda, such wasn't the case.

It was Natalie's mother who came to the door after Michael rang the bell. Lucinda, who looked like he imagined Natalie would in thirty years — still thin, her gray hair slowly replacing the darker shades — opened the door and gave Michael a confused stare. She was wiping splotches of flour from her hands onto a patchwork apron tied around her waist. Lucinda was a master when it came to baking, and Michael was always mindful not to overindulge on his visits. A lemon scent came wafting out from the kitchen, coupled with, of all things, a strong smell of vanilla. The odor momentarily sent Michael back to the hotel, to the traumatizing events he now had to share with Natalie's parents.

"Michael," said Lucinda. "What are you doing here? Did you come back early? Natalie didn't call. Is everything all right?"

Lucinda instinctively looked over her son-in-law's shoulder, searching for her daughter and the children. Michael watched her expression morph into a look of concern. *This is going to be horrendous,* he thought. *No, what's worse than that?* A few choice words came to him before he settled on *shocking* and *appalling.* The fear would soon follow.

"Hello, Lucinda," he said. He'd forgo her nickname, Lucy, as it felt too informal, and their relationship had never quite made it below the permafrost layer. "Is Harvey at home? We all need to talk. It's important."

Lucinda called out in a troubled voice, "Harvey, its Michael. He's here at the house. I need you to come to the front door right away. Something is wrong."

Moments later, Harvey appeared in the living room. His khakis and polo combo looked rather dapper, especially for a guy who wasn't going anywhere that day, or the next for that matter. Since retirement, Harvey ventured out of the house only to play golf, but he still dressed like every day was casual Friday at his law office.

Coming up behind his wife, Harvey placed a hand on Lucinda's delicate shoulder, a gesture of compassion and connection that came as naturally to them as breathing. A stab of guilt hit Michael like a sharp pain with no point of origin. It was just everywhere, radiating in every nerve of his body.

It was hard to see his in-laws like this, moments away from having their world rocked. They should be seated for this news, but that suggestion went nowhere.

"Tell us right here and now," Harvey said in the commanding way he'd perfected in the courtroom. "What's going on? Where are Natalie and the kids? Has something happened to them?"

The emotion imbedded in his voice came out raw and ripe. Lucinda didn't speak, but she nodded her head in vigorous agreement as if those were her words, too.

Harvey's hand intertwined with Lucinda's. Facing off with his in-laws, watching the tenderness between them, seeing all that through new eyes — it made all Michael's justifications for his choices (*I was lonely . . . I deserve love . . . I'm too young to be in a sexless marriage*) ring even more hollow. The lies he'd built upon lies now felt like a crushing weight for him to lug around.

"Let's sit down," Michael said again, but Harvey wasn't budging.

"Where is Natalie?" he asked.

For a man who'd once been larger than life during his professional career, Michael now saw in Harvey the fragility of a flower.

"I don't know," he confessed.

Lucinda seized Michael's arm, her grip tightening as her nails dug into his flesh.

"What do you mean, you don't know? Where are the children?"

And so he told them, standing in the foyer of their spacious home, rocking back and forth on his heels. He told them about Teddy and the empty hotel room, his conversations with the NYPD, the Lexington PD, and how they wouldn't issue an Amber Alert. Harvey's ruddy complexion changed, chameleon-like, to the greenish hue of seasickness. Lucinda went white as an envelope.

"Why would she do that?" Harvey asked, focusing on the obvious.

Why, indeed? thought Michael.

The question from Michael's point of view was how much to share. He was always so adept at skirting the truth, he figured why stop now?

"You know Natalie has been having trouble sleeping," he said. "Her insomnia has gotten worse over the past few months."

"I told you it was a bad idea for her to take that trip," Lucinda said to Harvey. If she'd shared her concern with her daughter, it had never made it back to Michael.

Harvey barked, "What the hell did you do to her?" Michael recoiled at his accusatory

193

tone. "It's something, I know it, because it's not like Natalie to behave this way."

"It's not me. I think her sleep troubles were more severe than I realized."

Michael offered up his defense like a reflex, omitting much of the truth with an ease that unsettled him. "Nat's become paranoid over the last couple months. It can happen in extreme cases of insomnia like hers. Lack of sleep is known to induce hallucinations, too. Honestly, it can mimic severe mental illness. I think she has some of that going on, maybe quite a lot. I think she was afraid, but for no good reason."

"Afraid of what?" asked Harvey, who seemed to grow in stature before Michael's eyes. He stood straighter, became broader in the shoulders and back, inflating himself as if that would somehow protect his missing daughter.

"Of me," said Michael gloomily. "I think Natalie has become afraid of me."

"You?" said Lucinda, who was shaking now.

With his admission, Michael suddenly deflated. He felt vulnerable opening up and owning that he might be part of the reason for Natalie's disappearance. His in-laws noticed this shift in his body language. They finally invited him into the home to take seats in the living room. The home was nicely furnished, but far from cozy. The couch on which Michael sat had all the softness of a plank of wood. Decorating the room were plenty of framed pictures of Natalie, their one and only child, as well as photos of the grandchildren. On occasion, Michael would comment to Natalie that his face didn't grace any of these photos.

"You're not blood," Natalie would say in a teasing way, whenever Michael mentioned this observation. Family was everything to Natalie's parents, and as far as they were concerned Michael had one job: take care of their precious daughter and grandchildren. And he'd failed them all, profoundly. Normally, Lucinda would brew some tea, or Harvey would offer up a beer. Not today.

"Honestly, I'm not sure what Natalie is afraid of specifically," said Michael. "She could have invented any number of stories about me."

"Why leave from New York? Why not come to us?" Lucinda asked.

Naturally, that's how any parent would think, but especially a mother.

"I can't say what's going through Nat's head," Michael offered. "I think she figured Amtrak would make it harder for me to find her. She's not in any car we can track or trace. It must have seemed like a good way to just disappear."

"I can't believe what I'm hearing," Lucinda said, whose color had yet to return.

A familiar little voice sounded in Michael's ears. The devil was back on his shoulder, doing that whisper thing he did so well.

You really got game, you know that, Mike? said the devil. *It's not about the affair, and you know it. You can't admit to anything, can you? You can't admit even to yourself what you've done. You know damn well why Natalie ran. Tell them, Mike. Get it off your chest. Unload. It'll make you feel so much better.*

Michael shook his head like a boxer after a knockdown, and the devil's voice went away. If his in-laws noticed his momentary distress, they kept it to themselves.

"What now?" Harvey asked.

"She took five hundred from the file safe, half of what we kept in there so the missing money wouldn't be easily noticed, and then she made several withdrawals from our checking account, hundred here, a hundred there, over the course of several weeks. The money won't last her forever. Eventually, she'll have to use a credit card, and then we should be able to locate her that way. If she bought a ticket on Amtrak, we'll get the destination soon enough."

Harvey didn't look impressed. "We've got to call the police," he demanded. "Michael, why aren't the police out looking for them?"

His anger was rising. Michael explained again how legally it's not an Amber Alert situation and it was unclear if any laws had been broken.

"It isn't considered abduction if Natalie and I share equal parenting rights."

Harvey was on his feet, inflating himself once more.

"I don't care what the law says," he growled in a low voice. "I have contacts at the damn FBI. I'll get them on the job." He glared at Michael as if to say, *Because you failed.*

"That's great, Harvey," Michael said. "The more help, the better. I'm going to put the word out on social media. See if we can get a post to go viral."

Lucinda took this as her cue to assist.

"I have pictures," she said, a hitch in her voice. "I'll get them off my phone. And I'll help you write the post."

Lucinda went to the kitchen, muttering to herself, wringing her hands nervously as she left the room. Michael heard her open and close the oven door. She had to take out the lemon tart. He knew that signature dessert by smell alone. She returned to the living room moments later carrying her phone on a tray that also held a pot of tea, three small saucers, and cups. To his surprise, Lucinda, even under duress, couldn't help but do as she'd always done — serve the tea and baked goods.

Harvey didn't bother leaving the room to make his call to the FBI. He spoke in a stentorian voice while sending telling looks Michael's way, as if to say, *This is how a man handles a crisis, how a real father protects his family.*

Michael knew how Harvey could be, which was one reason why he had dreaded coming here to break the news. He wasn't a puppy. He didn't need his failings shoved in his face like a mess on the carpet. And besides, he knew Harvey's FBI contact would give him lip service and nothing more. Michael had done his homework, and despite what Harvey thought, he'd already made the right calls to the right people.

While Lucinda poured the tea, Michael asked the question that had been on his mind all day.

"Can you think of anyone Natalie might stay with? An old friend of hers when she was young, someone maybe not in her current circle?"

Lucinda shook her head no before handing Michael his cup of tea. Her hands trembled, creating tiny waves that rippled across the steaming water. He thanked her dutifully as he would have at any other visit.

"Nobody I can think of off the top of my head," she said. "But I'm not thinking clearly, so maybe a name will come to me. Let's get the post up."

Harvey took a slice of the lemon tart before taking his phone to another room, while Lucinda busied herself with her own phone. It pained Michael to see his mother-in-law's hands continue to shake so uncontrollably, and was reminded of how he'd been when he first realized his family was gone.

He imagined what Natalie might be saying about him to the children, tried not to go there, but he couldn't help it.

Dad doesn't want to see you anymore.

It's better for all of us this way.

Your father has done some terrible things.

That last one wouldn't have been a lie.

As if reading Michael's thoughts, Lucinda said, "The children must be so confused and frightened. It's just not like Natalie to do something like this."

"Of course it's not," said Harvey, his booming voice carrying as he stormed back into the room. "What I want to know,

199

Michael, is what really happened. Did you hit her?"

Michael's eyes flew open wide.

"Harvey, God, no! I'd never."

Harvey had seen his fair share of charlatans and liars through his legal practice. Michael's strong denial didn't appear to appease him.

"Let's work on the post, okay?" Michael said. A focused task might keep the accusations to a minimum, and hopefully would help him hold his anger in check.

We both know what happens when you lose control of your temper, Michael, said the devil.

Lucinda, who kept her attention on her phone, perked up when she found a family photo to use. It was of the four of them taken last summer on a whale watch boat out of Gloucester. The sun was at its magic hour, giving everyone that radiant, healthy glow.

"This is a beautiful picture," Lucinda said. "I always hate the ones people choose for these things — bad news, deaths, missing persons. They always look so sickly and sad in their photos. This is just the opposite. Everyone will want to share this."

Michael took one look at the photo that might soon travel the virtual globe, and fear gripped his chest.

"No," he said adamantly. "Let's use this one instead."

Out came his phone. On the display was the same picture he had passed around in New York, the one of just Natalie and the kids taken by the entrance to the hotel.

"That image is too dark," Lucinda said, offering a dismissive wave of her hand. "The one on the boat is perfect. I'll get my laptop and we'll do the post from my Facebook account. I'll ask the garden club, my book group, and the church to share it. That will get it started."

"No," Michael said, putting too much force into his voice, but he couldn't help himself. "We can't use that picture."

Harvey took notice of Michael's modest outburst. A dark cloud seemed to pass over his eyes as he stormed across the room. He took Lucinda's phone so he could study the image himself before sending Michael a scathing stare.

"This photo is perfect. Use it," he demanded.

A stare down ensued, sort of a high-noon moment between Harvey and Michael. They'd never raised their voices to each other, but this was unchartered territory.

"Harvey, no," repeated Michael. "We need to be a team here, and this isn't the right image. The focus has to be on Natalie and the kids. That's it. Just of them. And in my photo, they're wearing the same clothes they had on when they disappeared, so it might help with identification."

"Yeah, that's a good point, I guess," Harvey said with a grumble. "Luce, let's use the photo Michael suggested instead."

Michael breathed a silent sigh of relief. He couldn't be in any picture that risked going viral, and certainly couldn't tell his in-laws why.

CHAPTER 18

Natalie

Before She Disappeared

Michael's car wasn't in the driveway when Natalie arrived home just before eight. She made her way up the walkway with a slight spring in her step, thinking the only good to have come from having seen her husband at McDonald's with Audrey Adler was that she was no longer exhausted. In fact, she couldn't recall a time when she'd felt more awake. Adrenaline was coursing through her veins. She wished she could experience this energy at will, though without the heartache of her hurtful discovery.

Seeing the Audi (or believing she saw it — damn brain, damn insomnia) all but confirmed Natalie's worst fears. How men believed they could openly carry on an affair and get away with it was mind-boggling. Did Michael honestly think she was stupid, or that she paid no attention to the little details of their lives? She'd learned from experience that routines were quite adept at carving grooves into everyday life, laying down tracks for the day's events to follow. Anything that jumps the rails, so to speak, was going to get noticed.

Like those shirts Michael bought a little while ago — one a dress shirt, the other a jersey, both black. Natalie's first thought when Michael showed her his purchases (of which he was quite proud) was that he didn't wear black. In fact, Michael had exactly zero black shirts in his entire wardrobe, and suddenly he owned two of them, both from different stores.

When Natalie asked about his newfound preference for black, Michael offered only a shrug of his shoulders and a dismissive wave of his hand.

"Haven't you been reading the news lately?" he asked, with a devilish grin. "We should all be mourning the state of things." He gave a chuckle, like he'd actually said something quite funny, which Natalie didn't even acknowledge with a smile. She was having her own private conversation at that moment, one that had nothing to do with politics. Instead, she was revisiting all the signs she'd shared with Tina. The cheater's playbook, she'd called it.

Mr. Too Lazy to Get Out of Bed suddenly becomes Mr. Hard-Core Gym Rat — pretty much overnight. Weight loss suddenly becomes a real priority, as if he's just discovered that under the fat he has abs. Next he tries a new cologne after all these years, as if that was for the benefit of his wife. And now these stylish black shirts.

Fuck him.

One evening when everyone was asleep (and of course she was not), Natalie picked up Michael's phone. She was surprised when she was required to use FaceID to unlock the device. For security, Michael always used a code, 0702, representing the months of their children's birthdays. She knew his code because on occasion he'd ask her to check a text message or something when he was otherwise occupied. Natalie couldn't remember the last time she'd checked his phone, and he'd certainly never told her that he'd gone all James Bond with the biometric security stuff.

When she pressed him on it, once again Michael had an answer at the ready, so his explanation sounded quite obvious and logical. And maybe it was.

"Oh, that?" he said, downplaying it. "I read something about hackers figuring out those codes. FaceID is really the most secure, and since I use mobile banking, figured better safe than sorry."

He didn't stick around for more questions, she remembered that clearly. Instead, he offered a weak smile before slipping off into another room of the house, his phone naturally clutched in his hand.

Bastard.

Signs.

Natalie was on the lookout for them when she entered her home. She was pleased to see everything was as it should be, which was to be expected given the skill of her nanny. The kids had been fed. The dinner cleanup was done. The dishes had been washed and put away, counters wiped down. The children were in their bedrooms for reading time, a weeknight ritual that usually required an equal number of minutes reading as were spent cajoling them into the activity.

Of course it was Natalie who had found and hired the nanny, did the background checks and such. Michael didn't even offer to help with the search, and his only comment after meeting her (and this "her" happened to be a lithe, quite attractive twenty-four-year-old woman of Swedish and Scottish descent) was to say she was the embodiment of every sexy nanny cliché.

He'd made that remark years before he'd given Natalie so many reasons not to trust him, and now she found herself eyeing her hire with a hint of suspicion.

Her name was Scarlett, which was just as bad as the name Audrey in Natalie's book — assuming "bad" meant provocative. Scarlett seemed to take note of Natalie's lingering stare that evening, a look she clearly found unnerving.

"Is everything all right?" Scarlett asked. Her voice had a smoky, sultry appeal — an alluring resonance that Natalie hadn't noticed before. Suddenly, as if her own mind were attacking her, Natalie conjured a mental image of Scarlett on the floor of the living room where they both now stood, with Michael on top of her, panting and thrusting. A queasy feeling came over her, but she pushed the image away and composed herself.

"Yes, everything is fine," said Natalie, opening her pocketbook. Normally there'd be a friendly debrief after a long day, and she'd give Scarlett a chance to recap the events, but Natalie wasn't going to offer her that opportunity — not today. She had the cash already presorted in the billfold of her wallet, so it was a quick exchange, which judging by the look in Scarlett's eyes might have felt a little rude. Natalie didn't care. She couldn't shake the vision of Michael grunting on top of her nanny, and she needed the woman out of her house stat. Even if there were no truth behind the fantasy, any attractive female now felt like a threat.

"Are you sure everything is all right?" Scarlett asked tentatively as she took the money without counting it. She stuffed the bills into the front pocket of her jeans — tight-fitting dark jeans that showed off her curves, Natalie keenly observed.

"It's fine. I'm just tired, that's all." *Michael isn't the only one around here adept at lying.* "Thank you, Scarlett."

"Will you need me extra hours this week?"

Natalie finally caught herself. Scarlett had always been tried and true, helping her for years, and Natalie had no reason to be suspicious of her. It was Michael who should be on guard, not poor Scarlett.

"I'll let you know," Natalie said. She gave Scarlett's arm a gentle squeeze as if to say all was right between them. In her grip she felt the nanny's well-defined tricep muscle, and remembered that she, like Michael, was big into the gym. Suddenly, Natalie found her graciousness taking a minor detour. "I'll go up and check on the children. You can see yourself out," she said.

Upstairs, after saying a quick hello to Addie, Natalie entered Bryce's bedroom. Lying on his bed, she rubbed her son's back while she finished reading him the story he'd started on his own. She tried not to think of Michael driving away from that McDonald's, following Audrey's car out of the parking lot, but twice she lost her place in a kid's book.

When Bryce was sleepy enough to drift off, she headed back into Addie's room, which had recently been decorated with LED lights. The room glowed purple as if it were a Euro nightclub. Worried the mood lighting would strain her daughter's eyes, Natalie turned on a bedside lamp without first asking permission. She didn't look about as she might have done normally, didn't check out the magnetic board Michael had hung on the wall, which Addie often adorned with handwritten notes, musings that offered insight into her world, her way of thinking.

Instead, Natalie got right down to business with a slew of questions: "Is your homework done? Did you have enough to eat? What's on your agenda for tomorrow? Did you need my help studying for that spelling test? What about the belt to your dance costume, did you find it? I'm not buying another one, just so you know."

Addie adopted a defensive posture in response to the onslaught, arms folded across her chest, eye contact broken, and it took a moment for Natalie to realize she was doing to her daughter what she'd done to poor Scarlett. Fighting off a sting of regret, Natalie kissed Addie on the top of her head, inhaling her fragrant scent, and told her to turn off the light when she was done reading. She was in the middle of *I Am Malala,* a selection Natalie had bragged about to Tina.

"I didn't suggest it. Addie picked it out all on her own."

Tina, who'd had her children earlier in life, wasn't overly impressed. She been through the "Everything they do is a miracle phase" and was entering the "I don't think I love my husband anymore" time of her life. Natalie had always assumed she'd avoid Tina's marital travails because she and Michael were excellent communicators and great friends, too. Now she wondered if she'd been wearing blinders for the entirety of their marriage.

Addie said, "I got in trouble today at school because I didn't have my field trip form. Now I'm not sure I can go."

Natalie knew all about the scheduled trip to a mill-turned-museum because she'd signed that form along with a check for the required ten-dollar fee. Students were to learn about factory life during the industrial revolution, and Addie was looking forward to the experience in part because one of her American Girl dolls was from that era.

"What are you talking about?" Natalie said, adopting the same folded arm posture her daughter had moments ago. "I put the form and check in your backpack. I told you all that this morning."

"It wasn't there when I went to get it," Addie said, tears coming to her eyes, poor thing.

Natalie was incensed, not at Addie for having an overstuffed backpack, but rather at the teacher, who was being overly rigid and could have helped her find those documents. No matter.

"I'll take care of it, not to worry," Natalie said, before heading downstairs to email Addie's teacher. In her small office on the first floor, Natalie saw something that changed her mind about the wording of the email that she'd already crafted in her head. There, on top of a pile of papers, right near her checkbook, Natalie saw the signed field trip form along with that check for ten dollars. She sighed aloud, shifted her gaze to the ceiling, letting the fatigue behind her eyes drip down her throat like bitter medicine. Instead of a screed, she'd have to send an apology.

Dammit, she thought. *I'm not with it. I'm always with it, but now I'm not.*

Natalie sent her an apology email, and soon after received assurances from Addie's teacher that she could still go on the field trip. Addie, pleased with the news, could finally get to sleep. Thirty minutes later, Michael returned home looking quite bedraggled. Natalie noted the strain in his eyes. He strode into the kitchen stoop-shouldered as though whatever was weighing on his mind also weighed him down physically.

"Hey, hon," he said, acting like everything was normal between them, and he even gave her a kiss on the cheek. Natalie, who had yet to rid herself of the guilt for the field trip debacle and for being a bit of a zombie parent, didn't have much fight in her. Tomorrow she'd reach out to her doctor, maybe try a new sleeping pill.

Michael opened the refrigerator, poked his head inside.

"Anything to eat?" he asked.

With his back turned to her, he couldn't

see Natalie's eye roll.

"There's plenty to eat," she said. "It's just all in cans, jars, and wrappers, so if you open those up and mix them together in some procedural fashion, I'm sure you'll be able to create something edible."

Michael extracted himself from the fridge holding a hunk of cheese in one hand and a beer in the other.

"That almost sounded like sarcasm," he said, sending her a playful grin from across the room. "Are you hungry? Let me cook you something. Maybe we can have some wine, watch something on TV."

Now he was being generous and Natalie didn't trust it — or him. She was about to answer when Michael's phone rang. He checked the number, looking rather puzzled. She hadn't even had the chance to inquire as to his whereabouts that day, didn't get to drop hints that she knew whatever he said was a lie. Instead, she watched as his expression changed and concern flooded his eyes. He cupped his hand over the phone and turned his back to her, speaking in a quiet voice so as to not be heard. Still, she had a good guess what he was saying: *I can't talk here,* or something to that effect. He noticed Natalie's attention on him.

"It's work," he said. "It's a crisis."

He slipped out of the kitchen, Natalie assumed to his office. Maybe Audrey had called to complain about Natalie harassing her, or perhaps she and Michael were plotting ways to get the wife out of the picture. Natalie loved true crime shows, she just never thought her life would become the subject of one.

Natalie went outside while Michael was elsewhere having his "work" chat. She wanted a peek at the Audi A8 now parked in the driveway. Even in the dark she could see it clearly — on the right side of the bumper, just as she remembered, was that dent. But was it the exact shape and diameter of the dent she'd seen on the black Audi A8 leaving the McDonald's parking lot? Natalie couldn't say. Stupidly, her eyes had gone straight to that dent, and she didn't think about the license plate until the car was out of view. By the time she considered using her phone to take a picture it was too late, the car was out of sight.

An idea came to Natalie, a devious one at that. She raced back into the house to get her key fob. She had to hurry. That call wouldn't last forever. She got into the front seat of her Highlander and started the engine. All the instruments came alight. A moment later a woman's voice came through the car speakers.

"We can't do that," Natalie heard her say. Then, "Hello? Michael?"

The speaker fell silent.

Natalie gnashed her teeth together hard enough to feel them crack. Michael had paired his phone to her car, since he shared the kid chauffeuring duties on weekends. She was pleased to have remembered that the Bluetooth switched from the phone to the car speaker when the devices were in close proximity. The tech glitch happened infrequently enough to be easily forgotten, and it almost always resulted in confusion and laughter when a mysterious voice came blasting unexpectedly into the car. Only this time it wasn't so unexpected, and it was no great shock to Natalie to confirm the person Michael was conversing with was a female.

But was it Audrey?

Moments later, the front door opened and Michael stepped out into the damp evening air. She expected he'd ask what she was doing sitting in her car, but he was too distracted. Natalie got out of her vehicle to greet him. If he harbored suspicions that she'd overheard snippets of his conversation when the call appeared to have dropped, he didn't make them known.

"I have to go back to the office," he said

215

briskly. "We have a big security breach. It's all hands on deck. A real mess. I'm so sorry, Nat."

He kissed her on the cheek, hard, as if he really just wanted to get it over and done with as quickly as possible. The next moment he was in his car, and Natalie was watching his taillights (and that dent) vanish into the gathering darkness. She waited awhile, arms limp by her side, wondering what to do, when an idea suddenly came to her. She returned to the house, got her phone, glanced at the time — just after nine now — and called a number from memory.

"Scarlett, it's me, Natalie . . . no, no, everything is fine. But I was wondering if you might be able to come back tonight. Something has come up and Michael and I both have to go out."

Scarlett gave her consent, but couldn't get to the house for a half hour. Natalie told her that would be fine. She was certain Michael didn't have a work emergency, but had a good idea where he was headed and figured he wouldn't be leaving anytime soon.

While it was painful to consider, she was grateful too, because tonight was the night she'd learn the truth about her husband once and for all.

CHAPTER 19

Natalie

In the light of morning, things looked different to Natalie — a whole lot less gloomy, that's for sure. The motel room was still on the seedy side, and without the cover of darkness, the dust and dirt were even more obvious. When Natalie opened the curtains, allowing in a bright swath of sunlight, she felt a shift take place inside of her. For a moment, the nagging fear and worry were gone, as were her ever-present fatigue and exhaustion from yet another sleepless night. It was as if the sun had vanquished those feelings like a magic trick, and in its place came a new sensation, a strange one at that: hope.

A new day meant new possibilities, and Natalie felt certain that her plan was going to work.

Natalie estimated Elsberry, Missouri, and Kate's farm would be a thirteen-hour drive from here. They'd have to break up the journey into two legs. She figured on doing an eight-hour stint with a couple of stops and a break for lunch, but it would be a long day for all. The children didn't budge even when the sunlight hit their faces. Natalie let them sleep. She wanted to get on her phone, check the news, search for any mention of a missing family from Lexington, but that could be a costly mistake. Her phone would ping cell towers, and those pings could get traced back to her. So instead, Natalie kept her device powered off as she went rummaging through the bags from Walmart. From one of those bags, Natalie removed a brand new Tracfone still in its packaging: an iPhone 11 Pro in a black case.

She'd done her best to think things through, to plan and cover her bases. From her research, she'd found out phones and credit cards were the two easiest ways to track someone down. Since there was no registration process for a Tracfone, Natalie was free to roam the internet anonymously.

She got the phone powered on, went through the activation process, and connected to the motel's Wi-Fi. Even crappy motels like this one had free Wi-Fi. As it turned out, they hadn't made the news, but a Google search of her name pulled up a Facebook post about her and the kids. Natalie didn't log into her account, thinking Michael could trace her that way. Instead, she used a new Gmail address to create a Facebook account, one her husband wouldn't know about. She wanted to trace the origin of the "Help Find Natalie Hart" post, which already had plenty of shares and was on the precipice of going viral.

After some digging, Natalie determined that it was her mother who had initiated the post. To read her mom's words, to experience the pain of her plea — *Please help. My daughter and my grandchildren are missing. They are my world. We are devastated beyond words* — bore into the most primal places in her heart.

Naturally, she could have involved them in her plans, but had decided after much contemplation, that the less they knew, the better. As she saw it, Michael was going to contact them no matter what, and if he suspected that they were hiding information from him, who knows what he might do?

Natalie quickly justified away her worry. Once they knew the truth, they'd understand her reasons for running. Not only would she be forgiven for putting them through this ordeal, her father would praise her ingenuity and resilience. "I raised a real fighter," she could hear her dad say with beaming pride after all this was behind them.

Natalie sent Kate her new number but didn't offer details. Let her friend inquire, she decided. The less she knew, the better. She put her phone away just as Bryce was waking up. His hair stuck out in a variety of angles like that of a newborn bird.

"When are we seeing Daddy?" he asked in a parched voice.

Of course those would be the first words out of his mouth. Natalie returned a tight smile.

"Come on, sleepyhead," she said, slumping down on the bed to give him a tender kiss on the cheek. "We've got a long drive today and there's a lot to do."

She was thinking about the picture of them on Facebook, which had probably gone elsewhere in social media land. Twitter. Instagram. She remembered Michael taking that photo in the carport of the Marriott Marquis. Seemed like a lifetime ago.

"I'm hungry," said Bryce.

"We'll get McDonald's on the way out of town. I know how much you love their hash browns."

McDonald's was a treat, and Bryce probably understood this was some sort of a bribe to ensure his cooperation. From the adjacent bed, Natalie heard sheets rustling as Addie began to stir. No troubles with breathing meant a good night's sleep for her. What Natalie wouldn't give for one of those! A sudden loud bang drew Natalie's attention to the front door. She jumped at the sound and thought, *Michael.* She was the only one who seemed to have heard it.

"Don't move," she said to the kids, speaking in a tight whisper. "Nobody say anything."

She proceeded cautiously toward the door, put her hand on the knob before placing her eye up to the peephole.

"What's wrong, Mom?" asked Addie, nervously.

Natalie blinked to make sure her vision was clear, that she wasn't missing something, because there was nobody at the door. She turned the knob and cracked open the door wide enough to poke her head outside into a warm April morning and the pleasing scent of spring. But she was on her guard and searched first to her left, then to her right. Nothing was happening outside. There were no cars idling nearby. Nobody was ambling down the walkway leading to the other rooms. The whole area appeared deserted. Still, Natalie was so sure she'd heard something — a loud knock, to be precise.

She looked for some object that might have blown against the door, but saw nothing. The other possibility was harder for her to fathom.

It was all in her head.

Now, she could add a mystery knock to her growing list of uncertainties.

Natalie rubbed at her tired eyes. Tonight she'd get good sleep, she promised herself, but only after she put in the miles.

"Everyone up," Natalie said, clapping her hands cheerily. "Time for the day to begin."

"What are we doing today?" Addie asked in a tiny voice fragranced with her endearing innocence. "Are we going to see Daddy?"

"Not today, love," said Natalie. "But we are going to play a game before we leave here."

Addie was interested right away.

"A game? What kind of game?"

Bryce wanted TV and those promised hash browns. Rather than pack, Natalie let him find a show to watch. This was going to be rough enough without her having to contend with his complaining.

"It's a game I'm calling Dress-Up," said Natalie.

That got Addie's attention, but not Bryce's.

Once more, Natalie went to those Walmart bags, and dumped the contents of one in particular onto Addie's bed.

"Who wants to go first?" she asked.

If Addie had wondered what her mother was buying at Walmart, she hadn't brought it up, probably because she was too exhausted from the day's travails. Now, seeing everything spread out before her, it was apparent she had some questions.

She picked up a spray bottle of B-Crazy!! temporary hair color. There were four spray cans of dark brown to choose from.

Natalie scooped up the box of brown hair dye.

"Dyes aren't for kids, they're not safe, but these spray-on colors are fine to use. It's going to be so fun."

You just can't look like you anymore, she held back from saying.

"Wait, are we really dyeing our hair?" asked Addie.

"Well, it is family makeover day. We have to go all in, or else it won't be any fun. And I have real, big girl makeup to put on you, too. It'll be like coloring our Easter eggs, only this will be our hair and faces. You'll look so beautiful, like a real princess."

Natalie had never put on a smile that felt so forced, and Addie didn't seem at all convinced of the promised fun.

"Will it hurt?"

"No darling. It's just a spray."

"What color can I have?" she asked, seeing only brown. There was a hint of trepidation in her voice, but not as much as Natalie had feared.

She handed Addie the bottle labeled Cinnamon Shimmer. "We're all going to be a family of brunettes."

"But I don't like that color," said Addie.

A mantra ticked away in Natalie's mind like the countdown to an explosion.

Move. Move. Gotta keep moving. Don't stay in one place too long.

An anxious feeling welled up inside her, and she raised her voice sharply.

"Well, you don't have a choice," she said. "We're all going to have the same color hair, and we're going to do it right now before we leave here."

A sick feeling came over Natalie when she caught the pain in Addie's eyes. Would she spend her time on the run hurting everyone she loved the most — first her parents, now her kids? She vowed to make amends, but later. Their picture was everywhere now, and she and the children had to look different for the remainder of the trip, so a family of brunettes they'd become.

"Sweetheart," Natalie said, taking Addie's hand, softening her tone. "I promise, we will have so much fun changing our hair color. And then we can show Daddy. He'll be so surprised."

She stroked Addie's long, straw-colored hair, using her fingers like the teeth of a comb, tugging gently on the roots. In the photograph making the rounds on social media it was obvious that Addie had long hair, so that was going to have to change, too.

"Another part of family makeover day is that we're going to have to cut your hair shorter, maybe to here."

Using her hands, Natalie lifted Addie's hair to the new, shorter length that she had in mind.

Addie's eyes sprung open, wide and filled with fright.

"No," she said, pulling away. "I'm not cutting my hair."

Natalie wasn't going to push the issue. She didn't want to scar her children. She was trying to save them.

"Then you'll have to wear your hair in

braids for a while, okay? But let's color it!"

Natalie clapped her hands together as if that made the whole idea that much more palatable.

"I'll go first, okay? You can help me?"

Addie left her bottle of spray-on brown on the bed as she followed her mother into the tiny bathroom. Bryce stayed put, oblivious to what was going on, happily gorging on cartoons.

Natalie hadn't washed her hair in the last forty hours, knowing the natural oils would help the dye stick to her follicles. Because she was an adult, Natalie opted to use the far messier real dye rather than the spray-on kind. She placed a towel on the floor and another draped around her neck like a cape to catch any dye that might drip off her hair in the process.

Addie helped brush Natalie's long, chestnut-colored hair that would soon become a much deeper, darker brown. With careful precision, Natalie applied a coating of Vaseline to her hairline, ears, and neck to make it easier to wash off any dye that got on her skin. Gloves came with the kit she'd bought, along with a bowl to mix the dye with developer. Once that was done, she separated her hair into four sections, then applied the dye to each section, careful to follow the instructions. Afterward, she put on a shower cap and set a timer for thirty minutes.

Watching her mother's process made Addie ready to move forward with her own makeover.

"Do me next!" she begged, clapping her hands delightedly.

Natalie obliged, but not in the bathroom. Chemical aerosol would fill the tight space like tear gas and could trigger an asthma attack. She might have been utterly exhausted, but she wasn't entirely out of it, which again made her think of that knock on the door. She was feeling more certain now than before that it wasn't all in her head.

But who would it have been?

She had no good answer. She considered going outside to do the spray, but that felt too exposed. Cars zoomed past the motel en route to the highway. An off-duty police officer could be riding in one of them, someone trained to be observant, who'd see a mother coloring her child's hair. It would be an odd enough sight for them to backtrack and have a second look.

A voice in Natalie's head rose up sharply.

Hurry. Hurry.

"Cover your eyes," she instructed Addie, who sat on a chair they dragged next to an open window. She was draped in a sheet Natalie had bought at Walmart for this very purpose. Addie covered her eyes as instructed.

A blast of color spit out from the spray bottle's nozzle and quickly coated Addie's golden locks a dark shade of brown.

"How does it look?" Addie asked excitedly.

"Gorgeous," answered Natalie, who realized she'd applied too much spray to one part of Addie's hair, so much so that the color appeared uneven. It looked like dried blood on her scalp. Natalie's mind immediately jumped to that terrible night — not so long ago — and to the vision seared into her memory. For the rest of the effort, Natalie was far more precise with her application, but she was still shaken by the flashback, that horrifying experience. How could she ever forget?

The spraying stopped. Addie turned her head.

"Mommy, you're crying," she said.

Natalie wiped her eyes with the back of her hand.

"No, darling, it's just spring allergies causing me to get teary. Let's finish, okay? It looks beautiful!" She forced a smile onto her face.

When Bryce saw his sister, he was all giggles and delight.

"I want brown hair, too," he said, bouncing on the bed like a rubber ball on asphalt.

"You're in luck," said Natalie, who still had her shower cap on.

Fifteen minutes later, Bryce was a brunette just like his sister. They were making faces in the mirror, laughing hysterically at their new appearances. Next, they tried on their new wardrobe, which Natalie had made as plain as possible. No flashy colors or logos of any kind. It was to be jeans, tees, and sweatshirts for both her children. From this point forward, they'd not be allowed to wear anything from the photo being shared online. New clothes. New hair. They each had sunglasses, too, as well as baggy coats that would help keep them concealed.

Was it perfect? No. But for Natalie it was one less worry to keep her awake at night.

Addie got to experiment with the makeup, while Natalie went to the bathroom to rinse her hair in the shower. Rivulets of brown, the color of dried blood, cascaded down her body, making a snaking path toward the drain. She watched as the dye pooled beneath the faucet, swirling as it disappeared.

For a moment, Natalie felt like she was standing near that pool of blood all over again. She got out of the shower and towel dried her now–dark brown hair, leaving behind stains on the white fabric. Reminders of blood were everywhere, following her, and would probably haunt her dreams if only she had any. The knock might have been in her head, but that body was as real as anything.

Natalie pushed the shock and fear of that memory away so she could focus on her children.

"Come here," she said to them, pulling them into her arms. "Let's look at ourselves."

They gathered in front of the mirror above the dresser, three brunettes now. It was hardly a professional job for any of them, but it would do the trick.

"Okay," said Natalie, "let's pack our bags and go. We've got a long drive ahead of us."

"I can't wait to show Daddy," said Bryce.

"Me too," Addie concurred.

Natalie took one more look in the mirror, noticing how the dye from her hair had bled onto her scalp. To her eyes, it looked like an open wound, almost like a prelude to her murder.

CHAPTER 20

Michael

Even though it wasn't yet noontime, Michael arrived home from his in-laws' utterly exhausted, enervated in a way he'd never experienced before. He noted (the irony not lost on him) that he was probably too tired to sleep, and if he tried he'd only be frustrated. Of course this brought to mind Natalie's plight. Melancholy enveloped him in a cocoon. What might he have done better to support her?

Somewhere along the bumpy road of life, Michael knew they'd veered onto separate paths. Sure, they'd managed to keep each other in sight, but how is it they had operated for so long as a couple and yet not as a team?

What he wanted out of life were the simple things: a woman to love, children to raise, new experiences, and a family to share it all with. And he had wanted to be smart and thoughtful about the partner he selected. Such was not the case with Natalie, who had swept him up in a whirlwind of feelings and emotions. He had gone along for the ride, eschewing his thoughtful intentions in the process.

In Michael's view, people weren't meant to walk this planet alone, and yet here he was now, all alone in his own house, blanketed in a profound silence. It was as if he'd just returned from his family's graveside.

The devil was on his shoulder again, whispering uncomfortable truths, reconfirming Michael's greatest fear about karma having a very long memory.

Ten minutes after he walked through the front door, Michael's cell phone buzzed, imploring him to answer. It was the fifth call he'd received in the last twenty minutes or so. Like the others, the caller wasn't someone in his contacts, and the number wasn't one he recognized. Four of the calls had been from strangers who'd seen the Facebook post and wanted to reach out with a prayer or word of support. Perhaps this caller would be different.

"Hello, Michael Hart here," he said, with enthusiasm and hope in his voice.

All he heard was breathing.

It was Harvey who had suggested Michael

include his cell phone number in the Facebook post about Natalie and the kids. That post was already starting to amass a lot of views, which explained the flurry of calls he'd received in short order.

"People will need a way to get in touch with you immediately, right?" Harvey had said in that commanding voice of his. The subtext there: *this is my daughter and it's not up for debate.*

Michael's initial reaction was a hard "No," but he was diminished from fatigue, and relented. Still, he had a good notion of the potential consequences of reaching out to the general public with his phone number on display. Last he checked, there were a hundred fifteen shares of Lucinda's post. There were a lot more eyeballs on the post than shares, so chances were a wide net would catch a few crazies along with those thoughts and prayers.

Michael spoke again.

"Hello, is this about Natalie?"

More breathing.

"Hello? Who is this?" Michael demanded. "I'm going to hang up if you don't answer me."

"You hang up and she's dead. Your kids, too."

A gravelly voice, low and menacing, issued the threat with little emotion. Michael felt a clamp around his heart like a cold hand squeezing inside his chest.

"Who are you?"

All Michael heard was more breathing, heavy and slow, each breath long and drawn out.

"I have them, all of them, your beautiful wife and two precious kids. They're in the back of a truck and I'm going to do terrible things to them if you don't do as I say. You listening, Mike?"

The man spoke quickly in a clipped voice, almost like he was reading from a script.

"I'm listening."

Michael gripped the kitchen counter for balance. Terror surged through him as he thought of those terrible things.

"You and I are going to make a little transaction, otherwise it's gonna be the bad things. Don't make me, okay?"

This was his worst nightmare coming to fruition — his family out on their own, him not around to protect them, and now they've become prey. As if to add an exclamation mark to his blossoming fear, Michael heard in the background a blood-chilling scream.

"Help me!" The raw and primal voice overpowered his phone's tiny speaker.

"Please help!" While the speaker distorted the words, he could still make out what was said. He tried to match the scream to Natalie's voice, but his mind was racing, thoughts scattered like shrapnel. Michael couldn't tell. He'd never heard his wife scream with such terror, so he had no point of reference.

"Listen to me carefully," said the man. "We have Natalie, Addie, and Bryce."

No, you have their names that I put out on the internet for all to see, Michael thought as he considered the possibility this could be a scam.

"You're going to pay us a ransom or we're going to cut off Natalie's toes using pruning shears. Strong shears. We'll do it toe by toe, slowly, painfully, until you pay us what we want. Do you hear me, Michael?"

What Michael heard was an accent he couldn't quite place. Had Natalie gone south, or maybe toward Miami? He could only speculate. His phone buzzed in his hand. He was getting another call. Of course, he'd let this one go to voicemail.

"Don't hang up on me," the kidnapper instructed, as if he knew about that incoming call. "We have to do this quickly or else."

A second scream, this one more chilling than the first, demanded he comply.

"You're going to wire fifteen hundred dollars to an account. I'll give you the number."

Fifteen hundred? Michael thought. *Why so low?*

"Got a pen? You write this down. I'm staying on the line with you until we get the money."

"Let me talk to my family first," Michael said, feeling emboldened. "I want to hear from Natalie. I need to know she's okay."

The man scoffed. "Hey, who's in charge here, me or you? You know what, fuck it. Cut her. Take the little toe."

A moment later, another scream tore through the speaker and Michael's heart at the same time.

What if this isn't a scam?

He thought: fifteen hundred dollars is a small price to pay for security.

Usually it was Natalie who let her imagination get the better of her, always concocting worst-case scenarios, mostly about the children. But now it was Michael doing the imagining, seeing Natalie and the kids locked up in the back of some sweltering box truck in the middle of God knows where. The mind-movie was back, and this time the feature film playing in his head showed a deranged man holding a pair of pruning shears. The man's body rippled

236

with muscle, arms adorned in tattoos, his grimy T-shirt soaked through because the truck had no air circulation. He saw Natalie thrashing about as another man held her down. The blades of the shears slipped between her toes. A dark, twisted look entered Muscle Man's eyes. He closed the shears with one strong thrust. And then came the scream.

At that exact moment, Michael heard another sound, this one a doorbell — his, to be precise. He raced to the door to tell whoever it was to go away, but to his utter astonishment he saw, of all people, Detective Sergeant Amos Kennett from the New York City Police Department. Kennett had come dressed casually in a rumpled blue shirt and jeans. He stood with hands on his hips, looking slightly impatient.

Michael whipped open the door, pointing wildly at his phone, mouthing the word "Kidnapped!" over and over so that Kennett would understand. To his bewilderment, the detective did not act overly concerned.

"Mike, you still with me?" said the kidnapper. "You want us to do another toe?"

Another scream followed, this one louder and more disturbing than the others, and on the heels of that came a female's desperate plea.

"Please . . . please help."

Kennett pointed to the phone, then to his ear, and then over to Michael who understood he was being asked to put the caller on mute. He was worried though. He remembered Kennett in New York as quite arrogant and feared the detective might do something rash, dangerous even. He couldn't help but see Natalie's blood painting that truck red, her severed toe nearby, and another one about to come off.

"Hang on," Michael said sharply into the phone. "I'm here. I'm just getting a pen."

"Hurry, Mike," said the kidnapper. "She's bleeding bad."

Michael thought it over. Kennett was a cop and that was the trump card. Michael tapped the mute icon on his phone.

"What's going on, Mike?" said Kennett. "I called your cell. You didn't answer. I was sitting in my car outside your house, but I could see you pacing about in here. You looked worried. Figured I'd come check on things, make sure you're all right."

Kennett pointed to the front door, which was open, allowing Michael to follow the trail of his finger to where a dark SUV was parked curbside.

"Is this something I might be able to help

238

you with?"

"What are you doing here, Detective?" Michael asked. A nervous flutter filled his chest. *Why is a detective from New York City at my house?* Less than twenty-four hours since he officially reported his wife missing. Odd didn't begin to address it. Michael reasoned if Kennett knew something about Natalie he'd have called. No matter. Kennett was here now, and Michael reasoned the detective might be able to help with his immediate crisis.

"A man on the phone," Michael said, spitting out the words, "claims he's got Natalie and the kids. He's cut off one of Nat's toes, and he's threatening to do it to the others."

"Well now," Kennett said, keeping any alarm out of his eyes and voice. "Did he ask you to wire him some money . . . a small amount, say, less than two thousand?"

"Yeah, they want fifteen hundred dollars."

Kennett nodded like he's heard that story before.

"Short money makes it easier to make a decision."

The anxiety building in Michael's chest let go, allowing a spurt of anger to take its place.

"Michael, this is a scam," Kennett said matter-of-factly. "Did you happen to hear a

239

scream?"

Michael returned a glum nod.

"That's a recording. It's called virtual kidnapping, and the virtual part is real, but the kidnapping part — eh." Kennett gave a dispirited headshake. "Not so much. How about you give me the phone, Mike?"

Michael handed over his phone without further prodding. Kennett took the call off mute.

"Hey, Jackhole," Kennett said, talking in an animated voice. "I don't know where you're calling from, or how you got this number." He looked to Mike and mouthed, *internet*? to which Michael nodded. "Okay, the internet. Got it. So you target a desperate dad. Pretty low even for you lowlifes."

"Who is this?"

"I'm your worst goddamn nightmare, that's who I am." Kennett paused, maybe to let the threat sink in. Then, a wide grin broke out on his face. "Ah, I'm just screwing with you. That tough talk is from the movies. But I do know that you're gigantically full of shit, and I'm technically in law enforcement, so I guess what I said isn't entirely a lie. But look, I'm not going to bother tracking you down. Frying small fish is a waste of your time and mine. But do us both a favor, amigo, will you? Don't call back."

Kennett handed the phone to Michael. He heard the breathing again before the kidnapper ended the call.

"Your wife's toes are fine," Kennett assured him. "These scammers." He shook his head more derisively this time. "You put your phone number out on the internet, give these sharks a whiff of desperation, let them smell blood in the water, and they'll come find you."

Michael glanced at his feet.

"Don't be hard on yourself, Mike. Lots of people fall for this nonsense. It's why they do it. But putting your contact info out there for all to see isn't a great move. There are better ways to source leads than having bottom feeders trying to get in touch with you."

"What are you doing here, Detective?"

Michael couldn't keep the edge from his voice.

"What? Can't I check up on you? See how things are going?"

"From New York? A day after I left the city? I'd figured you'd call if you had information."

Kennett cracked a smile.

"Normally that's right, but I happen to

have a cousin, lives close by. I had some vacation time and we both like to fish. Figured we'd hang out a bit, and since I was in the neighborhood, I decided I'd stop by, check in on you, see how things are going with your missing family. Guess I got here just in time to save you fifteen hundred bucks."

Michael shot Kennett a questioning look. It was obvious the detective had an ulterior motive and a game was afoot. What that game was, Michael couldn't say.

"Clearly you're too verklempt to thank me. Well, you can thank me later," Kennett said. "I'm going to be hanging out around here awhile . . . with my cousin. Maybe you and I could hook up. Go for beers. I can help you come up with strategies for finding Natalie. I've got some know-how there. Say, what are you doing right now, Mike? No time like the present."

Kennett offered a toothy smile. Michael took it in, and swallowed hard.

What's the game? he was thinking.

"What town does your cousin live in?" he asked.

"Medford," Kennett said. "You know that town, Mike?"

Michael couldn't speak. He knew plenty about Medford, but the fact that jumped out to him immediately was that Audrey Adler lived there.

Holy shit, Michael thought. *He knows. Somehow, some way, Kennett knows.*

Michael said, "Give me a few minutes, will you? Let me just take care of a couple of things."

He left Kennett in the foyer, thinking of the old adage: *Keep your friends close and your enemies closer.*

CHAPTER 21

Natalie

Before She Disappeared

Magoun Avenue was less than a mile from the spot of Paul Revere's famous midnight ride, which ran along Main Street in downtown Medford. It was the same street where Natalie now sat parked in her SUV across from Audrey Adler's home, a two-family converted into condos. Seeing the little red Kia in the tandem driveway, Natalie assumed Audrey was inside her first-floor unit. The night air was cool, but Natalie had stripped off layers of clothing, which were piled on the seat beside her. Her simmering rage kept her plenty warm.

The clapboard home featured a columned entranceway that supported a balcony on the upper level. Black shutters fronting square windows looked like eyelashes against the exterior's stark white paint. Gauzy curtains aglow with warm lamplight kept Natalie from peeking inside. She had a pretty good idea what those curtains were concealing, but to her chagrin she hadn't seen Michael's car in the driveway. She didn't even know for certain that he'd come to this address.

Natalie had called him, of course. He'd answered, saying he was still at the office, but that could have been a lie. She'd keyed in on the anxious flutter in his voice. He was hiding something. She could tell. Perhaps she should have installed a GPS tracker on his car (a bit psycho, she knew), or somehow used his phone to reveal his true location.

She cursed Scarlett softly under her breath. If the nanny had shown up sooner, Natalie might have made it here in time to catch him in the act.

No dice. No luck.

She thought back to his mysterious phone call, snippets of which she'd picked up through Bluetooth.

We can't do that.

What did "that" mean? More important, was it Audrey's voice that she'd heard? She told herself yes, and expected there was a good chance he'd stopped over for a quickie. Michael knew he couldn't stay long, otherwise he'd risk raising the suspicions of his already suspicious wife.

What was it that drove men to go to such lengths to do something they could easily take care of by themselves in a locked bathroom, with a lot less risk, time, and effort? Men were either incredibly complex or (and this she believed to be more likely), supremely simplistic. It was all about the conquest for them, not the relationship. The thrill of the chase, and to the winner goes the spoils! And what were the spoils? A broken marriage, a devastated family, vows that could not have been any more meaningless.

Several minutes passed, during which Natalie watched the home from the relative safety of her car. She was thinking maybe Michael had gone to get a bottle of wine, or takeout from one of the many restaurants dotting Medford's Main Street. She passed the time thinking of what she'd say if given a chance to confront him.

So, you're Audrey's 'Chris' came to mind, though Michael might not immediately get the reference. It would be Michael's name Audrey cried out in ecstasy, not Chris's, a name she'd used purposefully to hide her paramour's identity.

God, the thought of it all made Natalie sick.

Since indirect wasn't going to work, Natalie settled for the more obvious.

You shit. You lying, devious asshole. How could you? How dare you?

The thought of confronting Michael so gloriously brought a smile to her face. She imagined Audrey hearing the commotion before emerging from her condo with a wide-eyed look of shock. Neighbors would peek out their doors and windows. Maybe the cops would show up.

Good. Let it be a big deal.

Later, she'd kick Michael out of the house and he'd go willingly, without complaint, probably straight back to Audrey. He'd leave his wife and children behind like he was being the noble one, doing Natalie's bidding for her well-being, or so he'd say. In reality, he'd come back here with a bow on his head, and perhaps another ribbon tied elsewhere, like he himself was a gift.

Some gift.

Eventually, Natalie got tired of waiting. She texted Michael.

Where are you?

He didn't respond.

247

How long does it take to get Chinese food or fancy wine? she asked herself.

What time will you be home? she texted.

Again, no answer.

She got out of her car to have a stretch. Let Audrey see her, she decided. What would HR say? You can't be out and about in a free country? Natalie paced up and down the street, thinking . . . thinking. Her poor brain felt so gummed up that the best she could manage was a single notion, a thought set on repeat.

Confront. Confront. Confront.

But whom could she confront? Michael wasn't here, or at least his Audi with the dent in the bumper wasn't.

She went through it again — the "tells" Audrey and Michael had given her.

The gym. Chris. Brown hair. Fit. Trim. Super attractive. Married. Two kids. Nervously drums his fingers. Their strong reactions to the photos. Natalie didn't need to see Michael's dented car to know.

It was enough, more than enough to confront *someone,* and seeing as Michael wasn't available to be on the receiving end, Natalie settled for person number two on her hit list.

Audrey Adler herself.

The time had come. Enough of this, she told herself.

Inhaling a deep breath to inflate her resolve, Natalie climbed the stairs to the front door. She rang the doorbell, folding her arms across her chest as she waited. She heard no footsteps. Nobody came to the door. She rang the doorbell again, two chimes sounded, hollow to her ears.

But Natalie was set on her mission and decided to turn the knob only to discover the door was unlatched. Before she could process what she was doing, Natalie was giving the door a gentle push to open it wider.

Staying rooted on the front stoop, she called out into a darkened hallway, "Audrey? Are you home? It's Natalie Hart. We need to talk. Now."

She slipped an edge of authority into her voice, but there was a hint of uncertainty as well. Something felt off. Emboldened, Natalie opened the door wider to poke her head just beyond the threshold.

I shouldn't be doing this.

She paused, feeling an unfamiliar beat of fear. Glancing down a darkened hallway, Natalie couldn't see past a table that held a vase with a few orange flowers in it.

I shouldn't go in, but I have to.

She took out her phone to check the time. 8:37. She told Scarlett she'd be back by nine thirty at the latest. There was plenty of time to figure out what was going on. A car zoomed by and the word "witness" came to Natalie's mind.

Witness — because you shouldn't be here, she told herself.

"I can see your car in the driveway," Natalie said to no one. "I'd like to speak with you, and you know what it's about."

An eerie feeling washed over her. The apartment was as still as could be. Her heart beat erratically. Sweat dappled the nape of her neck. She took a cautious step inside and headed to her right, through a doorway into a living room, which held little more than a couch, love seat, and TV resting on a console table. A lone floor lamp was the same one that backlit those gauzy curtains. She used her phone to take pictures of the room. Right now she was too nervous to search carefully for evidence of Michael's presence, but perhaps the photos would reveal something of consequence she'd catch later, when she could view them under less precarious conditions.

"Hello," Natalie cried out again, her voice

echoing in the stillness. "Audrey, are you here?"

She had a passing thought that Michael and Audrey had left together in his car, and forgot to shut and lock the door on their way out. An oversight. Great sex could addle the brain, same as lack of sleep.

"Audrey?"

Natalie reentered the foyer, took a few more pictures, before venturing down the unlit hallway farther into the home. All appeared normal, but something felt off. She had an intense feeling, unsettling to say the least, and she couldn't ignore that type of intuition.

"Hello?"

Natalie's voice sank into the gloom. She took each step slowly, carefully, pausing to listen. As she proceeded, Natalie noticed a set of framed photos hanging on the walls. All three photographs were of two girls — the older one was somewhere in her late teens, utterly gorgeous, with long strawberry-blond hair and a delicate face. The younger girl, her arms draped around her companion with a smile like the sunrise, was no doubt Audrey Adler in her much younger years.

Who is the older girl? Natalie wondered.

Curious, Natalie used her phone to take a

digital picture of the framed photographs. While the photos clearly had nothing to do with Michael, at that moment Natalie wanted to know everything she could about the woman who was more important to her husband than she was.

What other mysteries did the house contain?

Checking a closed door to her right, Natalie poked her head into a small bathroom. She kept the light off, didn't bother looking around, nothing to see here. She closed that door before making her way deeper into the condo. Another door to her right revealed a bedroom. The duvet was on the floor; the sheets were rumpled. Natalie felt sick to her stomach thinking about what took place on that bed. Too sick to take a picture, so her phone went back into her pocket. She picked up an odd odor, a musty kind of smell, not the scent of sex. It was coming from somewhere else, so she backed out of the bedroom, focused now on a bright glow spilling out from a doorway at the end of the hall.

Natalie swallowed hard as she looked for, and found, the source of that light. Her heart stopped nearly mid-beat at the sight. Audrey Adler was spread out supine on the kitchen floor, floating in a lake of blood.

The white blouse she'd worn to work that day was soaked in crimson. The blood appeared to have come from multiple wounds to her abdomen, but the stained blouse made it hard to tell where the bleeding had originated. Shards of a broken green plate littered the floor near Audrey's inert form.

A low moan like a rattling wind escaped from Natalie's lips. She stood in the doorway, arms and legs shaking with fright. She'd never seen a dead person before, and really shouldn't have assumed Audrey was gone, but she knew. Maybe it was the odd angle of her head, or the faraway look in her eyes, or perhaps the stark paleness of her face that told her Audrey Adler had breathed her last breath.

Natalie took a few shaky steps down the hall, away from the body, and stopped. She forced herself to go back into the kitchen. A fierce tremor shot up her spine when she saw Audrey for a second time. She took a tentative step closer, then two, until her body froze and she could move no more. The heavy thud in Natalie's chest wouldn't abate. Thoughts came at her, piercing like the tips of darts.

Michael did this.

You left your house in a rush.

HR knows you've been harassing Audrey.

Michael will say you've made accusations about him and Audrey.

He'll turn you in for his crime to save himself.

You shouldn't be in this apartment, but now your fingerprints are everywhere.

Her hands felt like blocks of ice as she grabbed a roll of paper towels off the kitchen counter along with a nearby bottle of spray cleaner.

What had she touched?

She thought back to moments ago — the bathroom doorknob, the one to the bedroom, the front door. That was it. Not much. It would be easy to clean. Her gaze traveled over to Audrey, splayed on the floor. The milky look of death in her eyes bore into Natalie with a cutting force. Her mind clicked out of its raw shock as her survival instincts took over.

The kids. Addie and Bryce. They need a mother. I'm so sorry, Audrey. I'm sorry for everything.

Natalie backed out of the kitchen slowly before starting down the hallway again, clutching the cleaner and paper towels. Prickling fear stayed with her every step of the way. It felt as if at any moment Audrey's cold dead hand would latch against her shoulder, pulling her back to the kitchen.

Pushing her fear aside, Natalie stood at

the threshold to the bedroom. *Call the police,* rang an angry voice in her head. But no, she couldn't risk it. Not even an anonymous call. No, that could still be traced back to her.

Into the bedroom she went. She had to wipe off both doorknobs, inside and out. It was while she was wiping off a second application of cleaner that she glanced at the dresser. It was there in plain sight, neatly folded inside a clear plastic Ziploc bag. The design on the navy-colored T-shirt might have gone unnoticed were it not so familiar to Natalie.

She hadn't seen Michael wear his favorite shirt from his alma mater, University of Oregon, for a while now; didn't remember seeing it in the wash, either. Now here it was, secured inside a clear plastic bag on Audrey's dresser. Natalie was sure the T-shirt belonged to Michael, but she picked up the bag to check, careful to use a paper towel to avoid leaving prints. The coloring looked right. It was an old, faded tee, well-worn, a favorite workout shirt of Michael's. Why was it in a bag? Because Michael had left it after one of his trysts here, and thoughtful Audrey washed it for him and put it in a storage bag so it wouldn't get mixed up with the other clothes, Natalie decided. She was being kind and caring, and her payment was a knife thrust into her body over and over.

For a second Natalie had forgotten there was a body lying in a pool of blood just down the hall. Her breathing had grown shallow and rapid. Waves of dizziness came and went. Natalie had been certified in first aid and recognized the symptoms of shock, but she didn't have time to go catatonic. She had a few more doorknobs to wipe clean. The faces of her children flashed in her mind like the strobe light on a fire alarm, keeping her upright and moving.

Confused and dazed as she was, Natalie was with it enough to ask herself one question: *What triggered the attack?* She'd experienced Michael's anger before, but it had never resulted in violence.

Never, until today.

She had no clear answers, but then another thought came to her, a single word: *evidence.* If the police could trace the shirt to Michael, using his DNA perhaps, they'd put it all together and come after her, not him. She'd be the jilted wife who took matters into her own hands. Natalie couldn't let that happen.

The bag fell from her grasp — sweat and fear weakening her grip. She bent down to retrieve it, and that's when she saw the key. It was on the floor under the dresser. Natalie slid the key out from underneath, not worried about her fingerprints. The number 774 was engraved on one side of the red plastic key chain, and on the other side were the initials *OAC,* which Natalie took to mean Oakmont Athletic Club.

She'd seen this exact key in her house before, the key Michael had lost.

Natalie put the key in the same bag as the shirt. After finishing with all the doorknobs, she exited, looking both ways for cars containing more potential witnesses. The street was clear.

Natalie got back in her car. She tossed the bag with the shirt and key inside on top of her pile of clothes. A few moments later, she was driving off into the darkness, back to her children, to her home, and of course, to her husband.

Chapter 22

Natalie

The new hair color was going to take some getting used to. Natalie would catch a glimpse of herself in the rearview mirror as she drove the speed limit on I-70 and think: *Who am I?* Wanting to go as unnoticed as possible, she hadn't bothered with makeup this morning, and she found herself focused on the lines and wrinkles, the pasty white look of exhaustion she wore like foundation — and of course, her hair.

The dye job was hardly professional, but it was definitely better than what she'd given the children, who looked like they'd been playing with finger paint. There were still fading marks on their skin where the dye dripped past the hairline. The kids didn't seem to mind the new color, and Bryce even asked to go green next time, but both had refused haircuts. Addie had been especially adamant. Natalie could have forced them to comply — of course she could have, she was their mother after all — but she supposed the dye had done its job. From a distance the trio looked a lot less like the picture circulating on social media.

One problem solved, but another remained.

Sleep.

The road was doing that hypnotic thing again, making it hard for Natalie to focus on driving. Lines dividing the highway blurred from solid to dotted and then back again. How many hours of sleep did she get last night? Two? Three? No . . . probably less.

She tightened her hands on the wheel, but her eyes still felt heavy. Why was it she could sleep where she shouldn't and couldn't sleep where she should? She felt like the butt of a cruel joke.

Her gaze softened as her attention drifted from the road to nothing at all. It was some distance later that Bryce asked when they could stop, and only then did Natalie realize she was behind the wheel of a car, going sixty, with her two kids in the back.

Holy shit, she thought.

She bit the inside of her mouth hard enough to make her eyes water, but at least she was awake and alert again.

"We'll stop soon," she told Bryce.

Bryce didn't seem to like the answer and retorted: "When will we see Daddy?"

Kids know, thought Natalie. *They just know how to make it hurt.*

"Soon," she said, hating herself for the lie.

"When's soon?"

"Who needs a bathroom break?"

When in doubt, change the subject. Bryce raised his hand, and thinking she'd get to a rest area, Natalie followed a sign to a country highway. Away from the interstate the landscape changed with farms and fields on either side, and while this route offered nicer scenery, the road seemed to stretch on forever. Natalie felt herself driving toward some invisible edge — not only in this physical world, but in her mind as well. Her thinking was muddled, but at least she was keeping the car in its proper lane. Eventually, she pulled over onto the side of the road so that Bryce could do his business. No cars passed.

Everyone had a stretch, and Addie groaned about getting back in the car, a sentiment Natalie shared, but that was the extent of it. They had to keep driving. Complaints from the kids died down with the start of yet another game of I Spy.

"I spy with my little eye something . . .

green," Bryce announced.

Natalie glanced out the window.

Green . . . no shit.

Everything looked green to her. The trees. The grass. The houses. Hell, even the cows looked green. Natalie felt utterly disconnected from everything and everyone, as if she were having an out-of-body experience while behind the wheel of a two-thousand-pound car.

I'm going crazy, she thought. *Bit by bit. Drip by drip. I'm going insane.*

This line of thinking was as predictable as the dawning of a new day, and it served only to usher in waves of doubt.

Am I doing the right thing?

She reminded herself how easily Michael had slept that night after what he'd done. She knew she had no choice.

Her mantra came to her as it always did in moments of uncertainty.

Move. Move. Move. Keep on moving.

Her other thoughts: *get to Kate's farm. Rest and recharge. Turn the evidence over to the police, but do it from a place where Michael can't find us.*

Kate had replied, "ok," in response to the new number, hadn't asked any questions, which meant she hadn't seen the Facebook post. Good. She'd learn the truth soon enough.

Five or so hours and a few stops later, Natalie drove into Zanesville, Ohio. Finally, rest was imminent. No way could she make the full eight hours she'd planned on driving.

Brightly colored religious messages and neon-lit crosses greeted the family at every turn as they drove along the wide, quiet streets lined with white clapboard homes and their welcoming front porches. Natalie noted the overall Americana charm of the place, and without warning, a torrent of sadness rose up inside her. This was the life she'd imagined for herself when she and Michael first got serious. Lemonade stands and ball games. Good neighbors and cookouts. Campfires and cuddles. A husband who adored her — and didn't lie about everything. This was what she'd always wanted: a modest but decent existence in a town just like this one.

She drove through the town center in what she guessed to be under four seconds. It was approaching one o'clock in the afternoon, but the streets were eerily empty. Maybe everyone was at church. Natalie couldn't help but take in the multitude of spiritual messages peppering the sides of buildings and antiquated farmhouses, reminding her to pray.

She checked out three different motels, until finally selecting a modestly priced Fairfield Inn. The kids were all energy as they bounded out of the car, desperate to give their legs a good stretch. They ran in circles, chasing after each other on a patch of grass in something of a courtyard fronting the inn. Perhaps because the air tasted extra fresh out here, Addie didn't seem to have any breathing troubles, though Natalie's deep inhales were hardly rejuvenating.

After issuing instructions to both children to stay close by, play only on the grassy area. Natalie went to check in.

The receptionist greeted Natalie with an affable smile that could have advertised a dental practice.

"Checking in?"

A gritty film covered Natalie's eyes, as though she'd driven through a dust storm. Road-weary travelers had to comprise the bulk of the Fairfield's guests, which would explain why her bedraggled appearance attracted no special attention from this clerk.

"Yes, but I don't have a reservation," said Natalie.

The receptionist began tapping away on her keyboard with the precision of a concert pianist. Several moments later she announced room availability as if it were a stroke of good fortune. The parking lot was mostly empty when they'd arrived and Natalie doubted this establishment ever sold out.

"We just need a credit card to authorize for incidentals and a driver's license and I'll get you checked in," the receptionist said.

Natalie only half heard as her attention was focused out the window on the patch of lawn where Addie twirled Bryce by his arm. Both kids had big smiles on their faces, but Natalie thought the play was too rough. She remembered Bryce's elbow injury his father had inflicted upon him, and thought a hospital visit could be as disastrous as a speeding ticket. With her focus elsewhere, Natalie absentmindedly handed over her credit card.

While the receptionist busied herself with the check-in process, Natalie headed outside to round up Addie and Bryce.

Moments later, she returned to the counter with two grumbling kids in tow, both of them angry at having had their fun cut short. The receptionist returned the credit card and driver's license. She didn't seem at all perplexed that Natalie's new hair color didn't match her license photo, nor did her name raise any suspicions. That brought a measure of relief to Natalie, who felt she was in the clear here. They were safe. She could sleep tonight. Maybe.

But as Natalie put her card back in her wallet, something clicked in her mind. A sickening feeling swept over her as anxiety kicked in and her body began to tremble. She knew she'd made a terrible mistake, one from which she could not easily recover.

"Can you cancel that transaction?" Natalie asked the receptionist with urgency.

"Sure," came the reply, but Natalie thought it over, realizing that probably wouldn't work, wouldn't erase the transaction in the system.

Briskly, she snapped her wallet closed before shoving it into her purse.

Because Natalie had applied for the new credit card independently, the card company used her salary, not their joint income, to establish the credit limit, which was considerably less than she would have preferred. For that reason, Natalie kept the old credit card handy for emergency purposes only.

She thought she'd made all the right moves. The bank account she opened to pay bills would keep Michael in the dark about the new card, and she even had the foresight to use a PO box address for her application, as well as going paperless to hide the new credit card statements from him. As an added precaution, Natalie religiously kept the old card in a special slot in her wallet to avoid any mix-ups like the one she'd just made.

She'd been in a total fog, her brain clicked off, when she mistakenly handed the clerk the old credit card, the wrong damn card, the one Michael used as well.

Sirens blared in Natalie's head, and self-castigation soon followed.

You dummy! You idiot! You screwup!

A look of concern swept into the clerk's eyes.

"Are you okay?" she asked.

Heat like a fire burned through Natalie, turning her cheeks red. She couldn't get out any words. But that voice in her head was back, screaming at her like a drill sergeant: *Go! Go! Go!* He'd know. Natalie wasn't certain if an authorization would show up as a transaction on a statement, or if it might even trigger a fraud alert. Given the efficiency of the credit card company, it very well might. If so, Michael would see the charge or get the alert, and he'd know it was his wife checking into a hotel, and more significantly he'd know her exact location.

Then he'd come for her, and he'd track her down. There were cameras here, too, had to be, though Natalie didn't spot them on the way inside. She'd lulled herself into a false sense of security. But she was secure no more. Michael would see everything. The car. The license plate. He'd see it all.

Natalie's mouth went dry. She grabbed Addie and Bryce by their arms and pulled them toward the door.

"I'm sorry," she said to the clerk as she took several lumbering steps backward. "We won't be needing that room after all. Something's just come up."

"What's going on, Mommy?" asked Bryce, keying in on his mother's distress. "Is it Daddy? Do we have the wrong hotel?"

"Yes," said Natalie, twisting her body to face the door, moving faster now. Panic fluttered in her chest. "We have the wrong hotel."

"So that means we'll see Daddy soon?" asked Addie, her eyes shimmering with delight.

"Yes," Natalie said, talking with a faraway voice. In her mind she was plotting: *how to recover?* "We'll probably be seeing Daddy sooner than we think."

CHAPTER 23

Michael

Michael and Detective Kennett sat down at the bar of the Friday's restaurant in Burlington just in time for lunch. Kennett ordered a basket of wings along with a cold pilsner. Michael got a Coke and a burger, figuring he'd need a cool heart and clear head for this meal.

Service was swift, and before Michael knew it, Kennett had a frothy beer in front of him. He swallowed a gulp while letting his gaze linger too long on Michael's face for his comfort. The detective's stare seemed intended to intimidate, but the ensuing conversation was, for the most part, light and breezy. They talked about the scammer, Kennett telling him about other similar ruses he'd encountered, but that conversation came to an abrupt end when the food arrived. Kennett eyed the basket greedily before taking one steaming wing into his hand.

"So, Mike, tell me where you're at with the search for Natalie and the kids," he asked. "Any leads? I mean, real ones? No box trucks."

"Nothing," Michael said before taking a sip of his drink. He wasn't surprised that the Coke didn't make his throat feel any less parched.

"Nothing on her credit card, huh?" asked Kennett, as he licked buffalo sauce off his fingers before going to the napkin.

"I'm watching for transactions, but no. There's been nothing."

Kennett mulled that over.

"Smart. She thought this through, Mike. She's got a bank account somewhere. I bet anything on that. You do joint checking?"

Michael nodded.

"Right. So she's siphoned money. Guarantee it. Financial infidelity. Ever heard the term?"

Michael shook his head, didn't feel like sharing that Kennett was right about Natalie.

"Yeah, guessing you can figure out the meaning," he said.

"Better money than a man I suppose," said Michael.

Kennett cocked his head sideways. "Some would disagree," he said before gobbling down another wing. "Besides, it could be both."

Well, that hurt.

"You think she took the kids to be with her new lover?"

Kennett offered up a shrug.

"Mike, I don't have the foggiest idea why your wife ran away."

The left corner of Kennett's mouth ticked upward. A taunting look entered his eyes. It was the closest thing to a wink without being one that Michael had ever seen. He assured himself it wasn't a guarantee that Kennett knew more than he was letting on, but it was damn worrisome.

"Does she use direct deposit?" asked Kennett. "Lots of raises don't get reported to the hubby or wife and end up in a new bank account instead. That's another trick of the trade."

"Yeah, she does in fact use direct deposit; we both do," said Michael. His eyebrows arched slightly as he imagined Natalie skipping the celebratory promotion dinner because she'd never told him about it in the first place. "What are some other tricks?" he asked.

Michael was curious now. He didn't care

270

about the money; he just wanted his wife back, so he wondered — make that hoped — that knowing the tricks could somehow help him track her down.

"Cash back, and lots of it," said Kennett without hesitation. "An extra forty bucks every time she goes shopping can add up over time. The total charge shows up online, not the cash back amount."

"Clever," Michael said, feeling too queasy for the burger the bartender had finally put down in front of him. Natalie did the bulk of the shopping, which would make that money grab an easy one to pull off.

"She probably has her own credit card," Kennett said, almost offhandedly. "That's why you're not seeing the transactions. It's easy enough to do." Again, Kennett skipped the napkin to lick the wing sauce off his fingers. "You look a little sick, Mike. You feeling all right?"

Michael finally chomped down on his burger. He offered a nod to indicate all was okay as he chewed, but secretly wondered if he could keep the food down.

"I'm assuming her social media account has been pretty dormant," said Kennett.

"She's not posting any selfies, if that's what you're asking."

Kennett gave a throaty chuckle.

"Yeah, figured that."

More wings for Kennett. More burger for Mike. The silence felt worse than the conversation.

"So what *have* you done, Mike? Give me the rundown. Have you called on her friends and family? Checked all of Natalie's acquaintances?"

"Some, not all," Michael admitted. "I don't know them all."

"Well, maybe you should get knowing. You call friends of friends and you'll reveal her entire network. And you've got to call them all. It's legwork, Mike. No shortcuts here. What about hiring a PI?"

"I've been thinking about it."

"Probably a bit more effective than a Facebook post with your phone number on it."

This time Kennett gave a real wink that was both playful and sinister to Michael's eye. Even so, the detective wasn't wrong. Michael's phone had blessedly stopped ringing since he asked Lucinda to edit that post, removing his phone number. Any Good Samaritan could still get in touch with the family via the messenger app, or they could always call the police. As for the police, Michael thought about pressing Kennett again for his true purpose in being near Lexington, but he decided against it.

Perhaps it worked in his favor that they were both playing games.

"What about your family, Mike?" Kennett asked. "Have you been in touch with them?"

That taunting look found its way back into the detective's eyes. Michael chewed on his burger as he contemplated his response.

Is he fishing, or does he know?

"My father left us when I was a kid. Walked out on my mom and me. My mom, she died a long time ago, cancer."

"When you were a kid, Mike . . . or was it more like college age?"

Michael swallowed hard. Could be an innocuous question, but Michael suddenly doubted it.

"College," he said. He was trying to be mindful of his eyes (not too much blinking), of his posture (arms not folded), of his hands (not drumming his fingers). He didn't want to give Kennett any indication that he was sniffing around some deeper truths.

"Sorry to hear."

Kennett indeed sounded sorry.

Michael took that as a good sign, a signal that the detective didn't have another agenda.

"Anyway, it was a long time ago," added

273

Michael.

"Don't be so dismissive of your trauma. Your mom dying, and someone vanishing like your dad did, it's like a death of sorts . . . and death makes time stop, Mike," Kennett said. "You don't really get to move on from that. That's what the loved ones tell me, anyway, when they ask about their cases. They think they want justice, but really what they want is for time to start moving again. And it never does. Never. Even when the perp is behind bars, that eleven-year-old kid who had his brains blown out in a drive-by, he's still eleven . . . and always will be."

A faraway look seeped into Kennett's eyes, and for the first time Michael felt a spurt of sympathy for the man. This detective had a hard job to do, one that came with a lot of baggage. But Michael had baggage too, and he doubted Kennett would have much sympathy for any of that. Still, he wanted to know the man's angle, and frustratingly, he felt no closer to the truth.

"There's been some death around here, a murder," Kennett said, as if that wasn't a jarring segue. "At least according to my cousin."

"Yeah? I'm not much for the metro section of the news," said Michael.

274

"Audrey Adler. That name mean anything to you, Mike?"

A million thoughts rushed through Michael's head, but he couldn't articulate any of them. Kennett's hard stare made Michael shift uneasily on his barstool.

Fuck.

"Audrey," Michael said, giving his dry lips a lick.

No tells.

"I know that name, sure. She worked with my wife at Dynamic Media. A real tragedy."

"So you do watch the news."

"It was a few weeks back, but yeah, that one hit close to home."

Hopefully, Kennett doesn't know how close, thought Michael.

"Like you said, a real tragedy," Kennett replied.

A high-pitched whine rang in Michael's ears.

"So did you know her personally, Mike? Audrey Adler?"

The sound in his ears became as loud as those bells hanging in the tower at Notre Dame. Michael swallowed hard. The air in the bar tasted stale and oppressive.

"Not personally, no."

Kennett's eyes darted over to Michael's fingers, which he was drumming against the

275

bar's varnished surface. Michael noticed him looking before he pulled his hands to his lap.

"My cousin is a cop," said Kennett. "He's not on the case, but he knows about it. No good leads. No motive. Nobody wanted to do her any harm. Those are the hard cases, Mike. The ones without good answers." Here, Kennett paused. "Not that the answer will be any good."

"Well, I hope they catch whoever did it," Michael said. His vision was obscured. He wasn't seeing Kennett clearly anymore. Michael shivered, and it wasn't because of the air-conditioning blasting overhead. He was puzzled. *Had* this detective put it all together?

Michael had certainly given the detective a few verbal and visual cues to indicate he wasn't being entirely truthful, but didn't think he'd given away anything big. It seemed both he and Kennett were holding their cards close to their chests. Michael's phone buzzed on the bar. He picked it up. It could be about Natalie, so he had to look. The buzz was to let him know that he'd received a text message from his credit card company regarding potentially fraudulent activity on his account. Michael couldn't take his eyes off the display screen.

"Something interesting, Mike?" Kennett asked.

"Might be Natalie," he said, showing Kennett the text he just received, thinking there was no harm in showing the detective. As Kennett said back in New York, it's good to team up when things take a surprising turn.

With a touch of his finger Michael launched the app for his credit card. After entering his username and password into the corresponding fields, Michael waited for the application to load. Kennett kept his focus on Michael the entire time. His eyes held all the warmth of a winter night. Michael read the message asking if he had authorized a charge, and if so to click a button to dismiss the alert. He showed Kennett.

"Fairfield Inn," Kennett said, reading the alert. "Zanesville, Ohio. So, looks like your wife is in Ohio, Mike."

Michael put two twenties on the bar. Time to go.

"Where to?" Kennett asked, though the answer had to be obvious to him.

"I'm going to Logan right now," Michael said. "Catch a flight to Ohio. Find my wife."

Kennett nodded while taking a leisurely sip of his beer.

"Let me go with you," he said.

"What?"

"Yeah, I'll swing by my cousin's place, grab my stuff, and I'll go with you."

"Why would you do that?" Michael asked, feeling an anxious twist in his stomach.

"I took an oath, Mike, to be of service. And to be honest, you seem like a guy who could use some help."

"I'll do fine on my own," Michael said, wishing his heartbeat wasn't thundering. The way Kennett eyed him told Michael to be wary.

"Ohio is a big state, Mike. You got a lead, but that's probably not going to be enough. I've got contacts in law enforcement I can get a hold of with the push of a few buttons. I think you'll want my help."

"Why would you inconvenience yourself like that?"

Kennett brushed the question aside with a wave of his hand like it was crazy to even ask.

"Hell, you'd be doing me a favor," he said with a laugh. "My cousin can be a real pain in the ass."

It occurred to Michael that there wasn't any cousin from Medford, and Kennett had come here specifically because of Audrey Adler. If that were the case, not only was Kennett way out of his jurisdiction, Michael might also be way out of his depth.

Michael mulled it over. Maybe Kennett had an ulterior motive. Maybe this was exactly what it seemed to be — a setup, a trap of sorts, but it was also an offer that could be extremely helpful. As Kennett said, Ohio was a big state, and Michael had no experience with the business of tracking down missing persons. The stakes were too high.

"You can police out of your jurisdiction?" Michael asked.

"No, Mike, but I can vacation wherever I want," Kennett said.

The dual message Michael read in Kennett's second wink was easy enough to interpret.

I'm your best hope and your worst nightmare.

CHAPTER 24

Natalie

Before She Disappeared

Somehow, Natalie made it back home in one piece. She didn't have any real memory of making the trip from Audrey Adler's condo to Lexington — she thought she may even have blacked out for a time — but before she knew it, she was pulling into her driveway. There was a light on in the kitchen, but all was dark upstairs, meaning the children were fast asleep. She noticed Michael's car wasn't in the driveway or garage. Fine. Natalie was done texting him anyway. She knew he'd be home at some point, and that thought now gripped her with fear.

She couldn't imagine where he'd gone to wash the blood off his hands, change his clothes, get himself cleaned up. Perhaps he'd eventually made it to his office as he'd told her. Or maybe he cleaned up in Audrey's condo, still near the woman whose life he'd taken.

Natalie pictured Michael drying himself off, then driving to the woods or to some lake to rid himself of the murder weapon. Maybe someone else committed the crime, but Natalie doubted it. Michael was her lover. His shirt was there, and his locker key, too. Something happened between the time he'd left in a rush and when Natalie finally got to Audrey's place, something violent and unholy. To Natalie, he was now a man capable of anything.

Numb and reeling, Natalie climbed out of her car in a daze.

She found Scarlett in the kitchen. Natalie noticed the nanny's skimpy halter top and exposed shoulders, took in the curve of her hips, and again had the thought that Audrey Adler might not be Michael's one and only secret lover. She decided tonight would be Scarlett's final night working for the Hart family.

"Hello, Mrs. Hart. Are you all right?"

"Yes, I'm fine," she said flatly. From her purse, Natalie retrieved the money she owed Scarlett and made the exchange without banter before sending the nanny on her way for what would be the very last time.

Natalie listened for her car engine, hearing it rumble to life before the sound vanished into the night. Only when she was certain Scarlett was gone did Natalie let her legs relax enough to carry her to the kitchen, where she sank to the floor, resting her back against the cabinet containing the pots and pans. There, she let herself go, at last uncorking her bottled-up fear. Heaving sobs rattled her ribs as thick tears fell from her eyes. Pain gutted her inside and out.

Exhausted, she eventually settled. Using the counter for support, Natalie hoisted herself back to her feet. She considered going up to check on the children, but from the bottom landing, the stairs looked towering, and her legs felt too weak to make the climb. Instead, Natalie leaned against the railing, heaving heavy sighs.

She was still propped up on the railing when she heard a car coming down the road. Natalie's heart raced. She knew that engine's whine. Moments later, headlights cut through the darkness to illuminate the foyer where she stood. Natalie sucked down several shaky breaths before wiping her eyes clean with the back of her hand.

He can't know I know, she told herself.

Natalie found her way back to the kitchen before Michael opened the door. She poured water into the kettle and then hit the switch at the base to apply heat.

"Babe?" Michael called out tentatively. "I'm home."

A tangy smell of blood tickled her nostrils. A trick of the mind, she told herself.

"Babe?" Michael said again before appearing in the kitchen. "Hey," he said, upon seeing her. He set the black nylon travel bag that he used to shuttle work papers to and from the office onto the floor before approaching her with an impish grin.

"Sorry I ran out on you like that," he said. "Damn hackers. The tech guys are playing whack-a-mole. They knock down one attack, another pops up somewhere else, and I've got to be on-site to help calm down our high-net-worth investors. The attacks seem to be nonstop these days. Good for job security, I guess." He planted a warm kiss on Natalie's cheek. She worried he'd taste the lingering salt of her tears, but he said nothing. Her gaze went to that workbag. *Does he have papers inside, or something else?* She blinked away a vision of a bloody knife wrapped in a soiled cloth.

"Everything all right?" Michael asked, running his fingers down Natalie's arm. His touch almost stung.

"I'm fine," said Natalie, briskly, thinking she'd failed to muster much conviction.

283

"Yeah?" Michael stepped back to appraise her from a different angle before setting the back of his hand against her forehead. "You feel clammy. You sure you're all right?"

"Yeah, just tired is all. I had to run out to the store because I didn't have anything for the kids' lunches, so I asked Scarlett to come back over, keep an eye on things. Maybe it was too much after a long day."

Scarlett. She had to mention the nanny in case the kids mentioned her to Michael.

"Scarlett again?" A note of doubt came to Michael's voice. "That's odd. You haven't done that before. We usually make do with what's here."

A single thought burrowed into her head with the velocity of a gunshot.

He can't suspect me.

"Anyway, I'm not surprised you're tired," Michael said. "Comes with the territory when you don't sleep. This has got to be driving you crazy."

He tried pulling Natalie into an embrace, but she held her ground, locking her legs, her body stiffening in an involuntary response.

"Hey," Michael complained, pulling her harder. "It's me, babe. Relax."

His words cut through her. In response, Natalie let herself sink into him, albeit reluctantly and only for a second. She forgot herself and wondered what her lack of sleep might be doing to her.

Michael pressed his warm lips against the top of Natalie's head, taking a deep inhale. He let out a soft moan as he pulled her against him, tightening his hold. Natalie felt him stir at the same instant that pungent smell of blood tickled her nose. Maybe it was a trick of the mind, or more likely he wore Audrey's death like cheap cologne.

"The kids are asleep, the house is quiet," Michael whispered. "Why don't we go upstairs and let me give you a massage."

He rolled his tongue along the outer edge of Nat's ear in a gesture he knew from years of lovemaking would get her fired up. Instead of a soft moan like she might have let out in the past, her body went rigid before she pulled away.

"Hey," Michael said, looking and sounding hurt. "What's going on with you?"

"I can't," Natalie said. "I just can't."

She was looking him over from head to toe for any defensive wounds. Scratches. Red marks. Blood on his fingernails. He'd done a thorough job cleaning himself up, and poor Audrey probably never even had a chance to fight back. Sweat beaded on her brow.

Again, that thought: *he can't know I know.*

"Nat," said Michael, his voice holding growing frustration. "We are husband and wife."

"Thanks, but I don't need the reminder," said Natalie.

"And I don't want to have a sexless marriage," Michael retorted. "It's not what I signed up for."

Natalie turned her back to her husband, keeping her arms folded across her chest. Michael stepped forward. He wrapped himself around her from behind like a blanket.

"Look, I'm sorry," he said, rocking her in his arms as he breathed his apology into her ear. "I don't know what I can do to make you trust me. Is this about Audrey Adler again?"

Natalie's body tightened at the mention of her name. She thought it a good thing that Michael couldn't see the terror brimming in her eyes.

"How many times do I have to tell you I don't know that woman?"

Natalie resisted the urge to scoff. She wanted to go to her car, get his T-shirt and gym locker key, throw that bag in his face, and ask him to explain it away, but prudence won out.

She didn't know how well Michael had cleaned his tracks, and she needed time to think through all the possibilities before risking any suspicion being cast on her. Her mind raced ahead. If Michael learned she had been to Audrey's condo, taken his shirt and locker key, he could turn it around and paint her as the jealous wife who suffered from insomnia and lost control. She played out the scenario. Michael would call the police from the house, looking her straight in the eyes.

"My wife hasn't been well," she imagined him saying to the dispatcher in a dispassionate voice. "She's accused me of having an affair and now I think she may have done something quite horrible . . . Audrey Adler, yes that's the name. I believe she lives on Magoun Avenue. You should do a welfare check on Ms. Adler. I'm honestly worried."

He'd end his call with a cagey look on his face. Later on, evidence would surface that Audrey had filed a stalking complaint with HR against Natalie. That's all it would take for the police to hit her with a murder rap.

Natalie imagined her kids crying as she was being led away in handcuffs, the trial, the guilty verdict, Michael in the courtroom looking crushed as she was being escorted to her prison cell. Go to the police with the key and shirt and risk becoming a suspect, proof she'd been in the apartment on the night of the murder, keep them hidden and Michael could turn the tables on her. Damned if she did, damned if she didn't. Rock meet hard place.

"I'm going to sleep in Addie's room on the trundle," Natalie said with ice in her voice.

"Nat, babe."

Michael adopted a pleading tone as he took hold of her arm, too forcefully. She pulled free from his grasp.

"Don't," she said. "I'll see you in the morning."

She trudged up the stairs knowing full well that she'd see the sun catch fire without catching a single minute of sleep.

How could she go on living with a killer under her roof?

Her next thought was even more jarring.

How could she keep her children safe from their father?

She needed help. She had to tell someone.

Come morning, she would.

CHAPTER 25

Natalie

Rain.

Oh, hell, why did it have to start raining?

Natalie blasted the radio and the air-conditioning simultaneously, but the noise and cold couldn't offset the soothing sound of rain.

Pat-pat-pat-pat-pat.

Just like before when she was trying so hard to stay awake in the McDonald's parking lot, she felt the pull of sleep as the steady rhythm of rain sent Natalie into a trance. Her bleary eyes began closing, but snapped open as soon as she caught herself. She'd always hated driving in bad weather. Now, her bone-weary state made every second of this journey a sheer test of will.

Twenty minutes outside Zanesville, she thought of the Fairfield Inn as an oasis, one that had turned out to be a mirage. God, what she wouldn't give to be snuggled in that bed right now. She glanced in the rearview. All looked normal in the backseat with Addie and Bryce. The children gazed absently out their respective windows, watching the rain coming down in sheets.

In a matter of a day, confusion, chaos, and constant motion had become their new normal. And yet, they'd adjusted to it, leaving Natalie in awe of their adaptability. They weren't questioning her every mile as they had at the start of this journey. They'd come to terms that Mom had a plan, some plan, whatever it might be, and they'd be fine as long as they did as she instructed.

Poor things were utterly guileless and trusting, and their mother was so not. But her mantra was in charge: *Move. Move. Move.*

The rain was falling even harder now. One minute the roads were wet, and the next there were puddles everywhere as thick drops fell from black clouds. From off in the distance came the sound of thunder and a few streaks of bolt lightning. Like the crows from her nightmare, Natalie took the severe weather as a sign.

Michael.

He was coming.

She was sure of it.

During a brief stop at a convenience mart,

Natalie used her Tracfone to check her credit card account. Just as she feared, her inbox contained a fraud alert. Computers were quick on the draw. Michael, she knew, would get the same alert, probably sent to him via text message. She'd probably received one as well, but didn't dare turn on her cell phone to confirm.

No matter. Natalie had to assume Michael knew she had been in Zanesville. What he'd do with that information was anyone's guess.

Water sliding off the front windshield distorted the taillights of the cars in front of her as the wipers struggled to keep pace. The sound of rain hitting the roof reverberated inside the car like steady applause. She was driving west on I-70 in the left lane of a two-lane highway, zipping past the barren flats going five miles over the speed limit, wishing she could do fifteen.

Bad idea in this weather.

Natalie tried to ease her foot off the gas, but it was no use. She was hard on the pedal, pushing the speedometer needle higher than it was safe to do in the rain. From the backseat, Bryce sneezed a hearty *achoo* into his new teddy bear. The noise smacked her back to reality. The kids. She was doing this for them.

Even with two packs of Sno Balls bought at the mini-mart providing a sugar rush, her children would never make eight hours on the road. Meanwhile, Natalie wasn't sure she could make it eight more minutes. The rain splattered and plunked. She thought of Michael, departing for the airport, be it La-Guardia, JFK, or Logan, coming to get her.

Then what?

The clerk at the Fairfield could give him a description of her and the kids — the dye jobs weren't that helpful. Dammit. Maybe they'd change color, maybe go darker? She needed to ditch the rental car, too, thinking she might do that in Columbus at some Avis location. Then, she'd rent from Hertz or one of the other car companies, didn't matter. The license plate was the problem, not the vehicle.

Back to Michael.

She wasn't certain he'd have enough to go on to find her, but she couldn't risk making a beeline for Elsberry and Kate's farm. Perhaps he'd already scoured her life, looked up all her friends, new and old. Maybe he'd remembered that party, how they'd met, and how it was her work friend Kate who had taken her there. She worried he'd use a map to plot potential destinations. He'd cross-reference that to anyone who lived near I-70 in Zanesville. That would give him all he'd need to figure out where she might be going. Best she could do was detour. She thought about heading north to Bloomington, make her trail go cold before venturing south again. But the miles were getting harder to travel.

Thank goodness the rain stopped almost as suddenly as it had started. Natalie breathed easier. No sooner had the rain gone than the sun came out. Right away the kids started an earnest search for a rainbow.

All the while, Natalie was desperate for something else. *Sleep, sleep, sleep,* whispered a voice in her head. It felt like her eyelids were being pulled down by weights attached to her eyelashes with tiny chains.

"Mommy, you okay?"

Natalie lifted her head like the tail end of a whip. Beneath her she heard a heavy *whomp-whomp-whomp.* It took a moment to realize that the driver-side tires were off the road and bumping along the grassy, gravelly median. Pulling the wheel to the right, Natalie course-corrected back onto the highway, just as she caught a flash of red and blue lights in her rearview mirror.

Shit, she thought.

Her heart leapt to her throat when she saw a state trooper's patrol car closing in fast. Natalie took in a deep breath and held it. No use. She couldn't ease her rising panic. The kids saw the lights, too, and despite being belted in, spun full around to get a better look.

"Police!" cried Addie, who sounded far more nervous than excited. Natalie kept her daughter's inhaler in the center console compartment. A thought came to her that if Addie suffered an asthma attack, the cop might think she was reaching for a gun. She was fully alert now. Carefully, she got the inhaler out from the console. By that point, the patrol car was basically riding on her bumper. Natalie changed lanes when it was safe to do so, and both vehicles came to a rolling stop in the breakdown lane.

"It's okay, kids," said Natalie, adopting a confident, assured tone, despite how she was really feeling.

Bryce looked quite unsettled while Addie appeared downright petrified.

"Easy does it, sweetie."

Natalie scanned her daughter's face. All seemed okay. Addie's breathing appeared normal, but to ease her worry, Natalie moved the inhaler from the seat beside her onto her lap. Better if the cop saw it. It might even engender some sympathy. It also gave her a story.

The words "license and registration" pounded in Natalie's head.

My name will come up in some system. They'll know. Maybe. Or maybe not.

She had planned her escape like a game of chess, always thinking a few moves ahead. What she'd done was legally murky at best. She'd counted on Michael filing a missing persons report right away and perhaps even going to court to obtain a temporary custody order so he could use that to file parental kidnapping charges. The latter would take time, and Natalie remained doubtful that Michael had reached that stage of desperation so quickly.

Checking her rearview mirror, Natalie watched the patrol officer approach her car with an outlaw's swagger. From the shape of the hips she could tell that this officer was a female. She donned a cavalry gray campaign hat as she neared.

"I see a gun," Bryce announced with a mix of awe and delight in his voice.

Natalie tightened her grip on the wheel. Turning her head, she again caught that frightened look in Addie's eyes. Poor darling.

"It's all right, kids," she said, reaching behind her to place a reassuring hand on Addie's knee.

The trooper stood outside Natalie's door, seemingly unfazed as cars whizzed by. Natalie lowered her window. Sunglasses hid the trooper's eyes, but Natalie could feel her accusatory stare. She was young. A rookie perhaps? That might help. Bryce leaned forward in his seat, "Is that a real gun?"

The trooper didn't bother with an answer, so Bryce fell silent. Pinpricks of fear darted across Natalie's neck.

She'll see my name, she'll know . . .

Natalie fumbled for her purse. Her hands shook enough to make the clasp feel like a puzzle. From the glove compartment, she retrieved the car's registration, which was the rental agreement. She handed that document, along with her license to the trooper.

"I'm sorry officer, I took my eyes off the road for only a moment. I thought my daughter might be having an asthma attack."

Natalie took a guess as to why she'd been pulled over. The trooper raised her head ever so slightly. To make her story add up, Natalie indicated to the inhaler resting on her lap. The trooper glanced at the medicine, before checking out the patient in the backseat, which she did behind those sunglasses that hid her thoughts as well as her eyes.

She took the documents with her as she headed back to the patrol car. Natalie watched her go. She still couldn't catch her breath.

"Are we in trouble, Mommy?" asked Addie.

"No honey, we'll be fine."

Natalie hoped the quaver in her voice didn't betray the lie.

While the trooper ran the license, Natalie confronted her genuine remorse.

She shouldn't have been driving. Now that decision was going to cost them all. Time slowed to a crawl. She imagined the trooper on the radio, calling for backup. Before Natalie knew what she was doing, she had her hand on the key in the ignition.

Her thoughts chattered.

One turn. Then go. Hit the gas. Move! Move! Move!

She applied some torque against the key. Doubt filled her. If the engine rumbled to life, would she go the distance? Would she press her foot to the accelerator and make a run for it? In her mind, Natalie envisioned car wheels spinning against gravel as her vehicle lurched forward. The patrol car would come after her like a barracuda tracking down its prey. Of course in her fantasy she got away, but reality came knocking back hard. It was a crazy notion. She wouldn't put her children at risk. She was trapped with no way out.

Now, Natalie was thinking handcuffs. The pressure building up in her chest felt ready to explode.

She heard a door close. Glancing in the mirror she could see the trooper approach with steady strides. Natalie's insides compressed. She went stock-still. It was over. She knew it. Deep inside she knew this was the end of the road. Dread overwhelmed her as the trooper rapped her knuckles against her window. A gentle breeze entered the car that might have been refreshing anywhere else but here and now.

"You've come up as a missing person," the trooper said matter-of-factly. "Want to tell me what's going on?"

Natalie went cold inside. It felt like there were two hands wrapped around her throat. She looked back at the children.

"Can we talk in private?"

The trooper opened the door for Natalie to get out. She followed the trooper to the passenger side of her vehicle where they'd be safe from oncoming traffic.

"So, talk."

The trooper didn't look like she knew how to smile.

By this point, Natalie's thoughts were churning wildly. Her name must have come up on some screen with big red flags waving.

"I'm on my way to my mother's in Indianapolis," Natalie said. "I'm leaving my husband. He's horribly abusive and — it's not safe for me at home." She put in a dramatic pause for effect. "He's the one who filed the report, but I'm not missing. I'm in danger."

Tears sprang to Natalie's eyes. Mustering the emotion wasn't hard because what she'd said wasn't exactly a lie.

"If you report me to him, I'll be forced to go back there. Something terrible could happen to me, to the kids. Please, please," Natalie said. Her voice came out raw, thick with fear. "You have to believe me."

"Okay, just relax," said the trooper. "Nobody is going to put you in harm's way. I just need to call this in. I'm going to have to hold you for a time until I get further instructions."

No, thought Natalie. This was a worst-case scenario. Detention. Holding. Reporting. Michael would find her for sure.

The trooper was about to speak, offer assurances most likely, when the radio latched to her belt crackled to life.

Natalie couldn't make out all the words, but she heard: "OSHP, respond to I-70. Gratiot. Multi-vehicle accident. Injured parties."

Having thought so much about places to stop en route, Natalie had a good portion of the Ohio map stored in her brain. Gratiot was a village not far from their current location. The trooper's face went slack. She took off her glasses, revealing brown eyes that held more than a modicum of compassion.

"I'm going to put a call into the agency, let them know you're fine. Since I found you, you're technically no longer missing. I laid eyes on you, spoke to you, you seem fine to me, not suicidal, not a danger to yourself or others, so no reason to keep you detained. Closest patrol car to that accident is twenty miles away, so I'm going to have to hurry. I suggest you call your husband. Tell him you're alive and well. Then, get to where you're going safely."

With those parting words the trooper raced back to her patrol car, turned on the lights, gunned the engine, and was gone in a flash, her siren blaring. Natalie felt the pressure leave her body like an air leak.

The word "safe" flashed through her thoughts, but she knew better.

Safe was nothing. Safe didn't exist.

Just like that bed in the Fairfield Inn and the rest that was finally within her reach, safe was a mirage.

Chapter 26

Michael

There was a four o'clock direct flight from
Boston to Ohio with two available seats.
From his home, Michael paid for the tickets
while Kennett made a call to the hotel. He
confirmed that there was not a Natalie Hart
registered at the Fairfield Inn in Zanesville.
Getting an employee to identify a family of
three would be better done in person, so to
Ohio they'd go.

"She could be registered under a different
name and sleeping soundly," said Kennett,
offering up an encouraging note.

"I agree she could be there," Michael
replied, "but I highly doubt she's sleeping."

The flight itself proved uneventful. Kennett spent most of the time in the air reading a Michael Connelly novel he'd bought
in the airport bookstore.

"Cops read about fictional cops?" Michael
asked.

"Connelly gets it right," Kennett replied matter-of-factly.

"He does, eh? So tell me, would Harry Bosch get on a plane with a virtual stranger to help him track down his missing wife and kids?"

Kennett chuckled at that.

"Everyone counts or nobody does," he answered wryly, reciting a familiar Bosch refrain.

"Hmmm," said Michael, sounding doubtful. "Can't help but think I might be counting a little *too* much. You have so many cases, why are you paying so much attention to mine?"

"What is it that they say about gift horses?" asked Kennett.

"I believe that expression is about gratitude, not trust."

"Are you saying you don't trust me, Mike?" A deceitful twinkle slipped into Kennett's eyes — good cop or bad cop, it was hard to say.

"Not really," said Michael, jostling as the plane hit a bump of turbulence.

"Well, what if I told you that a long, long time ago my wife disappeared, ran off like yours did, and I've been looking for her ever since? In my own fractured mind, you're a chance at some kind of redemption."

Michael sent Kennett a sideways glance.

"I don't think I'd believe you," he said.

Kennett smiled fully and broadly.

"You keep that skepticism of yours, Mike," he said. "It'll serve you well down the line."

Kennett went back to reading and didn't talk much until the plane landed.

The drive from John Glenn Columbus International Airport to Zanesville took over an hour in a rented gray Ford Focus. For much of the drive Kennett was on his phone, didn't engage in conversation, which gave Michael the distinct impression he was being tested somehow. All Michael knew for certain was that Audrey Adler's name had come up in conversation, once to be exact, which was one too many times for his comfort.

They pulled into the parking lot of the Fairfield Inn sometime after eight o'clock in the evening. Michael's stomach felt tighter than a face full of Botox. They caught the sunset, a wash of pale orange and yellows that cloaked the darkening sky. The leaves of the red buckeye trees planted out front of the hotel swayed in a gentle breeze.

Kennett had his car door open before Michael came to a full stop. They made their way to the entrance together. Michael watched Kennett do up a button on his blazer as if he were performing some ritual that helped him get into character. Whatever he did, it worked. Kennett seemed to have upped his tough guy New York City detective air by several degrees.

"Let me do the talking, Mike," Kennett said gruffly.

When they reached the front desk, Kennett flashed his badge to the clerk, a young man with hair the color of the towering hay bales they'd seen dotting farmers' fields on the drive here.

"I'm Detective Sergeant Amos Kennett. This is Michael Hart."

The clerk gave Kennett's shiny badge a quick once-over, and if he saw New York City on the ID it didn't occur to him to ask why he was in Ohio.

"Around one o'clock this afternoon a woman and her two children may have checked into your hotel," Kennett said. As he slipped his badge back into the inner pocket of his blazer, Michael caught a flash of the holster and concealed weapon Kennett carried. Once again he got a reminder of the serious nature of his business. From a different pocket, Kennett produced his phone. He showed the clerk the display screen, holding the device so that Michael caught a glimpse of the same picture used in his mother-in-law's Facebook post. "Her name is Natalie Hart," Kennett said, "but she could be here under a different name. Do you recognize her? Did she check in to this hotel, and if so, is she still here?"

The clerk shook his head. "I didn't see her," he said, "but I just came in a few hours ago." He began tapping away at his keypad. "And we don't have a guest here by that name."

"Yeah, I know, we called earlier," said Kennett. "Got that answer. Like I said, they may have checked in under a different name, changed their appearance somehow. Different clothes, different hair, a hat perhaps."

Michael's heart sank, but not too deeply. He knew Natalie wouldn't be here, but even so, getting confirmation stung hard. Knowing his wife as he did, Michael figured she took off the moment she realized her mistake. Kennett didn't appear particularly flustered.

"Who was working at lunchtime?" Kennett asked.

The clerk seemed rattled.

"Let's try it another way," said Kennett, a bit edgier. "Do you have a work schedule handy? I'm assuming you do. If you want to switch shifts, you've got to know who to call, right?"

The clerk, acting nervous now, nodded several times in quick succession.

"Yeah," he said. "But maybe I should get my manager."

"Maybe you should go look at that schedule and tell me who was working at the time of this transaction."

He showed the clerk a screen grab of the alert Natalie's credit card company had sent. The clerk went stock-still, as if Kennett had performed some kind of Jedi mind trick from *Star Wars* on him. Thoughts of that movie made Michael think of Bryce — it was a favorite film of his.

God, how he missed his son, his daughter, and yes — even his wife. He loved Natalie, truly loved her. Which was why he'd done what had to be done. For everyone's sake, Michael had to find them and set things right. No matter how unpleasant that righting would be.

The clerk edged backward before slipping into an anteroom that Michael assumed functioned as a small office. Michael stayed quiet, letting Kennett take the lead doing his cop thing. The clerk returned a minute later.

"Nancy was on," he announced.

Delight danced in the detective's eyes.

Michael could tell Kennett got off on the chase, any chase.

"Okay," said Kennett, adopting a softer voice. "What's your name, son?"

"Jerry," said the clerk nervously.

"Jerry, okay, Jerry. I want you to get Nancy on the phone for me."

"I really . . ."

"And while you're at it," said Kennett, interrupting. "You have a camera that looks out at the parking lot. I need to see footage that coincides with the time of this alert."

Michael hadn't seen any cameras on the way into the hotel, but he didn't have Kennett's trained eyes either. Glancing through a bank of windows, Michael peered into a parking lot full of nondescript rental vehicles like his.

"I really need to speak to my manager," Jerry reiterated.

"What you need," said Kennett, his voice hardening again, "is to do what I said. Call your boss after. Time's a-wastin', son."

Kennett's goatee partially hid a slim smile, though Michael figured the clerk was too intimidated to have noticed.

"Yeah . . . yeah, okay . . . but you'd have to come back here to look at the security footage. We have software for that."

"Now we're getting somewhere," said

Kennett, who brightened considerably.

Michael followed Kennett into the anteroom behind the check-in counter. On one wall hung a corkboard papered with announcements, including a printed schedule — most likely what the clerk had referenced to figure out who was working at the time Natalie came in.

Why Ohio? Michael kept asking himself. Michael had made a Facebook profile to source leads, but Natalie's settings prevented him from seeing her friends, which limited his ability to cross-reference the people connected to his wife who lived in or near this state. As a countermeasure, he'd asked Harvey and Lucinda for their help in identifying individuals from Natalie's past who might be living in the vicinity of her last known location.

"Mike, you look at the software. Make sure you match the date and time. See if you get a license plate on Natalie's car. I'm going to call Nancy."

Kennett departed after the clerk gave him Nancy's home phone number. The clerk must have assumed Michael, too, was a New York City detective, because he set him up on the computer without hesitation. The application to review the black-and-white security camera footage was relatively intuitive and easy to use, but the clerk helped Michael anyway.

As Jerry got the footage up on the screen, Michael thought of the hotel manager in New York. Not that long ago, Dan White had held a viewing of similar security camera footage from the Marriott Marquis. This time it was Jerry controlling the playback. Michael watched as cars came and went like a time-lapse movie. He kept an eye on the date and time stamp displayed in the upper left corner of the screen. Minutes before the suspect credit card transaction took place — at quarter past one o'clock in the afternoon — a sedan pulled into the parking lot. Soon after that, Natalie exited from the driver's seat.

It was beyond surreal to see her on camera. It couldn't be Natalie, he told himself, but then out stepped the children, dispelling any doubt. Michael welled up at the sight of his family. He was relieved to see they were safe, seemed healthy, happy, and even playful. He asked himself: *How had this come to be their life?*

Why had Natalie driven a car all the way from New York to Ohio? Why had she dyed Bryce's hair several shades darker, which is how it appeared in the grainy security camera footage? Was she trying to disguise his appearance?

"This is Natalie. She's my wife," Michael said, pointing to the screen. "And these are my kids, Addison and Bryce."

Jerry was at a loss for words. He sported a vacant expression and looked quite uncomfortable on his feet. Michael got it. Jerry was pretty much a kid himself.

"She's on the run," he said, not caring if Jerry was tuned in or not. "I'm trying to find them."

Michael resumed the video playback, and the scene had changed. Addie and Bryce were visible in the background, coming in and out of the frame as they played on a strip of grass in front of the hotel. A great wave of sadness washed over Michael. His throat closed up as tears sprang to his eyes. Through his watery vision, Michael could see Jerry eyeing him warily. Holding up his hand, Michael hoped to convey the words he couldn't get out.

I'm okay. I'll be all right. Just give me a minute.

In an act of compassion, Jerry took several steps toward the door, which happened to be the only way he could get out of the room, trying to give Michael a moment of privacy. Before he could depart, Kennett showed up. If he noticed Michael drying his

311

eyes, Kennett didn't offer any commentary.

"Nancy wasn't much help," he said, "but she did share that your kids had dark hair."

Michael finished rubbing his red eyes.

"I saw that in the video."

"You handling this okay, Mike?" Kennett asked a bit tentatively.

"No, not really."

Kennett patted Michael on the shoulder, didn't bother with words of encouragement, leaving Michael to guess that was how the detective showed empathy.

For a change of subject, Michael reversed the footage and replayed it from the point of Natalie's arrival.

"Here's the car she's in," he said. "The footage is fuzzy, so I can't read the plate number."

"No need," said Kennett. "I've been texting with the Staties since we got here."

Michael thought: *So that's why you were being quiet on the drive.*

Kennett continued.

"Finally got word from headquarters that a few hours ago a state trooper pulled Natalie over on I-70. She came up in the system as a missing person, which should have meant she'd be detained and we'd be done, but there was a multi-vehicle accident nearby and she caught a lucky break. The trooper called it in though, so at least we have her plate number and more."

"Pulled over for what?"

"Erratic driving. Natalie said she got distracted thinking Addie might have been having an asthma attack. She's driving a rental car. Avis. Picked it up in New York. Told the cop who pulled her over that she was headed for Indianapolis."

"She never went to the train station," Michael said, thinking it through.

"Nope," said Kennett, offering a slight shake of his head. "She's being all sorts of slippery — kind of impressive, actually, gotta give her credit there. Can you think of anyone she might go see in Indianapolis?"

Michael gave it some thought before shaking his head no.

"She's probably going to dump the rental now," said Kennett. "Gives us something to work with. We'll need to keep calling Avis drop-off locations nearby, focus on the one at the airport if she's headed west."

"How do we track her from there?" Michael asked.

"Carefully," Kennett replied. "We track her very carefully."

CHAPTER 27

Natalie
Before She Disappeared

The morning after she found the body, Natalie made a teary confession in Tina's office.

"I followed Audrey after work that day you said she reported me to HR. She went to the McDonald's on 128, seemed like she was waiting for someone, and then Michael showed up — or at least I think he did. I fell asleep in the parking lot and when I woke up I saw the two of them driving off together. Michael came home after I did, but then he left again, and in a hurry. I overheard him talking to a woman on his phone, so I figured he was going to Audrey's to do . . . whatever. I got the nanny to come back and look after the kids, and I went to Audrey's to catch him in the act."

Tina's eyes were clear and focused as Natalie recounted her version of the events that followed, which she did without sparing any detail.

"Oh, my God, Nat," said Tina, all color drained from her face. Both Tina's voice and expression conveyed her utter shock and disbelief.

"You're telling me that Audrey Adler is dead and you saw her body?"

Natalie managed a grim nod.

Tina glanced over Natalie's shoulder, peering through her office window into an array of cubicles as if she expected to see Audrey strolling through.

"Are you absolutely sure you saw what you saw?" Tina asked as she continued scanning the room.

Natalie returned a snort of disgust.

"Are you suggesting I imagined it?"

"You haven't been sleeping well, and you've told me you've seen or imagined things that weren't there."

"I get that I haven't been sleeping, but I'm not that messed up, T," Natalie said defensively. "I know a dead, bloody body when I see one."

"Right," said Tina, who breathed out the word while fixing her gaze on her tidy desk.

"I don't know what to do," Natalie continued in a quavering voice. "Michael killed her. I'm sure of it. I found his shirt and

315

missing gym locker key inside Audrey's place — in her bedroom, no less! I have them in a plastic bag under the front seat of my car. Obviously, I can't put them back where I found them, so now I have no way to prove to the police that Michael was there, that he did it, but he did. I know it in my bones. Maybe I did the wrong thing — maybe I should have left the evidence there. But I wasn't thinking clearly. I was afraid it would point to me, the jilted wife."

Tina set her fingers against her temples as if she'd been blasted with a migraine.

"We have to call the police, Nat . . . we have to —"

"No . . . no, we can't."

Tina's eyebrows rose in a look of reproach. Her stern expression conveyed a clear warning: *lower your damn voice.* Some conversations must not be overhead.

"I'll be charged with murder," Natalie continued in a whispered tone. "Don't you see? I've been stalking Audrey at work; HR knows about it. I've accused her of sleeping with my husband, and I put myself at the scene of the crime. I can't call the police, Tina. And please, please, don't turn me in. You're the only one I can trust. I didn't do anything wrong."

Tina did not look at all pleased to have

been anointed her sole confidante. "Honestly, Nat, I wish that you had told the police and not me," she said.

After swallowing a shaky breath, Tina nervously tapped her fingers against her desk, thinking, thinking. It looked to Natalie as though she were crunching numbers in her head, her face a picture of pure concentration as she carefully mulled over her next move. In the ensuing silence, Natalie despaired.

"Michael will make sure I take the fall for what he did," she said. "He'll sacrifice me to save himself."

Natalie's plea seemed to resonate with Tina who could now, finally, look her friend in the eyes.

"I hear you, sweetie, and I think I know what to do," said Tina. "But I'm not letting Audrey just rot on her kitchen floor. My God." Tina covered her mouth as she looked away in disgust. "I'll call the police. Ask them to make a welfare check because we can't reach her. She didn't show up to work, didn't call in, and that's not like her."

Natalie nodded in agreement.

"That'll work. But what about me . . . and Michael?"

"Oh Nat," said Tina, slapping her hands together in a show of prayer. "I want to get up and give you a big hug, but don't want to call any attention to us, or this moment. I don't want anyone to even know that you're upset. This is going to be very complicated. It's dangerous what we're doing. The truth is always the safest way to go."

While Natalie remained unconvinced about the truth being her best path forward, she was more focused on something else her friend had just said. Tina had used the word "we" as if to imply they were in this together, a team of sorts. With that Natalie felt lighter and far less alone.

"I appreciate what you're doing, helping me," Natalie said, now on the verge of tears. "Trust me, Tina, you've got to believe me here: when it comes to this situation, the truth would be very bad for me."

"Right," said Tina. "I get it. I really do. I'm still thinking about what else to do."

Tina fell silent again for a stretch. Each second that Natalie spent sitting, watching, waiting — it all added to her mounting anxiety. She had to remind herself several times not to hold her breath. Eventually, a bright look came over Tina's face and her eyes widened, as if an idea had at last surfaced.

"Michael is the key. If he did it, then we

need to make sure we help the police link him to Audrey without implicating you in the process."

"And how do we do that? We're not professional detectives. Should I hire a private investigator?"

"Maybe so," said Tina.

"How do we find a good one?" asked Natalie. "I've never done this before."

"Leave that one to me," said Tina.

Later came the following day, when Tina informed Natalie she had something of a plan. When Natalie arrived at work, she could see pain etched on the face of the receptionist who was typically quite cheery in the morning. A noticeable pall had settled over the offices of Dynamic Media, and the energy, usually charged even at this early hour, had the feel of a late-night winter storm after a blanket of snowfall had silenced the world.

Guilt invaded Natalie's body. She was certain that her coworkers could smell it on her. Reflexively, she looked away anytime she caught the strained look in their eyes.

They know, she told herself. *They know what I've done.* But only one person knew, and that was Tina.

Chances were many of her colleagues had watched the news just as she'd done that morning, or they'd read the email from Steven Zacharius, the company CEO:

Dear Dynamic Media Employees,
It is with a heavy heart that I must inform you that while conducting a welfare check, the Medford police discovered the body of our colleague and dear friend, Audrey Adler. Details of Audrey's death are not readily available, but I can share that she appears to have been the victim of a homicide. The Medford police are actively investigating this crime, and they've asked anyone with information pertaining to Audrey's murder to contact them immediately.

The note from Steven went on to provide contact information for the Medford police along with details about accessing grief counselors, whom he said would be on-site for the next several days. He concluded his brief message with more words of sorrow and sympathy.

Natalie reread Steven's email half a dozen times. She kept having flashes of Audrey's lifeless body swimming in a sea of red on her kitchen floor. Despite her perpetual brain fog, she could recall many of the horrific details: the unnatural angle of Audrey's head, a pungent smell of blood, the pattern of the splatter, a burned-out overhead bulb, even the color of the broken plate littering the floor near her inert form. All these memories were seared into Natalie's consciousness.

Most of her meetings were canceled that day, and Natalie found herself with too much time on her hands to sit and think. She'd come to work specifically for one meeting, one that wasn't officially on the company calendar, one that wasn't going to be canceled.

At the appointed hour, Natalie made her way to Tina's office. Seated at the small conference table inside was a woman Natalie had never met before. She rose when Natalie entered, greeting her with a generous smile. Tina stood as well.

"Natalie, this is Sarah Fielding."

Standing nearly six feet tall, Sarah Fielding struck quite an imposing figure. Her dark blond hair was stylishly trimmed, adding to her professional air. Her skin radiated with the healthy glow of someone who paid particularly close attention to what went into her body. She had on form-fitting attire — a black shirt tucked into pleated black pants, an outfit best worn by those with a strong devotion to physical fitness. When her smile dimmed, there was no real warmth to Sarah Fielding, no aura of congeniality. She gave off the hardened exterior of a police officer. For a moment, that's who Natalie feared she was, until she remembered what Sarah did for the company and why Tina had set up this meeting in the first place.

"It's so nice to meet you," Natalie said, managing something of a smile. "But honestly, I'm glad we haven't met before."

Sarah returned a pleasant laugh. She got it. As the company's chief internal corporate investigator, it was Sarah's job to look into any employee wrongdoing. Natalie hoped her issues with Audrey Adler stayed with HR and had not yet made its way to Sarah's department.

"Usually I'm tracking down petty theft from expense reports, or too much porn on company time," said Sarah. "When Tina asked if I could recommend a private investigator, I had some names in mind, but I wondered if it had something to do with the company.

"Then she told me it was a case of infidelity involving one of our employees and your husband, and that got my attention. Last time we had an outsider looking into one of our own, we had a PR nightmare on our hands when the investigator uncovered some intellectual property theft. We would have preferred to have handled the situation internally, but instead it made the six o'clock news and cost us one of our largest accounts. Rather than risk letting that happen again, I agreed to take a look into this matter myself."

Natalie's strained smile conveyed her gratitude.

"Thank you. I really appreciate your help. I mean, what I'm dealing with is such a small thing in light of what happened to Audrey."

Natalie watched Sarah's jaw tighten.

"It's just awful," Sarah said. "I didn't know Audrey personally, but from what I read she was quiet and lived alone. The police don't even have any suspects."

Natalie noticed that Tina's eyes were red and there were crumpled tissues on the table where she'd been sitting.

"I'm so sorry, Tina," said Natalie, who then gave Tina a long embrace.

"I just can't believe it," Tina said, swallowing a sob. "She hadn't worked here long, but I knew right away she'd be one of the stars in my department."

Natalie squeezed Tina's hand gently.

Turning to Sarah, Natalie said, "It's often a husband or a boyfriend, someone close to the victim. Do you think that's the case with Audrey?"

"It's hard to say," said Sarah. "Could be."

Natalie caught a look in Sarah's eyes as if to suggest she already suspected Michael.

"I don't know if she was seeing someone," continued Sarah. "If so, it's not mentioned in any of the news reports that I've read."

Natalie couldn't resist exchanging a knowing glance with Tina.

"But I guess we're here to talk about your husband. What makes you so sure he's having an affair with someone who works for the company?" asked Sarah.

"We know it's someone who uses the corporate gym," Tina answered for Natalie. "And that's really all we know. There's a chance it's an outsider, but maybe not."

"I can run some database queries an outside party wouldn't be able to do. If there are no hits internally, I guess I'd pass you off to a licensed PI, since it wouldn't be a company matter after all. Seems harmless enough, and not hard for me to do. I at least can get the ball started."

Natalie returned a bright smile.

"That's great. Thank you so much. Let me know what I can do to help."

"Absolutely," Sarah said. "I'll be in touch. I'll start with some basic keyword searches and go from there. You'd be amazed what people write to each other on our corporate email, which, by the way, is *not* considered private."

"Sounds good," said Natalie. Her good feelings didn't last, as she was now faced with the inherent dangers of technology when it came to keeping secrets. "What about cell phones?" she asked Sarah, because she'd had her phone with her inside Audrey's apartment.

"What about them?"

"Can you track a person using a cell phone?"

"Not easily," Sarah said. "To get those records police need to get a subpoena, and phone companies will fight hard on that."

"So pings aren't helpful, no easy work-around."

Sarah shrugged off that concern.

"A cell phone sends out a radio-frequency signal to the towers within a radius of up to about twenty miles. Routing depends on topography and atmospheric conditions. There are too many variables and too many signals for the police to track anybody that way."

"Okay, got it. Thanks so much for your willingness to help," Natalie said. She was trying to rein in her emotions, thinking

Sarah might find it odd if she looked as relieved as she felt. "Anything you need from me, please let me know."

Sarah said she'd be in touch, then gathered her things and departed. Tina and Natalie stayed quiet. They'd debrief later, perhaps over margaritas at La Hacienda. Drinks or no drinks, Natalie could breathe easier for two reasons: the police wouldn't be able to put her at the scene of the crime, and she'd no doubt that Tina, inadvertently or not, had found the right woman for the job.

CHAPTER 28

Natalie

Natalie arrived at the Avis rental return in the Columbus, Ohio, airport five hours before sunset. She didn't like the strategically positioned security cameras recording her every movement as she and the children completed the car return, but there wasn't a damn thing she could do about it. Natalie paid her bill using the right credit card this time, so even if Michael had seen the transaction from the Fairfield Inn, he'd see no others.

She would have preferred to leave the car in Indianapolis, as she had told the trooper she would, and let her trail go cold from there. But that was a long drive, and Natalie was worried about getting pulled over again. As fatigued as she was, it simply wasn't safe for her to be on the road. The safest thing to do after the drop off would be to get a room at the airport hotel, but that would

327

mean more hours in Ohio, and more opportunity for Michael to find her. After
ditching one car, she'd get another and
hightail it out of here.

As she left the Avis facility, Natalie half
expected to hear the employee behind the
counter shouting after her, "Wait! Stop!
You're wanted by the police!" To her relief
— sort of — the only shouting came from
the kids, who were complaining in earnest
now about being hungry.

In addition to his grumbling tummy, poor
Bryce also bemoaned his missing teddy
bear. The replacement offered him little
comfort. "I want Teddy and I want Daddy
now!" he said, stomping his way out the
door en route to the shuttle bus area. Tears
filled his downcast eyes. He was running on
fumes. They all were. With his head bowed
and shoulders stooped, Bryce reluctantly
wheeled his luggage to the bus stop. According to the posted schedule, the shuttle that
would ferry them to Hertz made a stop here
every ten minutes. Airplanes rumbled overhead, streaking through the hints of blue
that peeked out from behind a scattering of
cloud cover.

Natalie shifted her focus from the sky to
the road, keeping a lookout for the bus
while trying to ignore her children's ongo-

ing complaints. Eventually (thank goodness!) a shuttle arrived, rumbling to a stop precisely at the scheduled time. The kids boarded first, moving nimbly up and in, finding seats in the back. Natalie struggled to get her heavy bag up those same stairs. Unsurprisingly, the surly driver wedged in her seat didn't offer a smile or assistance.

After storing her luggage, Natalie settled herself behind the children, where it would be easier to keep an eye on them. She tried not to dwell on how the misfortune of others, the terrible accident that had called the trooper away, spared her a near disaster. Even so, her name was probably flagged in some system, and a database search could easily reveal that she'd returned her rental to the Avis location at the airport. From there, Michael would check with every rental company in and around Columbus to find her next ride out of town. Damn. How to get away?

Natalie's anxiety felt like it sprouted wings and took flight. What would Michael do to her and the children if he found them?

She knew. In her heart, she knew.

It took thirty minutes in adult time — a thousand years, kid time — to get a new car from Hertz. Natalie ignored the steady grumbling and complaining of her charges as she loaded the luggage into the back of a blue Nissan Rogue. The kids cried out with delight when they drove by a Johnny Rockets located within the airport confines. Natalie made a U-turn. They had to eat.

A strong odor of grease greeted Natalie upon entering the restaurant. The smell made her pause. She knew strong odors could be an asthma trigger, but the kids were protesting too loudly for Natalie to make good on her suggestion they go elsewhere. She was also tired of fighting, so tired in general, that it was easy to ignore her better judgment. She allowed Addie to pick a booth in the back. At least they were away from the kitchen and that smell.

Both children ordered cheeseburgers from a chipper waitress with a welcoming smile that fit the Midwest stereotype. Natalie drank black coffee and later wolfed down a Snickers bar in a bathroom stall, hoping the sugar would give her a quick boost of energy. While the kids busied themselves with their iPads, Natalie desperately wanted to ditch the new rental and find some other way to get to Kate's farm — a way that would make them harder to track. They still had some five hundred miles to go.

The food arrived minutes before the kids started eating each other. Both plates of burgers and fries looked dishwasher-clean in a flash. If Natalie hadn't had to hunt down her waitress to get the check, she might not have seen the airport shuttle bus rumble on by. As she returned to the table, she realized that sometimes the most obvious answer was the easiest overlooked.

Natalie used her Tracfone to search the Greyhound website for one-way trips departing from Columbus. There was a bus leaving at 11:45 that night, which would get them to St. Louis at 6:30 the following morning. A second bus would take her to Wentzville, and from there they could catch a cab the rest of the way to Elsberry.

Good luck tracking that, Michael, she thought, smiling to herself.

Natalie's smile vanished quickly when Addie glanced up at her mother, scowling.

"I want to see Daddy today," she demanded.

Bryce got in on the action, nodding his vociferous agreement as if the two had planned a mutiny while she went for the check.

"Soon. I've told you that," Natalie said.

"But when is soon? I miss Daddy and I want to see him now."

Addie choked down a sob, her cheeks flushed with red.

"We have to do a little more traveling."

"I'm tired of traveling," Addie whined. She gulped down a breath, her chest heaving beneath her pink cardigan.

Natalie felt a familiar pang of anxiety inside her. The grease was bad enough, but now, agitated, Addie could easily suffer an attack. Addie tried again for a good breath, but coughed twice. Natalie shot to her feet and gripped her daughter's bony wrists in her hand.

"Sweetheart, are you okay?"

She knew the answer was no, and sure enough, Addie struggled to get out the word herself. Each shaky breath Addie took in was soon followed by a wheezing exhale. Terror bloomed in Addie's eyes. She placed her small hand to her chest as if that would ease the pressure building inside her. Natalie searched for, and eventually found, the rescue inhaler. Addie placed her lips around the mouthpiece and took in a blast of albuterol, which should have smoothed the swollen tissues inside her airway.

Somehow, Natalie had the wherewithal to toss two twenties on the table before she dragged her daughter from the booth toward the door. The medicine might not be enough.

"Bryce, let's go!"

Natalie barked her order while keeping her head on a swivel, looking to her daughter, then to her son, who was lagging behind. Each step brought a strangled new breath that only served to heighten Addie's mounting terror. Natalie's heart seized when she saw her daughter's near-bloodless complexion. The medicine should have put some coloring back in her cheeks by now.

Natalie got everyone settled in the car.

"How are you feeling, honey?" she asked, her voice drenched with worry. In answer to her question, Addie took another blast from her inhaler before exhaling a shaky, wheezing breath.

"It's not working," she croaked with panic.

Addie puckered her lips, sucking hard, only to get down sips of air.

"Hold on!" Natalie shouted, mostly for her own benefit. She barely checked her mirrors. Tires squealed against the pavement as she jammed the car into reverse.

She shouldn't have been on her phone while driving, but once again Google proved to be a miracle worker. Nationwide Children's Hospital was only a twelve-minute drive, giving Natalie a measure of calm.

"Can you breathe?" Natalie asked while switching her focus from her phone, to the road, to the backseat. She sent a silent prayer out into the universe: *please don't let me get into an accident. Don't let anything happen to my baby girl.*

"I can't . . . get . . . one."

Addie struggled to get out those few words.

The panic was palpable even for Bryce, judging by his wide-eyed stare. Seconds felt like minutes, minutes turned to hours.

"It's all right, sweetie," Natalie said. "You're going to be fine. We're close to the hospital and they'll give you the right medicine."

Natalie had to block out her other concern. The hospital would put her name into some database. That alone might call up her missing persons report, and this time there'd be no car accident to save her.

Addie's breathing grew so labored that by the time Natalie arrived at the hospital she couldn't risk parking her car. She left her vehicle out front with a valet before rushing Addie and Bryce inside. Bursting into the waiting room, Natalie dashed to the receptionist's window, dragging Addie behind her. Addie's breathing came out shallow and quick, her wheezing even more pronounced.

Maybe the receptionist could hear those strangled sounds, or she saw the panic in their eyes. Either way, she got on the phone without prompting, and a nurse appeared through a nearby set of double doors. The nurse, with the efficiency of a seasoned practitioner, rushed over to them and checked Addie's vitals while standing in the middle of the crowded waiting room. Nobody looked at them askance for receiving preferential treatment, as Addie's labored breathing was obvious to all.

The nurse reported that Addie's blood oxygen saturation was eighty-nine percent, far below normal. Addie was breathing more than twenty times a minute, too, which wasn't right for a healthy, young person. Her coloring remained pale, but thankfully her lips weren't blue.

"We'll get her seen right away," the nurse informed, "but don't worry. She's not in any life-threatening danger."

Addie seemed to breathe easier. Natalie did the same, even more so because after giving the receptionist her name nobody mentioned that she'd come up in a missing persons database.

Moments later, Natalie and Bryce were huddled together in one of the treatment bays with Addie on the bed. Another nurse started a nebulizer treatment and put an IV with fluids into a vein in her right arm.

Some minutes later, Natalie was giving

Addie's medical history to the doctor, a perfectly composed woman with corn-colored hair who seemed too young to have a medical license. In the back of Natalie's mind tumbled thoughts of that Greyhound bus. They had hours before it was scheduled to depart, but that depended on her daughter's condition, which thankfully appeared to be improving.

After careful monitoring and consideration, the doctor decided to let the nebulizer do its job before adding additional medication or ordering more tests. It took another fifteen minutes of treatment (fifteen precious minutes in which a computer could alert the authorities to her whereabouts) before Addie's breathing returned to normal. The news got better. Addie's oxygen saturation had shot above ninety-seven percent, well into the acceptable range. Natalie was more than a little relieved when the doctor gave word that the only additional procedure she wished to perform was a chest X-ray.

"We're supposed to be somewhere in a few hours," Natalie said. "Should I call them to change our plans?"

The doctor offered her assurances that the X-ray wouldn't take too long.

Natalie checked the time. They could still

make the St. Louis bus, but what to do with the car? She decided to leave it at the hospital, make it harder for Michael to figure how they left town. She'd leave the key in the car and call Hertz from Kate's place. Whatever additional fee they'd charge for retrieval, she'd pay it.

By nine thirty that evening, Addie was ready for discharge. Natalie had waited on pins and needles for permission to go. There was one last thing she had to do. Natalie found the doctor.

"Thank you so much for everything you've done for Addie," she said. "We're off to meet up with a friend of mine who lives in Toledo. Addie is so excited to meet my friend's daughter and see Toledo. I know she'd be heartbroken if we couldn't go."

"I'm just glad she's all right," said the doctor, with a look of satisfaction.

Natalie, too, looked satisfied.

She'd picked a city to the north, a reasonable distance to travel. The doctor would remember her. The conversation would stick in her mind. Twice she'd mentioned Toledo. Natalie was certain that by the time Michael was headed north, she and the kids would already be on a bus going south, destined for St. Louis.

CHAPTER 29

Michael

They stopped at a Johnny Rockets located inside the John Glenn Columbus airport for a meal. Good thing the airport location kept later hours as Michael had gone there with hope in his heart. They had a Johnny Rockets at the Burlington Mall, close to home, and it was one of his kids' favorite restaurants. It was conceivable that they'd begged Natalie to go there on the way out of the airport, but they weren't seated when he and Kennett arrived.

It was a half hour before closing, and Kennett was starving so they stayed; Michael willingly faked an appetite. When the food came, Kennett took a giant bite of his hamburger. He chewed slowly, no sign of worry or hurry. Michael watched with mounting concern. He sensed a shift take place in Kennett, as if his helper was revealing himself, morphing before Michael's eyes

338

into an adversary. He'd catch a telling glance here and there, Kennett's gaze lingering too long, a cagey expression hinting at ulterior motives. Michael could breathe easy only because Kennett hadn't brought up Audrey Adler's name since their time together at the Friday's bar in Burlington, but something told him that wouldn't be the case for long.

"You're not eating, Mike," Kennett said, as he dabbed away a dollop of ketchup that clung to a corner of his mouth.

Indeed, Michael's burger sat cooling on his plate.

"Relax and eat, Mike," Kennett encouraged. "We've got her new license plate number. She's going to turn up soon. We're almost at the endgame."

Michael should have had faith. After all, Kennett had guessed correctly that Natalie would ditch her rental. Skill and experience had directed him to check the Avis location at the Columbus airport. After confirming his theory, they'd checked three other companies before learning that Natalie had rented a Nissan Rogue from Hertz. Now, thanks largely to Kennett's efforts, the police had a description of her new vehicle along with a license plate to track. It wasn't a stretch to think it would only be a matter of time before they located his family.

Still, Michael was worried, not only about Natalie and his children, but about Kennett as well.

"Why are you doing this?" Michael asked.

He finally managed a bite of his burger, but the food had the flavor of cardboard.

"Doing what, Mike?" replied Kennett, as if he didn't know.

"Helping me find my wife."

"Going back there, are we?" Kennett gave a sly smile along with a wink. "Can't just accept my altruism, eh?"

"Not really. No. So how about you tell me the truth?"

"The truth?" Kennett's eyebrows shot up. "That's a good one, Mike. Okay. All right. Let's talk *truth.*"

Michael shifted uneasily in his seat.

"Your mother. Tell me about her."

"My mother?"

"Yeah, my mom died of cancer, too."

If Kennett was still grieving, it didn't show on his face or in his voice.

"I'm sorry to hear."

"It's not your doing," Kennett said with an indifferent shrug. "Eventually, we all end up in the same place, right? Some of us just get there quicker is all. So what was it?"

"What was what?"

"The cancer. What kind?"

"Um, breast cancer," Michael said, fumbling for the words. "It was extremely aggressive."

"Sorry to hear," said Kennett.

"Not your doing," Michael replied, which coaxed out another slight smile from his companion.

"She died when you were in college, right?"

"Yeah, that's right. It was tough."

"I bet it was," said Kennett. He spoke languidly, as if his thoughts were elsewhere. "Where'd you go to school?"

"University of Oregon."

"U of O!" Kennett's expression brightened as he rapped his knuckles several times against the table. "The Ducks."

"Go Ducks," Michael responded unenthusiastically.

"So, you grew up near there?"

"No, I, um, grew up in Charleston."

"South Carolina, a Southern boy."

Michael's stomach tightened.

Where was this going?

"Never been to Charleston," Kennett continued. "Nice place?"

"You should go," Michael said. "The city has great restaurants, pristine beaches. Yeah, I'd say a pretty nice place to visit. Even bet-

341

ter place to live."

"But not nice enough for college." Kennett offered his assessment dryly.

Michael bit down hard on his burger.

"I wanted to see a different coast."

"So tell me, did you go to the West Coast looking for your father?"

"My dad?"

"Yeah, you told me he walked out on you when you were young. Maybe you thought he headed west, so you went looking."

Hometown. College. Parents. This wasn't good.

"No, I never saw my father again after he left us."

"Not even after your mom died? Didn't he come back for the funeral? What a heartless prick, right?"

"Maybe he didn't hear. Why are you so interested in my family? My past?"

Kennett had no qualms about talking while he was chewing.

"Just making conversation, bud," he said, his words coming out garbled. "What else are we going to do on the road? Would you rather tackle the word search on the kids' menu?"

"I just think it's curious you're so inquisitive about my life, is all."

"What do you want to talk about, then?"

342

asked Kennett.

Since Michael was using Kennett as a means to an end, he thought it best to shift the focus away from him and back onto Natalie.

"How about finding my wife. What's our next move?"

"You got that list of friends and family? How many of them have you called?"

From the pocket of his jeans, Michael fished out a folded piece of paper. There were some fifty names on it, addresses too, mostly older friends and relatives he'd sourced from Harvey and Lucinda. Half the names were crossed out.

"I've gone over this list repeatedly and called every name we both knew. The rest don't live anywhere near Ohio."

Michael slid the paper over to Kennett, who studied it intently.

"Good detective work here, Mike," Kennett said, as he scanned the list. "The job looks glamorous to outsiders, but really it's a lot of gumshoe and tedium. I say call them all, even the ones living far away from here. They may know somebody you don't, might give us a new lead."

"Right," Michael said. He took the list from Kennett, slipped it back into his pocket.

They finished their food, eating mostly in silence. Michael kept ruminating on Kennett's keen interest in his past. Was it all just small talk? He couldn't decide. But from experience, Michael knew the inherent risks that came with keeping secrets. Secrets had the potential to make even the most innocent things — a comment, a look, an innocuous gesture from another — feel like a threat.

A waitress, still light on her feet after Michael had seen her bounding about from table to table, stopped by to check on her customers.

"Anything else, boys?" she said in a singsong voice.

"All set," said Michael. "Just the check, please."

The waitress was about to leave when Kennett held up a finger.

"Hold on a sec," he said. He sent her a flash of his badge. Michael watched some color slip from her face.

"My partner here is a trainee. Doesn't quite have the moves down yet. We're looking for someone," Kennett said. "Wondering if she might have stopped in here with a couple of kids." Kennett shifted his attention over to Michael. "Waitresses and waiters see more people and things than anyone,

Mike. They know what's up, so you should always make it a point to ask them." To the waitress Kennett said, "ABT — always be teaching, that's my motto." He sent her one of his trademark playful winks before switching his focus back over to Michael.

"Got that picture, Mike?"

Michael pulled up the picture he knew Kennett was referring to and gave his phone to their waitress. She studied the image of his family intently for several moments while Michael studied her eyes. There he saw what he'd hoped for — a look of recognition.

"Yeah, she was in here at the start of my shift," she said. "I didn't take their order. Jeannie did, but she's gone for the night."

Michael's whole face lit up, but Kennett maintained a neutral expression. Nothing could faze him.

"But the kids had dark hair," said the waitress. "I noticed because it wasn't a great dye job. I'm studying to be a hairdresser and I said to Jeannie, who the heck does that to their kids?"

"Someone who doesn't want to be found," Kennett answered dryly. "When did your shift start?"

"Five hours ago," the waitress said.

"Okay, so we're pretty far behind her. Did

she happen to say where she might have been headed? Maybe said something to Jeannie?"

"My guess is they went to the hospital."

Michael let out a gasp.

"Hospital? What was wrong?" he asked. A current of anxiety barreled up inside him.

The waitress returned a shrug. "I dunno," she said. "It looked to me like the girl was having a hard time breathing."

"Addie," Michael whispered to himself.

"Thanks," Kennett said, "you've been extremely helpful." He was already looking at his phone instead of the waitress. "Pretty sure she'd have gone to Nationwide Children's. Let's go, Mike."

Twenty minutes later, Michael and Kennett were face-to-face with the doctor who had treated Addie.

"They said they were going north to Toledo. I'm sorry, officer. We're happy to help law enforcement with runaways and missing persons, but we don't always get notified."

"Right, not a worry, you've been really helpful," said Kennett, parroting what he'd told the waitress not long ago.

"So what now?" Michael asked Kennett as the two made their way out of the hospital.

"Now, I guess we go to Toledo," Kennett said. "I can give the police a more focused area to search. Maybe we get lucky."

"Right," said Michael, who wasn't feeling nearly as optimistic. "Why the hell would Natalie go to Toledo? And why wouldn't she take I-80 from New York? It's more direct. Columbus is quite the detour."

All Kennett could do was offer up a shrug.

"She told the Statie she was headed to Indianapolis, but she'd have to know that detail would get back to you. Could be she's still trying to throw us off course, or maybe she has her reasons for heading north. Either way, it's the best lead we got, so we gotta follow it."

"I'm just glad Addie is okay." Michael breathed out his relief. "But damn." He shook his head in dismay. "Nat's putting too much stress on the kids. We've got to find her before something really terrible happens."

"We will, Mike," Kennett said assuredly. "I've got confidence. Natalie's been pretty slippery, I'll give her that much, but the sun doesn't shine on the same dog's butt every day."

Michael came to a hard stop, a quizzical look on his face. "What the hell does that mean?" he asked. "Is that cop talk or something?"

Kennett sent Michael a crooked smile, staring him hard in the eyes.

"It's a Southern expression, Mike," Kennett said, his voice carrying a hint of menace. "I had an aunt who lived outside of Atlanta, I'd go there most summers. It's a pretty common phrase down there. It means sometimes you win and sometimes you lose. I'd think a Southern boy like yourself would know that, but I guess you've moved around a lot. Right, Mike?"

Kennett patted Michael on his shoulder in a patronizing gesture.

Holy shit, thought Michael, a burning in his belly. *He knows. Kennett knows.*

And with that, the game got a whole lot more dangerous.

CHAPTER 30

Natalie
Before She Disappeared
Natalie, Tina, and Sarah Fielding gathered at La Hacienda. It was good for Natalie to get out of the office. She was having a hard time focusing at work — a hard time doing much of anything, really, including being at home. Michael had been acting like all was normal, which made everything he did feel even more sinister. His every action, from taking out the trash to doing the dishes, seemed layered with menace. He'd smile at her, kiss her on the cheek, on the mouth, and she'd see a knife in his hands; could almost feel him plunging the blade into her body instead of Audrey's.

"What's wrong, babe?" Michael asked one evening after dinner. According to him, she was being cool and distant again.

"Nothing. I'm fine," said Natalie, sounding

349

anything but.

"Yeah?" Michael's eyebrows rose. "The kids are asleep. Why don't we head upstairs and you can show me just how fine you really are?"

Natalie pulled away from his pleading touch.

"Not tonight," she said, turning her head.

Michael grunted in disgust.

"You know, we don't have much of a marriage anymore," Michael said. "I'm trying here, I really am. I want to blame all our problems on your sleep troubles — your irritability, your distance and forgetfulness, the lack of sex or touch of any kind, but you know what? This is destroying both of us. We may live in the same house and parent the same kids, but there's nothing between us anymore. This isn't what I signed up for."

"Yeah, well, maybe if you weren't getting your needs met elsewhere I'd be a little warmer."

Natalie delivered her assessment with cool indifference.

"You just won't let it go, will you?" Michael seethed. "Maybe I should go and do just that so you can be right about me for once."

"Please have the decency to divorce me first before you do." Natalie tried to leave the room, but Michael lunged, grabbed her arm, and pulled her back toward him with force. He put his face close to hers. She felt an anxious flutter in her chest.

"I'm not going to blow up my life over your damn delusions about me," he said. "Honestly, I'm worried you are not in your right mind. Let me ask you, Nat, where'd you really go that night Scarlett came back here? Maybe you were getting something somewhere else. Got a receipt for the peanut butter you bought? Oh, I bet you paid cash."

"What are you getting at?"

"What I'm getting at, Natalie, is that it doesn't feel good to be the object of scorn and innuendo. This is my family too, and I'm going to keep it together no matter what. So don't try to leave me. It won't work out well for you. I'm not the one who can't sleep, who's seeing things, acting irrationally. A judge might not look on that too favorably."

Natalie felt a sputter of fear. She had heard him loud and clear. He hadn't made a demand of her. No, he had made a threat.

Natalie spent the night on the trundle bed in her daughter's bedroom. The next morning, Michael gave her a tender kiss on her cheek on his way out the door.

"I'm sorry about last night," he said with sincerity. "I know it's been a lot on you . . . our marital stress, the sleep troubles, all that. But believe me, I'm on your side, not in your way.

We're a team, and we need to stay a team for the sake of our kids, for all we've built together, my love for you . . . we need to ride this out and find a way to come back together."

Natalie heard a different message: keep quiet, soldier on, and this too shall pass.

Dead Audrey flashed in her mind. Both she and Michael had motive, method, and opportunity.

Michael was sending her a second message, she realized: they were in it together now.

"I love you, Natalie," he said, looking her in the eyes. She felt his words, his love, and wanted to cry.

The La Hacienda waitress took their food and drink orders. Unfortunately, Natalie's order didn't include a margarita this time, because Sarah had warned her that she'd want to be clearheaded for what she was about to hear.

"I guess I should start with my database search," Sarah began.

Bright mariachi music played in the background, in sharp contrast to the somber expression on Sarah's face.

"Natalie —" Sarah paused, collecting her thoughts. "This is going to be difficult for you to hear. I think there may be much more going on with Michael than a case of infidelity."

What little appetite Natalie had brought to the restaurant vanished entirely. A chip dipped in fresh guacamole lay on her plate, untouched. She had a good idea where this conversation was headed. Judging by Tina's taut expression and knowing glance, her friend must have been thinking along the same lines. Audrey Adler.

The look Sarah sent Natalie was partly empathic, partly something Natalie couldn't decipher, which put her on guard. In the back of her mind lurked a gnawing fear that she hadn't been so perfect in erasing all evidence of her short visit to Audrey's home.

Worst-case scenarios flittered in and out of Natalie's thoughts as Sarah pulled out a manila folder thick with papers and set it on the table next to the basket of chips.

"I've uncovered evidence suggesting your husband was involved with Audrey Adler."

Natalie was careful not to let her face reveal that she'd already known about the link between Audrey and her husband — and Tina followed suit.

"Michael was with Audrey?" Natalie said incredulously.

"Well, I can't say for certain what type of relationship they had," Sarah answered.

"But they were definitely in communication. Take a look. Here's the first message she sent him."

Sarah removed the top sheet of paper from the manila folder. She handed it to Natalie, who quickly read the message from Audrey to Michael. It was short and to the point.

We need to talk. You know what it's about.

Natalie noticed the date and time stamp on Audrey's email — not long after Natalie had shown her Michael's picture, and around the time she had shown him Audrey's.

"Is there more?" Natalie asked in a strained whisper before handing Tina the correspondence to read for herself.

"A little, yes," said Sarah. "But Natalie, you know that I'm a trained investigator. You must have realized I'd find out that Audrey had reported you to HR for stalking, and that you'd accused her of having an affair with your husband. Why didn't you bring up Audrey's name at our initial meeting?"

Natalie froze, but said a silent thank you when Tina came to her rescue.

"We didn't want to cloud your work with any confirmation bias," Tina said. "It was only our suspicion. We thought it might

354

come to this, that Michael and Audrey were seeing each other, but it's still a real shock to have the proof."

"Unfortunately, that's not the only shock you're going to get today," Sarah said.

Natalie returned a grimace. "Please tell me there aren't pictures of the two of them in compromising positions," she said.

"Worse," said Sarah without a smile. "Much worse, in fact. But before we get to that, I should show you Michael's response back to Audrey."

Natalie examined the next page in Sarah's stack, an email from Michael back to Audrey.

Don't email me. Not safe. Use Telegram.

His email contained a link.

"What's Telegram?" asked Natalie.

"It's a cloud-based instant messaging app," Sarah said. "You can have messages purged from the system, so it gives users a way to auto-delete their communications without having to remember to do it for themselves. Unfortunately, I suspect Michael suggested they use that app because it's not his first affair — if that's what this is. He knew how to stay in the shadows."

The waitress returned to fill their water glasses, sparing Natalie from having to respond immediately. A second waitress arrived carrying their entrees. Natalie's was a plate of tacos that she knew she couldn't eat.

"Is there more?"

A shiver began working its way up Natalie's spine.

"There are no more messages between them," said Sarah. "I guess because they stopped using our corporate email server and likely switched to Telegram."

Judging by Sarah's expression, Natalie was fairly certain where this conversation was headed: that the police now had eyes on Michael as their prime suspect in Audrey's murder. Natalie could think of no other reason why Sarah would tell her to prepare for the worst.

"You should know that I've given what I found to the Medford police, and they said they'll take it from here," said Sarah, as if reading Natalie's thoughts.

"I can't believe what I'm hearing," said Tina. "Do you think he might be connected to Audrey's *murder*?"

"Well, that's a leap, but I think the police need all the information that's available."

"There's got to be a mistake," Natalie said softly, almost as an aside. "It can't be true." She was stunned at how easily the lie came out, and even more so at how convincing she sounded. "It just doesn't make any sense. Michael has never been in trouble before."

Sarah cocked her head slightly, a grimace showing. "I'm not so sure that's true," she replied.

Unlike Natalie, Sarah had an appetite. She had no trouble putting away a taco. Bits of lettuce and tomato squeezed out the back as the shell cracked between her pearly white teeth. She chewed, swallowed, downing a sip of water before she spoke.

"I usually do a deep dive on the subjects of all my investigations," she said. "I know that Michael wasn't my focus here, that I got involved to safeguard the company, but I admit I was intrigued. I figured I'd do a little more digging into Michael's life just out of . . . well, morbid curiosity, really."

Sarah tapped her hand against the table in a rhythmic pattern like a steady drumbeat. Natalie had a thud of her own going on inside her chest. She couldn't imagine what a deep dive into Michael's life might have revealed, but clearly it was something of consequence, enough to make Sarah anxious about presenting her findings.

"I started with the present, Michael's employment history, current address, that sort of thing. I was looking for bankruptcy filings, criminal records, maybe unusual property transactions, something that would give me insight into his character."

"And did you find anything?" asked Tina.

"Not exactly. But I sort of hit a brick wall."

"A brick wall? How so?" Natalie's voice carried notes of her trepidation.

"Usually I can go back pretty far, all the way to childhood," said Sarah. "If you give me an hour, I'll tell you the first car you owned, what street you lived on when you were in grade school, that sort of thing."

"That's a wee bit unsettling," said Tina, who'd finally found the stomach for a few bites of her food.

Sarah nodded emphatically. "And that's a common reaction to just how much information is available about each and every one of us. But with Michael, I didn't find anything about him that predated his nineteenth birthday. Not a single bit of information."

"What does that mean?" asked Natalie. She'd wrangled her napkin into a tight corkscrew.

"It means that from a document trail standpoint, Michael came into this world as a teenager. It's more than bizarre, and it suggests something you might not like to hear — unless of course it's something you

already know and my worries are misplaced."

"And what's that?" Natalie asked quietly.

"That your husband, Michael Hart, wasn't
always Michael Hart."

Natalie met Sarah's gaze head-on. She
searched her eyes, but they were flat, revealing nothing. She looked to the corners of
her mouth for a slight uptick of a smile, but
her face was grim. There was no levity to be
found in Sarah's expression, leaving Natalie
to conclude she wasn't joking.

"What do you mean by that?" Natalie
asked.

Sarah scratched the back of her head,
pursing her lips together.

"Ah, damn, this is hard for me to say."
Sarah winced to show her discomfort. "I
like getting the bad guys, but I sure don't
like giving bad news to good people."

"What bad news?"

Natalie held back the urge to lurch to her
feet. Instead, she corked her fear while holding a breath.

"Usually in these cases, at least the few
times I've run into this problem, I find out
the subject of my investigation legally
changed their name. Now, you'd think I
could get the original name — the one they

were given at birth — easily enough, but I can't."

"Is it hard to do? Change your name?" Tina asked.

Sarah shook her head.

"No, people do it all the time," she said. "Marriage, divorce, there's a host of reasons for doing it. And unless it was sealed, there should be a public record of any official name change, but that doesn't make it easy for me to find."

"What would you need to know?" asked Natalie, who sat frozen across from Sarah, staring at her.

"For starters, I'd need to know the county where Michael resided when he changed his name."

"That should be easy enough. He's from Charleston, South Carolina," Natalie said.

"Is he?" Sarah retorted.

Natalie paled.

"You think Michael lied about where he grew up?"

"Why not?" asked Sarah. "Have you been to Charleston with Michael? Seen his hometown? Have you hung out with friends of his from high school? Ever looked at his high school yearbook?"

Darkness swelled up in Natalie. She shook her head. It was a no to all.

"I've seen family photos, though," she said, her voice lacking confidence.

"Any of those pictures make it clear that he was in Charleston, South Carolina, when they were taken?" Sarah asked.

Natalie thought hard before shaking her head again.

"He didn't have many photos. It's not like men to keep family albums and keepsakes, memory books, that sort of thing. When we got together he bragged about using milk crates for bookshelves, because he could turn them over and technically he'd be ready to move. He didn't own much, didn't bring much to the marriage other than himself."

"You know what his mother and father look like?"

"Sure," said Natalie. "I've seen photos of them, but we never met. His father ran off when he was young and his mother died from cancer before we got together."

Sarah's eyebrows went up in a way that made Natalie feel sick to her stomach.

"You think his father may still be around? Or that his mother might not be dead?"

Sarah bit at her bottom lip.

"I'm saying it's a possibility," she offered in an apologetic tone.

Tina sent Natalie a crumpled look.

"Natalie," Tina said, leaning forward to cup Natalie's hands in her own. "Let's not jump to conclusions."

"It's good advice," said Sarah. "I don't have any real facts about your husband before he became Michael Hart, so we shouldn't assume anything. Maybe he changed his name for career purposes. For all I know it could be that he started calling himself Michael Hart without doing a formal name change. If he did that, there'd be no public court record for us to track down. Basically we'd be at a dead end, unless we got Michael's cooperation."

Sarah's assessment gave Natalie a second jolt.

"So what am I supposed to do? I sleep next to this man. You're saying it's possible he's a killer — and he's not even who he says he is?"

Sarah gave her a slight shake of her head.

"Natalie, I am so sorry to bring you this news." She tapped a finger on the folder. "This is all the information I've gathered on your husband. Have a look. See what aligns with what he's told you. Start there. You give me whatever you can get — a real birthplace, maybe his birth certificate — and I can go from there. Most states will indicate when an amendment has been made to a birth certificate. Some states even cross out the old name and put in the new one."

"Okay," Natalie said, sounding quite unsettled as she locked eyes with Tina.

"I'll help you," said Tina. "You won't be in this alone."

"Thanks," Natalie said. She felt utterly hollowed out, numb, as if all feeling had been drained from her body.

"I guess there's one other bit of advice I should give you," Sarah said cautiously. "I can't say for sure if Michael had anything to do with Audrey Adler's murder, but I'm a hundred percent certain that he changed his name. If I were you, Natalie, I would put some serious thought and effort into figuring out why."

CHAPTER 31

Natalie

The bus trip was the best part of her journey so far. The kids were tired, she was tired, and for once everyone slept. For Natalie, it was a deep, dreamless slumber. There were no lights in the back of the bus, and the darkness hid their identities far better than the dye job ever could. For a blessed six or so hours on the road, she and the children were safe.

When Natalie's internal clock woke her, they were somewhere outside St. Louis. Off to the east, glimmers of dawn cast an orange streak across a glowing horizon. She stretched creaky limbs — her neck was especially tight — before checking on the children, who were sleeping beside each other, their tiny heads touching. She wanted to hug them, caress their arms, their hair, but they needed rest as much as she did, so she let them sleep.

She got to her feet carefully, checking her balance, well aware that a few hours of shut-eye wouldn't be enough to offset the long-term effects of her insomnia. She knew from experience that a full night's sleep could actually make her symptoms worse — and sure enough, Natalie felt groggier now than she had before. What she needed was a consistent sleep schedule, but that would have to wait until they were settled at Kate's place.

The Greyhound station in St. Louis was a massive, modern, glass structure that had the appearance of a sports arena. Natalie woke the children fifteen minutes before their scheduled arrival so they could adjust to the daylight. All three exited the bus in silence and began the long walk down an emerald green–tiled corridor to the exit.

At some point, Natalie had the where-withal to phone Kate and tell her they'd be arriving by bus now, knowing her friend would insist on picking them up at the bus station in St. Louis. Yes, it was an inconvenience, and for that Natalie felt a little guilty, but the children needed a break from the hard travel, and Kate had insisted an hour's drive each way wasn't a big deal at all.

There were few cars in the passenger

pickup area when they arrived, making it easy for her to locate her friend. Kate, dressed in blue jeans and a red T-shirt adorned with the Hildonen Farms logo, a cow sporting a toothy grin, stood next to a dust-covered four-door pickup truck. When she saw them, her face lit up.

"Nat!"

Kate came running over, arms open wide, and wrapped Natalie in a tight embrace. The warmth of Kate's touch, the imperative of her hug, made Natalie want to cry. A flood of emotions, mostly relief and gratitude, overwhelmed her. She didn't realize how much she'd been holding in until that moment.

"Hey there, you all right?" Kate whispered in Natalie's ear. "You're trembling."

"I'm fine," Natalie assured her in a low voice. "It's been a hell of a trip, is all."

When they finally broke apart, Kate turned her attention to the children, who were gazing uncertainly at the woman with the round face and genial smile standing before them. She placed a calloused hand upon Addie's slender shoulder.

"Look at you two," Kate said, a tinge of awe in her voice, her bright blue eyes beaming. "Your mother and I haven't spoken in quite some time, but I've seen pictures of you both — and, well, if you two aren't the cutest things ever, I don't know what. I bet you're hungry though. What do you say we stop at a doughnut shop I know? The frosted glaze will perk up even the weariest traveler."

Addie nodded a bit tentatively, while Bryce looked quite eager.

"I like doughnuts," Bryce said with an earnest grin.

Kate smiled back warmly and brushed bits of hay onto the floor of her pickup as she helped the kids get settled into the backseat.

"Well then, you'll really like these."

Natalie tried to reconcile the Kate she'd known back when they were young urban professionals living in Boston with this solidly built, square-shouldered woman. Natalie guessed her friend's ruddy complexion was a byproduct of working outdoors under the Missouri sun, something Kate had sworn she'd never do. "My dad wants me to quit this damn job and get back to the farm," Kate would lament at least once a week. Then one day Kate didn't show up for work, and the next Natalie heard she was gone, back home to run the family dairy farm after her father had suffered a near-fatal heart attack.

For a time, she and Kate stayed in touch.

Natalie would share anecdotes of the office life Kate had left behind — who was dating whom, who got fired, who should get fired — while Kate regaled her with tales from the farm, everything from early morning milkings to details on how to inseminate cattle, which included a picture of Kate with her gloved arm buried deep in the vagina of a cow.

Kate's father died nine months later from a second coronary. Natalie sent a condolence card, but by then their emails were sporadic, and communication trailed off from there. Back in those days, Natalie was consumed with Michael, building a life with her future husband. Even friends who lived close by had drifted into the background of her life, while acquaintances like Kate faded almost entirely out of the picture.

It was a short drive to the doughnut shop. The four inhaled their purchases, which lived up to the hype, and then did a drive-by viewing of the Gateway Arch, which failed to inspire the children.

"I'm sorry I haven't been in touch," Natalie said, compelled to offer her apology. "I should have reached out. I mean, I didn't think to look you up on Facebook until I needed your help, and that's just shameful."

Kate gave Natalie's leg a few gentle, placating pats.

"You've got nothing to apologize for. I was thrilled to hear from you, and I'm happy to help. When we get to the farm, we'll get you all settled in your rooms and then you can tell me what's really going on."

The drive to Elsberry passed with a scattering of conversation, mostly from Kate, who, despite having no children of her own, proved quite adept at engaging with Bryce and Addie. She asked about their respective schools, favorite subjects, and what foods they liked to eat.

"You're gonna have to try my toasted ravioli," she said. "And of course I'll fix you up some St. Louis–style barbecue."

The landscape grew wider the farther from the city they drove. If Natalie had tried on her own to follow the directions Kate provided, she most certainly would have missed the turnoff to the farm, which was hidden by an overgrowth of shrubs and weeds. The pickup turned onto a road that wasn't much more than a wood-lined rutted path and went jouncing over rocks and potholes before entering a clearing, which revealed a wide green pasture. Wire fencing tacked to rustic posts ran in all directions, stretching out beyond Natalie's line of sight.

"Welcome to Hildonen Farms," Kate announced proudly.

With a flourish, she gestured with one hand toward a rectangular building that Natalie presumed housed a number of dairy cows. Off to her right stood a large, white clapboard farmhouse built atop a gently sloping hill. The home featured a wide wraparound porch on which hung a swing that was so folksy it made Natalie thirst for a lemonade. It was an idyllic setting, Natalie thought, and the rustic home reminded her of the one in *Field of Dreams,* a movie Michael watched anytime it came on cable.

Kate was more interested in talking about her cows than her home.

"There are six hundred and fifty Holstein milk cows on the farm, and that gives us around six thousand gallons of milk each day. We milk twenty-four hours a day in three-hour shifts, and then we ship off to a plant in St. Louis. It's always a thrill when we get to see our friends and neighbors using our product."

She beamed a smile back to the kids who *now* looked to be in awe, far more so than the famed arch had rendered them.

"After you get settled in your rooms we'll walk the fence together so you get a sense of things, see how our lives really revolve around these fine animals. We have a simple motto here on Hildonen Farms: the more we take care of our cows, the more our cows take care of us."

"Do they ever get away? The cows, I mean," Addie asked.

Kate returned a hearty chuckle.

"Well, I assumed you didn't mean Chuck — that's my husband. Though I reckon there are times he'd like to make a break for it." The sound of Kate's wholehearted laugh made Natalie remember how easily her friend always cracked herself up.

Every minute in Kate's company made it possible for Natalie to breathe easier. She embraced the feeling of sunshine streaming in through her open window. Along with that warming sensation came a breeze carrying the scent of grass and farm life. The strange blend of smells reminded Natalie that the world was larger than her troubles. It was a vibrant place full of hope and possibilities.

A sense of peace enveloped Natalie like a comforting hug. Kate's farm was a gourmet feast for the senses, easing Natalie's perpetual stress and fatigue, and at last she could relax.

As if attuned to the shift that had taken place, Kate sent Natalie a gentle smile that seemed to convey the words she'd longed hear: *you're safe now.*

"To answer your specific question, Addie, we use RID tags on all our cows. Not only do they help us track where they are, those tags tell us all sorts of things about our animals."

Kate pulled over to the side of the road, where a large black-and-white cow grazed on a patch of grass. The bovine appeared undisturbed by these young visitors clambering out of the truck, doors slamming behind them as they rushed over to have a closer look.

"This is 1752," said Kate. "That's her tag. The tag transfers all the data to my computer and phone. You two use computers, right?"

"We have iPads," Bryce replied chirpily.

"Well, there you have it," said Kate. "Now, let me tell you about 1752 here." Kate checked her phone.

"This one here is pregnant. Hundred twenty-two days. Our cows usually have a calf every thirteen months. 1752 was born on July third, almost Independence Day, a big celebration around these parts, and she weighs in at a slight eight hundred and twenty-two pounds. Good and healthy."

"I think 1752 is a terrible name for a

cow," Addie said mournfully.

Kate set her hands to her hips.

"Oh? And what do you think we should call her then?"

"Call her Teddy," Bryce said emphatically. "That's the name of my bear that's missing. Is Daddy going to meet us here? Will he bring Teddy?"

Kate and Natalie exchanged glances.

"We'll talk about plans with Daddy later," Natalie said brusquely before ushering the kids back into the truck.

Kate put the vehicle in gear.

"Bryce, I'm going to add a note to the system that from this day forward, cow 1752 shall henceforth be called Teddy. We'll make it short for Theodora so there's no confusion."

"That's from *Hamilton,*" Bryce shouted from the backseat. He seemed quite pleased to have known the reference.

"That's Theodosia," Addie corrected him sternly. "Not Theodora." Bryce stuck his tongue out at his sister. Mother radar helped Natalie catch the gesture in her peripheral vision, but she didn't correct the behavior. Rather, she welcomed the bit of normality it represented.

"Either way, we will call her Teddy," said Kate, as she made the turn onto the driveway leading to the house.

"We do farm tours for kids all the time here," she added, with glee in her voice. "I'll have Hank, our chief farmhand, show you two around. Your mom and I need to talk and catch up."

The interior of the farmhouse was mostly wood throughout, warm and inviting, with a few well-worn rugs and comfy furniture that made Natalie feel right at home. After so many hours and days spent in close quarters, the kids rejoiced at having bedrooms of their own.

"I want to milk a cow," Bryce exclaimed with delight as he gazed out the window of his second-floor bedroom at the cow-dotted pastures.

"How about feeding a baby calf?" Kate said, clapping her hands together, eagerness shining in her eyes and face.

"Really?" Bryce's expression brightened.

"Really."

Some minutes later, the kids were off with Hank, a wiry man in his late fifties who Natalie thought wore a cowboy hat as well as Clint Eastwood did. After everyone was gone, Natalie and Kate retreated to the kitchen. Kate made tea and the two women sat at a pinewood table in the center of the airy room, catching up on years in a matter of minutes. Eventually, they got to the heart of the matter.

"So Nat, why did you come here? Talk to me. Whatever it is, I'll help you in any way I can."

Natalie guessed Kate hadn't seen the Facebook post, so had no idea her friend was a missing person. Natalie bit her bottom lip. Her eyes stung with the salt of gathering tears. Kate grabbed a box of tissues from a counter so Natalie could continue.

"I have to leave Michael," she said. "We need to divorce, right away, but it's complicated."

"I'm so sorry to hear, but okay," Kate said. "Lord help me, but I feel responsible. That night."

Natalie managed a strained smile, thinking about that party Kate had dragged her to when she and Michael met.

"Not your fault. Nobody could have known."

"Known what, that you'd end up divorcing?"

"No, there's more to it than that. I guess I should just come right out and say it . . . my husband is a killer. He murdered his lover, Audrey Adler, who worked for my company, Dynamic Media."

Kate's ruddy complexion went pale.

"Holy hell, Nat," said Kate breathlessly, putting her hands to her mouth. "What about the police? Aren't they involved?"

"It's complicated," Natalie said. She proceeded to explain her dilemma — how she'd come to learn about the affair and later found her way inside Audrey's apartment, how she had stalked Audrey at work, and how because of all that, she feared Michael would set her up for a murder rap.

"So what's your plan of attack?" Kate asked after Natalie finished listing her litany of concerns.

"If you don't mind having us around for a while?" Natalie asked, sounding uncertain. "I want to stay here if we can, hide out really. I'll file for divorce from here and try to get full custody of the kids from a safe place."

Kate got up from her chair to give her friend a comforting embrace. "Now, I need to check with Chuck, because this is complicated and potentially dangerous, but that man always thirsts for a bit of excitement. I suspect he'll be quite agreeable and you'll be welcome to stay here, long as you need. Chuck and I love each other, but honestly we've run out of things to talk about." She capped her quip with a grin to make certain her joke was understood.

"I just need somewhere to be until I get the process going. And honestly I'm hoping that the police will do their jobs and arrest him first."

"Okay, like I said, I'm here to help."

"That's all I need to know."

There was more to the story, much more, but Natalie didn't share it. Only so much a person could take in at once, she reasoned. At some point, she'd tell Kate the whole truth.

Audrey Adler hadn't been Michael's first victim.

CHAPTER 32

Michael

They had arrived too late to do much looking, so Michael and Kennett crashed at a
Renaissance hotel in downtown Toledo for
the night. The accommodations didn't quite
fit Kennett's budget, so Michael paid both
room charges.

In the morning, they drove the city streets,
checking as many hotel parking lots as they
could, looking for Natalie's rental car, and
coming up empty. They paid visits to all four
police departments — Erie Street, North
Cove Boulevard, Nebraska Avenue, and
even the department at the University of
Toledo. At each stop, they got plenty of assurance that the officers would keep an eye
out for the vehicle and its occupants, which
engendered no great feelings of hope in
Michael.

"Do you think she's even here?" he asked
Kennett as they headed back to the car after

stopping at a Wendy's for chicken sand-
wiches and fries — road food.

Kennett returned a shrug.

"I'm a cop, Mike," he said. "Not a genie.
Gumshoe and persistence, those are the
tools of my trade."

After several more hours of fruitless
searching, they had to stop for gas before
heading for the hotel to rest and recharge,
plan their next moves. Michael heard Kennett's phone chirp while he was filling up.
Kennett leaned his head out the open window.

"They found her car," he announced.

Michael perked up. "Where?"

He could feel the heat coming off him as
his heart revved up.

"It's back in Columbus," Kennett said
with no joy in his voice. He held out his
phone, which Michael grabbed like a relay
baton. He read the text even as Kennett was
telling him what it said. "Security at the
hospital found her rental parked in the visitors' lot and reported it to the police, who
then reported it to me."

The look on Kennett's face was equal
parts frustration and reverence.

"She misled us," Michael said, his voice
falling. "She must have told the doctor her
plans, her lie, thinking we might track her

to the hospital. Dammit."

Kennett left the car. He came over to Michael and patted him on the shoulder.

"Hey, don't worry, Mike. Gumshoe and persistence, remember?"

"But we don't even know where to look now," Michael bemoaned. "She could be anywhere."

He slammed the gas nozzle back into the pump, cursing under his breath. Kennett's patience and optimism weren't rubbing off on him. The car had the odor of a dorm room. They both needed a shower, and Michael was thinking about a stiff drink to follow. Heavy traffic made the drive back to the Renaissance a slow one. Michael filled the silence with his own thoughts and regrets.

The affair was one thing. It was an awful thing, a terrible choice he couldn't unmake. The moment he set his lips to those of another woman, undid the zipper of her dress, slipped his hand down her waist, he had stepped into a new realm, a bizarre landscape that held him prisoner. A voice in his head trumpeted plenty of warnings, told him to step back from the edge, but there was that devil on his shoulder, goading him on.

You're a person with feelings too, Michael,

said the devil. *You have needs that should be met. You've tried with Natalie, tried so hard, but you are two ships passing in the night.*

Michael wasn't ignorant. He knew all that chatter was nothing but fancy excuses.

People are fallible, Michael was thinking as he drummed his fingers against the steering wheel.

Kennett keyed in on his nervous habit. "What's on your mind, Mike? You seem troubled," he said. He downed a sip of water from a plastic bottle, swished it around like mouthwash.

"Just thinking, is all," Michael replied, as he changed lanes.

"Thinking. Sounds dangerous."

"I'm thinking you're breaking a lot of rules helping me on this search," said Michael.

"Perhaps."

Michael chuckled softly.

"Do cops always break the rules?" he asked.

"Do husbands always lie to their wives?"

Michael flinched.

"Why'd you say that?"

Kennett smiled back languidly.

"Come on, Mike. Your wife takes off on you like that. She had to have a reason. I've spent a good amount of time with you now. I don't think you were beating her. Don't see you abusing drugs and booze. Haven't seen you obsessively checking lines on your sports betting app, so I'm willing to forgo a gambling problem. Why not come clean with me? You cheat on her? She find out and get kinda teed off?" Kennett grimaced in a way that was both sincere and a bit mocking at the same time. Michael tried to hide his reaction but evidently didn't do a great job of it.

"Yeah, I thought so," said Kennett, his expression turning more somber. He craned his head to have another look out the window. "It sucks. Shitty thing to do, Mike, cheating and all."

"I'm not proud of it," said Michael.

"Not a thing to be proud about," said Kennett matter-of-factly. "But look here, Mike, shit happens. You had your reasons, am I right?"

"It's not an excuse."

"Nah, I suppose not," said Kennett with a shrug. He grabbed a warm Pepsi they'd bought at a gas station yesterday and popped the top. "I'm not a saint, Mike. I cheated on my wife — ex-wife, I mean," he said. "Had my reasons. No sex. No communication. All my pressures at work, no release valve, yadayadayada. Know what I didn't have, Mike?"

"What's that?"

"Courage," said Kennett with regret. "I should have had the damn courage to say to Janet, 'Hey, we need to split. I'm not happy, you're not happy, and we need to live a different kind of life before we have no more life to live.' "

"Yeah, that was probably the right thing to do, but I'm not sure my circumstances were exactly the same as yours. I didn't *want* to leave my wife."

"Well, what did you want then?" Kennett asked.

"Comfort," said Michael, pausing to think it through. He also wondered why he was confiding in this cop, but the need to speak his truth trumped his better judgment.

"Love, touch, connection," he continued. "I don't know. I wanted something different from what I had, that's for sure." Michael sighed deeply and then continued. "Natalie's work stress, plus kid stress, put a lot of strain and distance between us, then her insomnia kicked in, made a bad problem a whole lot worse, and I couldn't reach her anymore no matter how hard I tried. And a lot of it is my fault. Once I broke down and gave in to temptation it was like Natalie somehow knew. Without any evidence she became obsessed with the thought and fear of my cheating on her. And I guess I also didn't have the courage to tell her the truth."

"There's nothing you could have done to save it?" Kennett asked with a look of true concern.

"Maybe if I owned up to what I did, Natalie could have stopped obsessing and half doubting me, half doubting herself, and we could have dealt with our troubles head-on, and she might have gotten a good night's sleep for once. Maybe."

"I'm guessing she somehow found out about the cheating."

"There was a note," Michael said. "I found it in a shoebox. So yeah, she finally got the confirmation she was after."

"Damn shame," said Kennett.

"A damn shame is right," said Michael. He was thinking about his kids. The pain he felt in his chest was like a puncture wound. He kept ruminating over all they'd lose out on, all the family memories they wouldn't have. Snapshots of what would never be flashed in his mind. His kids getting older in each vision, Natalie getting older, too. He saw the four of them growing older together, on vacation at some resort somewhere, together at Christmas, Thanksgiving, his kids coming home from college, settling into their old rooms like birds returning to the nest, all smiles and beaming, perfect for Instagram. But Michael knew all too well that behind those social media smiles, all the pictures posted by strangers, acquaintances, and friends, there was often hidden pain, suffering, sadness, loss, grief, and yes, betrayal.

He knew he and Natalie were headed for divorce; the tension in the house before they went to New York had been unbearable. Was the note in the shoebox the reason Natalie ran? He highly doubted it. If it had been about the note, she should have thrown him out, asked for a divorce, and that would be that. Finished.

"The thing about adultery, Mike, is that you can't undo it," Kennett said. "It happened, right? So what are you going to do about it? How do you move forward? Should you just put a bullet in your head because you screwed up? Seems harsh, don't you think?"

"I guess," said Michael, mulling over his regrets. There was no way to hide what he'd done. He felt lonely in his marriage and had a fling with the beautiful woman he met at the gym, those were undeniable facts that came with mountains of regret. "Sometimes

I think a bullet is what I deserve."

"Well, you don't." Kennett clapped him on the back, looking Michael squarely in the eyes so he'd know he was serious. "Don't ever say that again. Your kids don't deserve a lifetime of heartache for your momentary lapse of reason. I've been to too many funerals to listen to that bullshit, you hear me, Mike?"

"I hear you," Michael said. He figured Kennett's spurt of kindness was out of compassion for Michael's kids more than anything.

"What you have to do is come clean," continued Kennett. "Own what you did, all of it. Own it and accept the consequences of your actions — and make a promise to yourself that you won't ever repeat those same mistakes again. You can't force Natalie to forgive you. The only thing you can control is yourself. It's not easy, Mike. Don't fall into the trap of beating yourself up, thinking you're a bad person. That kind of self-abuse is counterproductive. You don't need Natalie's permission to forgive yourself. Look at what you've done, learn from it, and change for the better. That's honestly the best you can do. If Natalie never forgives you, that's going to be her problem, her burden to carry, not yours."

Michael let out a heavy sigh.

"I don't think you're a bad guy, Mike. I think you did a bad thing. But marriage is complicated, and it really takes two people to make it work, or otherwise . . . bad things may happen."

"Yeah, maybe that's right," Michael said. "Maybe not."

"Is there anything else you want to get off your chest? Lighten your load? Anything you want to share? That's part of the healing process, Mike. Come clean."

Kennett flashed his teeth in a crooked smile. Michael bristled inwardly as he glanced at the speedometer, which showed him going twenty over the speed limit. He let up on the gas.

Kennett's smile only deepened.

"The thing about guilt is, Mike, no matter how fast you go, you can't outrun it."

CHAPTER 33

Natalie

Before She Disappeared

It was Saturday afternoon, just after her lunch with Tina Langley and Sarah Fielding at La Hacienda. Papers were strewn about Natalie's usually tidy home office. She'd gone to the attic to retrieve several boxes of documents, most of which deserved a shredder more than a half-assed filing system. Those boxes were filled with old insurance invoices, bank statements from banks where they no longer had accounts, telephone bills for phone numbers no longer in service.

She wasn't entirely sure what she was looking for. Maybe something with a mention of South Carolina, a yearbook from one of the local high schools with Michael's picture in it, perhaps receipts or old invoices that showed a home address from Charleston. She'd come up short all around. Sarah

Fielding could have sped up the process, but Natalie was hoping to keep her personal pain and office life separate as much as possible. As far as she was concerned, Sarah had linked Michael to Audrey and that was enough for her, at least for now.

Michael was out for the afternoon, running errands. The television was doing an okay job at keeping the children occupied, but Natalie knew it wouldn't be long before she was needed again for this or that. She sat cross-legged on the floor, papers crinkling beneath her as she shifted position to get more comfortable, all the while thinking about another document she couldn't find.

Where was Michael's birth certificate?

Only now, after Sarah's big reveal, was Natalie aware that his wasn't in the file safe along with the others. That box contained their most important documents: passports, insurance policy information, their respective wills, keys to the safety deposit box, and a thousand dollars in emergency cash.

Had it ever been in the safe? She hadn't looked at his birth certificate when they obtained their marriage license all those years ago — a town clerk had overseen the document exchange. Did Michael intentionally keep it from her? It was impossible to say who had handed the clerk the documents back then, but conceivably Michael had orchestrated it.

Natalie realized she'd had no occasion to review the official certification of her husband's birth until an investigator tasked with scouring Michael's life, his past, had given her one.

Natalie heard Michael's car in the driveway, and after greeting Addie and Bryce, who sounded far more interested in the TV than they did their father, he strode into her office.

"Love what you've done with the place," he said, with a sardonic grin. "Did you download a homemade confetti recipe off Pinterest?"

Natalie gathered some loose papers into a neat pile, but it didn't make the slightest difference to the overall mess.

"Back already?" she asked, trying to appear calm.

"Yeah, Home Depot didn't have what I needed. What on earth are you doing, hon?"

Natalie knew she was handling a bomb, a man with a secret, a threat to her and to her children. She hadn't demolished her office without formulating an answer to the question she knew Michael would ask.

"I'm looking for your birth certificate."

Natalie had hoped it was all a big misunderstanding, that Michael would happily clear the air, get the document (wherever it was), prove it wasn't annotated with a name change, and give her one less reason to distrust him. Now it was clear — that was wishful thinking.

Michael took a threatening step forward. Natalie saw how he kept his body positioned in front of the door to block her only way out.

"What do you want that for?" he asked.

She took note of an icy detachment in his voice.

"I thought it would be a good idea to get our passports renewed," Natalie said, again grateful that she'd preplanned her story. "Mine is expiring and yours is only good for a couple more years, so I figured we should all get new ones. You took care of that the last time, thought I'd return the favor. But I need our birth certificates for that, and yours isn't in the safe."

She rose from the floor to make her way to the hefty blue box on her cluttered desk. The lid was open. Three birth certificates topped the stack of papers within. Natalie fanned them out for Michael's benefit.

"Where's yours, Michael?"

She was unable to keep an accusatory edge from her voice.

Michael advanced, the shadow in his expression only deepening.

"I brought it to work a while ago," he said after a brief hesitation. "Don't remember when. I needed it to redo my I-9 form and I just forgot about it. Left it in a file drawer there."

His explanation seemed reasonable. Perhaps he was telling the truth — or perhaps he had this story at the ready to shore up his deception.

"Okay, well, maybe you can bring it home. We should really keep all the important documents together."

Natalie followed up her suggestion with a tight smile.

"Sure," Michael said. "And I'll happily take care of the passport renewals for you. You do enough around here. But you don't need our birth certificates for that. Figured you'd know that."

Helpful or evasive? Natalie had her suspicions.

"Guess I forgot," she said. "You know . . . maybe instead of going abroad, if that's what we end up doing, we could take the kids to South Carolina, to Charleston this summer. Let them see where you grew up. I'd like to go. You've never taken me."

Michael's mouth formed something of a frown.

"Charleston has bad memories for me," he said with an edge. "I lost my mom *and* dad there, and high school wasn't exactly my happiest time. I couldn't get far enough away from that place. You know that. And yet, here you are, asking to go to Charleston, of all places. What are you after? My birth certificate, my hometown, all these papers — why don't you tell me what you're really up to?"

Michael gestured to the mess. His voice carried harsh notes of accusation. Reflexively, Natalie stepped back from him as he approached. Audrey's lifeless form flashed in and out of her mind.

"What's this all about?" he said, his voice rising.

She observed how he stood, arms akimbo, hands latched to his hips, eyes narrowed. Lack of sleep made it hard to trust her judgment. How far could she press him before he snapped? Natalie felt compelled to pull back.

"I told you what I'm doing," she said, rubbing her hands against her pants to wick away the moisture that had collected on her palms. "And thanks for taking care of the passports when you can."

She closed the lid on the safe and turned the key, then shifted her gaze to the floor so that Michael couldn't read her eyes. He came over to the desk anyway, where he pressed his palms against the paper-covered surface.

Michael reached a hand out and set it gently on her shoulder, holding her back. His touch was tender and loving. What happened to the menace she'd felt radiating off him moments ago?

"You don't seem well," Michael said as he stroked her cheek in a loving way. "I'm concerned about you."

"I'm fine," Natalie said, finding it hard to sound convincing.

Michael eyed her skeptically.

"I'm not so sure that's true," he said. He cupped her face with his hands, gazing deeply into her eyes. "You look so tired, honey. I'm really worried."

He didn't sound sincere.

"How much sleep did you get last night?"

"Don't . . ."

Natalie caught herself.

"Don't what?" asked Michael.

"Try to make this anything more than it is. I just thought about taking a trip, is all."

"Yeah?" Michael didn't look remotely convinced. "A trip, a birth certificate, my hometown? I'm getting this strange sense that you don't trust me, do you, Nat?"

"You know our problems."

"Problems? More like an obsession of yours, I'd say."

"It's not," Natalie said, stepping away. She didn't like him standing so close to her.

"Yes, it is," he replied. "You're a terrible liar, especially when you're so exhausted."

Natalie thought of blood on a kitchen floor, a broken plate nearby. A shudder tore through her as she contemplated when the police would come knocking at her door. She'd done as she intended and put them on his trail. At some point soon, Michael would have to answer for his actions.

She had to move cautiously here. A man with that kind of violence in him could do terrible things in a sudden fit of rage.

"Maybe you should take a trip on your own," Michael suggested. "Let me look after the kids for a while. You need to get some *real* rest, and Addie and Bryce need their mom functioning at a hundred percent."

Something about his suggestion, a subtext she noted, made Natalie perk up.

"What's that supposed to mean?" she asked.

"Nothing," said Michael, sounding defensive. "I'm just saying the kids need their mom healthy and well, that's all."

"Are you implying that you're worried about my fitness as a parent?"

Michael scoffed at the insinuation.

"No, babe, I'm worried about you as a person, you and your health. You've been under a lot of strain, and you're sounding kind of paranoid now."

Was she?

Natalie took a few steps back from Michael to get a better look at him. The threatening behavior she thought she'd seen mere moments ago — a menace lurking in his eyes, the intimidating way he carried himself, an unsettling timbre to his voice — wasn't there anymore. What she saw now was unfiltered empathy pouring out of him in waves.

"Look, if you want to go to Charleston, if it means that much to you, then we'll go." Michael tossed out his concession as if it were nothing to him now. "It's got a lot of great beaches and restaurants and a lot of bad memories for me, but whatever. If you think that's what you need to get better, then I'm all for it. But you need to think about the children. You have to do what's best for them, and sometimes that means putting yourself first."

Michael's eyes were kind, but in his voice,

she heard the distinct undercurrent of another threat.

Get your shit together, or I'll get the kids away from you.

She could confront him on it, push him for his true intentions, but Natalie didn't want things to escalate. She returned what she hoped was an appreciative nod.

"Thanks for caring," she said as sweetly as she could manage. "I'll think about that getaway . . . and your other suggestion."

"Good," Michael said, as if that had settled matters. "You want help cleaning up?" He gestured to the mess.

"I've got it, thanks," said Natalie.

"Okay, then I'll get dinner started." He planted a quick kiss on her cheek before departing.

After she was sure he was gone, Natalie slumped into her office chair, decompressing. Michael may have left the room, but his words (*his implied threat?*) lingered.

Natalie set about her cleanup effort thinking, planning what to do next. Sarah had done a deep dive on Michael, but not on Audrey Adler, which made sense. The police were looking into Audrey's life, and it was more as a favor (or morbid curiosity, as Sarah had put it) that she went looking into Michael's.

Now, Natalie wondered what an investigation into Audrey might reveal. Was there more to her gruesome murder than a secret love gone sour? Sarah had mentioned investigating all kinds of corporate misdeeds. She hated Michael for his affair, his many betrayals, but it would still be a relief to get proof that the father of her children wasn't a killer. Perhaps Audrey had gotten herself caught up in something nefarious, which might mean Michael wasn't responsible for her death.

She suspected this inquiry into Audrey was a waste of time, but what did she have to lose? While she wasn't a trained investigator like Sarah, and a Google search had revealed nothing of consequence other than what the newspapers had already reported, she did have the pictures she'd taken with her phone inside Audrey's home. She breezed through the photos of the living room and foyer. Nothing there. But who was the girl in the framed photographs decorating Audrey's hallway? She was someone important to her, that much was obvious. The papers had made no mention of Audrey's family, but that girl had to be her sister. Natalie took out her phone and confirmed that the likeness between the pair was too similar to be anything else. Both girls had reddish hair, a similar mouth shape, full lips, a dappling of freckles.

Why was there no mention of a sister, or parents for that matter, in the news reports?

Natalie thought of calling Sarah Fielding for guidance, though she would first attempt this on her own. Could she identify a person using a photograph, a web search for facial recognition? She googled that very subject on her phone and got plenty of hits. One site in particular seemed especially promising — BitEyes advertised itself as a reverse image search. The instructions were simple enough: upload a photo and find where images with that face appeared online.

Creepy, Natalie thought, but she did just that, uploading a cropped image of the girl she presumed to be Audrey's sister. She knew Audrey, a murder victim, would get plenty of hits.

The reverse image search completed in a matter of seconds, returning a series of images that depicted the mystery girl's face. She *was* online. In fact, she was all over the internet, it seemed. But who was she? To get that information, the corresponding URLs for each image returned in the search required Natalie to pony up $19.99 for a one-month subscription, which she had no problem paying.

The problem came moments later when Natalie clicked on the first image in the results. As the webpage loaded, the headline immediately jumped out at her:

FORMER BOYFRIEND CHARGED IN MURDER OF WESTCHESTER'S BRIANNA SYKES

A color photograph below the headline showed a young man dressed in jeans and a blue T-shirt, with the words *Rye Wrestling* stenciled in white. His hands were shackled in front of him and a uniformed officer kept a tight grip on his arm. The young man appeared to be in shock, his eyes blank, staring straight at the camera. There was a second image overlapping that one, a photograph of a girl — the victim, Natalie supposed. She had no doubt this was the girl whose photos hung in Audrey's hallway.

But the boy. An icy chill came over her as she studied the young man in handcuffs. His face wasn't just familiar, it was seared into her being. It was older, now weathered from years of toil and struggle, but it was him, she had no doubt about it.

It was her husband, only so much younger.

But the name printed below his picture read: *Joseph Jacob Saunders.*

CHAPTER 34

Natalie

It was her first night sleeping — or more accurately, trying to sleep — at the farm.

A symphony of night critters, crickets, and katydids had come out after the rainstorm passed. They called to each other outside Natalie's bedroom window, making an incessant cacophonous buzzing like the steady rumble of a subway train. Wind rustled the leaves of a giant maple in the yard, and the sound of its branches scraped her ears. Every groan of a pipe or creaking wood plank, the sounds of a house settling for the night, all made it impossible for her to sleep. An antique wall clock ticked off each second she lay awake like a cruel taunt.

Natalie sat up in bed, rubbing her eyes. She turned on a bedside lamp. There was a stack of old paperbacks underneath the nightstand — maybe she'd read herself to sleep. Everything suddenly slipped out of focus, and for a moment Natalie felt quite disoriented. Her vision soon cleared, and as she reached for a book, Natalie caught sight of a slim shadow passing in the hallway outside her bedroom door.

It couldn't be the children. Was Chuck awake at this hour?

Natalie felt a stirring of fear. The shadow passed by quickly, silently too, allowing the hallway light to once again seep in underneath the door. She let go of the breath she'd been holding. It had to be Chuck, out doing something at this late hour.

She then heard a squeak, like a shoe dragging against the floor as it pivoted. The shadow outside her door returned, and this time it lingered. She heard the soft rapping of knuckles against wood.

Natalie jumped, pulling the covers up to her chin.

"Yes, who is it?" Her voice shook.

She got no answer. A gnawing worry raised the hair on her arms.

She heard another knock.

"Hello," she cried out. "Who's there? Chuck, is that you?"

Again, no answer.

Natalie willed herself out of bed. She stood, not feeling at all steady on her feet. With cautious steps, she approached the door. Sips of light from the hallway seeped into her bedroom from around both sides of the hovering shadow that lingered there. Fear made her skin tingle all over. It couldn't be him, couldn't be Michael. Was it possible he'd found her? Was it?

No, it's Chuck, Natalie told herself as she reached for the doorknob. Michael wouldn't knock. He'd come barging in, most likely in a violent rage. Setting one hand on the knob, the other on the door itself, Natalie contemplated what to do. Should she open the door or barricade herself inside?

She listened for a sound. Before she could take action, the shadow moved away again. Natalie waited a few seconds before daring to open the door. She stepped into the hall, spinning in the direction of the staircase, thinking she'd catch sight of whoever had been lurking outside her bedroom, whoever had knocked, but all was perfectly still. She immediately went into the children's rooms, not bothering to be quiet about it, and found them both fast asleep, peaceful as angels.

She returned to the hallway, confused and disoriented. She thought about checking on Kate and Chuck to make certain they were okay, but she didn't want to risk waking them. Explaining herself might make her confront the deeply unsettling possibility that the only things she'd seen and heard had come from her exhausted mind.

Damn sleep.

Natalie made her way downstairs despite her trepidation. She worried that someone *could* be in the house. But no, every room she checked was empty; all was quiet save for a knocking sound, the source of which she determined to be an old cast-iron radiator. Is that what she heard upstairs? Natalie thought of Camo Man in the Pennsylvania Walmart — her perceived stalker had been nothing but an innocent shopper. The flash of silver she thought was a knife had been only a stick of gum. She was losing it, and she knew it. At least she was safe here at the farm, or so she hoped.

Natalie returned to the kitchen, where the savory smells of dinner lingered — a delightful meal of chicken and biscuits that Kate had insisted she prepare without assistance. Even Bryce, who could be such a picky eater, had devoured the green beans (perhaps because they were drizzled with butter).

During dinner the children, both of whom wore their brand new Hildonen Farms T-shirts featuring that smiling cow, chattered tirelessly about their first day on the farm. Chuck, a barrel-chested man with a booming laugh that shook the house, listened intently, hanging on their every word as if they were delivering an important address. Natalie especially enjoyed the stories of Hank the farmhand, who had been kind enough to teach them some basic animal husbandry skills.

"The calves are the cutest," Addie said from her seat across from Natalie at the dinner table. "I want to take one home with me. Can we, Mommy? Take home a cow? I'll care for her I promise. I know how to feed her now. I promise, promise, promise she'll be happy."

Natalie laughed jovially.

"I don't think there's room in the house for a cow," she said.

"We'll keep him outside," Addie answered as if that should have settled it.

"I can't wait to show Daddy the cows!" Bryce announced.

At the mention of Michael, Kate flashed her a look of concern.

"Did you know a cow eats a hundred ten pounds of food a day?" Addie said to her mother.

"That's a lot of mashed potatoes," said Chuck as he shoveled a spoonful of that particular food into his mouth, a dollop of which got caught in his beard. Kate rolled her eyes and pointed to his face.

"I think you need a napkin, love," she said, motioning for him to wipe his beard clean.

Thinking about that meal inspired Natalie to check the refrigerator, though nothing called to her. She wasn't particularly hungry, more looking for something to do to make her forget the shadow, the squeak of a shoe, the knocking, forget that she might be cracking.

From a cupboard, Natalie got a drinking glass and poured herself some water. She tried to keep quiet, but Kate had already given her permission to make as much noise as she wanted.

"I get that you don't sleep well," she said before turning in for the night. "But I'm like a rock when the lights go out. Hardly move at all. You know, maybe you should work at the farm for a while, Nat. I've never slept so well until I started exerting myself the way I do with these cows."

Natalie sipped from her glass while ruminating on Kate's offer. Perhaps she would start working here while she rebuilt her life. She could picture herself waking up before the dawn, overalls on, carrying buckets of milk in her mud-caked hands.

It could be a nice life. A new start.

According to the time on the stove clock, it was nearly three in the morning. Kate and Chuck would be awake in a couple of hours to tend to their cows. She knew resting could still be beneficial without sleep, so Natalie prepared to return to the warmth of her bed before she had to get up at dawn.

As she was leaving the kitchen, from outside came the distinct sound of a stick snapping in two. She froze the way a deer might when sensing a predator. Peering out the window over the kitchen sink revealed only a canvas of black. Any moonlight was well concealed by cloud cover. She pushed herself up on the counter, leaning her body forward to try to get a clear look outside.

She was fully awake now. That sound was too real to have been imagined. Natalie listened with intense focus, but all she heard were those damn bugs. Perhaps an animal had passed by, a cow that got loose, or a coyote if those hunted in these parts, or maybe a bear or a fox.

She pondered those possibilities while pressing her face against the window, but it was no use. She couldn't see anything outside.

Then, she heard it again.

Crack.

There was no mistaking the sound of

wood splintering. Once again, she could clearly imagine a boot, something heavy soled — a sound which no longer seemed at all imaginary or the product of a rusty radiator.

Recoiling, Natalie fell away from the window as she dropped back to the floor. She tried to land silent as a cat, stifling the scream rising up her throat. Something was out there, or someone, stalking the house under the cloak of darkness. She had to know.

Quietly as she could, Natalie opened the back door on its well-oiled hinges (*thank goodness for that silence*). Slipping sideways, she ventured out into the chilly night air. The rain that had fallen earlier turned the ground spongey beneath her feet, and her eyes soon adjusted to the darkness.

She could now make out the shape of a nearby tree, its branches like spindly arms scraping the sky. The chirp of tree frogs filled her ears, but Natalie wasn't interested in any of these sounds. She was on the lookout for whatever creature — or person — had broken that stick. Her eyes scanned the foreground, her nerves on edge. Nothing. No sound. No movement at all.

A dream. She must have suffered another one of her waking dreams.

Call it what it is, she told herself. *A hallucination.*

She was about to head back into the house when the sensation of movement behind her made her turn around and look at that tree again. She was sure something was there. The wind picked up. Branches swayed. When the wind died, all went still. Then it picked up again, and as it did, a slim shadow slowly emerged from behind the tree. Natalie had hoped for an animal, but this figure appeared to stand on two legs.

Soon the shape of a man came into sharp focus, long and lanky, his arms dangling limply at his sides, no hurry in his body language. He was no more than thirty feet from where she stood. Even from that distance, Natalie could see the gun in the man's right hand, the barrel like a finger pointing toward the muddy earth. His arm rose, and before Natalie knew it, that gun was pointed right at her.

She gasped as the shadowy man moved toward her. Without hesitating, Natalie dashed back into the house, slamming the door behind her — as if that would shield her from a bullet. She raced up the stairs, her feet thundering on the wood steps. Terror clutched at her throat.

"Wake up! Wake up!" she banged on the

doors to her children's rooms. Kate heard the commotion and burst into the hallway, disoriented and frightened. She was dressed in a white nightgown, her hair a Medusa-like tangle.

"What's going on?" she asked breathlessly.

Natalie could barely get out the words.

"I heard someone inside the house," she said in a panic-drenched voice. "I thought I might have dreamt it, but then I heard a different sound, a stick breaking outside, so I went to have a look, and saw him, a man. He's here, Kate. I don't know how, but Michael's found me."

"Chuck," Kate cried out as she rummaged through her bedroom closet. "Get up. We've got trouble."

Moments later, Kate emerged from her closet wielding a shotgun. Addie and Bryce had stepped out from their respective bedrooms into the hallway to join the commotion, both groggily rubbing at their eyes.

"What's going on?" asked Addie with an anxious tremor. Fearing another asthma attack, Natalie found a measure of calm.

"It's all okay. Come with me, children," she said, as she ushered them into her bedroom. Natalie closed the door behind them, shutting her kids inside, while she remained in the hallway to debrief Kate.

"He was hiding behind the big tree outside the kitchen," she said. "He has a gun."

"You stay here with the kids." Kate spoke with authority — an order, not a request — before turning her attention back to her bedroom. "Dammit, Chuck, hurry up!" she cried out.

"Shouldn't we call the police?" Natalie asked nervously.

Kate laughed to highlight the absurdity.

"Out here? These parts? By the time they got here we'd all be Swiss cheese."

She hefted the shotgun in her hands.

"This is the only authority we need. Chuck! Let's go!"

Chuck, wearing an untied camel-colored robe, his patterned boxers showing along with an ample belly, came plodding along with shuffling steps.

"Yeah, yeah, yeah," he said, checking the gun in his hand, a pistol of some sort, to make sure it was loaded.

"I need someone to guard the kids," Natalie said. "Chuck, can you wait out in the hall? I'll come with you, Kate. I'll show you where I saw him."

Kate seemed to know when a fight wasn't going to go her way.

"Okay," she said. "Chuck, keep an eye out."

Moments later, Natalie and Kate were standing together on the rain-soaked ground in the back of the house. Kate wielded a powerful flashlight she had procured from the kitchen on their way outside. She trained the beam at the tree out back, moving from left to right then back again.

Nothing.

Emboldened, Kate went to the tree. Natalie stayed behind.

"Kate, be careful."

Kate was shining the light on something Natalie couldn't see, so she approached.

"The wind may have knocked down this branch," Kate said.

Sure enough, a long branch swayed back and forth close to the ground, clinging perilously to the tree by a sliver of wood. Kate aimed her flashlight at the base of the tree.

"Honey, the ground is muddy from rain, but there are no footprints here," she said.

The flashlight cast a glow, allowing Natalie to see sympathy brimming in Kate's eyes.

"Nat, did you get any sleep tonight?" she asked. "Have you been sleeping at all?"

Natalie pursed her lips in a tight grimace.

"I didn't imagine it," she said. "I saw a shadow in the hallway. I heard a knock, footsteps outside my door. There was a man out here." She pointed to the tree. "I saw him. I heard him."

Kate tugged at the branch.

"With everything going on, this could easily look like a person. And this branch here might look like a gun."

She pulled Natalie into an embrace.

"Nat, whatever you heard, whatever you thought you saw, it came from your mind, not from behind this tree."

There was a moment, brief as a breath, when Natalie could pick up her friend's thoughts hanging in the silence between them.

Have you become paranoid? Is the threat of Michael real or imagined?

Natalie now feared that she'd come to the wrong place. Hildonen Farms wouldn't be her safe harbor if Kate believed the children could be in danger under her care.

CHAPTER 35

Michael

He found Kennett hanging out in the bar at the Renaissance Hotel in Toledo, where they decided to spend another night to rest, recharge, and come up with a new game plan. The bar, like the hotel itself, was more serviceable than fancy. Fine place to sit and have a drink and decompress — which Michael desperately needed to do.

His hair still felt damp from a refreshing shower, and from the looks of it, Kennett had cleaned up as well. Wearing a blue polo, signature blazer draped over the back of his barstool, Michael got a good look at the detective's fit physique. Kennett sipped a drink idly from an ice-filled tumbler, appearing quite relaxed for a guy who'd been chasing bad leads across the Midwest. Kennett's cop sense must have kicked in when Michael arrived, because he spun around on his stool to issue him a greeting before

414

Michael had a chance to say a single word.

"Hey there, Mikey," Kennett said as he patted the stool next to him. Before Michael could get settled in his seat, Kennett handed him a drink menu.

"Get anything you want, Mike," Kennett said, "and by anything, I mean nothing that costs more than twenty bucks."

Kennett gave a little chuckle, but Michael knew he was also being serious, so he ordered a Wild Turkey, neat.

"How you doing there?" Kennett asked. "I know it's hard to come so close and yet be so far."

Kennett eyed Michael up and down carefully the way a doctor might when giving a patient an exam.

"I'm a little discouraged, to be honest," Michael admitted. "I don't think I'm cut out to do your job."

He took a long, slow drink of his bourbon, embracing the burn as it settled in his throat.

Kennett huffed his agreement — or disagreement, Michael wasn't entirely sure.

"Look, I appreciate everything you've done to help me. But maybe we should end it. I'll pay for your flight back to Boston, New York, wherever you want to go. I'll stay and look for Natalie and the kids because

I'm sure they're somewhere in the Midwest. You've got big violent crimes to solve. I'm grateful for your help, I really am, but this is my problem to solve."

Michael would have paid double the airfare to rid himself of the uncertainty and guilt that came with having Kennett's help.

"To be honest with ya, Mike," Kennett said with a laissez-faire air, "looking for your wife has made me rethink my job. I guess I didn't realize how much I needed a break from the violence. Seeing what people do to each other, how callous and cruel they can be, living with that day in and day out *really* gets to you."

Again, Michael shifted uneasily in his stool. He didn't like the way Kennett kept looking at him, as if he were a part of that problem.

"I imagine those cases stay with you," said Michael, who spoke too brightly for the subject, but he'd done so with the hope of easing some of the odd tension between them.

"Stays with you like ghosts," Kennett answered wistfully. "Even when you put the bad guys where they belong, it doesn't take the sting out of it. You still saw what you saw. That never goes away. No matter how much time a perp spends behind bars, the memory of what they did lingers."

"I bet," replied Michael, who kept his response intentionally brief. He hoped his message to Kennett was clear: *let's change the subject.* To drive that point home, Michael turned his attention to the TV above the bar, which was broadcasting some sports game — didn't matter what or who was playing. Better that than meeting Kennett's hard stare, which Michael could feel like a cold hand gripping the back of his neck.

"You know what's really hard to take, Mike? What sticks with you the longest?" Kennett said brusquely. He didn't seem to mind that he was addressing the back of Michael's head.

Michael didn't want to ask, didn't want to avert his gaze from the TV, but Kennett rapped his knuckles against the bar to make sure the focus went to him. "I'm talking the *really* hard cases."

Once again, Michael felt forced to face Kennett. "No," he said, as a tight band closed around his throat.

An unsettling gleam entered Kennett's eyes. He seemed to be relishing Michael's evident unease.

"I bet you think it's the cold cases," said Kennett. "Most people do, and sure, those are tough, but you still have a hope you'll get your perp. It could be next week, next year, a decade from now, and that kind of keeps you going."

"I'm sure it does," Michael seconded.

"The hard cases, Mike," Kennett went on, as if he were giving a lecture, "are the ones when you *get* your guy, dead to rights, you've got 'em, you know who did it, and yet they still walk free. A technicality during the arrest, a blown case in court — whatever the reason, you have your killer, no question about it, but they walk. Those are the cases that really haunt you. That's the shit you don't ever forget. I've got a long memory for that kind of thing. That's what I've got. A long memory. Blessing and a curse."

Kennett downed his drink in one long gulp. Michael heard the ice cubes rattling inside the tumbler like a pair of casino dice, a reminder that accepting Kennett's offer to help find Natalie was definitely a gamble. With the drink gone, Kennett tapped the bar, ordered another. It felt as if a harsh wind had blown through the room, chilling Michael to the bone.

"It's only happened a handful of times in my career, but the first one — now that was the hardest of them all, because it was personal."

"I guess we're going there," Michael mumbled to himself, feeling pressured to look Kennett in the eyes. Again, he didn't like what he saw.

"I didn't find the body," Kennett began. "A jogger did. Hell, that's why I don't run. Joggers always find the body."

If that was supposed to get a laugh out of Michael, it didn't.

"She was sixteen years old, beautiful girl, whole life in front of her. I wasn't much older, twenty-three at the time, new on the force, a rookie cop who came from a family of cops. Her killer strangled her and then slit her throat from ear to ear before dumping her body in a marsh. She'd been missing for two weeks. Wasn't a pretty sight when we found her."

"Grim," said Michael, trying to ignore his growing unease.

Ghosts.

Michael tried to calm himself.

It's going to be a serial killer . . . not a boyfriend . . .

"Didn't take long for us to lock in on a suspect," said Kennett. "The boyfriend. Dated her two years and she'd recently called it off."

Oh shit . . .

Where was it? When did it happen? Her

419

name . . . what's her name?

Michael wasn't sure how to ask those questions without implicating himself in the process.

Kennett continued.

"Phone records showed the victim was in touch with this guy at least three times before her murder. The mother wasn't too keen on the relationship. Didn't want her daughter dating anybody. Real strict, religious type — not that there's anything wrong with that, but it created a lot of friction at home."

Mother's name is Helen.

"Mom tried a number of times to force a breakup, but the boyfriend always managed to win her back, until that one time he didn't."

Michael sat stone-faced and still as the dead. Every word Kennett spoke upped his anxiety another degree.

"I wasn't a detective back then, but I was on the case, helping out, doing my part, whatever was asked of me. See, I knew the girl, Mike — went to the same church. Knew her and her sister from a distance. Nice family, everyone knew them."

"Where was that?" Michael asked. An anxious flutter entered his belly when he

420

thought, *Rye. He's going to say, Rye, New York.*

Instead, Kennett waved off the question.

"A city in Westchester County, you probably haven't heard of it, doesn't matter anyway." His expression told a different story. Michael let it slide. He got his answer. Rye was in Westchester County.

"The boyfriend was persistent. Gotta give him that. Kept calling her at work, harassing her, that sort of thing."

"Young love can be tough," Michael said, forcing the words out of a throat so dry it hurt him to swallow.

"Or, it can be a deadly obsession."

Kennett's face remained grim as Michael let his gaze drift to the floor.

"She had a big heart, though, told her friends she was going to go see him after her shift ended. She scooped ice cream for a job."

Michael thought: *Sweet Licks on Bartlett Avenue.*

From out of nowhere, Michael caught the scent of vanilla. It wasn't the same air freshener the Marriott Marquis used to spruce up their hotel rooms. No, this vanilla smell was a blend of cream and sugar. It was a scent from his past, a spectral fragrance that wafted in the air before it

421

dispersed into nothingness. Kennett didn't seem to notice Michael's attention drifting to another place and time; didn't call out the pain that crossed his face. If Kennett did observe these changes he ignored them intentionally, as if to bask in Michael's growing discomfort, not wanting it to end.

A light above Michael's head seemed to grow brighter. As it did, he heard a strange hum, like a buzz from a surge of electricity. He knew it wasn't the room lights going wonky, at least not any lights in this room. No, these were lights from a different place and time, a police interview room from long ago. The buzz that rang in his ears was a sound that haunted him; all these years later, Michael could still hear that buzz.

Detective Troy Emmett expressed skepticism by way of the cold stare he sent Joseph's way. Four feet of table was all that separated him from his interrogator. Joseph didn't know how many hours he'd been in that cramped room — more than four — and he felt like they were going in circles. Judging by Emmett's exasperated sigh, the hand he ran through his short, dark hair, the detective was feeling the same.

"I just want to know the why, Joseph. Why did you kill her?"

"I told you, I didn't," Joseph said.

He was eighteen. An adult. Mom and Dad couldn't come to his rescue. He was on his own.

Emmett's dark, expressive eyes narrowed. An overhead light buzzed like a bug trap zapping a kill on a summer's eve.

"Come on now, Joseph. I'm not stupid, and neither are you. We both know she went to see you. You two broke up. From all accounts, it was a pretty charged split, too. Lots of emotion. Did she say something to you? Did she embarrass you? We try to answer the whys. That's why we're still in this room. Maybe you just went to meet up with Brianna and you snapped, you freaked out, not saying you planned it. It was a moment when you lost control. I'm not going to bullshit you, Joseph, there are consequences regardless, but it could be vastly different if it's manslaughter."

"I told you. I went to meet her at the park, but when I got there she was gone. I saw a car, a red one, but I don't remember the make or model, parked next to her car. Maybe she's got a new boyfriend. I dunno. I just know she wasn't there when I showed up."

"A lot of people use that park, Joseph, so the car doesn't mean that much to us. But her going there to meet you does, and now she's dead. Someone cut her throat open."

Emmett again showed Joseph a forensic

photo of Brianna Sykes's mutilated body. As before, Joseph held a placid expression despite the shocking grotesqueness of the visual. He knew Emmett was trying to get a rise out of him, and Joseph was too aware to take the bait.

Emmett continued, "The door is closing on your chance to tell us the truth. This is the time to tell your story, before the entire town forms a story of its own. I can only throw you the rope, man. You've got to grab it."

"I told you the truth, I went to meet her, and when I showed up she wasn't there. There was this red car parked next to her car. I went looking for her, and when I came back to the parking lot the red car was gone, and I never found Brianna."

"What about those scratches on your hand, Joseph? Where did those come from?"

The police had already photographed his hands and wrists. He didn't need to be a criminologist to know the police believed they were defensive wounds.

"I went through a bunch of thickets, branches, whatever, looking for her."

"Because that's what you do when your friend doesn't show up for a meeting? You search the bushes?"

"Her car was there. I thought something had happened to her."

"Something happened to her all right."

Emmett had already read Joseph his Miranda rights, several times in fact. He didn't have to talk, but he wanted to, because he knew what everyone in town was thinking — what his parents were thinking, too, though they didn't come right out and say it. They thought that he did it, that he, Joseph Jacob Saunders, had murdered his ex-girlfriend Brianna Sykes in cold blood.

"It's pretty uncommon to have a sixteen-year-old murdered in a small town like ours," Detective Emmett said. "So you can imagine how upset people are about this case. They want answers, Joseph. And you're going to give them, one way or another."

Joseph shook his head.

He wanted to cry. He desperately wanted those tears to come. They would look good for the detective.

"Not a moment goes by when I'm not thinking of Brianna, when I don't ask myself what would have happened if I wasn't late getting to the park, if I got there even five minutes sooner. Would she still be alive?"

Emmett didn't have to roll his eyes for Joseph to know the detective wasn't buying it.

"Tell me again why you were late?"

"I stopped to get us sandwiches. And there was a line. It took longer than I thought."

"You have the receipt for those sand-wiches?"

"No, I left. Like I said, it was taking too long."

He heard Emmett mutter, "How convenient."

"I don't want to talk to you anymore," Joseph said.

"Are you exercising your right to remain silent?"

"I am."

"Okay, then. The interview is over."

It was back to his holding cell. His arraignment was in the morning. He didn't want his father there. His father came yesterday, and it was no surprise he made it all about himself, making a point to say how hard it was to be the talk of the town.

Joseph lost his temper, of course he did. He screamed at his father to go to hell and the guards had to come subdue him. That temper, always getting him in trouble — but his dad asked for it, didn't he? It was Joseph's life on the line, but somehow his dad was the one suffering the most.

He could do without seeing his mother, too. She'd smile tightly, tell him she loved him, but he could read her eyes just the same. And those eyes of hers would say one word:

Guilty.

The memory faded. Michael was back in

the bar, but the interview room and Detective Emmett were never far from his thoughts. Any doubts Michael had harbored about Kennett's motivation for helping him find Natalie were gone. This wasn't about his missing wife — Kennett was here because of him. The story he'd told about the girl in the marsh might in fact be the first honest thing to come out of the detective's mouth since the start of their journey.

Kennett was here because he wanted what the courts couldn't get: justice for Brianna.

"She told her coworker they were going to meet at the park. She was going to try to calm him down," Kennett said with the dispassion of a police report. "I guess he was really upset about the breakup. She was a sweetheart; very thoughtful girl. If you knew her, you'd know she'd care, put his needs before her own. When she didn't come home, her father called the police to report her missing. Then, weeks later, that jogger found her."

"What about the boyfriend?" Michael asked, willing the shake from his voice.

"He was put on trial. We thought we had a good case. Really strong. He was at the scene of the crime. He had a motive."

"But no murder weapon."

Michael said it like a statement, not a

question, because he knew the answer. He could have finished Kennett's sentences about the case and trial if he wanted to.

"Nope. No weapon ever found. There was a second car, or so the boyfriend claimed, a red one, make and model unknown, and some grainy surveillance footage to back up his story, and that helped put additional doubt in the mind of the jury."

"And no forensics, either, I bet," said Michael.

"Good guess there, Mike," Kennett said. "No forensics. But that was a long time ago. DNA testing wasn't much back then."

"So are you going to try the guy again with new evidence?"

Kennett smiled wickedly.

"Can't do that, Mike, you know that. Double jeopardy."

"So how you gonna rid yourself of that ghost?" Michael couldn't mask the tension in his voice. "It's a lot for you to carry around."

"Once a killer, always a killer, Mike," Kennett said calmly. "Unfortunately, that means someone else will have to die before I can get my man. Not wishing for it, of course, but like I said, once a killer, always a killer. I'd say the odds of it happening again are kind of in my favor."

CHAPTER 36

Natalie

Before She Disappeared

She told Michael she was going on a business trip.

To sell her story, Natalie did what was expected. She packed an overnight bag, her small black one, since she'd only be gone a day. She made sure Michael had the number of the hotel in Connecticut where she'd be staying. She'd made arrangements for Addie and Bryce to stay with her parents. She sold this as a benefit, but there was no way she'd allow her children to be alone in the care of a murderer.

"Mom's been wanting them for an overnight for ages, and weekends are so busy lately," Natalie explained, giving it her best acting job, worried that she was laying it on a bit too thick. "Let them miss a day of school. What difference will it make?"

None. Michael agreed readily without

argument, probably because he didn't want the responsibility. Natalie mused that maybe he already had a new woman on the side.

She took all the right precautions. If Michael got suspicious for any reason and checked the hotel, there wouldn't be a problem, as she'd made and paid for the reservation, but there was no meeting to attend. Instead, she headed across state lines into New York.

The day was warm. Bright sunshine filled the sky, though her mood remained dark. Each mile traveled put her that much closer to an encounter she wasn't sure she could handle.

Port Chester Harbor loomed on her right as she traversed the bridge on the Connecticut Turnpike, but a steady stream of construction projects soon obstructed the view. Eventually, she found herself navigating the leafy streets of Rye, New York, which featured sprawling colonials right up next to each other on nicely manicured lawns. A GPS phone app guided Natalie to her destination, 14 Rockaway Road, on which stood a single-story, cedar-shingled home, far more modest than any of the neighboring homes.

Natalie parked in the driveway behind a silver Mercedes. She got as far as putting

430

her hand on the door handle, but couldn't muster the courage to exit her car, so she made a phone call instead.

"I can't go through with it," Natalie lamented to Tina.

"Yes, you can," her friend offered encouragingly. "You have no choice."

By this point, Tina knew the whole story. She understood why Natalie was here, and why it was so difficult to take that next step.

"Okay, okay, I'm going," Natalie said as if she were about to leap from a plane. "I'm doing it."

"That's my girl," replied Tina with a smile in her voice. "Call me right after. You got this."

Natalie said a brief goodbye, then let out an audible exhale. She exited her car and headed for the front door, taking purposeful strides as though she were expected, which she was not.

She set her finger on the doorbell, her heart beating wildly. She hesitated. Pressing that button meant no turning back. Natalie thought of leaving, driving home, forgetting everything, but she stayed right where she was. She'd come here on a mission, partly to get answers, and partly to give them.

She rang the doorbell, then waited with her arms folded across her chest. Even though she wasn't at work, Natalie had come dressed for a business meeting, in a single-button blazer, gray turtleneck, and slimming dark pants. She paid special attention to her hair and makeup. It was important to her that she made a good first impression.

A few moments later, an older woman came to the door. She was slender, in her seventies. Hers was a pretty face, although deep worry lines suggested the years had taken a toll. A pair of ice-blue eyes peered out at Natalie through the glass of the storm door.

The older woman appraised her visitor questioningly, making it quite clear that she didn't recognize Natalie, had never even seen a picture of her. The woman looked familiar to Natalie though. She had Michael's prominent nose, the round shape of his eyes, and dimples that had been passed on to her son.

She opened the screen door wide enough to be polite, while maintaining some barrier between them.

"May I help you?" the woman asked. speaking in a low tone that carried an air of sophistication and culture.

"Marjorie Saunders?"

"Yes? I'm Marjorie."

A hint of concern seeped into the older woman's eyes.

What's this about? she was asking.

"I was wondering if I might have a word with you." Natalie clasped her hands together in front of her waist, feeling moisture collect on her palms.

"Do I know you?"

There was confusion in Marjorie's face and voice.

That confirmed it. Michael had never told his mother that he had a wife, probably hadn't shared that he had children — her grandchildren. Chances were this poor woman, whom Natalie believed had died of cancer decades ago, hadn't seen or heard from her son since the day he changed his name.

"We don't know each other," Natalie said quickly, her voice coming out soft and uncertain. "We've never met, but I know you — well, I sort of know you. God, this is awkward." She paused, sighed, while collecting her thoughts. Finally, she gave up on tact and settled for a more direct approach. "Maybe it's best if I get right to the purpose for my visit. I'm your son's wife, Natalie. I've been married to your son for nineteen years, though I know him as Michael Hart, and I've only recently found out that he

433

changed his name."

Marjorie's controlled manner held, but her face lost all expression, as if she'd slipped into a shell for protective purposes. It wasn't long before the color returned to her cheeks. She appeared to be dazed, slightly off-kilter. Natalie too was feeling unsteady on her feet, as if the ground beneath her had given way. Eventually, Marjorie pressed her hands together, setting them to her lips in a silent prayer.

"I should have been prepared for this," she said. A shift took place before Natalie's eyes, as if Marjorie had resigned herself to her fate. "You're pretty," she said. "I'm not surprised. My son always had a thing for the pretty girls."

"Thank you," Natalie said, feeling quite awkward and unsure how to respond.

"I saw the news reports," Marjorie continued. "This is about Audrey Adler, isn't it? The murdered girl from Massachusetts."

"Yes, it is, in a way," said Natalie.

"I see." Marjorie lowered her head. "I was afraid of that. I knew her as Audrey Sykes. I guess Adler is her married name. She lived down the street, she —" Marjorie looked to her right, as if she could see into Audrey's home. When she met Natalie's gaze again, her eyes had reddened, but in them fired a fierce determination to maintain control. "He did it again, didn't he? That's why you're here."

Natalie's heart dropped. She felt suddenly faint, almost needing to seize the railings for support.

Again . . .

It was a breathtaking punch to the gut. Part of her had come here hoping for a story that would exonerate her husband, a mother's assurance that her beloved boy was innocent of all charges, that he'd been framed. But no, Marjorie all but confirmed Natalie's worst fears.

Again . . .

Pursing her lips together until they compressed into a thin red line, Marjorie stepped aside to make room for Natalie to enter.

"Please come in."

A sniffle, then a dab at her eyes with her finger, were the only indications that Marjorie's stoicism wouldn't hold for long. Natalie felt deeply sorry for this woman she didn't know, pained to come here bringing her nothing but more grief and sorrow.

No turning back now . . .

Natalie entered the home feeling a burgeoning curiosity about the place where her husband grew up. What was he like as a boy?

What stories would his mother tell? What would Natalie learn of him, and of the woman who should have been her mother-in-law — who, legally, was?

A palette of light blues and whites gave the interior the feeling of an ocean cottage, but the pleasing aesthetic did nothing to soften Natalie's lingering apprehension and worry.

Marjorie escorted Natalie into the living room, where she offered her a seat on a pearled leather armchair. She excused herself to go make tea, giving Natalie a chance to survey her surroundings in an uncomfortable, weighty silence. The home décor had the touch of a professional designer. Everything was visually pleasing, from the vases lining the built-in shelves to the soft wool throw draped over the arm of a pristine couch, but the room itself lacked a personal feel.

Natalie noticed mostly what wasn't there. No pictures of family. No trinkets or knick-knacks of any kind, no mementos from vacations or family gatherings. It was a home that managed to feel both inviting and lonely at the same time. The house and the woman who occupied it appeared to be fitting companions: both were perfectly put together on the outside, but with something notably lacking on the inside.

Marjorie returned some minutes later, bringing with her two tea mugs and a small decorative pot, all of which she carried on a lacquered tray.

"Cream or sugar?" she asked.

"No," said Natalie, who moved uneasily in her chair. She was having a difficult time meeting Marjorie's gaze. "Thank you for your hospitality. I know this is a lot to take in."

Marjorie nodded solemnly.

"It is," she said, managing to maintain her control, which Natalie took to mean that Marjorie was either still in shock — or she had the game face of the century.

"So what did he tell you about me?" she asked.

"The truth?"

"Please."

Natalie's eyebrows slid up an inch as that uneasy feeling found its way back into her stomach.

How will she take it?

"He'd said that you had died when he was in college. Cancer."

"Did he now?"

Marjorie winced slightly, but her expression quickly reverted to one of impassivity.

"I see," she said.

"He also told me that he grew up in Charleston, South Carolina," Natalie continued, "and that he had a difficult childhood, lots of upheaval and bad memories, which was his excuse for why we never went to visit. Part of those memories involved you."

"And what of his father?" Marjorie asked, shielding her eyes with a lengthy sip of tea. She couldn't as easily hide her hands, which were trembling.

"He said that he'd run off and left you when you got sick."

Marjorie returned a nearly imperceptible nod.

"Well, I suppose that's true, at least in part," she said, adopting a slightly clipped tone.

"What happened to him?" asked Natalie.

"By him, do you mean Joseph or Joseph's father? I'm sorry . . . you know him as — ?"

"Michael," answered Natalie. "Michael Hart. And I guess my question applies to them both. But you know what?"

"What?"

"Let's slow down."

She was seeing Marjorie in a different light, not as a person who had answers, but someone in need of loving kindness and goodwill. Using that as her guide, Natalie decided on her next course of action.

Rising from her chair, Natalie crossed the room over to Marjorie. She placed a hand gently on the older woman's bony shoulder, sending her a look layered with sympathy.

"Before we get into all this history," Natalie said, "I brought you something from my home that I'd like to share. Let me go to my car and get it. Let's start with a lighter topic."

Marjorie sent Natalie an appreciative look, and with that she was off, returning moments later with a white photo album clutched to her chest.

"I'd like you to get to know your grandchildren," she said, encouraging Marjorie to join her on the couch. She did, sitting close enough for their shoulders to touch, and Natalie placed her hand atop of Marjorie's, feeling the delicate bones underneath cool skin thin as rice paper. A lump appeared in Natalie's throat. Her eyes welled. Blinking back tears, she could see Marjorie's eyes filling as well.

"Their names are Addison, Addie for short, and Bryce," Natalie said, giving Marjorie's hand a gentle squeeze.

"Those are very lovely names," said Marjorie as she pried open the album.

After an hour of sharing pictures and

stories of the children, a few tissues needed along the way, Marjorie and Natalie felt more at ease with each other, both relaxing on the couch like two old friends catching up. Following a brief pause in conversation, Marjorie sat up straighter, seemingly resigned to diving into the topic they'd been avoiding.

"I'm not sure where to begin," she said quietly. "You deserve answers, and I'll tell you everything you want to know."

Natalie returned a succession of grim nods.

"Thank you," she said. "I guess what I want to know is what really happened. Why did he change his name and tell me that you had died? I know what I've read in the news reports, but I want to hear it from your perspective."

Marjorie clenched then relaxed her jaw.

"It was a terrible time for us all," she began, breaking eye contact to look out the window, perhaps refocusing her vision on the past. "Joseph and Brianna were dating back then. It didn't seem like there was anything unusual about their relationship. He was older, a senior, and she a sophomore — that was something to keep an eye on.

"The real problem was the mother, Helen. She was a very religious woman, quite strict, and Brianna was something of a rebel, a black sheep, especially compared to her sister, Audrey, who was very much the good girl. Helen worried that my son and her daughter were sexually active, and I don't think she was wrong to be concerned. I believe they were.

"Anyway, she kept coming between them, and eventually she convinced her daughter to break it off for good with Joseph. He was utterly devastated. Wouldn't eat, couldn't sleep, it was just terrible. As a mother, I felt helpless. I just couldn't reach him. He slipped into a dark depression. I'd never seen him so broken."

Natalie felt a stir of sadness thinking of her husband suffering as a teen, flashing on how she'd react if Bryce one day fell into a similar state of despair.

"As you can imagine Brianna's murder was all the town could talk about, think about. There was no escaping it. As soon as Joseph became a suspect, we became prisoners in our own lives."

Marjorie detailed the harrowing search efforts in which Joseph participated, but whispers followed. She shared some of what was said.

He did it. He killed her. He's pretending to cry, to care. Look at him. His hands are cover-

441

ing his eyes because he doesn't want other people to see his guilt. Watch how he's pulling at his shirt. He's nervous. He's literally trying to loosen his collar to get more oxygen.

"I'm ashamed to say that after a while I had a hard time shutting out all the doubters and naysayers. In my heart, I knew my son was innocent — or that's what I told myself. He couldn't have done anything to hurt Brianna. He *loved* her."

Natalie didn't voice her view that love could be a twisted person's reason for murder, a punishment for rejection. It was why she'd been afraid to leave Michael outright and simply ask for a divorce. She feared his retribution.

"His father wasn't nearly as convinced of his innocence. And Joseph had something of a temper. He could be quite explosive at times. His father tried to force a confession out of Joseph. One night I had to call the police because the two got into an extremely heated argument, and I was worried for their safety.

"A few days after that fight, Joseph moved out. He went to stay with a friend; he wouldn't talk to us anymore. My marriage fell apart not long after that. I couldn't stand the sight of my husband. How could he turn his back on his own son? But the damage was done. Joseph, your Michael, wouldn't talk to me anymore. He'd convinced himself that I didn't believe him either, that I was saying one thing to his face and another behind his back."

Marjorie's shoulders were slouched, her face set and sad. Natalie put her mug down on the coffee table. She'd been curious about Michael's father, but wasn't about to ask to see a picture of the man. Let him be a mystery. It was hard enough dealing with the ghosts in this room.

"Our house was vandalized multiple times," said Marjorie. "I couldn't go out, not even to the market, couldn't see friends either. My son was all over the news. The press hounded us day and night. It was relentless.

"Then they found Brianna's body in the Marshlands Conservancy. She was half naked, badly decomposed, her throat slit. Police were able to put Joseph at the scene of the crime, and they felt they had enough for an arrest. What they didn't have was any forensic evidence, and the jury acquitted him on all charges, but that was hardly the end of it. Nobody believed the verdict.

"I was in the courtroom that day, not that Joseph wanted me there. We weren't on speaking terms by that point, but I was there, of course I was. I cried when the verdict was announced. The jury was ushered out of the courthouse under police protection, that's how intense it was, the outrage was everywhere. Even today the verdict still stuns and upsets people — former friends who can't believe my boy walked free and then just disappeared."

"Why did the jury acquit him? Did you ever find out?" Natalie asked, sounding surprised.

"Oh yes." Marjorie gave a derisive little laugh. "The jury felt a pressing need to explain themselves. The problem, they said, was that the prosecution didn't give enough evidence to convict. They gave a lot of circumstantial evidence that made them think that Joseph was involved, that he could have done it, but not beyond a reasonable doubt. The lead prosecutor was also quite vicious and arrogant, and that didn't help the prosecution.

"It didn't hurt that Joseph had a great attorney. He might not have wanted to speak to his parents anymore, but he had no trouble taking our money to pay for his defense. But enough about the past — tell me about Audrey?"

Marjorie sounded desperate to change the subject.

"I'm not sure what to tell," said Natalie, feeling a rush of blood to her ears.

"How did they reconnect, do you know?"

"She worked for my company, they were both members of my corporate gym. I think that's how it happened."

"I see," said Marjorie. She poured more tea into her mug. "I wasn't close with the family for obvious reasons, but I knew that Audrey absolutely adored her older sister."

Natalie felt a heavy weight settle in her chest, one she felt compelled to push off.

"He slept with her," she blurted out. "Michael, my husband, he had an affair with Audrey."

Marjorie's gaze was an abyss, dark and impossible to read.

"I see."

"I don't think she knew it was your Joseph. I think maybe she found out after, and that's why he killed her."

Marjorie nodded her agreement.

"I guess she might not have recognized him — it was so long ago, and she was so young — but he would have remembered her," Marjorie said. She closed her eyes tightly, a portent of more tears, which gave Natalie a sharp pang of guilt for adding to her misery.

"I'm glad you told me," Marjorie said

eventually, which did little to absolve Natalie of her discomfort. "I can't speak to his motives. I don't know my son. But perhaps he was trying to relive his love for Brianna through her sister."

That notion did not sit well with Natalie, who felt nauseated all of a sudden. The idea of Michael's affair serving as a macabre proxy for his first love and murder victim chilled her to the core. While she might not have understood what drove her husband, Natalie harbored no doubts that he and Audrey were romantically involved. What else explained Michael's shirt and gym key inside her apartment? Why else would they have met up in the McDonald's parking lot? What other "Chris," the parent of two children, drummed his fingers nervously? Given the list of parallels Audrey had rattled off that day in Buckley's, it was quite obvious her strong reaction to seeing Michael's picture had come not from a glimpse into her past, but rather one into her present.

"I'm sorry to have laid all this on you," Natalie said, following a tense silence. "You've been through so much, suffered such a terrible ordeal."

Marjorie smiled back sadly.

"Don't feel so sorry for me," she said, a haunted look slipping into her eyes. Her vacant stare only deepened.

"But you've done nothing wrong," Natalie countered. "Michael — I mean Joseph, made his choices."

Invoking the wrong name did not appear to rattle Marjorie. "Don't be so sure of yourself," she answered in a detached manner.

Natalie clutched at her chest.

"What do you mean?" she asked, tentatively.

Marjorie went very still, long enough for Natalie to grow deeply uncomfortable.

"Is everything all right?" Natalie asked.

"Yes and no. Mostly no. Wait here a moment, will you?"

"Of course," said Natalie.

Minutes later, Marjorie returned to the living room, carrying an object wrapped in a terry cloth towel. She lifted one corner of the towel as though unveiling a painting. The falling fabric uncovered a large knife with an intimidating, razor-sharp blade. "I'm sure you know what the red stain is, and I promise you it's not rust.

"It was in his room. I was cleaning it after Joseph moved out, and found it under his mattress when I was making the bed. Soon after, the police showed up with a search warrant, but by then I'd already hidden the knife."

"Is that . . . ?" Natalie couldn't find the words.

"The murder weapon? The one used to kill Brianna? Yes, I believe it is."

"You've . . . you've had it all this time?"

"Yes," said Marjorie, whose eyes had filled again. "And I've kept it hidden for my son all this time. I'm the reason that he got acquitted, and apparently the reason Audrey is now dead. Don't you see, Natalie? I'm no grandmother; I'm no mother at all. I'm as bad as my son, as evil as he is. I've kept this secret all these years, and now I'm giving this to you to do with as you see fit. I don't care what happens to me anymore, honestly I don't, but Natalie, promise me something."

"What?" Natalie said, still unable to believe that she held in her hands a knife with such weight and power. The silver blade had old bloodstains running from the tip all the way down its serrated edge.

"Please protect my grandchildren. No matter what you decide to do with me, with this knife, don't let anything happen to them."

Marjorie began to weep.

CHAPTER 37

Michael

After leaving Kennett at the bar, Michael, utterly shell-shocked, returned to his hotel room in Toledo. But he did not get a minute's sleep — he lay awake in bed, tossing and turning, thinking that any moment Kennett would show up at his door, joined by the officers from the Toledo PD. In Michael's fearful fantasy, Kennett would be dangling handcuffs and a warrant for his arrest, and once again he'd hear his Miranda rights read to him as he was taken back into custody.

The charge would be murder. The victim would be Audrey Adler, aka Audrey Sykes, aka the sister of his first true love, Brianna Sykes.

Michael thought back to the day Natalie had showed him Audrey's picture on her phone. It had been quite a shock when she accused him of infidelity. Of course it was true, he had strayed, but it was so much more.

Some things done can never be undone.

Gazing fixedly at Audrey's picture on Natalie's phone, at those all too familiar blue eyes, Michael was shocked at how close Natalie was to the truth. Just for a moment, he let his guard down, allowed his emotions to take over — and, judging by the way Natalie eyed him with hurt and suspicion, her accusations that quickly followed, it was a moment too long. She knew something was amiss, that Audrey was involved, and that Michael wasn't being completely honest with her.

And he wasn't, not by a long shot.

Michael tried to recover, to stuff his emotions back inside the metaphorical box and adopt a more imperturbable expression. After long years of use, he'd strengthened his lie muscles the way bodybuilders did their biceps.

Forget the affair, Michael told himself. If Natalie knew the truth about him, there'd be no coming back.

Then, everything got worse. Much worse.

He recalled the night he got that phone call. She was hysterical. Demanding that she see him, or else. She'd tell. She'd tell everything. He left the house in a rush, and the next day the news came out.

Audrey was dead. There were no suspects.

He doubted that would stay the case for long, but it did. Nobody figured it out. The police got in touch with him because of one email exchange, but so far nothing came of it because there was nothing tying him directly to the crime.

Even so, he should have guessed Kennett's ulterior motive from the start. He'd even mentioned Audrey's name in the bar that first night. The threat had pulsed before Michael like a neon sign, but he was too consumed with fear about Natalie and the kids to listen to his intuition. Best he could do was to pretend he had nothing to hide when Kennett essentially invited himself into Michael's problem.

Now his greatest threat was sleeping in the room next door — or, if he was like Michael, failing to sleep. Every few minutes, it seemed, Michael found himself out of bed, pacing his hotel room like a prisoner in a cell, peering out the peephole at a fish-eyed view of an empty hallway, then out the third-floor window. There he looked out onto a bleak parking lot, expecting at any minute to see a swarm of police cars rolling in at high speed. But there were no strobe lights, no sirens, and no police came that night.

When would Kennett drop the other shoe? Michael kept asking himself. Obviously he had no intention of arresting him for Brianna's murder. Double jeopardy kept Michael safe there, but Audrey was a different matter. Michael wondered if that was Kennett's angle. Was he playing a game, working Michael undercover, gathering evidence he could later use to make an arrest? Perhaps. But he was also helping to track down Natalie, so Michael decided to tackle one problem at a time.

It was almost morning, and Michael's sleeplessness began to take a physical and mental toll. He felt it in his bones, like a sickness he couldn't shake, a weakness he couldn't overcome. He was utterly out of sorts in both body and mind.

Poor Natalie, he thought. Once again he was reminded of his thoughtlessness in ignoring her suffering — or worse, losing his temper when she couldn't do the simplest tasks. Insomnia was an insidious beast, a predator of the mind.

If he got out of this quagmire, if he somehow managed to fix the unfixable, Michael vowed to change. He was done living a life of lies. He'd come clean about everything.

Well, almost everything.

As dawn came, Michael decided to shower. He didn't know what the day would bring, but he was going to be clean and shaved when he faced it. Toledo was obviously a dead end, but where to go from here, Michael couldn't say. All he knew was that the more time he and Kennett spent together, the more chances there'd be for him to say or do something incriminating.

The shower's scalding water didn't wash away Michael's worry. He stood under the showerhead, hands braced against the slick tile, thinking of memories Kennett had conjured up for him of another time many years ago, a party Michael had attended when everything started to unravel.

Without that party, Michael wouldn't be in Toledo with Kennett, would probably be married to someone else, have different kids. Without that party, and what happened that night, his life would have been entirely different.

The place was packed with sweaty teens. A teacher was there, too. Mr. Oman. He was cool, though. In his twenties, not long out of college, taught chem, wasn't a dick. He was drinking out of a red plastic cup like everyone else. Nobody was going to rat on him. He could score weed.

The party punch was spiked with so much vodka that a match held too close might have set the place ablaze. They were partying at Toby's house because his parents were out of town and they didn't give a shit anyway. Rye had just beaten Harrison 34–14 and after the game, everyone gathered at Toby's for a big celebratory party. That's where he first saw Brianna. She was young, just a sophomore, but he didn't let that stop him.

She was a cheerleader, hot as hell, with legs longer than a mile and a smile like a sunbeam. He'd had his share of girlfriends (a benefit of being athletic and good-looking), but Brianna was something else. Sure, she was young, but he didn't let her age or those pom-poms deter him. She was confident. Wasn't at all intimidated to talk to a senior, much less one who was captain of the soccer team, member of the National Honor Society, yearbook president, and spent four years in honors choir.

He sought her out, waited until she was alone, before approaching. She wasn't drinking, but he offered her some of his. She refused.

"It's not my thing," she said. "My mom would kill me if she caught me drinking."

He didn't know much about her mother back then, but he'd find out later just how uncompromising she could be.

Brianna had no trouble holding her own in conversation. She was flirtatious, playing with her hair, giggling at his jokes, and sending lingering looks, which he quite enjoyed, but he sensed there was something underneath her bubbly exterior. He was intrigued to find out if his instincts were right.

"So, is your mom really that strict?" he asked.

"She's super religious," Brianna said, sounding annoyed, like religion wasn't her thing. "Let's just say she'd be really upset if she knew I was here. I'm not allowed to go to parties with boys."

He almost spit out his drink.

"What party has only girls? Hell, I'd like to go there."

That got another coquettish laugh.

"What I mean is she really wants me to just hang out with kids from my church."

"Well, that certainly isn't me," he said. "Last time I went to church I think Jesus was alive."

She laughed again. They talked for hours that night, and after a while it felt like there was nobody else at the party but the two of them. Nobody else mattered. She was easy to talk to, bright as could be, so well-read,

455

and she understood it all, too. English was his worst subject. He didn't get a sense that she was too hung up on her religion when they kissed as the party was coming to an end, his hands traveling up and down her body, their tongues greedily finding each other.

They began dating, hot and heavy, and he got to know her mom, Helen — aka "Bane of his Existence" — pretty well. She kept coming between them, trying to force a breakup, but by then Brianna was hooked on him and he on her. He'd never done heroin, but he'd learned about it in health class, and felt certain that for him, she was that drug in human form.

Days blurred into weeks, into months, until his time in high school was coming to an end, but not his time with Brianna, or at least that was his desire. Once again, they were at Toby's place, this time for the big blowout end-of-the-year party.

Most of the kids there were headed off to college in the fall. That was his plan, too. He was eighteen. Wasn't sure where he was going. It was already spring and he hadn't decided on Rutgers or Penn State, or what he'd major in — probably econ — but he was open to general business studies, too. It had been a good run, four years at Rye High. He'd done his share of soccer games, three years of lax, before "senioritis" set in hard and he gave it all up for more time with friends, red plastic cups, and most importantly, Brianna.

But Brianna was being quiet that night. She didn't want him to go off to college and find another girl. At least that's what he was thinking when she pulled him aside, away from a loud crew playing beer pong, to step onto the patio and talk in private about something important that was on her mind.

"I can't see you anymore," she blurted out. No buildup, no warning, just a punch delivered right to the solar plexus. For a moment he couldn't breathe.

"My mom is serious this time," she said. "If I keep seeing you, she's going to send me away to a Catholic boarding school."

"She can't do that," he replied with hurt in his voice. "She doesn't run your life."

"Tell that to her," said Brianna sorrowfully.

"Screw it, let's run away."

"I can't." Brianna pulled her hand free from his grasp. "I'm going to be a junior. I'm not running off to get married."

"Who said anything about marriage?" he said, sending her an endearing smile.

She socked him in the arm.

"This is serious," she said. "I can't be with you anymore."

It was as if she took her hand and drove it straight through his chest.

"We're not breaking up," he insisted. He grabbed hold of her arm, squeezing it hard enough for her to wince. He worried his grip might have left a bruise, but he was thinking of the summer, the beach, Brianna in a bikini, all the talking, cuddling, touching, and more that they'd do. He couldn't live without her, that's what he was telling himself.

"I'm sick about it," Brianna said as tears flooded her eyes. "But my mom is insisting. If she even knew I was here seeing you, she'd kill me. But I had to come. Tonight was my only chance to tell you in person. It's got to be over between us."

She bit her bottom lip trying to hold back the tears, but still, they streaked down her face.

"I love you," he said, holding her hands as he gazed deeply into her eyes. The hurt tore through him. He thought he might get sick. In his mind he could feel her body against his, in his bedroom, after having sex — such incredible sex, he'd never had that overwhelming feeling before, and he knew with certainty that he'd never feel this way about another person again.

"Please," he said, pulling her against his chest. He was tearing up as well, but didn't care that his emotions were spilling out. It didn't matter to him that all eyes were on them, watching their every move. They were clearly making a scene. "I can't be without you."

Before Brianna could answer, an angry and all-too-familiar voice called out in the distance.

"Brianna? Brianna? There you are."

Brianna went pale. She turned in the direction of the voice, looking panic-stricken.

"It's my mother."

A moment later an imposing woman stepped into the floodlights from the darkness beyond the patio. She glared at Brianna with eyes ablaze.

"I thought you were here."

Brianna hung her head, saying nothing.

"Let's go," her mother said, taking Brianna by the arm, pulling her away.

Before she could depart, he reached out a hand, seizing hold of Brianna's other arm, pulling her in the opposite direction toward him like she was the rope in a tug-of-war. Brianna wrung herself free from his grasp.

"Don't make it worse," she implored. Turning to her mother she said, "How'd you find me?"

"Audrey overheard you talking to your friends about this party, and her guilty conscience finally got the better of her. You could learn a thing or two from your sister about honesty. We'll talk more when we get home."

"She doesn't have to go with you," he said.

Brianna's mother approached, radiating enough anger to throw off heat.

"Don't you dare tell me what to do, young man," she scolded him. "Brianna told me that you two had broken up months ago. I guess that's just more of her lies. I've said from the start that she is way too young to be dating. And if she's ever going to date again it will be someone from church, not someone like you with shallow morals and a predatory nature.

"Now let's go, young lady."

He watched, enraged, as Helen dragged Brianna away. He ran after them, but Toby, who had fifty extra pounds on him, locked him in a bear hug.

"Let it be," he said.

When she was gone he smashed a beer bottle on the patio. Glass shards scattered in all directions.

"It's not ending this way," he seethed to Toby. "I won't let her leave me like this."

Months later, Toby would recount that conversation for the jury while on the witness stand.

The memory sat in Michael's throat. He toweled off, still thinking about that party, of Brianna, but soon found himself reminiscing about another party — this one from the night he met Natalie. He hadn't thought

460

of that night in quite some time, but memories can be like an avalanche, one triggering another.

In his mind, he was back in his friend Morgan's crowded apartment. He was at the tail end of his mid-twenties, living in Boston of all places (odd, given his prior love for the Yankees and New York sports teams in general), figuring out life, working his first job in finance. In she came, and it was like Brianna all over, a light surrounding her like a glow around the moon. She was different, special, he could tell with just one look.

He and Morgan worked together, so he knew most of the people at the party. They were part of a party circuit, with the same people, same drinks, different locations. This particular woman had never come to any of those parties before; he would have remembered her. He was curious now, all these years later, how Natalie came to be at Morgan's that night, setting his life on a different path.

He dried off, put on clothes, got ready for the day, whatever the day would bring, still trying to recall why she was there. Who brought her? She'd come with someone who knew Morgan, but he couldn't remember who it was. His vague memory slowly formed a picture of a blond woman at Natalie's side, cute as well, but they were young and everyone was cute back then.

He tried to recall if Natalie had mentioned this person's name on their walk around the block that night, or what they even talked about. It was no use. He remembered their first conversation had been a good one. Same as with Brianna, they didn't stay in the shallow end of the pool for long.

Michael wouldn't have given that night much thought if he hadn't been obsessed with finding his wife. Every name mattered now. Even though it was early, he decided to text Morgan. He and Morgan weren't particularly close anymore, but she was still in his contacts, and he was on her Christmas card list.

After apologizing for maybe waking her, he asked if she remembered how Natalie had ended up at her party on the night they met. He told her it might be important, but that he'd explain later. As it turned out, Morgan didn't have to think long to give him a name.

Kate Hildonen, she wrote back.

Michael remembered the name. Morgan reminded Michael that Natalie and Kate were once college roommates, and that they worked together before Kate had moved back to her family's dairy farm. It was coming back to him now. The woman who had technically introduced them wasn't at their wedding. He recalled that Natalie hadn't seen Kate after she moved away, but they had been very close beforehand.

Morgan texted back that she hadn't been in touch with Kate in years, but thought that her farm was located in Missouri. Michael searched the name on Google, and sure enough, he found Hildonen Farms in Elsberry.

Michael sourced his list of names, all of the friends and acquaintances that he and Natalie had in common. Most of the names were crossed out. Kate's name wasn't even on the list. But she was the only one who lived in the Midwest.

Michael thought: *She sent us north while she went south.*

He thanked Morgan. Told her he'd be in touch. He left his hotel room and went to Kennett's. He knocked on the door, half expecting Kennett to greet him with handcuffs.

Screw it, Michael said to himself. He was in too deep to back out now.

Kennett opened the door dressed in a gray suit, white shirt, and tie, like he was going to work.

"Mikey," he said with a cheerful smile and tone, not looking at all like a detective about to make an arrest. "I was just going to call you for breakfast. Get any sleep last night?"

He gave him a telling smile, which set Michael ill at ease. He ignored the insinuation and his own discomfort.

"I think I know where she is," he said.

He told Kennett about Morgan, the party, and Kate Hildonen.

"Damn good detective work, damn good," Kennett said. "I like it, Mike. Like the lead." Kennett went to his closet, got out his suitcase, tossed it on the bed, and threw some clothes inside. He looked over at Michael, who stood impassively in the doorway, watching.

"What are you doing, Mike?" Kennett asked. "Go pack. Time's a-wasting. We've got to get ourselves to Missouri."

Four hours, two pee stops, one driver change, one fast-food drive-through, and one gas station refill later, Michael's cell phone rang. The caller ID came up: *InLaws*. He answered the call, finding Lucinda, not Harvey, on the other end of the phone.

"We know where she is," Lucinda said. "I just got off a call with her friend Kate Hildonen. She's very worried about Natalie's health. Said she's not well and may need help."

Michael sent Kennett, who was doing the driving at the time, a big thumbs-up. He mouthed the words: *We got her.*

"Thank you, Lucinda," said Michael. "Please get back in touch with Kate. Make sure she doesn't say anything to Natalie. We were actually headed to Kate's farm when you called. I had a feeling she might be there. We should arrive soon enough. This nightmare will be over very shortly."

CHAPTER 38

Natalie

The morning brought a day full of bright sunshine along with cloudless blue skies. The chatter of farm life chorused in through her open bedroom window. Natalie's ears tuned into the sounds of cows lowing in their enclosures, the steady hum of machinery, and the noise a breeze made as it rustled the trees and grassy fields. The smell of damp soil held a rejuvenating freshness, as if last night's rainstorm had come to wash the earth clean. A new day should have felt like a new start, but Natalie still carried memories of the night before. She pondered shadows that were never there, knocks that never sounded, and snapping branches that echoed like a threat.

Up from the kitchen wafted the smell of bacon sizzling on the griddle and buttery pancakes hot off the stove. Natalie had mercifully fallen asleep at some point and didn't hear the children go downstairs. She arrived in the kitchen to find Addie and Bryce greedily eating breakfast. Out the window she spied Chuck working on the banged-up old tractor Bryce loved to sit on and pretend to ride.

"Chuck thinks he can get it to run again," Bryce said, beaming. "He said he'd take me for a ride on it."

"Sounds wonderful," said Natalie while checking over the sorry state of that vehicle, thinking if anyone could fix it, she'd put her money on Chuck.

"Have you seen Kate?" Natalie asked Addie.

The time had come.

"She left with Hank," Addie said.

A knot of worry formed at the base of Natalie's neck, but she told herself it was nothing, unrelated to her fear that Kate was no longer her trusted confidante.

"Oh? Did she say where?"

"One of the calves got sick and she had to bring it to the vet in a trailer. She left in a hurry."

"I see," said Natalie.

She sent Kate a text asking about the calf and got an answer right away that she was going to live, but they'd be some time at the vet. Natalie took care of the breakfast dishes while Addie and Bryce set off to go sweep the barn, a chore that Kate had assigned them that morning.

Some time turned out to be most of the day. During that period, Chuck made good headway on the tractor, managing to get the engine running again.

"I'll let Bryce put his hands on the wheel, but I'll do the driving," he said, with a chuckle.

Natalie was watering the garden when she finally crossed paths with Kate, but the air between them hadn't cleared in their time apart. If anything, it felt worse — almost like Kate, who was barely able to maintain eye contact, wished she'd avoided the garden altogether.

Nevertheless, Natalie decided for the direct approach.

"We need to talk," Natalie said firmly, encouraging Kate to follow her into the house, and then to the living room. When they got settled in chairs, Natalie raised her concern. "Something is up between us," she said. "It's quite obvious to me, and I suspect it has to do with last night. I admit my imagination may have gotten the better of me, Kate, but there's a reason I'm not sleeping, something I think you should know."

Natalie straightened her body as if

strengthening her resolve.

"Okay," Kate said. "Talk to me."

Natalie reminded Kate of Michael's affair and how she'd come to believe he was responsible for Audrey Adler's death.

"What I didn't tell you is that Michael knew Audrey from before, from long ago."

Kate listened intently as Natalie recalled discovering Audrey's body, Sarah Fielding's investigation, her search for the missing birth certificate, and the reverse image search that led to a shocking discovery. Then Natalie made her big reveal: that Audrey was the sister of the woman Michael had murdered, that his mother hadn't died of cancer, that Michael was born Joseph Jacob Saunders, that he wasn't from South Carolina but rather New York, that he'd gotten off at trial but everyone remained convinced of his guilt, and that Audrey had died at his hands because — and this Natalie said was speculation on her part — Michael's cover was about to be blown.

"If Audrey wasn't murdered, I wouldn't have involved Sarah Fielding and I never would have learned the truth about Michael," Natalie told Kate, who sat stunned and motionless in a checkered wingback chair.

"Honey, is this true?"

Natalie nodded vigorously.

"Of course it is. Why? Do you think I'd lie to you? It's all true, Kate."

To drive home her point, Natalie showed Kate her correspondence with Marjorie Saunders that confirmed every bit of her story. Any lingering doubts Kate may have harbored regarding the veracity of Natalie's story were swept away by the barrage of corroborating evidence — including a picture of young Joseph Jacob Saunders being led away in handcuffs.

Kate put her hand to her mouth, a stunned look on her face.

"What is it?" Natalie asked, sensing her friend's distress.

"I've done something," said Kate.

Natalie's stomach tightened.

"What did you do?" she asked.

"You've been acting so off. Seeing things, hearing things, and then Chuck and I found out that Michael had reported you missing, and included in that report was mention of your insomnia and that you might be delusional."

Kate cut short anything more she had to say. She wrung her hands together with nervous apprehension.

"What did you do?" Natalie repeated, speaking slowly, holding back her panic.

"I called your mother," Kate confessed, blurting out the words. "I got her number. She's been posting about you online, so it wasn't hard to find her. I was worried about you, and the kids, and your mental health and —"

"No!" Natalie was up from her chair in a flash. "Tell me you didn't. Tell me, Kate. Tell me it's not true."

"I'm so sorry, Nat. I didn't understand. Given everything I —"

"You thought I was lying about Michael? You thought I made up a story about him being a murderer?"

"It just seemed you weren't all right, emotionally that is."

"What did my mom say?"

Kate bit at her lower lip, deepening the grimace on her face.

"She told me she was going to get in touch with Michael. She called back some time later to tell me he was with someone, a policeman, and they were coming here, to our farm to get you."

"A policeman?" Natalie huffed. "That's a good one. Michael wants me dead. Oh, Kate, why, why, why did you do that?"

Kate's eyes held much sorrow.

"I was frightened for you," she said. "I'm so sorry."

471

"When?" Natalie barked, snapping back into herself. "When did you make that call?"

"I called right around lunchtime while I was at the vet."

Natalie frowned, hating that answer.

"Where was he? Do you know? Did my mother say?"

She loomed over Kate who sat dazed, absolutely still.

Natalie collapsed to her knees.

"Where is Michael?"

"Your mom called back, told me he was just outside Indianapolis," Kate said. "He was coming from Toledo."

"Toledo, of course he was," Natalie muttered to herself. She didn't bother explaining to Kate that it was her ruse that had sent him there.

"Evidently, Michael had already figured out you were staying here. He was driving to Elsberry when your mother reached him."

"He's been on the road most of the day," Natalie realized. "That means he could be here any minute now."

"Chuck knew I was going to call your mom," Kate continued, still trying to justify her actions. "He encouraged it. He was worried about you, same as I was."

"Well, now you can both worry a whole

lot more," Natalie retorted as she rushed out of the room.

"Where are you going?" asked Kate, following behind. "Please, talk to me."

They were three-quarters of the way up the stairs. Natalie whirled around, sending Kate a fierce glare.

"You want to help me?" she said. "Go get my kids. I'll pack their stuff. I need your truck."

"Where are you going?" asked Kate.

"I'm going to do what I've been doing for days now," said Natalie with bitterness. "I'm going to run."

CHAPTER 39

Michael

It took two tries before Michael found the small white sign advertising the entrance to Hildonen Farms. He drove too fast down a rutted dirt road, avoiding potholes and rocks like he was in a video game. Kennett's probing gaze scanned in all directions as if he expected Natalie to emerge from the dense forest lining the road. Michael caught his squinting stare in his peripheral vision. He seemed troubled by something.

"What's on your mind?" Michael asked, his eyes on the road ahead.

"Dust," said Kennett.

"What?"

Michael drove over a large rock that sent him bouncing and caused his seat belt to lock tight.

"Dust," Kennett repeated, sounding troubled for reasons Michael didn't understand.

"What about?" asked Michael.

474

"It's in the air in front of us," said Kennett.

"And? We're on a dirt road. I think that's to be expected."

Kennett pointed to the trees whizzing by on Michael's left.

"No wind," he said.

Michael still wasn't getting it. Kennett's musings, as well as this road that seemed to stretch on forever, were both trying his patience.

"A car came through here, Mike," Kennett explained, speaking as if he were giving a weak student the answer. "It was going fast, too, I suspect. Can't say if it was coming or going, but all the dust means it couldn't have been that long ago."

Michael would have asked Kennett to elaborate, but just then the road brought them to a wide clearing, from which he could see both cow-dotted pastures and a white farmhouse not far up ahead. It was a beautiful vista, resplendent as a pastoral painting.

Natalie was here, hiding out from him. *What did she know? What had she told Kate?* For the entirety of the drive, Kennett hadn't once mentioned the name Brianna Sykes, and yet Michael sensed it was on his mind, a shadow lurking just below the surface.

Michael pushed his worries aside — he still needed Kennett's help. They drove up to the house and exited the car together, like partners accustomed to the routine of answering dispatch calls. Kennett did up the button of his blazer, his focus switching between the farmhouse in front of them and the dust cloud still clinging to the air.

As they approached the house, a stout blond woman trotted down the front stairs. Michael assumed this was Kate, but he couldn't say for sure. There were too many years and miles between them for that kind of clarity, not to mention his dim recollections of anyone but Natalie from the night they met. The woman came outside as though she'd been waiting at the door, expecting their arrival. Michael found her eagerness disconcerting.

The woman greeted Michael and Kennett at the halfway point between their car and the house.

"Hi there," she said, her voice bright as the midday sun.

Too bright, too chipper.

Kennett sent Michael a telling glance. *She's hiding something,* that look said. Michael may have missed the dust clue entirely, but being around Kennett offered him some sort of detecting ability by osmosis.

"Hey there," said Kennett before flashing his badge. "Are you Kate Hildonen?"

"I am," said Kate, still cheery.

Michael noted how she stood, hands clasped together white-knuckled in front of her, a smile that looked plastered on. Whenever Michael got anxious, he'd drum his fingers against any surface. Perhaps hand-clasping was Kate's way of showing her unease.

"I'm Detective Sergeant Amos Kennett from the New York PD, and this here is Mike Hart, who I think you know already."

"Michael," said Kate, her forced smile faltering for only a moment. She let go an audible exhale. "Yes, it's been a long time. And Detective, you've come a long way. What are you doing here, Mike?"

"You know why we're here," said Kennett in a tone that clearly implied an eye roll. "Where is she?"

"I don't know —"

Michael put up his hand like a stop sign.

"Kate, let's not, okay?" he said, holding back his ire. "Let's just not. You called Lucinda, and Lucinda called me. You know why we're here. I figured out where she'd gone, so we were already on our way to your farm when I got that call. Now, where's my family?"

Kate shifted her attention back to the house, where a barrel-chested man now appeared on the front porch.

"That's my husband, Chuck," said Kate.

Michael's eyes followed the big man as he bounded down the stairs with a grace that belied his size. He approached with a hand extended, eager to greet these visitors.

"Chuck MacLeod," he said in a resonate baritone. Michael took the proffered hand and gave it a shake. Kennett did not. His focus was back on the road, still eyeing that dust.

"They're here for Natalie," Kate said, adopting a more subdued tone.

Chuck nodded vigorously while sending Kate a glance that all but screamed to Michael that they'd preplanned their stories. "Yeah, well, she and the kids are gone," he announced, shifting uneasily in his heavy-duty work boots.

"Yeah? When?" asked Kennett, not sounding convinced.

Chuck scratched at his beard with a forced look of contemplation, but Michael knew it was an effort to sell his lie.

"A while ago, I'd say."

He turned to Kate, who nodded in agreement.

"What's a while?" inquired Kennett as he took another glance at the road.

"I'd say an hour or so," answered Kate. "We didn't know you were coming for her."

"Because I told Lucinda not to tell you," Michael answered quickly. "Where'd they go?"

"I don't know," Kate answered — too quickly.

More lies.

"Do you know if she's planning to come back?" asked Kennett.

"I assume so," Kate folded her arms, maybe not realizing she'd taken a defensive posture.

"Did she say why she came to Missouri without me?" Michael asked. He hoped his steady stare would force Kate to look him in the eyes, windows to the soul Kennett might say, but she shifted her gaze to Chuck instead.

"She told us you were having marital troubles," Chuck answered.

"Missouri is a long way to go to escape a bad marriage," said Kennett, effectively dismissing that lie. Michael heard him take in a calming breath. "How about some truth," he continued. "Did you give her a car?"

"Yes, she borrowed my truck. But I'm sure she's coming back here in a few hours. I think she took the kids to the river."

"Now you remember where she'd gone?" said Kennett.

"It slipped my mind," Kate said, brushing off his insinuation. "They'd never seen the Mississippi before. Bryce is really proud he can spell it. It's so cute. Anyway, we had to let her go because she was being so insistent. Mike, she doesn't know that we called her mother, so I think we're all good here. Natalie will come back soon, so why don't you two come inside and we can wait for her? I'll fix you something to eat, brew us some coffee. We can catch up."

"Yeah, are you gonna show us their clothes and suitcases in their bedrooms?" Kennett asked, sounding as if he already knew the answer.

Kate couldn't suppress a grimace.

"Thought as much. What's she driving?"

"I told you, my truck," said Kate.

"I mean make, model? Color?" he wanted to know.

"Ford F150. Blue."

"Got it," he said. "I'm going to double-check that. I'm police, remember? Are you sure that's what you drive? Hmmm?"

Kate broke eye contact, then said to nobody in particular, "Dodge Ram, gray. Need the license plate, Detective?"

"Please," said Kennett.

"You shouldn't have gotten involved, Kate," Michael said. "This wasn't your problem to fix."

"I think I can make my own decision in that regard, Michael," Kate answered coldly.

Chuck went to get Kennett the license plate number. While he was gone the rumble of an approaching engine broke an uncomfortable silence. The whine grew louder as a dust cloud bloomed from its source. Soon an ATV came into view, driven by a lanky man draped in denim. With his long hair and thick mustache, Michael thought he could have been a roadie for the Eagles. The driver brought his vehicle to a hard stop a few feet from where Kate stood, dismounting his ride as though it were his trusty steed.

"What's going on?" he asked.

"We're looking for Natalie," Kennett interjected before Kate could coach him. "I'm a cop. This is Natalie's husband, Michael." He thumbed over to Michael.

"Yeah? Police?" said the man, who spoke in a drawl. He introduced himself as Hank,

481

a long-time employee of Hildonen Farms. "She done something? She seemed a bit off to me."

"Yeah, I bet," said Kennett. "Have you seen her recently?"

"I told the detective that Natalie had gone to the river with the children," Kate said. The notable rise in her voice all but confirmed Michael's suspicion that she wanted to make sure they had their stories straight, but Hank appeared utterly oblivious and somewhat perplexed.

"The river?" he said with surprise. "Uh, I don't think so. She just drove past me headed west on 358. Last I checked, the Miss is east of here."

"Hank," Kate replied tersely, but it was too late. The damage was done.

Kennett, who had gotten the license plate number from Chuck, brushed Kate with an admonishing look that sent her gaze to her feet before she glared angrily up at Hank. It was obvious he wasn't part of whatever discussions Kate and Chuck had had prior to their arrival.

Michael was on the move, headed for the car. Kennett did the same, making it clear he wanted to be the one driving.

"We don't give chase. We don't do anything that puts Natalie and my kids in danger, is that understood?"

Kennett gave a firm nod.

"Absolutely," he said. "Safety first."

Michael opened his car door, pausing long enough to send Kate an angry stare.

"Please stay out of this, Kate. She doesn't need your help. She needs mine."

"Whatever you say, Joseph," Kate shot back.

Michael recoiled as though he'd been shot. Kennett was already halfway in the car, but came back out to send a sardonic grin Kate's way.

"You must be mistaken," Kennett said dryly. "This here is Michael Hart."

There was no wink, no smile, no explanation given, just a stony expression that Kennett took with him back into the car. Michael climbed into the seat beside him, still reeling.

"Buckle up," said Kennett. "I promise no chase, but it might still be a wild ride."

He slammed the car into reverse, and they were off.

CHAPTER 40

Natalie

The truck wasn't far from Hildonen Farms when Natalie's Tracfone rang. The sound of it, like a clang of bells, startled her, but she soon realized that only one person had the number. Kate.

Natalie answered the call on the second ring thinking, *Trouble.*

"I'm so sorry," Kate blurted out, skipping the customary hello. Her breathing came through the phone's speaker loud and uneven. "Hank showed up and I didn't have a chance to explain things to him. He gave it away. Where are you? He said he saw you driving west on 358."

Natalie grappled with the implications. "What are you talking about?" she said testily. "What did Hank say? Is he there? Did *Joseph* show up? Was he alone?"

For the sake of the children, Natalie avoided speaking their father's name, using

484

Joseph as a code between her and Kate. Even so, she couldn't help but allow hints of fear to enter her voice. She took a glimpse behind her at the kids safely ensconced in the back of the truck, eyes glued to their respective devices. They appeared none the wiser, but Natalie knew better than to take those vacant stares for obliviousness. Devices or not, they were all eyes and ears — and on edge too, especially given how they'd been so unceremoniously rushed away from a place neither of them wanted to leave.

When Natalie broke the news to Addie and Bryce, that they would be leaving the farm, both children, as expected, protested vociferously. Addie stomped her feet in a regressive show of frustration. She so desperately wanted to stay and care for the animals, and Bryce (poor thing) burst into tears. Their obstinacy forced Natalie, under the pressure of time, to resort to a cruel lie that sickened her.

"We have to go to meet Daddy," she told them. "He's waiting for us and we have to hurry. If we don't, we might miss him."

The children were too excited at the prospect of a reunion with their father to question what they'd been told. Natalie embarked on a mad rush getting packed.

She jammed clothes into suitcases while scrambling from room to room, checking under beds, making sure Bryce's replacement bear wasn't left behind.

"I might not have much of a head start," Natalie said to Kate while pulling clothes from a dresser.

Go! Go! Go! That voice in her head again urged her along.

"I think the river makes the most sense," Natalie told Kate hurriedly. "Bryce loves the water. Tell Michael what I said about Bryce if he shows up. It will make it sound more believable."

When she was through getting her belongings together, Natalie had done such a haphazard packing job that her suitcase wouldn't close without Kate pushing on the top with both hands, applying considerable pressure.

"You're going to be all right," Kate offered encouragingly before bringing Natalie into a brief, albeit comforting, embrace.

Natalie pried them apart, though she held on to Kate's arms a beat longer, enough to send a look of gratitude and forgiveness.

"I know that you meant well," she said. "And thank you for all that you've done. Please, please, just do whatever you can to help us get away from him."

■ ■ ■

Whatever Kate had done, clearly it hadn't been enough.

"How much of a lead do I have?" asked Natalie, who drove with the phone pressed between her left shoulder and ear. Bluetooth wasn't an option because the children would listen in, and she didn't have a headset handy.

"Not much of one," Kate revealed. "They showed up here minutes after you'd gone. I'm so sorry."

"Don't worry about that," Natalie said. "Just help me. You know the area. There's got to be a place where we can hide."

Route 358 out of Elsberry snaked its way through a stark landscape of plowed fields and thin forest like an asphalt river. She was headed to 79, and from there didn't know if she would go north or south. Now she questioned if she could even make it to the main road.

"Talk to me, Kate," Natalie said urgently, forgetting for a second to keep her voice down.

"What's going on, Mommy?" asked Addie from the backseat. Natalie pulled the phone from her ear, spun her head to look behind her. Sunlight from all the outdoor time had transformed Addie's hair to an odd shade — nearly orange.

"It's nothing to worry about, sweetheart," Natalie said, imagining an asthma attack coming on at the worst possible moment.

"What street are you near? Can you see any signs?" Kate asked in a faraway voice, jarring Natalie back to the moment.

She put the phone back against her ear before glancing out her window.

"I just passed Oma Lane."

"Oma Lane, okay, okay, let me think," muttered Kate.

Natalie was thinking too, but the notion that she could outrun her pursuers was out of the question. Michael was with a cop — probably a dirty one — who could call for backup. She pictured state troopers swarming her, lights flashing, sirens blaring, and it was back to Ohio and the same problem with the law. She had her children with her, and their safety remained paramount.

A gray sedan came out of nowhere and started to close the gap, fast. "I think they found me," said Natalie, panic in her voice.

Kate described a car that sounded just like the one coming up on her tail.

"Give me something, anything," Natalie pleaded as she turned onto North Fifth, headed south. She didn't know the area, didn't know where to go.

"Where are you now?" asked Kate.

Natalie gave her position as she watched the gray sedan accelerate.

"Okay, you should be coming up to a Baptist church on the right any second," Kate announced. "It's just before Commerce Street. Turn in to the parking lot when you see it."

Natalie saw a large building up ahead, no steeple, but the sign out front confirmed it was the right place. She didn't use her blinker, waiting until the last possible moment before making the turn.

"Drive straight through the parking lot," Kate instructed. "There's no barriers, just drive right onto the grass, and take a right onto North Sixth Street. They may follow you, but they'll be confused for a moment. It'll buy you some time. I think I know what to do from here."

Kate issued her directives while Natalie was already bounding over a grassy patch at the back end of the parking lot.

"Mom! You're off the road," Bryce shouted.

"Right, honey," said Natalie nonchalantly as she drove onto the street behind the church. "Wrong turn. Here's the real road, all better now." She paused to catch her breath. Into the phone she said, "Okay, I'm on North Sixth, what now?"

"Follow that road back and take a left back onto North Fifth. Then take your first right onto Powell," Kate instructed.

Natalie checked her rearview. There was no sedan in sight, but that might not mean anything. She assumed they'd see the tire tracks in the grass and would follow.

"I'm on Powell," Natalie said.

"Okay, that's good. I'm texting a friend who works nearby."

The gray sedan appeared again in Natalie's rearview. Any doubt that it might not be Michael in that car was gone. She felt her heart swim up her throat. Sweat gathered on her brow, her neck throbbing from the awkward angle used to hold the phone in place.

"He's still following," Natalie said in a whispered voice.

"Listen to me carefully," Kate said, speaking more forcefully this time. "Soon as you cross over North Second Street, you're going to take your first right onto a dirt road."

Natalie forced herself to slow down so she wouldn't miss the turn as she passed Dubois. She spotted what appeared to be some kind of cut-through for large trucks, judging by the size of the tire tracks left in the dirt. Kate was right to say it was a tricky turn to spot, but the driver of the sedan had seen where she'd gone and could follow her easily.

How was this going to help? Natalie wondered.

"Now, when you reach the end of the dirt road you're going to take a sharp right onto a paved portion that runs parallel to the dirt road. You're essentially going to backtrack the way you came until you reach the IGA parking lot. You'll be entering at the rear of the building. I know the manager and he's expecting you. I've been texting him while we talk. Drive my truck straight into the first open bay, the first one you come to. Don't hesitate. Just drive."

"We're off the road again," Addie cried out after Kate's truck slammed hard into a deep pothole that sent everyone bouncing.

"Sorry, I missed our street," said Natalie, with forced cheer in her voice. At the end of the dirt lane, she made the U-turn onto the paved road. The jouncing stopped thanks to the asphalt beneath her wheels. Up ahead the expansive brick façade of the IGA came into full view. Out of her passenger window, Natalie observed the sedan coming toward her now. Were it not for a steady line of shrubs and small trees separating the dirt road from the paved one, the sedan could have easily swerved to intercept her. Instead, they'd have to backtrack as Natalie had done.

The vehicles passed each other while driving on opposite sides of the shrubbery. Sunlight and the cloudless day made it possible to see inside the vehicle. Natalie confirmed her worst fear — it was Michael in the passenger's seat, traveling with a man she did not know.

Her truck bounded over a speed bump placed at the entrance to the rear lot of the IGA, which sent everyone up and down like they were in a traveling bouncy house. She was going too fast to safely steer the truck toward the loading bays. Instead she watched as the only open bay door fell away in her rearview mirror.

Natalie hit the brakes hard, seat belts locking, tires squealing beneath her. She jammed the truck into reverse, not wanting to waste precious seconds turning the vehicle around. Glancing over her left shoulder as she drove backward, Natalie let the phone and her lifeline to Kate fall to the truck floor.

She navigated toward the open door, sacrificing speed for precision. Off in the distance she could hear the revving engine of Michael's sedan headed her way. In seconds, it would come over that speed bump. He'd see her. Then it would all be over.

Natalie jammed her foot down on the gas. "Mommy, what are you doing?" cried Addie in distress.

Natalie was too focused to answer. The truck picked up speed, still going in reverse. A man dressed in beige coveralls emerged from the darkness of the warehouse space. He was big and burly like Chuck, waving his arms frantically in an effort to guide her.

Sunlight gave way to darkness as Natalie steered the truck successfully through the open bay door and into a cavernous building. She heard the rumbling roll of a steel door as it closed shut.

The children sat stunned and quiet. Natalie's nerves hummed inside her with an electric charge. A knock on her window drew Natalie's attention. Her savior in coveralls motioned with his hand for Natalie to kill the engine, which she did, but not before she rolled down her window.

"I'm Gus, friend of Kate's," the big man said in a deep, resonate voice. "I'll keep a lookout, so I'll know when that car is gone and it's safe for y'all to leave."

"Thank you, Gus," Natalie said, feeling both relief and profound gratitude.

"What do you mean, safe?" asked Addie from the backseat. "What's wrong, Mommy?"

"There's nothing wrong, sweetheart. There's just a problem with Kate's truck and it needs to be looked at. Gus here is going to help."

"We should go to a gas station then," said Addie, ever the wise. "This is a warehouse."

"Yes, I know it's a warehouse," said Natalie, finding her calm. "I was worried about the engine overheating, so Kate called ahead, said that Gus here could fix it," she added definitively. Natalie then thought of Michael, how one lie of his had led to another, and then another still, until he'd erected a city of them, where they all lived under the illusion of comfort and security.

Damn him to hell, she thought.

"We have to give the engine a chance to cool down, so I need you both to be patient and quiet," said Natalie. "You can play with your iPads while we wait."

The wait lasted ten minutes, maybe fifteen. Natalie was glad, however, when Gus returned to the truck after opening the bay door, which rose as nosily as a roller coaster going up a track.

"All set," he said to Natalie through her open window. "That car came and went. Hasn't come back. We've been keeping an eye out and the coast is clear."

"Thank you, again. I can't honestly say it enough."

"Don't ya mention it," Gus replied, drawing out each word. "Don't know what's going on exactly, but if Kate says you need my help, then I'm more than happy to oblige."

"Please tell Kate we're okay, and that I'll be in touch soon," said Natalie.

Following a head nod from Gus, Natalie drove the truck out of the warehouse, feeling great relief.

But what now? she asked herself while she was stopped at a red light.

She was at the intersection of Auburn Street and South Third, on her way to 79, lost in her private thoughts, when from the backseat she heard a yowl of delight. Then came the click of a seat belt and the metal squeak of a door swinging open. In her peripheral vision, she caught motion as she was turning her head to have a look. To her horror, she saw Bryce bounding out of the truck and onto the road, his face beaming with pure joy.

"It's Daddy!" she heard him shout as he bolted from the truck. She could now see

495

that he was headed for the gas station on the other side of the road. To reach the station, Bryce would have to safely navigate two lanes of traffic. He raced ahead, oblivious as the light turned and the traffic surged forward.

Natalie had never moved so fast in all her life. She was out of the vehicle and sprinting in front of her parked truck before her brain even had a chance to register what she was doing. Horns blared as cars swerved to avoid Bryce, who bounded across the road with a smile that wouldn't dim even in the midst of the danger.

"Bryce!" Natalie screamed, but it was no use. There was no way to stop him now. Natalie saw the car coming at a high rate of speed, Bryce in front of it. She heard the screech of brakes. A horn blared loudly. Her eyes closed tight, she fell to her knees and curled into a ball, unable to look, unable to move. Holding her breath, she waited for the sound, the collision.

Over the blare of another horn she heard Bryce's delighted little voice cry out, "Daddy! Daddy!"

Natalie opened her eyes to see that Bryce was now safely across the road and wrapped tightly in Michael's arms. She rose to her feet and crossed the busy street in a daze, ignoring the cars that maneuvered to avoid hitting her. She got to within five feet of Michael and Bryce before coming to a stop.

Her arms hung limply at her sides. She met her husband's eyes. In them she saw only love and relief.

"Babe," Michael breathed. "Thank God, Nat. We found you."

He stepped forward, arms out wide, but a man got in his way. Natalie recognized him as the man who was driving the sedan.

"Natalie Hart," said the man, taking hold of her wrist.

"Yes," she said weakly.

"I'm Detective Sergeant Amos Kennett from the New York City Police Department."

He placed something around her wrist, something cold and metallic.

"I regret to inform you," he said, locking the handcuffs in place, "that you are under arrest for the murder of Audrey Adler."

CHAPTER 41

Michael

He sat on a metal folding chair in a barren room located somewhere in the Medford, Massachusetts, police station. Through a grimy window, he could see into another empty room, where Natalie would soon appear. It had been an eventful twenty-four hours — or maybe more, he'd lost track of time — since Kennett had arrested his wife in Elsberry, Missouri. Depending on how her bail hearing went tomorrow, Natalie would most likely be transferred to the women's facility at MCI-Framingham to await trial on murder charges.

Michael hadn't slept much since her shocking arrest, catching an hour or so on the flight back to Logan, Addie and Bryce seated on either side of him. Natalie, accompanied by two U.S. Marshals, her handcuffs concealed by a coat draped over her wrists, was placed in the back of the

498

plane, along with Kennett.

Natalie's parents, Harvey and Lucinda, met Michael at the airport upon their arrival. It was Kennett's suggestion that the children remain away from the family home for a few nights, because reporters might catch wind of the arrest and make a scene that could leave a lasting impression on impressionable young minds. Michael readily agreed, and that was the last conversation he and Kennett shared.

The cat-and-mouse game Michael had thought he and the detective had been playing wasn't a game at all. Michael was never the target. Kennett knew who Michael was, of course he did, but now, in the aftermath, it was all quite clear —

Kennett had been after his wife from the start. His involvement in the case outside his jurisdiction made sense for someone with a long memory for justice. No way would he allow the murder of two Sykes women to go unsolved.

According to reports from Lucinda, the children were both distraught. Poor Bryce even wet the bed, something he'd outgrown years ago. At least his son finally had his teddy bear to comfort him. Michael told himself they were young, resilient, and they'd bounce back from all this, but in nearly the same breath, he could envision the road ahead, and his hopes would dim.

At last Natalie entered the room, led by an armed police escort. She looked utterly drained, a ghostly apparition, her eyes more sunken and darkly ringed than ever. She'd fought her sleep condition with a prizefighter's vigor, but in this gray setting she appeared as fragile as a porcelain doll. His heart ached for her. He felt deeply protective as he battled an urge to hoist up his chair and use it to shatter the glass separating them, pulling her to safety — or at least into his arms.

He found himself struggling to make sense of it all. She seemed utterly lost and confused, and he felt so unable to help. He pressed his hand up against the glass, fingers spread out wide, before picking up the wall-mounted phone to his right. Natalie didn't budge until Michael pointed to the phone on her side of the partition. His unblinking gaze watched her every move as she hesitantly lifted the receiver. She seemed to be in some sort of a trance, here with him in body only. She put the phone to her ear, saying nothing. Michael couldn't even hear the sound of her breath.

"Hey babe," he said eventually, his voice choked with emotion. He brandished something of a smile, hoping Natalie would put her hand to the glass to meet his, but hers remained fisted on the narrow counter running along the lip of the window.

There was nothing in her eyes, just icy detachment.

"How are you?" Michael asked.

She gave no response.

"The children are asking for you, of course they are."

Michael felt a twinge of apprehension, expecting that the mere mention of them would uncork whatever emotions Natalie had bottled up, but she sat like she might for a portrait, her hard stare boring into him.

"You haven't been sleeping, you . . . you haven't been yourself," he said in a whispered voice, even though he knew this conversation was being recorded. "We need to talk to some experts, get their opinion, it could be you didn't know what you were doing and —"

"Three things," said Natalie coarsely, though her expression remained quite controlled.

"What?" Michael screwed up his face in a show of confusion.

"Three things," she repeated into the phone. "That's our family game, right? So let's play."

"Nat, I don't think now is the time."

"I think it's the perfect time," she spat back in a clipped tone. "So let's play . . . *Michael.* How about you go first. Three things. What are yours?"

The way she said his name with such venom made him recoil. Michael fixed his wife with a curious stare, but he could see her resolve was firm. There'd be no talking to her until she got her way.

"Okay, then," he said, as he ran a free hand through his thick brown hair and then across the stubble dotting his chin. He hadn't shaved, hadn't slept, and no doubt he looked as bone-tired to Natalie as she did to him, but he was with it enough to engage.

"Three things," he said, needing a moment to remember the categories. "What went well today is that I got to see you. I got to set my eyes on you and know that you're all right."

"And what are you grateful for?" asked Natalie in a chillingly robotic voice.

"That you're unhurt," Michael said. "That our children our fine. That we found you before something happened to any of you. If it did — Nat, honey, I wouldn't recover. I love you so much it hurts. I can't bear to think of anything bad happening to you or the kids. I love you with everything that I am and that I have. I'm here for you and I'll stay by your side, no matter what. You haven't been sleeping, you can't be responsible for what happened to Audrey."

"Three things," Natalie said, still without a drop of emotion in her voice. "That's only two. You've one to go."

"Something I wish I'd done differently," Michael said, remembering the category. He gazed down at his hands as he thought how to answer.

Natalie offered him nothing but a hard stare.

"Okay then," he said. "I wish I had shown you more compassion these last few months. I wish I'd been more helpful to you. Your sleep troubles, your accusations, I thought it was all an excuse to avoid me, avoid us."

Natalie's eyebrows rose slightly on her forehead.

"I didn't understand what that kind of lack of sleep does to a body and mind. I do now, believe me, because I've been living it, and I'm sorry."

"So you get it now, do you?" said Natalie ratcheting up the contempt. "You couldn't sleep after I took off with the kids, is that it, Michael?"

"No, I couldn't. You planned it, didn't you?"

Natalie scoffed. "Of course I did," she said. "I knew you'd be delayed getting the pizza. I must have tested the delivery window a half dozen times before we left for New York. And I knew we'd have just enough time to pack up and leave the hotel while you were gone. I'm sure you thought we took an Amtrak train somewhere; that's why I made New York our departure city. I figured it would buy us more time as we got away, but I didn't think you'd remember Kate Hildonen. Good for you. If I hadn't used the wrong credit card, you probably wouldn't have had any idea where to begin looking for me."

"Why, Nat? Why did you run? Did you think the police were closing in on you for Audrey? You could have talked to me." He spoke in an imploring way. "We could have worked it out."

Natalie gazed back at Michael straight-faced, her expression blank as a new canvas.

"Three things," she said softly. "Now it's my turn."

She radiated a fierceness he'd never seen before. Michael's apprehension deepened with each moment of uncomfortable silence that fell between them.

"What went well is that I slept last night for the first time in ages," she said softly into the phone. "Eight hours straight. Here in a police station of all places, I finally got that elusive, uninterrupted sleep I've been craving. You know why that is, Michael?"

"No," said Michael, finding himself unable to meet her stare, and yet eager to know the answer.

Natalie gave him a few moments to marinate in his discomfort.

When she finally spoke, it was evident to Michael that she was choosing her words very carefully.

"I finally slept because I'm locked behind bars and these thick concrete walls." She rapped her knuckles against one of them. "Because locked up in here, I know without the slightest bit of doubt that you can't get to me, that in here I'm safe, Michael, safe from you, my own husband."

She layered on the sarcasm.

"Natalie, I —"

She held up a finger: *no words,* she was saying, *it's my turn at the table now.*

"As for gratitude, well, I'm grateful that my children are with my parents and not with you. That's another reason I could sleep well last night."

Michael clamped down an urge to protest.

The look in Natalie's eyes told him what was coming next, and he knew to stay silent, let it happen — take his medicine, so to speak.

"Three things," she said with an accompanying huff of air.

Michael drummed his fingers nervously against the counter, holding his breath, waiting for what he knew was coming.

He remembered her answers from the last time they played the game, seated around the dinner table on the evening before they departed for New York.

Today I got us all packed and ready to go.
I'm grateful for the truth.
I wish I'd done this sooner.

He understood what she was saying now. The first line about packing was for the kids, but the other two were definitely directed at him.

"What do I wish happened differently?" Natalie said, drawing out the words.

He was shaking now. Struggling to catch his breath. He had waited so many years for this moment, for his secrets to be fully exposed. He waited for it, to hear the names: Joseph, Brianna, perhaps even Marjorie, the mother who never believed in her own son.

Natalie stayed cool and reserved. Michael

found her impassivity more tortuous than her vitriol. It was a complete negation of him, as though he no longer mattered, alive or dead. To his wife, he was now an inconsequential being.

Natalie said, "I wish that I told you months ago to pack up your shit and get the fuck out of my house." She paused to send him a lopsided smile. "So I'm telling you now, Michael: go home, get your stuff together, and get out of our lives, forever. Because I'm getting out of here tomorrow morning, my lawyer is sure of it, and when I do, I'm coming home. I'm sure I won't be able to sleep well knowing you're out there somewhere, but some things I'm willing to live with. And you, my darling husband, are not one of them."

Natalie hung up the phone. She rose to her feet. A policeman let her out, and she was gone, never once looking back.

CHAPTER 42

Natalie

Hours after Michael left the police station, a Medford cop informed Natalie she had a visitor. Only after confirming it wasn't her husband or the children coming to visit (she didn't want them seeing her locked up, dressed in the orange uniform of a prisoner) did she agree to the meeting.

She was curious who'd come to see her. The lawyer her father had hired wasn't scheduled to visit. Her curiosity gave way to shock when the interview room door opened and in strolled the very man who had arrested her in Missouri, Detective Sergeant Amos Kennett.

Natalie wondered why the police had left her unsupervised, with no handcuffs, and those questions only grew more pressing now that she was in the presence of law enforcement. Surely the police would want protection from any detainee, even one as slight and slender as she.

"How are you doing, Natalie?" Detective Kennett asked pleasantly enough. His voice may have been as gritty as the city streets where he came from, but his eyes held a gentle kindness.

"Guess you could say I've been better," Natalie quipped back.

Kennett only nodded.

"Yeah, I imagine that's so."

Natalie glared at Kennett from across the table, her arms folded tightly across her chest.

"Why are you here, Detective?" she asked curtly. She didn't bother masking her anger. After all, this was the man who had humiliated her and separated her from her children. "Is this the interrogation portion of my arrest? Have you come here to offer me a plea deal? Leniency if I confess to a murder that I didn't commit?"

Natalie may have been all bravado externally, but inside she was hardly self-assured. It was obvious they had enough evidence to arrest her — fingerprints she'd inadvertently left behind, security camera footage from Audrey's house, or perhaps those cell tower pings Sarah Fielding had assured her wouldn't be a problem. Why a detective from New York City had taken it upon himself to hunt her down like an animal, Natalie couldn't say.

"I'm not here to offer you leniency," Kennett said matter-of-factly, "but I do have a deal of sorts to make. More of a favor, I guess."

"A favor?" Natalie eyed him, nonplussed. "I'm sorry, Detective, but I'm pretty sure you've got the roles reversed. I'm the prisoner."

"Are you wearing handcuffs?" asked Kennett, capping that with a sly smile.

Natalie held up her wrists, spreading her arms apart.

"You're not a prisoner, not at all. You're free to go, in fact. I actually have a car waiting outside to take you anywhere you wish. I needed to make it look and feel believable, but in fact your arrest was actually done for your own protection and that of your children."

Natalie barked out a mirthless laugh.

"My protection? Detective, you traumatized my kids. Forgive me if I don't express my sincere gratitude. And what the hell were you *'protecting'* me from?"

"From your husband, from Audrey Adler's real killer."

Natalie froze for a moment. Any anger she'd felt toward Kennett left her in a flash.

He knows the truth.

"So are you telling me that my arrest was staged? That you did it to make Michael think you were on *his* side?"

Kennett returned a slight nod.

"I think you already know some of the rather distressing discoveries that I have to share about Michael," he said.

Natalie replied, "You mean Joseph Jacob Saunders?"

"When did you find out?"

"Before I ran away," said Natalie without equivocating.

That elicited another nod of admiration from Kennett.

"I certainly don't blame you for running," he said.

"What's your deal here, Detective?" Natalie asked. "Why is a New York City police detective involved in all of this? Aren't you outside your jurisdiction? And before you answer that, I want you to know that I'm still royally pissed that you put my children through the trauma of seeing their mother handcuffed and carted away like a dangerous criminal."

"I understand your anger," Kennett said apologetically. "But I need your cooperation to get to your husband — and if it helps, it wasn't a decision we came to lightly. In fact, it took a lot of string pulling and interdepartmental cooperation to get the approvals I needed to launch this undercover op, mainly *because* of your kids and an abundance of concern for their well-being. Ultimately everyone involved agreed it was a case of the end justifying the means. We want Michael behind bars, Natalie. We want him where he belongs. And I want to be the one who puts him there."

Natalie held his unflinching gaze.

"Let me ask you again," she said. "What's your involvement in all of this?"

Kennett cleared his throat.

"Brianna Sykes, Audrey's sister, was the first murder case I worked as a rookie cop when I was with the Rye PD. I knew we had the right guy — your husband, Joseph, as he went by back then — but he went free as a bird, and I never got over it."

"I know all about Brianna," Natalie admitted. "I've been to see Michael's mother, too," she added.

"Marjorie Saunders," said Kennett. "Now that's a blast from the past. How is Marjorie doing these days?"

"I don't think she's over it, either," Natalie offered.

"No surprise there," Kennett countered. "But I sure as shit was surprised when one of my best detectives sends over a picture of a family to use for a 'be on the lookout alert,' wife and children gone missing, and I get a peek at it, and right away recognize the husband as Brianna's killer. Naturally, I decide to get involved, go to the scene. Your husband didn't recognize me, I'm sure of that. I was a nothing cop back then, but I pegged him in two seconds. I didn't reveal the connection, of course. That would have been showing my whole hand. You were wise to run away from him."

"You're not the only person from Michael's past he didn't recognize," Natalie said with conviction. "He and Audrey were having an affair. I don't think he recognized her as Brianna's sister, or maybe she didn't recognize him — that Michael was really Joseph. Either way it's pretty twisted."

Kennett's expression remained impassive.

"Yeah, we had our suspicions about their relationship, but nothing concrete," he said in a low voice. "I wouldn't be surprised if she didn't know who he was. She was so young back then, and people do change a lot in twenty-five years."

"But you ID'd my husband right away," said Natalie.

"I was older than Audrey, that's all. And truth be told, if it wasn't such a high-profile case, and if the case hadn't continued to haunt me, he might have been lost to me under the avalanche of scumbags that I've dealt with over the years.

"I guess you should know that while we were on the road together, Michael told me that he'd had an affair — an 'indiscretion,' he called it. Gotta say, I didn't imagine it was with his victim's sister."

"So you knew about Audrey, and figured her murder was somehow connected to my running away from Michael? Is that what made you go looking for me, Detective?" Natalie asked.

"Pretty much. Audrey's murder wasn't high profile, but I caught wind of it from colleagues who had worked Brianna's case back then," Kennett said. "Obviously I didn't know about you and Michael, not until he turned up at the hotel and I found out you two didn't live far from Audrey. So yeah, you're right. I got it in my head that he was involved in her death, and I came up with the idea of playing good cop to get him. I surprised Mike with a visit to your house, where I offered him my services to help him find you. When people let you in, that's usually when the secrets spill out. Didn't quite work out as I planned, so I improvised, came up with a new approach while we were on the road together."

"My arrest," said Natalie.

"Your *fake* arrest," Kennett corrected her. "You did a good job finding me. From what I gather you were already headed to Kate's farm when she called."

"Actually it was Michael who did most of the detective work. Hard as it may be for you to believe, I have a real sense from my time with him that he truly loves you. He's full of regrets, but he's also full of shit. He's a killer, cold-blooded and cruel. So tell me, Natalie, why do you think your husband and Audrey were involved?"

"Not think — I know," Natalie answered bitterly.

She then launched into her story about hearing a crying woman at work — how she'd invited Audrey to lunch, hoping to hatch a plan to catch her husband cheating, only to find out that the woman across from her was already sleeping with Michael.

"She tells me her lover's name is Chris, which is Michael's middle name, or the one he gave himself anyway, and that was just the start. There were all these arrows pointing to Michael as Audrey's lover. He fit the description she gave, same number of kids, same gym, same nervous habit."

She mentioned seeing Michael's car during a rendezvous with Audrey in the Mc-Donald's parking lot, but left out the part about how she'd fallen asleep, along with her many hallucinations. She didn't need Kennett doubting her, nor did she want to incriminate herself — which is why she neglected to mention her own crime. While it wasn't murder, breaking and entering into Audrey's home and taking those items was still against the law. Since her children were down to one parent, and the police had ample evidence against Michael, Natalie opted not to mention finding Michael's shirt and gym locker key in Audrey's apartment.

"I all but accused Audrey of sleeping with Michael, and she got visibly upset when I showed her his picture. He had basically the same reaction when I showed him hers," Natalie remarked.

"All this came on the heels of my receiving an anonymous note from someone at work informing me — out of the goodness of their heart, bless them — that Michael was involved with a woman at our gym. Later I found a second note shuffled in a pile of papers in my desk drawer. I have no idea how long it was there. It got mixed in with some files I hadn't looked at in a while. To me, it's a note from the grave. I'm certain it was Audrey who left it. Guess all my accusations got her conscience going, but she never had the chance to come clean to me in person. Michael didn't give her one."

"Do you still have the note?"

"Yes, it's at my house."

Also at her house was the plastic bag containing Michael's shirt and gym locker key. Eventually, Natalie would clean out the locker. Should she find something of consequence, of course she'd inform Kennett straightaway, and make up a story as to where she found the key. For now, less was more.

"I'd like to see that note if I may," Kennett requested.

"Well, I'd like to go home," Natalie replied curtly. "So what's the favor, Detective? What is it you want me to do?"

A slight frown darkened Kennett's expression in a clear warning that his ask wouldn't be easy.

"At first I wanted you to wear a wire and get a confession from Michael on tape for us, but Massachusetts has a two-party consent law that pretty much makes that plan a no-go unless Michael was also involved in organized crime."

"He can't even organize his sock drawer,"

Natalie tossed out.

Kennett couldn't suppress a laugh.

"So what then?" she asked. "No wire. What's your ask?"

"I want you to get a confession. We have evidence that Michael had been in contact with Audrey, communications suggesting he was concerned about certain things coming to light. It's some evidence, but not enough. I need his confession. Talk to him. Tell him that you love him. That you want to keep your family together, make it work."

"But he's a murderer."

"He killed Audrey to guard his secret, to protect you and the kids, the life you have together. You're going to tell him that you know what he did, and that while you're horrified by his crime, you understand why he did it. All you want is the truth so that you can move forward as a family again. As for your arrest, we're going to drop the charges against you — the story here is that your lawyer found errors with your arrest warrant. As a result, a judge is going to order your immediate release. You'll tell Michael you want to see him. Tell him almost losing it all has made you rethink your life. Now that you're better rested, you've had a change of heart about the marriage, even though you know he killed Audrey Adler."

Natalie silently mulled the offer over.

"Let me give this some thought. I think I can do better than that," she eventually said.

"Okay, well, I hope so. There are no other suspects. He's our guy and you're going to help us get him."

"And where will you be when all this is taking place?"

"Outside your house, waiting. You'll turn a light on and off two times and that'll be our signal to move. We'll come in, arrest him, and you can get on with your life. We'll want you of course to be a witness at trial."

"I'll think it over," said Natalie, even though she'd already decided.

"I appreciate it," said Kennett, who, judging by the slight twinkle in his eyes, might have been a mind reader. "One other thing, Natalie, if I may. If you do agree to help, and I hope that you will, we'd like to find out where Michael hid the murder weapon."

"If I agree to participate, I'll do my best to help you find it," she said.

Natalie was also thinking of a different weapon, one used to murder Brianna Sykes. She'd give that knife to the police as well, but not before it served another purpose, one directly connected to her newly formed plan to get Michael out of her life forever.

CHAPTER 43

Michael

He stood outside his house, unsure of what to do. Should he ring the bell or march right in? In the past, it wouldn't have been a question. The new normal, however, meant new norms that hadn't yet been established. His finger hovered near the button while another thought scuttled about in his head.

Where are the reporters?

He had expected a gauntlet of them to be camped on the front lawn, covering Natalie's surprise release after the charges against her were dropped. She got off on a technicality was all she told him on the phone. Perhaps that news hadn't yet made it to the media. It was the only logical explanation as to why his street held the same quiet stillness it always had.

He moved his hand from the doorbell to the doorknob after deciding he'd walk in as if these were normal times. From down the hall came the melodious sounds of soft jazz played through the Sonos speakers — a system he had configured years ago that was no longer his to enjoy. This place he once thought of as being home now seemed alien. The kids weren't around to greet him, which added to the strangeness. They were still staying with Harvey and Lucinda. Tonight marked Natalie's first time back in the house since they left for New York.

As he moved down the hallway, past the framed photos and artwork, Michael suffered again from that odd feeling of disassociation, as though he were a stranger marching through a strange land.

"In here, Michael," he heard Natalie call out to him.

Michael found his wife standing at the kitchen island, sipping red wine from one of their fancier glasses, looking gorgeous in jeans and a light-colored sweater. She'd let her dark hair down so that the wavy curls bounced gently off her shoulders in an alluring way. On the floor nearby were the red-soled shoes, the ones that she'd kept in the shoebox where he'd found the hidden note.

"Let me pour you some wine," Natalie said.

"Why are those out?" Michael asked,

indicating the shoes.

Natalie's gaze went to them and back again.

"Oh, those," she said dismissively. "I was going to get dressed up, wear that black dress to go with these shoes, soften you up a bit, but . . . I couldn't bring myself to do it."

"Soften me up for what?" Michael asked, curious.

"Later. Wine first," she said.

The lights. The music. The dress and shoes.

What was she trying to get out of him? Michael wondered where the anger was, her rage. What had changed in a day?

Against his better judgment, he allowed for a ray of hope to enter his heart. He didn't know why Natalie had asked to see him on short notice, she wouldn't say on the phone, but now that he was here he was wondering. Did she have designs on repairing their rift? Could his family be put back together in a new and different way?

Michael couldn't say why after all the venom she directed his way she'd forgive him for all he'd done, but something clearly had changed since her release from jail. *What could it be?*

"Dress or no dress, you look stunning,"

Michael said. He moved to a spot that put him directly across from her at the kitchen island.

"Thanks," answered Natalie coolly.

While she poured him wine, Michael had a chance to take in his wife's beauty, admire her form, absorb her quiet grace, thinking he would miss her always.

Unless . . .

Natalie handed Michael a nearly full glass, leaving the bottle nearby.

"Thank you," he said, clearing his throat, hoping to also clear away a deepening discomfort. Where could this lead? He felt his cheeks blushing.

"Feel like you're on the hot seat, honey?" Natalie inquired, no doubt aware of his unease.

"I do," said Michael, before taking a long drink. "I expected to find reporters hounding you."

"The DA did a good job of keeping a lid on everything," Natalie clarified. "She doesn't want the embarrassment hindering her reelection, I guess."

"What's the technicality?"

"My lawyer reviewed all the warrants and got the DA to agree that some key evidence was illegally obtained and, therefore, inadmissible in court. They had no choice but to drop the charges and try to get new evidence."

"Is there more?"

Natalie shrugged.

"Kennett dropped hints they do have something new, and big too — something with DNA. Kennett told me not to get too comfy at home, but for now, I'm free as a bird."

Natalie punctuated her assessment with a jaunty smile to accompany a celebratory hoisting of her wine glass. Michael followed suit, raising his glass, but they didn't touch rims.

"Well, that part is good news," he said. "I'm really happy about that."

"Lucky for me," Natalie clarified, sounding contrite. "But Audrey's still dead. Unlucky for her, right, Mike?"

Michael sighed out his stress. *Audrey. How much does she know?*

"What do you need me to say?" he pleaded.

She returned a tight smile, her lingering stare feeling cool and detached.

"Well, for starters, let's clear the air straightaway. I know everything, Michael, so I don't need any more lies about your poor dead mother. We had a lovely chat, just so you know."

While she hadn't come right out and said it during his jailhouse visit, Michael assumed Natalie somehow learned the truth about Joseph. Kate had called him by that name, but getting official confirmation from his wife incriminated him anew. Finding out that she'd also visited his mother only piled on the misery.

"So you met Marjorie?" he asked, feeling a tightness lash across his chest.

Natalie nodded in a delighted way.

"Where?"

"Your old house," she said. "That meeting I had in Connecticut? There never was a meeting. I just made that up and took a trip to Rye. Very enlightening."

She eyed him almost challengingly over the rim of her wine glass. She downed more of her drink, and he more of his.

"What do you want me to say, Natalie?" he asked. "It sounds like you now know everything about me."

"Do I?"

Natalie reached for her purse, which she'd left atop the island counter. From inside her bag she produced a folded piece of paper, which she then placed in front of Michael. Recognizing the stationery as a match for the one that he found in the shoebox, Michael unfolded the paper slowly, certain of the content. Sure enough, the words written there were ones he'd already committed mostly to memory. They ran together in a long string of blurred letters that set his heart racing.

"I know who it is, your affair," Natalie clarified, "the woman whose conscience 'can't take it anymore.' " At last she put some of the expected hostility into her voice. "It's sick what you've done, truly sick."

Michael knew his behavior was deplorably wrong, hurtful and deceitful to the core, but still, the arrows she'd slung felt outsized for his transgression.

"I was so lonely in our marriage," he said, pleading his case. "I admit it's horrible, and I know that's no excuse."

"Horrible?" The timbre of Natalie's voice rose with pronounced incredulity. "Lying to me about who you are for more than ten years is *horrible*. This?" She snatched the note from his hand, waving it in front of his face like a taunt. "This is on a whole other level of depravity."

Michael couldn't reconcile why Natalie's vitriol over his affair had eclipsed his other betrayal. There were two tigers here for him to tackle, but the tamer one appeared to be from his distant past, so he went there first.

"I *had* to leave Joseph behind," he said, his voice going soft. "He was stained. He couldn't have led a normal life."

Natalie scoffed.

"So now you're talking about yourself in the third person? Isn't that rich."

Her caustic tone wounded him.

"Mock me if you like," he said bitterly, "but Joseph is dead to me, same as my mother and father are both dead to me. They turned their backs on their only son when I needed them most. So yes, I lied to you, Natalie, but not without good reason. I wanted a new life, a fresh start. Is that so wrong?"

Natalie appeared to mull over his rationale, though he got the sense she wasn't exactly buying his justifications.

"First off, you may need to rethink your position on your mom," she said. "I'd say she *more* than had your back. Second, you're so full of shit it makes my head hurt."

"Why did you call me here, then?" Michael barked back at her. "Getting dressed up, pouring us wine, the music — why do all of that if you're done with me?"

Natalie paused, as if unsure what to say or how to say it.

"There's a lot more at stake here than your personal absolution, Michael," she managed. "Guess I can call you that, right? I mean, you'll always be Michael to me, and the real reason you're here, why I'm trying to soften you up with all this," she motioned first to the room, then to those shoes like it was a magician's reveal, "is that the police aren't done with me, not yet anyway."

"The DNA evidence," Michael said sorrowfully.

Natalie tossed her hands in the air as if all were lost.

"Maybe it's hair, or skin, or something; whatever they found, I think Kennett is convinced it's going to point back to me."

"And why is that?" asked Michael.

"Because I was there," Natalie said. "Inside Audrey's apartment on the night of her murder. I found your shirt and locker key in her bedroom, and then farther down the hall, in the kitchen, is where I found Audrey's lifeless, bloody body."

Michael's vision went momentarily white. When it cleared, the seriousness of Natalie's expression expelled any doubt in his mind as to her truthfulness.

"You were there? In Audrey's place? Why would you go there? This isn't going to look good for you."

"Right after you left the house in a rush, I called Scarlett and asked her to return to look after the kids so I could go looking for you. Only I got there a little too late. I didn't kill Audrey, Michael, but I'm scared out of my mind that I'm going to take the fall for her murder. So I need to know why did you do it, Michael? Please, please tell me."

"Nat, I —"

"Don't deny it, and please don't patronize me," Natalie cut him off. "Was she going to blow your cover? Did Audrey suddenly realize who she was sleeping with? Or was it something more banal, like love gone sour?"

"It's not that, no. I didn't hurt her."

"Hurt her?" Natalie's pinched face highlighted her resolute indignation. "You *murdered* her, just as you murdered her sister, Brianna."

"No," Michael shouted, slapping the counter with enough force to sting his palm. "That's not true."

"No?" said Natalie, her voice rising. Michael watched as she reached into her purse for the second time. From inside the seemingly cavernous bag Natalie produced an item wrapped within a faded blue wash-cloth, its nappy fabric pilled with age. Her shaky hands clutched a familiar black handle. She let the cloth fall away to reveal the dull silver of a sharp knife. Michael knew without making a close inspection that it wasn't rust that partially covered the blade.

"Where did you get that?" he asked. He stared slack-jawed at the weapon she wielded, his eyes gone wide.

"You know where I got it," Natalie answered harshly.

"Give me that," Michael said. He reached for her wrist, but Natalie pulled away quickly. "It's not what you think," he said.

"No? Let's see what a DNA test has to say about that."

"Natalie, stop. You've got it all wrong."

"Tell me the truth, Michael. Save me. You owe it to me to own up to what you've done. You killed Audrey Adler. Admit it. I can't go to jail for a crime I didn't commit. I won't do it. So please, be honest with me, here and now. Then tell me where you hid the murder weapon."

Michael's head was spinning. He couldn't think straight, couldn't see straight. He came around the island thinking he'd make another play for the knife before she got some crazy idea what to do with it, but Natalie took a hasty step in retreat. Instead of approaching her again, he seized a clump of his own hair, tugging at the roots in frustration.

"Are you *fucking* kidding me, Natalie?" he

shouted, taking a step toward her. "That knife is from the worst time of my life, and now you're going to threaten me with it?"

His face went red with rage, and try as he might, Michael couldn't find even a measure of calm. He felt his anger spiraling out of control. It was swimming inside him, rising up from his belly to his throat. Seeing the knife, the sudden rush of memories it brought back, all the stress of the last year, especially the last few days searching for his missing wife and children — all of it coalesced into something he couldn't contain.

Every emotion the knife evoked came rushing at him, overwhelming the circuitry in his brain, leaving him unable to think, barely able to breathe.

"This whole thing is so crazy, Natalie," he said, flashing her a look of pure, unadulterated rage. "You've been out of your mind for months, and now you tell me you were *inside* Audrey's apartment. You saw her body. Natalie, what have you done?" Michael glared at her with an inimical power.

"You want *my* confession? How about yours? What happened to us? Yeah, I made a mistake. I should have been honest with you about a lot of things. I know that's true. But there's no coming back from what you've done. Now, give me that knife,

Natalie, before this gets so much worse for us both."

Michael lunged forward, believing he'd catch Natalie by surprise, snatch the blade from her grasp before she did something she'd later regret. With his anger still burning hot, Michael wasn't thinking that his movement might be seen as threatening, intimidating, violent even. He was so focused on the knife, so utterly consumed with indignation, that he failed to take notice of how, in those moments, Natalie's demeanor went through a dramatic shift. Fear now overtook her.

He didn't give this shift much consideration, nor did he process what it meant when she put one foot behind her as if to brace for an attack while at the same time bringing the knife forward in defense.

One moment he was lunging at her, and the next Michael felt a strange sensation ripping through his belly. He came to a complete stop as a gushing warmth began to escape him. A sharp pain radiated from his stomach outward, and he tottered unsteadily from one foot to the other. His blurring vision made it difficult to regain his balance. He glanced down at the black knife handle now protruding from his belly, but could see no sign of the attached blade, which was now buried deep in his flesh.

Michael dropped to his knees, feeling nothing as he struck the floor hard. He gazed up at Natalie feeling utterly helpless and confused. With every heartbeat blood oozed out of him, turning his white shirt dark crimson. An irregular splotch formed, the knife handle in its center, growing larger by the second.

He couldn't breathe, couldn't hold a clear thought. Shock and pain had come forward to take center stage. From somewhere far away it seemed he heard a scream, a voice calling out his name, a sound that echoed in a vast chamber of nothingness, washing over him in waves.

Natalie sank down to kneel before him, her eyes welling. He felt her hand brush against his cheek, but couldn't take in any warmth from her touch. Cold was rooted in his bones.

"Michael," she said, sounding shocked. She cupped his head in her hands as she gently lowered him to the floor, down onto his back.

Natalie, he realized. This is my wife Natalie peering down at me. He felt weightless in his own body, rising up, drifting away, less anchored than a helium balloon.

"Michael, please, please hold on, help is

coming. I called for help. I thought you were going to hurt me . . . I didn't mean to, I didn't."

Her voice broke. She covered her mouth with her hands, but he could see her hot tears flowing like jeweled rivers down pale cheeks. He reached up to touch her face, wipe those tears away. It's okay, he wanted to say, but couldn't voice those words.

"You feel cold," she said anxiously, rubbing his skin to warm him.

He should have been afraid. He was feeling colder by the second. It was getting harder to breathe too, but something kept him going, a notion he had that it wasn't time to give up and fade to the black.

There was something he had to do.

Natalie continued pleading with him, urging him to hold on. Her voice grew fainter, until all he heard was a high-pitched whine.

He was dying. There was no question about it. Death was coming. It was near. But there was something he had to do before he let go. *What was it? What?*

He saw visions of light dancing before his eyes, the faces of Addie and Bryce coming in and out of focus. A flood of memories played about in his mind like a scattering of confetti, each piece containing a fragment of his story, a sensation, a feeling he had stored away for reasons unknown. A piercing pain radiated out across his body in all directions, the epicenter of it at his midsection, but even that couldn't eclipse the anguish he felt at not being able to do that one thing he was supposed to do before the blackness came to get him.

I need to help her, he thought. *I have to do what's right.*

Save her.

I'm dying.

"Michael, I'm so sorry . . ."

She was standing over him. People were entering the room in a frantic rush. They came to his side, kneeling down, pressing on his wound, saying things he didn't need to hear, taking vital signs, calling out numbers. All the while, he continued to take stock of his fading life.

I should have done more with the time I had.

"Michael, please don't go."

He heard her voice, like the call of angels. Yes, of course. He owed her something, didn't he? He could save her. He was glad there were people there. They'd bear witness to what he had to say, his final confession.

The truth doesn't matter now.

He waved his hand weakly, beckoning for her to lean down, to come to him, get close, put her ear to his lips. He remembered the scent of her. Time was running out. *Soon,* he thought. *Soon I'll go. But first* —

"Natalie," he whispered in her ear, lifting himself up off the floor ever so slightly, wincing against the pain, his voice strained and weakened like his fading pulse. "Listen to me, listen carefully. I'll help you." Michael hissed out the words. "Kennett." He remembered that name and then remembered another. "He has the wrong person. It's not you. It's me, Natalie. It's me. I did it. I killed Audrey."

There.

All better now.

He let go a breath as he collapsed onto the floor, but this time the ground didn't meet his body. He kept on falling, falling into the black, into a great nothingness, where the pain vanished — and so did he.

CHAPTER 44

Natalie

Natalie gazed in disbelief at the sea of tubes and wires strewn about Michael's cramped room in the ICU. A ventilator pushed air into his lungs while an attached apparatus did the breathing for him. Tina was with her, holding Natalie's hand, consoling her as only her dear friend could. The doctors had come and gone, providing brief updates on his critical condition. The penetrating abdominal wound he'd suffered — at her hand no less — had perforated the intra-abdominal vasculature as well as the small and large bowel.

His surgery had lasted almost eight hours. According to the surgeon, it had been a hell of a ride.

"He's as stable as we can make him right now," she said. "We're worried about the liver, but we need to give him some time to rest before we do another MRI."

Natalie lamented to Tina how there was no guarantee the tubes would ever come out, no timetable given for Michael's recovery.

"None of us are given any guarantees," Tina said darkly in response. "You just have to be there for him," she added. "And hope for the best."

Natalie sighed deeply as she thought over the implications.

"The best," she said, almost capping that with a derisive laugh. "If he recovers, he'll face murder charges. Meanwhile, Addie is refusing to go back to school. She's too afraid of what the other kids might say now that the story is all over the news. And Bryce — thank goodness he's too young to fully understand, but he knows something is very wrong."

Natalie's own feelings were mixed. While she didn't wish any further harm to come to Michael, she was certain her love for him was gone, buried forever under the sediment of his lies and sickening crimes. How could she have loved someone so wholeheartedly without ever truly knowing him? This question, she imagined, would haunt the rest of her days.

"What are you going to do about . . . that stuff?" Tina asked, keeping her voice low even though nobody could hear them.

From the conversation they'd had on the drive to the hospital, Natalie knew the "stuff" to which she referred was the bag with the shirt and gym locker key in it.

"I'll go clean out Michael's locker myself, hand over anything incriminating to Kennett," Natalie said.

"What if you find the murder weapon in there?" Tina asked. "God forbid John from accounting is doing curls and watches it fall onto the gym floor."

"Good point," Natalie admitted. "Maybe Michael got a replacement key after all. We have no idea what he did with the murder weapon. I doubt we'll find it in there, but I have a feeling we'll learn something, maybe about his affair. Can you go with me? I could just turn the key over to the police, but after all I've been through, I feel I need to face this myself first. We could go after hours. Don't company directors have twenty-four-hour access?"

"That we do," said Tina. "When would you want to go?"

Natalie didn't need long to think especially because the kids were still with her parents, taking them out of the equation.

"Can you go tonight?" she asked.

■ ■ ■ ■

Access to the Oakmont Athletic Club was through a set of double glass doors secured with a simple lock. Tina had the key as well as the code needed to turn off the alarm, which she did by pressing a series of numbers from memory.

While the club had closed at ten o'clock that evening, they'd waited until eleven thirty to show up, thinking there might be some stragglers still about. Natalie was relieved to have the place all to themselves, though wary about what she'd find in Michael's locker.

A heavy smell of chlorine from the first-floor pool perfumed the air. Tina informed her that the pool was locked after hours, but the rest of the facility was available for use.

"I used to work out here a lot late at night, and it was always a ghost town at this hour," she said. "Of course, we have to sign all these waivers so we can't sue the company if we drop a dumbbell on our head, but better that than sweaty bodies, grunting lifters, and long waits for the machines."

Natalie followed Tina wordlessly across an expansive tiled foyer toward a set of wide concrete steps that led to the fitness studios, weight machines, cardio equipment, free weights, and lockers that were available for a monthly fee. Tina sourced two flashlights from her shoulder bag, which they used to guide their way through the dark.

"God, I haven't been here in ages," Tina lamented a bit breathlessly as she and Natalie ascended to the second floor. "I really need to get back at it."

At the top of the stairs, Tina went to turn on the main lights, while Natalie used the flashlight to navigate her way through the weight room and over to a wall holding the bank of rental lockers. The lights came on with a blinding bright blaze. A hum of electricity soon filled the air.

Across from the lockers, on the other side of a cushy running track that circled the entire second floor, stood a white wall with a series of rectangular windows, all overlooking the twenty-five-meter pool a story below. Another nearby wall held a rack of dumbbells.

Natalie had only one thought as she fit the key into the keyhole built into locker number 774: *please don't let me find a bloody knife.* Natalie heard the click of the lock disengaging. She waited for Tina to show up to do the actual reveal, her hand poised to lift the latch. Tina came up behind Natalie, silent as a cat.

"What locker number is that?" asked Tina, who couldn't see over Natalie's shoulder. She sounded perplexed.

Natalie lifted the handle.

"774," she said.

"774?" Tina repeated slowly. "Are you sure that's the number?"

"That's what's on the key tag," Natalie answered as she pulled the locker door open.

It was dark inside the locker. Once Natalie's eyesight adjusted, however, she still couldn't make sense of the items within. It was hardly what she'd expected to find, as none of the contents appeared to belong to Michael.

On the top shelf was a line of feminine products and women's deodorant as well as Clinique face powder and hand creams from Aveeno and Burt's Bees. Hanging on the three-pronged hook was a pink hoodie and a pin-striped suit jacket cut for a female figure. On the floor of the locker stood a gym bag with the words *Dynamic Media* and their logo stitched on the side. Next to that was a pair of women's sandals and a folded-up blue towel.

At first Natalie thought she must have

opened Audrey's gym locker, but she recognized the suit jacket as one of Tina's favorites.

"Well now, I wondered where that jacket had gone to," Tina said after Natalie removed it from the locker. "I blamed the dry cleaners. Guess I'll have to apologize."

Natalie recalled Tina wearing that exact suit on the day she'd had her nightmare at work.

"Tina," Natalie breathed out, standing frozen in place.

Tina replied with an uncomfortable laugh.

"Yeah, this is pretty screwed up," Tina said to Natalie's back. "I really thought that was Michael's locker key you had with you. I *really* did."

Natalie couldn't move. She stood as still as a stone pillar, gazing into the locker, taking in the items before her, recognizing more of them as Tina's, while the pieces slowly slid into place.

"I just haven't been here in a while," said Tina, sounding as if she was talking to herself, running through a series of events, then finally coming to grips with how this all came to be. "I didn't even know I'd misplaced my locker key until this very moment. It didn't even occur to me to ask you what the locker number was before we came here.

"Ah, shit. What a mess, Nat."

Natalie recalled where she'd found the key: on the floor, under a dresser in Audrey's bedroom — a hidden place that a missing key might likely turn up. Panic gripped her.

"I mean, I knew Audrey had Michael's shirt because I put it there, but I didn't think it was my key you found. Stupid, stupid, mistake."

"You took Michael's shirt?"

Tina returned a nod.

"He made it easy, always leaving his bag on the bench when he worked out. Didn't look after it. Kept an extra shirt in there and so I took it. Audrey told me all about him, you know, after you showed her his picture, how his real name was Joseph Saunders — that people thought he killed her sister, Brianna, but she knew better. Joseph loved Brianna, or at least that's what Audrey told me. Said he'd never hurt her sister. Never."

"You knew . . . you lied to me."

"I kept the truth from you. That's not the same thing. And not without reason."

"What reason could you have for not telling me?"

"A good one, but it doesn't really matter now, does it?"

"I don't understand. Why did you put Michael's shirt in Audrey's room?"

"Because I figured the police would find it, not you, silly, and they'd come after Michael. They'd put a story together. Something about Michael leaving his shirt there. The shirt would back up your story of Michael and Audrey having an affair and the police would be on his tail. Linking the shirt to Michael was a concern, but with his background, I figured the police were likely to have his DNA in some crime database. If not, I'd drop them an anonymous tip and they could go get samples to make a match. However they got to Michael, there were several possible motives for him to murder Audrey. Maybe she figured out who he really was and threatened to expose him. Or it could have been a crime of passion. It happens with lovers. Whatever the motive, the police would be all over Michael. Then *you* took the shirt, and I had to improvise.

"When you said you'd found a key, I just assumed it was tucked inside the fabric folds and I didn't realize it when I put the shirt in the plastic bag."

"I found the key on the floor, under the dresser," Natalie breathed out.

"Well, no wonder I couldn't find it. That was an important detail you didn't share with me. Guess I shouldn't have assumed anything."

"Chris," Natalie then whispered to herself, thinking of assumptions *she* had made. "Not Michael Christopher . . . *Christina*. Or Tina for short. You. You're Audrey's Chris."

"Yeah," said Tina, followed by a sigh of regret coupled with a sad little laugh. "That was Audrey being clever. She wasn't going to tell you about us, not then anyway. We were still planning to stay a secret, and I'm sure she didn't know Michael's middle name, so — unlucky coincidence there."

Natalie's eyes traveled downward, noticing Tina tapping her fingers against her legs, moving them in a rhythmic pattern. It was something she'd seen her friend do countless times before, but when Audrey described it to her, she had attributed it to Michael.

Natalie replayed the numerous incorrect assumptions she'd made about Audrey's Chris, applying them now to Tina, not her husband:

Goes to this gym. Check.
Married. Check.
Two kids. Check.

Brown hair. Check.
Fit and athletic. Check.
Nervous habit. Check.

"It was your damn lunch with her that started all of this," Tina said with a scoff. "You got her thinking about living an authentic life, how secret affairs only perpetuate sorrow. Either come clean and be together or break it off, that's what she said you told her. But you didn't know her history, Nat.

"Suddenly, she wants to tell her mother all about us, finally come out of the closet, be her *authentic self.* I mean, Audrey marrying a man? What a laugh. She did that for her mother. She was so terrified of being rejected by 'Mama,' what with her super-religious views, and let's be honest — the Bible isn't really a playbook for living a gay life. So Audrey kept it quiet all these years, thinking she couldn't add to her mother's heartache by telling her she was a lesbian. Poor Audrey lived with such pain, so much *sadness.*"

"Tina, what did you do?" Natalie asked softly.

"Do? I had the best sex of my life, that's what I did. And that's what it was. Great fun. Exhilarating sex. But come on, I couldn't be Audrey's partner, not in real life! I have a husband, children, not to mention a job that I would certainly lose if it came out that I was sleeping with my employee."

"Tina," Natalie breathed.

"She demanded that I get a divorce," Tina went on. "Said she'd quit her job so that I wouldn't get in any trouble with our company, but that's not how it works, not in this day and age. No, I told her that was a big no, but she wouldn't give in, she kept on insisting."

"You did it," Natalie said.

"Come on, Nat," Tina spat back. "I couldn't let her destroy my life."

"She was stabbed I don't know how many times, Tina," Natalie reminded her.

"Her demands, her threats, made me kind of angry. I wasn't in my right head."

"I can't . . . I can't . . . I think I'm going to be sick."

Natalie's world tilted. She leaned against the locker for support.

"Michael went to see Audrey. He left our house to go see her," said Natalie, talking more to herself than to Tina.

"Honey," answered Tina, closing the short gap between them. "I don't know where Mike went off to that night, or who he was sleeping with, honestly I don't. But I can assure you, it wasn't Audrey, and he *definitely* didn't kill her."

Natalie understood Michael's admission then and there. He believed she was going to be arrested for Audrey's murder, because that's what she'd told him when she demanded his confession. Believing he was dying, he had lied to save her.

So many wrong assumptions.

And she couldn't blame them all on her insomnia.

"I wouldn't have come here with you if I thought you had *my* locker key," Tina said. "I wouldn't have brought you into this mess." She chortled her incredulity. "I would have found another way to pin the murder weapon on Michael, bury it in your yard or something. This just seemed too easy. Put it in his locker."

It took Natalie a moment for Tina's words to register. She repeated them to gain clarity.

"Put the knife . . . in his locker," Natalie said in a low voice, turning her head in that direction.

When Natalie looked back, she saw that Tina had slipped a latex glove over one hand. In that same hand, she now held a bloodstained kitchen knife, the kind used to carve up meat.

"I'm so sorry about this, Natalie," Tina said. "I really am."

CHAPTER 45

Natalie

"Is that what I think it is?" Natalie asked. Tina took a threatening step forward, wielding a bloodstained knife, her hand perfectly steady.

"The murder weapon I used on Audrey?" she said. "It is. Yes. Like I said, if I thought you had *my* key . . . if I had any idea that my key was even missing, this wouldn't be happening. But I was so excited because this was going to be too easy. I figured I could distract you and then just slip the knife into his locker, make it seem like you missed seeing it."

Tina had tears in her eyes.

"You brought the murder weapon in your bag to plant in Michael's locker?"

"I'm so sorry about all this," Tina replied, sounding genuinely contrite. "I don't want to do this, but this is a real mess now. How can I trust you to stay quiet?"

"I will, I will," Natalie assured her. "I won't say anything. I promise."

Tina didn't look at all convinced.

"And let Michael take the blame for something I did? You won't last. You'll crack like an egg. I know you too well. You've got too good a heart for that."

"What are you going to do?" Natalie asked. "Stab me? Kill me in cold blood?"

Natalie had come here already in a weakened condition after her string of sleepless months. How would she find the strength to wrestle a knife from someone well rested and supremely motivated? She had to think, plan her next move with extreme care.

"I don't know," said Tina forlornly. "This wasn't my plan. But I guess I'll say we found the knife hidden in your house. We were bringing the knife to the police when you suggested we should come here to look in his locker, see what else there might be. But we got into a fight because you got cold feet about turning on your husband and handing over the evidence. We argued. It got heated. You came at me with the knife.

"It was self-defense, yes, that's what it was. You already stabbed someone, they'll believe me."

Natalie realized that she was hearing a woman coming to grips with how she'd explain away a murder. Her murder.

Any hint of lingering fatigue left Natalie in a great rush. Thoughts of Addie and Bryce only added to her resolve. She'd do anything to be there for them.

With startling speed, Natalie shot her right hand forward, latching her fingers around the wrist of Tina's hand, somehow managing to avoid the knife blade. At the same time, she wrapped her foot around Tina's ankle. Pulling her leg back, mustering a strength Natalie didn't know she possessed, she sent Tina to the ground on her back. The matted gym floor protected Tina's body, but the bloody knife dislodged from her grasp upon impact.

Panic drove Natalie as she scrambled to her feet. She glanced at the knife, thinking she could reach it before Tina came to her senses. Natalie made her move, but Tina recovered quicker than she expected. In a role reversal, it was Tina who got a hand on Natalie's ankle. With a tug, Natalie went back down onto her knees, hard. Tina scrambled over her back like she was after a fumbled football.

"I have kids, too," Tina blurted out.

Natalie rolled onto her back, taking Tina with her. She grappled with Tina on the floor, moving her face from side to side to avoid her fingers, which Tina was trying to use like talons. Even so, Tina sunk her nails into Natalie's cheek. She pulled her fingers across the skin, digging in deep. Blood surfaced from the long marks gored into Natalie's flesh.

With an anguished roar, Natalie bucked Tina off her, but she fell back in the direction of the knife. By the time Natalie scrambled to her feet, she found Tina standing as well, holding the knife out in front of her, stabbing at the air.

With every step Tina took forward, Natalie took one in retreat, all the way until she was butted up against the rack of dumbbells. Instinctively, Natalie picked up a ten-pound weight to use as a weapon.

"Please, Tina. Don't. This isn't you."

"I killed before to save my life, my family. I can do it again."

Natalie threw the weight at Tina's head, but there wasn't much thrust. Tina had no trouble sidestepping the slow-moving projectile. Natalie picked up a five-pound weight and threw it harder this time. Tina ducked to avoid the strike.

Don't stop attacking.

Don't give her time to breathe.

Blood continued to ooze from the scratches running down Natalie's cheek as she picked up another ten-pound barbell. This time, instead of throwing it, she charged at Tina while giving her best warrior cry. Taken by surprise, Tina backpedaled quickly. She crossed over the running track before ramming up against the wall that overlooked the swimming pool below.

Momentum carried Natalie over the track as well. When she was within striking distance, Tina lurched forward with a lightning-fast counterattack. The blade of the knife landed on Natalie's forearm. Tina pulled her arm back, dragging the blade with it, producing a long gash. Natalie tried landing a punch at Tina's head with the barbell, but the shock of getting sliced open caused her to miss her target. Even worse, the barbell sprung from her grasp as if she'd thrown the weight. The window behind Tina broke in an explosion of glass that plinked as the pieces hit the tiled floor below.

A chlorine smell washed in through the shattered window. Tina came at Natalie with a fury, the knife hoisted high above her head. In response, Natalie wrapped Tina around the midsection, driving forward with her legs like she was pushing a weighted sled across the floor. Tina fell backward, stopping only when her legs hit the wall behind her. About three feet up from the floor, the wall became an open window that looked out onto the pool below. With the glass now in a million pieces, there was nothing to safeguard against a fall. Tina vanished through the opening, but Natalie didn't see what was happening in time to let go.

She was still holding on to Tina when she realized the momentum was too much. One moment her feet were on the ground, and the next she was tumbling over Tina before she, too, fell through the opening created by the shattered window. The fall lasted only a second, but it took a lifetime. Down she went, holding her breath, eyes closed, bracing to meet the floor below.

A sudden splash reverberated in her ears. Cold water covered her body. Natalie hit the pool with force, and intense pain radiated out from her shoulder before traveling up and down her legs, her back. She surfaced, choking, coughing water out of her lungs and spitting out blood. Wet hair curtained her eyes. She examined her arm, expecting to see a protruding bone. There was the gash, nothing more. But still, the blood was everywhere, pooling about her with the crimson sheen of an oil slick.

Then she saw the source.

Tina lay on the edge of the pool, her arms

splayed open in the shape of a cross, legs straight out in front of her, feet pointing toward the ceiling. Her shoulders hung over the pool's edge with her neck flexed at a grotesque angle, her head partly submerged under water. Even with a distorted view, Natalie could see that one side of her head was crushed and through a hole in her skull, poured a steady stream of blood.

Natalie caught a flash of silver glinting from the bottom of the pool, shimmering like a mirage. It was the knife used to kill Audrey Adler.

CHAPTER 46

Michael

He felt like he was drowning.

He couldn't breathe. There was something down his throat, choking him. He thrashed about in an unfamiliar bed, noticing now that there were tubes and wires hindering his mobility, so many that he felt like a puppet on strings. Alarms rang out. He heard commotion coming from the hallway outside his room. Then there was indiscriminate shouting, strained voices, and the high-piercing whine of several more alarms.

His eyes fluttered open slowly; everything appeared blurred. He shook his head from side to side, trying to dislodge the discomfort in his throat. No use. There was no getting rid of it. Soon there were hands all over him, tugging, pulling out the tubes. He gagged. Coughed.

"Michael, can you hear me? Take a breath, you can do it on your own now. Breathe in slowly, out slowly. Relax, Michael, you're okay."

He thrashed in his bed.

"We need to sedate him," he heard somebody cry out.

Michael understood what that meant. He had something important to say before they sent him back into the abyss.

"Natalie," he managed to croak out. "I need to see my wife."

Michael opened his eyes to find her standing at his bedside. Her arm was in a heavy-duty black sling. Bruises and scrapes covered her face but didn't dim her smile or her beauty. His heart lifted.

"Hey, you," Natalie said, running her hand across Michael's stubbly cheek.

"Hey, back," he said in a hoarse whisper. "What happened? You're hurt."

He lifted his arm weakly, gesturing to her sling.

"The old Michael would ask if I got the license plate of the truck that hit me," Natalie said.

"I'm still heavily sedated," he managed, which coaxed a little smile from Natalie. She got him some water, which he drank through a plastic straw.

"I'm so sorry," she said. "For what I've

done. I'm so sorry."

A few tears slipped out of her eyes.

Michael didn't know what she was sorry for, so she told him, enduring a fresh stabbing pain in his abdomen as her story unfolded.

"You told me that you killed Audrey."

Michael nodded, though he didn't quite remember.

"I was dying," he said. "You were all I cared about, you and the kids."

"Our kids are fine," she told him.

The pleased look on Michael's face disappeared as Natalie shared what had happened at the Oakmont Athletic Club.

"Tina . . . I can't believe it. She's gone?"

"Gone," said Natalie. "Died instantly when she hit the side of the pool."

They talked more about Tina and Audrey and the gruesome scene the police had found at the club; about Natalie's dislocated shoulder and the cut she'd sustained to her arm, which needed twenty stitches to close. She told him, too, about how Kate Hildonen got on the first flight out of St. Louis when she'd heard the news reports.

Then Natalie made her confession.

"I wasn't ever charged with Audrey's murder, just so you know. Kennett and I came up with the plan. We set it all up. Did it to try to trap you, make you think I was going to go to prison for something you did. We were playing to your conscience when we weren't even sure you had one."

"He played me well this whole time," Michael admitted. "So, I confessed, did I?"

Natalie answered with a nod. "Yes, you did it to save me," she said. With that, she broke into tears, heaving and sobbing, fighting for each breath, just as Michael had done when the tubes finally came out. He put his hand on hers.

"Is it too late to save us?" he asked. "Are we done, too? The doctors are pretty sure I'm going to get out of here alive, so you can't get rid of me that easily."

Michael coughed again. His throat felt like sandpaper.

Natalie touched his face. He saw love in her eyes — not a flame, but a spark, a hint that something could ignite again.

"We can talk about that later," she said. "When you're stronger, healthier. Now isn't the time."

"I need you to know the truth about me," Michael said. "I won't recover well if I'm holding it inside. Nat, I have to talk. Now."

"Michael, I don't —"

"Please," he begged again. "Please."

Natalie took time between his request and

her response.

"Okay," she eventually relented. "Talk. But before you do, I think you should know that your mother got in touch with me. She wants to come and see you."

"That would be good. Great, even," Michael agreed. He coughed, wincing through the pain. It hurt to take in air. Every breath felt like someone was pounding a fist against his ribs, but the pain he experienced now was nothing compared with the suffering he had caused others through his numerous lies.

"I had an affair," he blurted out. "It was brief. It was stupid. I don't deserve your forgiveness, but you deserve the truth. I'll take the consequences of my actions."

An inscrutable look came over Natalie's face. If she felt relief or anger at getting confirmation of her long-held suspicion, it wasn't for Michael to know.

"Do I know her?" she asked, sounding more curious than upset.

"I'm not sure," he said. "I met her at the gym. That part is true. She works for your company, that's true, as well. Does corporate investigations."

"Sarah Fielding?" Natalie spat out, disbelieving.

"Yeah, that's her. Sarah Fielding. You do

562

know her?"

Natalie told him about meeting Sarah, and how she may have used the lie of protecting the company as a veiled excuse to protect herself.

"She was probably worried that if I went looking on my own I would have very likely connected her directly to you," she told Michael.

"Good way to hide the evidence — doing the investigation yourself."

"But instead of a cover-up, she discovered what she thought was your affair with Audrey and more of your secrets. She wanted me to know everything. I think that's why she wrote her confessional."

"The note you hid in your shoebox," said Michael forlornly. "I found it while pulling apart the house looking for reasons why you ran."

Natalie returned a grim nod.

"She said it was to apologize, but really I think she wanted me to know you were unfaithful, hope that I'd leave you."

"She'd do anything to get back at me for breaking it off with her," said Michael. "She wanted our marriage to end, and maybe she got her wish. That night you went to Audrey's house, the night she was murdered, I was with Sarah. I'd already ended things with her, but she refused to accept it was over, and I was trying to talk sense into her before she did something destructive to you and me."

"I was sure you were with Audrey that night," said Natalie. "Were you two *ever* in contact?"

"We did exchange messages," Michael revealed.

"About what?"

"Audrey and I have been in touch for years. She knew I changed my name, but didn't know who I became. I kept everything very close to the vest. For my sake, our sake, the less she knew about my new life the better."

"She didn't know about me?"

"Not until you showed her my picture," he said.

"I see," answered Natalie.

"She thought of me like a big brother. In fact, I was the one who told her to apply for a job at Dynamic Media when she decided to relocate to the area. I encouraged it, and maybe even greased the wheels a little."

"Greased the wheels? How?"

"One night when Tina came over to the house for dinner, I pulled her aside, told her a friend of mine was lamenting the loss of his best employee who was trying to get a finance job at Dynamic Media. I asked her if an Audrey Adler had applied for a position there. So when Audrey went to interview she was already well endorsed because Tina loves you . . . or she did."

"Why did you want to help her so much?"

"Because of this."

Michael held up his wrist to show her the scar that he always hid with his watchband.

"The only blood on that knife is mine," he said. "After my arrest, I tried to kill myself. Made the cut, but I couldn't go deep enough. I wiped a lot of the blood off the blade, and then hid the knife. I forgot about it when I moved out of the house. I guess my mom found it, and naturally she thought the worst.

"I was going to try again, but I called Audrey instead. Audrey came to where I was staying and talked to me for hours. She told me that Brianna always loved me, and that if it weren't for their mother, she would never have ended things. She also said Brianna would want me to live. She was certain I didn't kill her sister, and believed that someday the truth would come out. I couldn't stop crying. I was so scared, but I didn't go through with it. Audrey saved my life that night. I truly believe that."

Natalie took Michael's hand.

"I need to know something, for my own sanity. Did you meet her at a McDonald's?"

"I did," Michael said, sounding surprised. "How did you know that?"

"I followed her there," Natalie admitted.

"We were trying to figure out what to do now that you were involved," he said. "We didn't want you to get hurt.

"Can you ever find it in your heart to forgive me for everything I've done? I love you. I love us. You, me, Addie, Bryce, you're my heart. You give my life shape and purpose. I don't know how I'll function without you."

"You'll always have Addie and Bryce," she said, peering down at Michael. "But I can't think about us right now, Michael. I just can't do it. Whatever is going to happen with you and me will take time to sort out. But tell me something, and tell me now, because I need to know. There's no going forward without it. And I need to look you in the eyes when you say it."

"What is it? Ask me anything."

Natalie gazed at him fixedly, undaunted.

"Did you murder Brianna Sykes?"

Without hesitation, Michael said, "I swear to you, Nat. I didn't kill Brianna."

Natalie looked deeply into Michael's eyes. She felt a shift take place within her as a powerful intuition took hold, and she knew with inexplicable certainty that this man, her husband, was telling her the truth.

"The kids," Michael managed, tears in his eyes. "When can I see them?"

"How about now?" said Natalie with a gentle hand on his shoulder.

Natalie left the room and moments later Addie and Bryce came bounding in with their bright smiles on full display. They crawled on their father, despite the warnings from Natalie and a nurse who accompanied them, undeterred even when Michael made a slight groan of pain.

"I love you both so much," Michael said, choking on emotion.

"I love you, Daddy," said Bryce in his sweet little voice. Then Michael felt something soft and fuzzy brush against his face. A blur of motion crossed his vision as Bryce placed Teddy on his father's chest. With the plush arms spread wide, Bryce play-acted his beloved bear giving Michael a hug, while he and his sister added hugs of their own that filled their father's heart with an unimaginable joy.

EPILOGUE

Newspaper clippings papered his dining room table.

When the police came — and come they would, because his mother would find him eventually — they'd see the clippings and maybe a smart detective, someone like Amos Kennett, would figure it out. But he left the police a suicide note on his desk anyway, because he wanted there to be no doubt about what he'd done and why. He had no ego to protect anymore. No secret he planned to take with him to the grave. In fact, he wanted to purge himself of all his secrets. He was always too scared, too weak to do the right thing and own up to what he'd done.

He was weak no more. The time had come.

It was the constant news coverage of Audrey Adler (Sykes, to him) and Michael and Natalie Hart that had ripped open this old wound. He'd done so little with his life. He never married. Never had kids. Never did anything substantial except to screw everything up. Now, he'd make amends in a way for all of his wrongdoings.

He clutched a Bible in his hand. He planned to hold on to the book until he couldn't, which wouldn't be long once it all got started.

Inside the Bible, he had placed a picture of her at Deuteronomy 5:17 to mark the passage, "You shall not murder."

Too late for that, he had mused, reading it over.

He entered his garage, where a thick rope hung from a pipe overhead. He'd tested the pipe plenty. It would hold him — not that he weighed all that much.

Skinny. Weak. Disgusting. Pathetic.

He wondered how his former students would memorialize him online. *Mr. Oman, the cool teacher who could score weed.* He could score other things too, including some of the students he managed to seduce, but only (always) after he got them high. He never loved the girls he slept with, but they made him feel desired, hot, and powerful. Even so, he didn't care about them, didn't care about much of anything — until she came along.

He cared for her all right. He cared too damn much.

He tried with her. It wasn't a crush; it was an obsession. The more she rejected him, the more he wanted her. He followed her. Learned about her relationship with Joseph. Oh, how he hated Joseph! When they split up, he thought he had a chance with her. No dice.

He followed her to the park that day. She told him Joseph was coming to meet her, that he needed to go away, leave her alone. He said he couldn't do that, told her he thought about her all the time. When he tried to force himself on her, she screamed. She threatened to tell everyone what he did, what he had done for years.

I know about the other students, she snarled at him. She called him a predator. Threatened to tell her mother about him, to tell the school. If she did that, he'd be done for. He'd go to prison. He couldn't survive in prison, he was too weak for that.

He didn't know what came over him. Maybe it was the hurt of rejection compounded with the pain of losing her, of losing everything.

One minute they were arguing in the park, and the next thing he knew he had his hands wrapped around her throat, choking her. He felt nothing, nothing but pure rage, when he reached in his back pocket for the knife he always carried.

He'd never killed anyone before, never killed anyone since — and in a way, he died that day, too. He'd been nothing since then, a pointless, useless person, and his self-hatred had only grown with the years. Couldn't hold a teaching job. Couldn't hold any job. A weed burnout, they called him when he went on disability.

If only they knew . . . if only.

Mr. Oman climbed the stepladder six steps high, holding the Bible in his right hand. He only needed one hand to slip the rope around his neck. He swayed back and forth on the ladder. The rope groaned creakily as it pulled taut before going slack again. Back and forth he rocked until the ladder rested on only two legs. One more shove and it went over with a crash. The rope immediately pulled tight as he dropped. His neck and head went up while the rest of his body went down. As with everything else in his life, he had misjudged, and badly at that. His neck didn't break — this was going to be a long, slow, painful death.

Mr. Oman's feet kicked out wildly, his legs bicycling in midair, desperate to find purchase. The pain against his throat was unlike anything he could imagine, and he had imagined the worst. He regretted his decision, regretted every damn thing about his life, but there was no turning back now.

His feet barely grazing the side of the only thing of value he owned: a beautiful, still shiny, red Ford Mustang Cobra. A common car back then was a collectible now, but he'd kept it parked in the garage at his mother's house since the day that boy, Joseph, saw him driving it away. Nobody ever came looking for that car, or for him. They had their person. They had Joseph.

Constriction reduced his windpipe to the size of a pea. He couldn't take in any air. Blackness soon filled his eyes. His feet stopped kicking.

As the Bible fell from his lifeless grasp, a picture within slipped out from the pages. It floated in the air, hovering it seemed, light as a feather, wafting its way downward, the face of Brianna Sykes gazing up to the heavens, beautiful, glorious, youthful, resplendent.

Forever sixteen.

ACKNOWLEDGMENTS

I welcome an opportunity to thank those who offered help, often in unexpected ways, in the creation of this work of fiction. In addition to my editor and steadfast supporter, Jennifer Enderlin, deepest thanks to:

Meg Ruley and Rebecca Sheer for always being sounding boards and trusted guides.

Jane Berkey for making JRA the agency of choice for the Palmer family.

Michael Palmer for his continued influence on my life and work.

Judy Palmer for her guidance, unwavering support, a commitment to helping me be the very best, and Richard Glantz for his fatherly wisdom and help.

Kathleen Miller for helping to open my heart to new possibilities and bringing invaluable energy, creativity, and insights to this novel.

Sue Miller for her careful read and remarkable attention to detail.

Zoe Quinton who helps make sure my words ring true. Same goes for Lani Meyer, copy editor extraordinaire.

The team at SMP — Danielle, Sarah, Sally, Christina, Lisa, and Paul who do all they can to support my novels.

My friends Erik Olsen, Don Dilego, Danielle Girard, Brad Parks, Phil Redman, Erin Copland, and Tom Wolfinger, who have been there for me in the best of times, and the worst.

My brothers, Matthew, Ethan, and Luke, and my aunt Donna who always have my back.

My children, Benjamin and Sophie, for giving my life shape, meaning, and unwavering purpose.

And of course to my readers who make all this possible.

ABOUT THE AUTHOR

D.J. Palmer is the author of numerous critically acclaimed suspense novels. He received his master's degree from Boston University and after a career in e-commerce he shifted gears to writing full time. He lives by the ocean in Massachusetts where he is working on his current novel. Besides writing, DJ enjoys yoga, songwriting, and family time with his two children and his ever faithful dog.

The employees of Thorndike Press hope you have enjoyed this Large Print book. All our Thorndike, Wheeler, and Kennebec Large Print titles are designed for easy reading, and all our books are made to last. Other Thorndike Press Large Print books are available at your library, through selected bookstores, or directly from us.

For information about titles, please call:
   (800) 223-1244

or visit our website at:
   gale.com/thorndike

To share your comments, please write:
   Publisher
   Thorndike Press
   10 Water St., Suite 310
   Waterville, ME 04901